The Mender

R. J. MOERSHEL

Cover art by Paul Thompson
www.paulwthompson.weebly.com

For Larry and Ellie
Best boosters ever

People at Flat Rocks (in order of appearance)

First newcomers
    Esri
    Zura
    Dagan

Original residents
    Tars
    Kai
    Piram
    Riga
    Nagar
    Saba
    Fenti-Dumu/Grilu

Barsa's Group
    Barsa
    Wilki (Wilki-Dumu)
    Nat
    Dara
    Grayla
    Jolam

Lost Children
    Sela
    Muni

Shell Bead People
    Ulun
    Hanu
    Otom
    Geslo
    Carthan

LEAVING THE BODE

The end of the world came in waves . . .

First, a far-off thunderous roar from beyond the horizon. It swept over them - again and again.

Next, a dense cloud, its leading edge blood red, slowly consumed the sky. It blanketed the sun, shrouding everything in deep twilight. It stayed and became the Always Cloud.

And then came the Ash Rain. Birds dropped from the skies. The people looked up and their mouths filled with ashes. Everyone and everything turned into ghosts. As the people fell, they believed it was the end of the world. What had they done to so anger the Ancients?

One of the last to fall thought about the old woman in his bode who knew too much. When the blood red Always Cloud came she told them to go into the forbidden depths of their cave. But few of them listened. He smiled. Maybe she would survive the end of the world. But would anyone else?

LOST TRAVELERS

"Has Angry Snake come?" Esri whispered.

A shrouded half-moon offered the only light, barely enough for Esri to make out Zura's hunched-over form in the Thinking Circle. Esri's hand brushed one of the large rocks at the entrance to the stone circle. In the near dark, she relied on touch as much as sight as she walked the familiar path from the cave.

"No, she hasn't arrived, but she still has time. Come, sit with me, Esri." Zura sat rubbing her fingers over the grooves of the Sky Bones. "If Angry Snake is the first Traveler to return it will be a welcome sign. She is one of the most powerful of the Travelers. The Sky Bones and Thinking Circle tell me that this is the night when Angry Snake's sky journey should begin again."

"But we haven't seen any Travelers since the Ash Rain and Always Cloud. And still you wait for the Travelers every night before pale Sun-Man returns. If the Travelers are gone, what use are the Sky Bones? Or the Thinking Circle? What does it mean, Zura?"

Zura said, "I believe the Travelers are only lost and will return to us. We need to watch closely for them so we can welcome them back."

Esri wrapped the extra animal skin she brought around the older woman. "It's so cold. You're shaking. Let me keep watch for Angry Snake.

Go back and lie beside Dagan and get warm. You know he has the heat of an old buffalo when he sleeps."

"Yes, one of his many gifts," Zura agreed. "I need to stay, Esri. Angry Snake may be weak if she comes. You might miss her. I've seen her many more times than you. I'm happy you came. You will keep me warm."

Zura stared in the direction of the Traveler's Guidepost, a tall, narrow stone pointing up, barely visible in the dark. It was positioned opposite her in the stone circle.

Esri sighed, "Though you're old, your eyes are better than mine. Even if the Elders Council allowed me to become a Skywatcher, I doubt I could ever be like you."

"But no one hammers a truer spear point. Or fills me with a sweeter song. Anyway, since I am the only Elder left now, I say that you can be Skywatcher if you want." Zura patted Esri's knee. "And what I want from you, is for you to start making your songs again."

Esri couldn't understand Zura's hopeful tone, "And what would I make songs about? The Ash Rain? How there are only three of us left? That we're cold all the time? And we have hardly any food?"

"But the Ash Rain ended and we're still alive, Esri. More plants are coming back. Perhaps soon even the big animals will return. Yes, it's still cold, but Sun-Man looks stronger. Maybe he's not leaving us as many feared. And see, even Moon-Woman brings a little more light." Zura pointed at the half-moon.

"So many died, Zura. I can't stop the sadness I feel all the time. And, I worry about something happening to you or Dagan. . ."

"I also mourn for those who died. But these nights as I sit waiting for the return of the Travelers, I've been thinking that if we are alive, there could be others who didn't die in the Ash Rain. We need to find them," said Zura.

"But where are they? How do we find them?"

"We walk. And keep walking, even to the Rising Sun land of the Ancients if we need to."

"Leave our bode?" Esri asked. "There's little to eat but at least we know where to look for food and the cave spring is still the only good water to drink. We can't leave, Zura."

"I walked to the River of Life yesterday, when you and Dagan were gathering roots, and the water tasted like before the Ash Rain. We can stay near the river and look for those we've traded with in the past." Zura turned to Esri, "Little Bird, we are too few. A bode needs many people to help each other. If we stay, we won't survive for long. It's better to try to find Others than die one by one in our empty bode."

Esri said, "I'm frightened to leave, but I'll do whatever you ask. It's because of you that Dagan and I are still alive. You saved us and took care of us like you always have since we were little and our mothers died."

"If only more had been saved, but they wouldn't stay deep in the cave and kept walking too far in the Ash Rain, drinking the bad water, eating rotten meat."

"And they were frightened," added Esri.

"Yes, they were frightened and stopped taking care of themselves and others. I wish it hadn't been so and I could have done more."

Esri leaned against Zura, and Zura wrapped her arm around Esri. They waited. The sun would rise soon. Once Sun-Man appeared, the opportunity to see Angry Snake would be gone for another day.

"There! There she is." Zura stood.

"Where?" Esri rose.

"There, those two small spots just above the Travelers' Guidepost are the beginning of her mouth." Zura and Esri stared at the two faint stars on the horizon. The women spread their arms and chanted rising Travelers' songs to Angry Snake, welcoming her back. It had been a long time since anyone had seen a Traveler.

In a short while, Zura said, "And now Sun-Man comes and Angry Snake leaves us but we'll see more of her tomorrow. This is the sign I've been waiting for. The Travelers have returned."

"I could hardly see Angry Snake," Esri said.

Zura smiled, "She is back and will be stronger soon. In time, the Travelers will all be back. Come, we must wake Dagan and start our journey today."

"Today?"

"You remember about Angry Snake? She moves quickly. It's a strong sign that she is the first Traveler to return. We must leave soon."

Esri and Zura walked back to the cave. The sun struggled to penetrate the Always Cloud blanketing the sky. Dagan stood at the cave entrance, "Did you see Angry Snake?"

Zura answered, "Yes. She is telling us it's time to leave and begin looking for Others."

Dagan glanced at Esri, "Now? How far will we go?"

"Until we find more people. Pack like when we go to the big-animal hunting site, except we won't come back here to the cave." Zura repeated for Dagan, "We will follow the River of Life. He'll give us drink, help us find plants to eat, and maybe Others with whom we have traded in the past."

Esri asked, "But Zura, the markings we made for the Ancients when we were hiding from the Ash Rain. If we leave, no one, not even the Ancients, will find them. They're so far back in our cave."

"We'll find other places to make markings. And I believe the Ancients will find our markings one day, and they'll see our story. Come now, let's gather what we need."

Using pouches slung over their shoulders and tied around their waists, they took what food they had - mainly roots; fire-making tools; Zura's remaining store of dried healing plants; a few flints; Esri's hammer stone for making more flints; the Sky Bones; and spears. They drank their last from the cave spring, filled animal bladders with water, and bundled up as many skins as they could carry on their backs for the cold nights ahead. They used sinew and vines to tie up the skins and create straps for carrying the skins wrapped around their other belongings.

"Will we go to the Rising Sun land of the Ancients?" asked Esri.

"I don't know, Esri, maybe. We would have to walk a long time. I want you to keep a Sun-Man Stick for our journey." Zura pulled a stick from the bodefire woodpile. "Here's a good one." It was less than half the length of a spear shaft. "Use one of your flints to carve a notch in the Sun-Man Stick each morning when you wake up."

Esri was honored to be the keeper of the Sun-Man Stick. Usually Sun-Man Sticks were marked by Zura or another Elder Skywatcher. They used the Sun-Man Sticks and Sky Bones and Thinking Circle to tell the bode when the rainy and dry seasons were coming, when animals would visit certain parts of the bode, and when it was time to go to the growing places of different plants. With the Ash Rain and cold days of Always Cloud, everything changed. All the large animals died, and so did many of the plants and Zura was now the only Skywatcher and Elder still alive.

Esri asked, "What will we do without a Thinking Circle. Will we make a new one?"

"Yes, when we find a place to make a new bode. It may take time to understand the skies in a new place. I'll bring the Sky Bones. Your Sun-Man Stick will help us know how far we have come."

They began their journey, following the River of Life. Throughout the first day they moved through landscapes that were familiar to them. The sun was muted but visible. When it was over their heads, they stopped to rest and drink and eat a few roots.

Late afternoon Dagan said, "I know of a small cave a little farther ahead. I've hunted near it many times. Let's stop there for the night."

For two more days after, they walked through places where they sometimes hunted. On the fourth day they began walking through places unknown even to Dagan.

In the morning, Esri said, "I want to go first today and be the first to see Others. Or at least see something we haven't seen for a long time, even a small bird. It's so quiet. I wish some of the birds would come back."

Zura whistled a few notes. "Maybe if we sing like the birds, they will hear us and come find us." The three took turns whistling and tweeting and squawking, imitating as many birds as they could remember. They began with those birds they could imitate perfectly, which were many, then some less than perfect imitations. Esri started walking backwards while trying to imitate the flight and sounds of a turkey vulture taking off.

Zura and Dagan laughed and then cried out in horror as the embankment under Esri gave way and just like that, she disappeared, plunging into the river below.

SOLITHH SIGHTING

Esri cried, "Help, help," first quietly, then a louder "help" and finally screamed longer and louder "Help me!"

Joe came barreling into Esri's room. Sound travelled readily through the thin walls of their apartment. He was half-awake and half-dressed but already into panic parent mode. He ran to the bed and gently pulled Esri into his arms.

"It's ok sweetie pie. It's only a dream, just a dream. Shake it off,"

Esri was now fully awake, "Holy, shit."

"Esri!"

"Oh, sorry, Dad. I know, shouldn't swear. I'm ok now."

"Bad dream?'

"Eee-yeah, sort of, I guess, at the end. Scared the you-know-what outta me."

Joe smoothed Esri's mass of thick, curly hair away from her face. "It'll be ok. It's been a while since you did that, called me in the night. Want to talk about it? Were you dreaming about your Mom?"

"No, not about Mom. I haven't dreamt about her in a long time. It's just that this dream seemed so real, it really freaked me out. Kinda weird but not weird. Anyway, what's with the 'sweetie pie'? I'm not a baby you know."

"Old habits. You should get some more sleep. It's still a while before you need to get up. Want me to sit here a minute?"

"Yeah, sure. Did I wake Jilly up?"

"Doesn't look like it. She's pretty zonked out," said Joe. They looked across the room at six-year-old Jilly sleeping peacefully, her mouth forming a small 'o'.

"That's good. Thanks for coming, Dad. 'Night – again," Esri kissed her Dad and snuggled back down in her bed.

"'Night Esri, I'll sit in the chair a little while." Joe slouched half-awake in the old bean bag chair until Esri's breathing slowed and deepened and then he quietly returned to his bed.

Next morning, Esri remembered the dream. And kept thinking about it throughout the day. Every detail. The touch of Zura's rough hands, her warm calmness, Dagan's large presence and watchful eyes. She especially remembered the hunger and cold, how they nuzzled together under the animal skins to stay warm at night. Esri wasn't able to talk to anyone about the dream. As soon as she tried, she'd get a catch in throat and couldn't speak. Maybe it was just as well. It was a pretty weird dream.

Where did all that stuff come from? Starting a fire without matches by twirling and pressing down on a stick into a thicker notched stick lying on the ground, foraging for edible plants and roots. In her dream, she knew exactly what to do.

Esri was distracted by the dream throughout the school day. She couldn't stop thinking about Zura and Dagan and worrying about what was happening to them. She kept telling herself to snap out of it, stay focused. People will notice.

Esri didn't have soccer practice today so her closest friends – Ada and Luka – were waiting for her after school. They all lived in the same low-rent high-rise apartment building. The three were friends since before they could remember. Their mothers met at the infant program at the local library branch when Esri, Ada, and Luka were babies.

Luka was a head taller than Esri and nearly two heads taller than Ada. Usually they walked with Esri in the middle. One of their friends referred to the three as The Stairs as the tops of their heads created a stair step effect when they were side by side.

Luka hugged Esri. He was a frequent hugger. "Hey you, incandescent true friend of mine," he said, "do you realize as of today we've survived our first month of high school and yours truly has not once been sent the office?"

"That's true," Esri hugged him back. "In-can-des-cent Luka. Good going. Are you saying Ada and I are out of a job?" She broke away from Luka and hooked her arm into Ada's.

Ada looked up at Luka. "You know how greatly it thrills us to become intimately acquainted with all the principals and vice-principals at our schools."

Luka grinned, "Well, I'm not exactly a little kid anymore, in case you haven't noticed. So even if I end up in trouble, you don't have to look after me like you used to. Though I do always like your company."

Luka was a hyperactive kid, and his overbearing exuberance frequently landed him in trouble. In earlier school years, he often ended up being sent to the principal's office, where the girls would collect him at the end of the day.

Ada said, "Library time, Mr. Incandescent?"

Luka groaned, "Sure. But you know, you two are kind of boring some times."

"And? . . . " prompted Ada.

"My Mom says she never could have raised me without you two. Ok, so study time, here we go. I'll race your short little legs there, Ms. Brainiac," said Luka.

Ada glared at Luka, then smiled, "I look forward to the day when I'm a famous neurosurgeon and they wheel you into the operating room after you've landed on your noggin' trying out for Cirque de Soleil. I'll make you retract every shorty comment you've ever made to me before I reattach your brain."

Ada and Luka walked on, continuing to banter back and forth. Esri lagged behind, thinking about her dream. How different it was to walk for days outdoors and see no buildings or sidewalks or cars or roads or power lines - and no stores, totally relying on eating directly from nature.

Ada turned around, "Hello? Esri, you with us? You look adrift."

Esri slowed, absorbed in watching a squirrel leaping between two trees. It was Luka's turn to speak now, "Yo, Es. That would be a squirrel - you know, rats with fluffy tails."

Esri turned to them, "Ohhh, just thinking. How would you go about catching a squirrel if you had to hunt them and didn't have a gun? Probably not a lot of meat. I wonder what they taste like?"

"Uck, disgusting," Ada grimaced. "Why would you even contemplate such a thing?"

"I dunno. I was wondering what if suddenly we didn't have any place to buy food. Like all the grocery stores or restaurants were gone. What would we do?"

"Well, we'd probably all start killing each other. Maybe start eating each other until only the baddest and meanest were left," said Luka.

"Thanks for that vote of confidence for humankind, Luka." Ada shook her head and then lowered her voice. "Hey, look, ahead of us. Isn't that Solithh?" It was their code name for Scary Old Lady in the Haunted House.

They watched the older woman slowly bumping her bundle-buggy ahead of her. She had a kind of rocking way of walking, like something was wrong with one of her legs. Though she was older and moved awkwardly, she emanated a certain energy. She had short grey hair, piercing eyes, no make-up or jewelry and usually wore a colourful tunic over her pants.

They were fascinated by her and a little bit scared of her, especially when they were younger. Her spooky house sat back from the street partially hidden by a tall cedar hedge. The ivy-covered brick house was two-stories with several leaded glass windows and a turret in front. For the three friends, it was something out of a Grimms' fairy tale.

Esri came out of her dream reverie, "That is so weird. You know, Jilly and I saw Solithh this morning, too, on the way to school. I was going to tell you guys. You hardly ever see Solithh away from her creepy house. Twice in one day. Very odd."

"Remember how we used to go to her house on Halloween, and most of the other kids were too scared?" said Luka. "She'd take forever to come to the door, give us the old Solithh stare, and hand us each a quarter." Luka turned around to Esri and Ada and did a dead-on imitation of Solithh peering around her door.

"Luka, stop it. She'll see you," said Ada

Esri teased, "And she'll put a curse on you, if you don't watch out."

'Ya, right. So now you think she's a witch. You used to think she was Amelia Earhart and that she hurt her leg when her plane crashed," Luka said.

"Ok, so I was a little off on my timing with Amelia Earhart but you must admit, there's something about Solithh that's intriguing. I'd love to know her story," said Esri.

They watched Solithh's rocking movements as she continued down the sidewalk. As they did, Solithh stopped and turned around. She stared at them, nodded several times, turned, and shuffled away.

"OH – MY – GOD ! ! ! What was that?" Esri shuddered.

"She only nodded at us, Es. Aren't you over-reacting a little? I thought that was my job," said Luka.

But Esri had seen more than just a nod.

RAVINE PATH

"Esri's back in la-la land," teased Luka. "Somebody looks at her and she starts a whole conspiracy."

"But, did you see what happened?" Esri asked.

"Yes, Solithh looked at us and nodded," said Ada. "C'mon, let's go. It's not that big a deal."

The encounter with Solithh disturbed Esri. "You know, you two are right. I am kind of out of it today. I'm going to skip the library. Sorry, I didn't sleep so well last night. I'll, I'll see you guys tomorrow."

"Sure, Es. You ok? You're not mad at us or anything, are you?" asked Ada.

"No, no, not at all. Never with you two, you know that," said Esri as she walked away.

Luka looked at Ada, "Now, that's almost weirder than seeing Solithh."

"Yeah. She's definitely not herself. Maybe she dreamt about her mom last night, I know Esri still gets these waves of missing her mom even though it's a long time since she died. I know I would sure miss mine," said Ada.

"Me too," said Luka.

Esri took the long way home, detouring through Taylor Creek ravine. She needed to clear her head and figure out what had just happened.

If Ada and Luka had seen what Esri saw, they would not have dismissed the Solithh encounter as something minor. During the several seconds that Solithh nodded at them, Esri saw a flaming vapor flare-up and pulsate around Solithh. Esri was certain that Solithh's stare was aimed directly at Esri, as if Solithh was sending her some kind of message.

The crazy, intense cave-people dream was bad enough. Now seeing flames pulsating from an old lady in her neighbourhood made Esri wonder if she was having some kind of mental breakdown.

The pathway through the wooded Taylor Creek ravine was Esri's ruminating place. The trail connected to Toronto's extensive ravine network. The dense foliage in the ravine largely muffled the city's sights and sounds. Right now Taylor Creek was a vibrant fluttering spectacle as the leaves were at their peak of fall colour.

Esri took her time, but was still early getting her little sister who stayed with a neighbor after school a few floors above them in the apartment building.

"How come you're so early?" Jilly complained. "Nasima and me just started being princesses-es-es"

"Nasima and I," Esri corrected and turned to Farhana, Nasima's mother. "I came home early today. But I guess I've interrupted fashion hour. Thanks for picking up Jilly. She loves coming here."

Farhana replied, "It's no problem. You know that, Esri. The girls keep each other totally occupied. My manager gave me some more fabric ends she can't sell so they're all excited today. They're already planning their Halloween costumes." She turned to Jilly, "I'll see you tomorrow after school, Jilly. You and Nasima still have lots of time before Halloween."

Esri and Jilly walked down the several flights of stairs to their apartment.

When he came home from work, Joe gave Esri a big hug. "You ok, kiddo? How was school? Were you kind of tired after that bad dream?"

"I'm fine."

"Sure?"

"Sure," Esri mumbled.

"Thanks for making supper."

"Sure."

They had a quiet evening. Joe read Jilly her bedtime story and came back in the living room. Esri had a book in her hands but it didn't offer the distraction she was hoping for. She had been staring at the same page for a long time. She looked up at her dad and realized that maybe she wasn't the only one having an off day. "Something bothering you, Dad?"

Joe smiled, "Sometimes you're so like your mom, the way you read my mind."

Unbidden, tears sprang into Esri eyes, "I miss her so much, Dad."

"Oh honey, I didn't mean to make you cry." He sat and put his arm around her. "I miss her too."

"She was so wonderful, always smiling and happy. Even at the end, we'd still sing together in the hospital. It makes me so sad that Jilly doesn't really remember Mom." Esri couldn't stop her tears.

"Yeah, Jilly was barely two when Sofie died. I've thought about that a lot. In some ways it helps us, Esri, because Jilly is just Jilly, a happy kid, getting on with life. Jilly doesn't carry the same sadness you and I have about missing your Mom. You know what Sofie would want us to do . . ."

"Start making some lemonade from all these lemons lying around. She was good at that, wasn't she?" Esri said. "I haven't cried about Mom in a long time. I don't know why I am tonight."

"It's ok. We keep carrying people with us, even long after they're gone. It's a way to have them with us for a while. But we're still doing ok, aren't we?" Joe said. "You had a rough night last night, so you're probably kind of worn out. Why don't you go on to bed?"

"Ok, Dad. I'll read in bed for a while." Esri got up and walked toward her bedroom. "Will you come turn out the light if I fall asleep?"

"Of course, honey. See you in the morning."

Esri turned back, "Love you." When Esri got in bed she remembered that she hadn't found out what was bothering her Dad - probably money.

As soon as she fell asleep, she began gasping for air.

RIVER SONG

Esri struggled to come to the surface, madly grabbing onto a rock, sputtering river water. Fortunately, the current wasn't strong where she fell in and her fall was partially cushioned by the animal skins she was carrying. Zura and Dagan peered over the ledge from above.

"Esri!" they both cried out.

Esri hung onto the rock and pulled herself out of the river. She lay panting and shaken but managed to smile up at the two worried people above.

"I'm all right. Just wet."

Zura looked at Dagan. "Angry Snake is warning us that we must be careful. We're fortunate that Esri is not hurt. She's young and light and quick. If it had been my old body or your large body, it could have been worse. Leave your things and go down and help her. We'll stop here for a while and let the skins dry."

Dagan nodded and carefully made his way down to Esri. "Are you all right?"

Esri was looking through her things. "Yes, just a few small scrapes. I lost my water carrier but everything else is here, even my spear. I dropped it when I fell and it landed by the river," Esri said.

"And your Huti stone?" Dagan smiled.

"Oh yes, that's tied-up with the flints." She pointed to the pouch looped around her waist. Zura and Dagan had tried to dissuade Esri from carrying the extra weight of the Huti stone. The stone had white veins running through it that formed a perfect outline of Huti, the large water bird. Esri had stopped using it as a hammerstone as she worried that continually striking it against the flaking stones would harm the Huti image. Hence, the stone served no practical purpose for their journey, but Esri was adamant about bringing it. "It was probably the Huti stone that saved me!"

Dagan shook his head. "I wish it was more powerful and stopped you from falling. Come, let's go back to Zura. We'll spread out your things to dry. I'll walk behind you."

Though Esri claimed to be all right, Dagan knew accidents could shake up your feelings inside as much as outward parts of your body, and he worried that Esri might slip again.

They thoroughly examined Esri for cuts and bruises, making sure she was all right. The skins that landed in the river with her were still damp when they left but the walkers didn't want to tarry longer. They were anxious to find a sheltered place before nightfall. By late afternoon they spotted a small shallow cave.

"That will do for the night," Zura said. "We can get some wood and brush from that grove of trees over there."

Esri used the spindle and base of the hand drill they carried to create a hot coal, gradually adding grasses, and then small twigs until the fire was hot enough to burn the larger sticks. They placed the fire near the front of the cave both for warmth and protection should there be any predatory animals that survived. They spread out the still damp animal skins hoping to dry them some more before going to sleep and ate most of their remaining roots. The three huddled together under the skins that were dry. They were exhausted.

Esri turned to Zura, "We've walked far from our bode and found no Others. What if there are no more and we're alone? What if tomorrow we can't find food? Our roots are almost gone."

Zura said, "The River of Life will provide for us but he can harm us if we don't watch him closely. We were wrong to turn our backs to him today. As long as Angry Snake travels with us, she'll protect us as she protected you today, Esri. I can see her entire head now before Sun-Man comes. She grows bigger."

Esri said, "Do you think we will be walking when the next Traveler comes?"

Zura paused, then said, "I don't know. The next Traveler is Spear-Thrower. When he comes we'll have walked farther than any from our bode have walked in a long time. No one since my brother, Barsa, who left before you were born, Esri."

"Maybe we'll find Barsa," said Esri.

"Yes, I would like that, to see him again, but I think something happened to him and his End Days came because he never returned from his last journey. We must be very careful on our journey," Zura's voice grew soft and sad.

"I think Barsa is waiting for us, Zura," Esri said. "And truly, I'm not hurt. You two sleep. I'll feed our fire and wake the great buffalo when I'm tired." She poked Dagan.

"And I'll sit with you when Angry Snake comes," Dagan said to Zura.

When the pre-dawn came, Dagan and Zura watched Angry Snake appear.

Zura said, "We're seeing more stars at night. If all of the Travelers return, I believe they will bring back the animals and plants that left with the Ash Rain. We need to be patient."

After Sun-Man shone, Dagan walked toward the river and found a few familiar plants growing near the water.

Zura said, "You didn't take them all, did you?"

He laughed, "No Zura, you taught me well. I only took enough. I left some so the plants can keep coming back."

The tender, new shoots were a welcome change from the tough, dry roots they had been eating for days. After yesterday's near catastrophe when Esri fell in the river, finding the crunchy, fresh greens brought badly needed hope to the three walkers. "Look, the River of Life provides for us. We won't turn our backs to him today," said Zura.

Before setting off, Zura began chanting. When Esri added her lovely, clear high voice and Dagan's baritone came rumbling in, it resounded down the river valley and gave them courage. The cadence and melody of the chant came from an ancient river song but many of the words were new as they beseeched the river to return their world to how things were before the Ash Rain and the Always Cloud. They took turns adding new verses, repeating them many times, hoping the River of Life would hear them.

> River of Life, bring back your clear water
> River of Life, bring back your green plants
> River of Life, bring back your fat fish
> River of Life, bring back your beautiful shells
> River of Life, River of Life, hear us, watch over us.

They continued singing as they walked. Though their pace was slow, it was steady and they soon covered a fair distance. The day passed, the terrain was new to them but not unlike their old home territory. Several times they ate more newly sprouted greens.

Late in the afternoon they saw the opening to what might be a large cave on a high ledge up ahead. It felt early to stop for the day but there was no guarantee they would find somewhere else before nightfall.

Esri slipped out of the animals skins strapped to her back, "I'll go look."

"Dagan should go," Zura said.

"I'll be all right."

Dagan said, "Let her go. We haven't seen large animals in many moon journeys and the signs of Others we've seen are old."

Zura agreed, "Yes, all right. The signs are all old. But be careful."

Zura and Dagan watched Esri scramble up to the top of the ledge to the cave entrance. As soon as she pulled herself upright in front of the cave, she gasped.

Lying inside were the broken remains of many people.

DRESSING JILLY

This time Esri didn't yell for help. She sat up in bed, wide awake. The dream was frightening and oddly real. What was going on? She didn't call for Joe. She could tell that he was feeling stressed out about work. It was only a dream, she told herself.

Esri looked around the room, felt the sheets, the comforter. She stared at the book shelves, desk, the old bean bag chair, Jilly snuggled up in her bed on the opposite side of the room. Everything was the same.

Esri went back to sleep.

"Come on, sleepyhead," Joe called into Esri. "I've got to get on the site early today so I need you up to take care of Jilly."

"Coming, Dad." Waking for the second time, Esri half expected to see Dagan lingering in the doorway.

"Bye, kiddo" Joe called from down the hallway. "Have a good soccer game. One of these days I'll get time off to come see you play."

"Bye, Dad." The front door closed. "Hey, Jelly-bean, you awake yet? I'm comin' to get you!"

Jilly giggled under her covers. She was infectiously good humoured in the mornings. "So does the exalted Queen of Fashion know what she's wearing to school today?"

Jilly jumped out of bed, "I want to wear what I got from Nasima's mom." Jilly pulled a strip of shimmery green silky fabric out of her dresser drawer.

"Ok, Jills but that might get kind of wrecked at school."

"But I told Nasima . . ."

"Ok, ok, maybe we can make a kind of sash out of it. And what else?" Esri started rummaging around knowing otherwise it would take Jilly forever to put together her ensemble. "How about these barrettes? They're green like your sash. I can put them in your hair."

Jilly danced around eager to get decked out for school, "You always look so boring, Esri. How come?"

"You make enough of a fashion statement for both of us, Jilly." Esri hugged her.

■ ■ ■

After her last class, Esri rushed to the soccer pitch. They were playing one of the toughest teams in the city today. She was thrilled and proud to be one of the regular team starters, and loved the recognition it gave her, particularly from the older girls on the team. It was a huge honor for someone in Grade 9.

Esri loved playing soccer. Especially playing mid-field and being a central part of the team – by turns setting up the striker or supporting the defense. She was blessed with a natural grace and agility that made her a skilled player.

Esri's team won, 2 – 0. The coach took Esri aside after the game. "You've got great vision for what's unfolding on the pitch, Esri, and you're unselfish about setting up others and working to their strengths. Well done. Keep it up." Esri couldn't wait to tell her Dad about the game and what the coach said.

She still felt the glow of the coach's words when she fell asleep that night.

CAVE DISCOVERY

Esri spun around from the horrible sight in the cave and looked down at Zura and Dagan. The distress on Esri's face alarmed them.

Dagan scrambled up to her. "What is it?"

"It's Others. They're long dead. Come see what's happened to them."

Zura forced herself to climb slowly and carefully, mindful of how important it was not to chance any accidents.

Finally, all three stood at the mouth of the cave. They were stunned by the sight in front of them. They had dealt with much death and sadness during the dark and cold times and were not surprised to see that Others were also affected by the Ash Rain. However, here there were signs of brutality.

Esri said, "I don't understand what happened. Some of these bones are badly broken. And I only see signs of Others, of people like us."

Zura said, "Yes, there are no signs of large animals."

Dagan spoke, "You know what happened here, don't you, Zura?"

"Yes," she spoke bluntly. "This is the work of Violent Ones. They came to this bode and killed those who did not perish in the Ash Rain, probably to take whatever food remained."

Esri cried, "But that goes against the Ancients! It could be a sister or brother they are hurting."

Zura said, "It's wrong. Those who kill their own kind break our promise to the Ancients. Violent Ones have no place in any bode - or anywhere." Zura raised her arms, stretched them wide, "Killing your own kind, kills everything. It kills the earth spirit."

"Did the Violent Ones bring the Ash Rain?" asked Esri.

"If they did, it would make them very powerful. But the Ancients are pushing back because the earth spirit is returning. We must help the Ancients."

Dagan spoke, "One thing we know now is that there are Others who survived the Ash Rain, and we are not the only ones. There could be more. We need to keep walking and find them before the Violent Ones do."

Zura said, "There are too many here to bury but we must honor them and help them on their final journey. We can cover them with sand and branches and sing of their End Days.'"

She walked around the remains, paused, and stared. "Oh no," she bent over and pulled out a small antelope skin pouch with a jagged design rubbed into the top edge. "This is a bag I made and traded for healing plants from an old mother at the last trading gathering. She must be one of the people lying here. These are Others I hoped we could find and join but they are all dead."

Using her hands as a scoop, Zura began flinging sand from the floor of the cave on top of the bodies. Dagan and Esri used flints to cut branches off of nearby bushes. As the three covered the dead people with sand and a layer of branches, they sang songs from their bode that were sung when someone died or was dying.

After they were done, Zura continued to sit outside the cave for a long time, rocking and chanting softly.

Dagan and Esri prepared a place to sleep in a sheltered spot a distance from the cave but near enough that they could see Zura. They sat and waited for her to finish.

She nodded her approval when she saw the bed they prepared. They were likely safe for tonight. The Violent Ones who killed the Others in the cave would have no reason to come back. Tomorrow the three would continue walking along the River of Life. The fearful discovery in the cave heightened the anxiety and urgency of their journey, but it also brought a sliver of hope that they were not the only ones to survive the Ash Rain.

Zura said, "You are right not to build a fire. There are no signs of big animals but we must be cautious and try to stay hidden. If we find Others, we need to watch them first and make sure they are not Violent Ones, and show ourselves very carefully."

DEAD MOUSE

It was Saturday morning and Joe was working, as he often did.

Esri said, "C'mon, Jilly, let's go see Ada at the coffee shop. She's working this morning. I'll split a cinnamon bun with you before we go to the park. I'll take my soccer ball."

"And we can jump in the leaves!"

Jilly bounced into the coffee shop in her light-up runners, with a tiara on her head, waving a wand.

Ada spotted her, "Wow, Jills, are you a princess today?"

"No, I'm a fairy godmother and I've come to grant you a wish."

"OK, I wish that this coffee shop would turn into a castle and I would be the queen."

"Lubbly lady, I will turn around and wave my magic wand and make your wish come true."

Jilly twirled around and round. Esri caught Jilly before she became too dizzy. Ada and several people in the donut shop applauded, including Ada's manager, Peter Chin, who asked Jilly, "and what would the fairy godmother like today?"

"Cinnabin bum," she said and he handed her one.

"No charge, Jilly, but I'm hoping to see this place turn into a castle by the end of the day," Peter said.

"It will!"

Esri thanked Peter and took Jilly to a seat by the window. They divided the cinnamon bun. Jilly thought hers should be the larger half because she was the fairy godmother. Esri sat thinking about the Zura/Dagan dreams. Last night's dream was disturbing about the Violent Ones. She had now had a few dreams about Zura and Dagan. Always so vivid. Would they keep coming and coming?

Esri caught a whiff of something unpleasant. It grew stronger and ratcheted up into an overpowering, sickening smell. It was like, what? Like a dead mouse smelled? Retch. And it was coming from the back corner of the donut shop. No one else seemed bothered by it. How could that be? It was nauseating.

A gaunt man in a suit and tie sat in the corner. His tall frame barely folded under the small table. He glared at Esri and Jilly. Esri scanned the donut shop. Still no reaction from anyone to the dead mouse smell. She looked back at the tall man. He was still watching them. His mouth now formed into a menacing sneer. He frightened Esri. She broke away from the man's penetrating eyes and whispered to Jilly, "We have to go. Don't make a fuss."

"No, Esri, I'm not done with my cinnabin bum."

"We need to leave. Now. We'll take it with us. Just be quiet until we get outside."

Esri wrapped the remains of the cinnamon bun in a napkin, stuffed it in her pocket, took the soccer ball, and grabbed Jilly's hand. Jilly was miffed. When they reached the door, she broke away from Esri and raced out of the donut shop.

Jilly ran straight into Solithh, nearly knocking her down.

CLEA

The front wheel of Solithh's bundle buggy had come off and she was bent over picking it up. Before Esri could stop her, Jilly catapulted right into the buggy which then tipped over. Solithh wobbled and Esri grabbed Solithh by the arm to steady her as the contents of the buggy scattered across the sidewalk.

"Oh my gosh, I'm so sorry. Are you okay?" Esri righted the bundle buggy. "Jilly, pick up her stuff and put it in the buggy."

"It's okay, I'm all right now." Solithh's voice was low and calm.

Esri made sure that Solithh was standing steady and quickly restored the contents of the bundle buggy. Esri was anxious about the tall, suit-and-tie man in the donut shop. Surely he was more than some random creepy guy. Something was not right with those glaring eyes, and what was that smell? Esri tried glancing back into the donut shop but was distracted by Solithh.

"If you wouldn't mind, I would be most appreciative if you could help me get my buggy and purchases home," Solithh said. She wasn't at all rattled or upset. "Give me your arm and tip the buggy forward on two wheels. You can tuck the wheel that came off into one of the bags. I don't live far from here. Just down there," and she pointed. "Do you mind?"

"Sure, we can do that. I'm so sorry we ran into you. Maybe I can fix the wheel on your buggy," said Esri.

"I think the cotter pin fell out again . . . somewhere . . . I might have something to fix it at home. Are you in a hurry? I see you have a princess with you. Is she on her way to a party?"

"I'm a fairy godmother! And I am taking care of Esri today," said Jilly.

"Oh my, aren't you lucky, Esri? And does the fairy godmother have a name?"

"Jilly."

"Well, Jilly and Esri, my name is Clea."

"Nice to meet you, Mrs. Clea," said Esri.

"No, no, just Clea. And I am very pleased to meet you too. I'm sure I've seen you around the neighbourhood."

Before they set off, Esri stared back into the donut shop, but the suit-and-tie man was gone. Had he disappeared? In the washroom? No, a teenage boy was coming out of the washroom.

Clea looked over at Esri, "Are you all right?"

"Yes, yes, fine. I . . . just thought . . . it's ok, we can go. C'mon, Jills."

Clea took Esri's arm. Esri dropped her soccer ball into the bundle buggy and pulled it behind her. Jilly skipped in front of them waving her magic wand.

Clea's front yard, once past the cedar hedge, was aglow with vivid fall reds and yellows. She opened the door to her house, which Esri noted was not locked.

The furnishings in the house were sparse and simple. It was lovely and light-filled. Jilly twirled slowly around. "This is a fairy godmother house, Esri."

Clea laughed. Esri also liked the house - not scary at all. It wasn't fancy, but felt like a place she would like to live.

"You have a nice place, Clea. Have you lived here a long time?"

"Oh, yes, quite a while. Come see the kitchen and the backyard."

She led them into a spacious kitchen at the back of the house. A large, round wooden table with claw feet stood in the middle, and the walls were lined with shelves and cupboards filled with glass jars, neatly labelled and organized with many grains and spices.

"It's like the Bulk Barn but nicer!"

"Jilly!"

Clea said, "I don't mind. It is a well-stocked kitchen. I enjoy cooking and baking and trying new things. But come, let me show you the garden."

Clea opened the kitchen door and Esri and Jilly stepped outside. The house was lovely and inviting but the garden was beyond anything Esri and Jilly had ever seen.

CLEA'S GARDEN

In the October sun, Clea's backyard was an explosion of dazzling autumn colour. Her yard, surprisingly large for a city lot, was filled with magnificent old trees and dense groupings of shrubs and plants. Fanciful vine-covered arbors created doorways to half-hidden nooks. Mosses, still brilliant green, outlined the irregular shaped stones on the pathways. It was like walking through a series of outdoor rooms with surprises at every turn.

Near the house was an open space where Clea had a large vegetable garden. Pumpkins and varieties of squash and gourds in many shapes and colours were sitting and waiting to be harvested.

Esri and Jilly looked around in wonder. Clea pointed out the grape-vines, fruit trees, and identified many plants they had never heard of. Everything had a use, whether to eat or drink or heal or simply for beauty. She pointed out which were the plants that were coming into their own now in the fall.

Esri couldn't remember even a tenth of what Clea told them but was excited and amazed. Jilly twirled and laughed. It was like a fairyland for her.

Esri asked, "How far back does your yard go?"

"All the way to the ravine. It overlooks Taylor Creek though you can't see too much of the ravine until all the leaves are down. It's a pretty steep drop. In the springtime, there are lots of wildflowers in the forest. You two will have to come back and see them," said Clea.

Clea watched the children exploring her outdoor world. "Esri, are you by chance looking for work? I could surely use help taking care of my yard. It's all gotten to be a bit much for me. And, during the winter there is much to do indoors, with preparing teas and breads. Is that something that interests you or would you have time?"

"I would love to have a job on the weekends, but my Dad often works and I need to be free to take care of Jilly."

"Bring her with you. That would be no problem. How about Saturdays? Say, 10 to 3, and you and Jilly could have lunch with me."

"Saturdays would work. But I have to ask my Dad."

"Bring him here and we can talk. He can meet me and, if he's agreeable, the three of us can work out a fair wage, the work, and the types of things I want you to do. I have lots to entertain Jilly. I'm sure she'll be no trouble."

"Wow, that would be great, Clea. I'm not sure how my Dad will feel about it but I'll bring him soon."

"Do. I'm sure it will work out fine. Bring him anytime. I'll be here."

Jilly listened intently, uncharacteristically quiet. She walked over to Clea, patted her leg. "He'll come, Clea, Daddy is a berry nice man and Esri is the best big sister in the whole world."

Clea smiled down at Jilly. "I look forward to meeting your dad and seeing more of you."

Esri and Jilly said goodbye. They hoped too they would be coming back - often. It felt like the beginning of something special.

Clea waved goodbye at her front door and watched them walk down her sidewalk to the street. She reached into her pocket and fingered the cotter pin from the front wheel of her bundle buggy.

ADDING NOTCHES

Despite the horrifying discovery in the cave, Zura, Dagan, and Esri slept soundly during the night, each in their staggered turn. By honoring the Others' passage back to earth, it took away some of the terror of what the Violent Ones had done.

Zura, as usual, rose well before Sun-Man returned, watching for the Travelers. Angry Snake now stretched far across the sky, more brilliant every day. If the Travelers were indeed returning, Spear-Thrower should be coming soon.

The three walked on for many days, following every bend of the River of Life. Twice more they found the remains of Others. Once, the remains bore signs of brutality by Violent Ones, and again, the three covered what was left of the bodies and sang their songs for the End Days.

At the other remains, there were no signs of violence, only one body, now largely decomposed, lying beside a fire long cold as if that person was the last of their group to survive the Ash Rain. Dagan found several lightly buried bodies a short distance away. The people in the bode likely perished soon after the rains began. Zura, Dagan, and Esri buried the body that remained and again sang the End Days songs.

"Will that be how it is for one of us? Tending a fire alone with no one to help us on our journey back to the earth spirit. No one to sing the End

Days songs over our body?" asked Esri. "We have come so far and not found Others to be with. Why do we keep going?"

Zura spoke sharply to Esri, "Sun-Man is warmer. Moon-Woman is brighter. The River of Life is bringing us food and now Spear-Thrower has returned. These are not our End Days."

Dagan said, "I'm not stopping until I find a buffalo to hunt. And a big cat for a fine fur blanket."

Zura softened her tone to Esri, "It's time you started a new song. You haven't for a long time. You used to make many songs for things as small as an ant carrying a grain of sand. Surely with so many new sights each day and the signs of so much returning, you could make endless songs."

Esri pulled out the Sun-Man Stick and carved another notch. "I might need another Sun-Man Stick before our walk is over." She sighed and offered Zura and Dagan the smallest of smiles, "All right, yes. I will begin a journey song today."

From then on, each morning when Esri added another notch to the many-notched Sun-Man Stick, she added a little more to her song. The days were hard but she could always find at least one good moment from each day.

The three travellers were encouraged by the small changes they saw in the world around them, and by Zura's positive radiance, Dagan's warm strength, and Esri's journey song. There was no denying that many days were tough. Food supplies ran low at times but they always managed to find something to eat, plants, roots, fruit. They were thankful that much of the plant-life still looked familiar though the terrain was new.

Dagan saw it first, "Look, a Huti bird."

"Where?" asked Esri.

Dagan pointed.

Zura laughed, "Ah, that's wonderful. If the birds are returning maybe soon we can sing about eggs."

"And I hope soon we will sing about big animals," said Esri.

"Yes, we need their strength," said Zura. "They will come back too."

One morning Esri awoke and saw that Zura was still sound asleep. Dagan was already up and busy organizing for that day's walk. It was not like the older woman to be the last one up. Esri gently nudged her, "Zura, Sun-Man has begun his day."

Zura barely opened her eyes, slowly shook her head, and closed her eyes again.

Esri rubbed her hands across Zura's face and neck. Zura had taught her that one of the signs of someone being unwell was if their body gave off extra heat. Indeed, Zura felt disturbingly hot. "Dagan, Dagan, Zura is sick. She cannot move today. We need to take care of her and make her well."

Esri and Dagan spent the day hovering over Zura, bringing her food and water though she had little interest in eating. They cleared away and fixed up their sleeping spot to provide a more comfortable place to stay for a while. Neither wanted to think about what it meant if Zura didn't get better.

"We need to make a small fire and use some of Zura's healing plants to make a tea for her," said Esri.

"Yes, we'll make a small fire, just enough for the tea," said Dagan.

Zura slept for most of the day. She woke the next morning feeling a little better though not well enough to continue.

Esri and Dagan were enormously relieved. Dagan told Zura, "Tomorrow you may feel much better, but we're not moving. You need to build your strength. And then the next day we'll only walk a little."

"Yes, no matter what you say, we're not moving," Esri insisted. And Zura finally agreed. Esri turned to Dagan, "Let's build Zura a small Thinking Circle."

The next day, Zura was much better. She got up in time to greet Spear-Thrower and positioned two sticks in the small circle to provide an alignment to where Spear-Thrower came up on the horizon.

Several times during the day, Zura sat rocking and chanting in the makeshift Thinking Circle, placing a few more stones here and there as she followed Sun-Man.

Esri quizzed Zura, "I thought we were leaving tomorrow but the Thinking Circle gets filled with more stones every time I look."

Zura laughed, "I know it's foolish to fix this Thinking Circle but at least for one day, I can use stick Guideposts to find Spear-Thrower. I miss our Thinking Circle. I'm glad you and Dagan made this for me."

Esri sighed, "And I miss our bode. The only things I know now are yours and Dagan's faces. In our bode, I knew everything, every sleeping place, where to get hammerstones, spear stones. And I miss how things were before the Ash Rain, when you and the other Skywatchers used the big Thinking Circle and Sky Bones to tell us when and where to hunt, find roots and plants, catch fish, sing to Sun-Man and Moon-Woman and . . ."

Zura broke in, "We don't have that anymore. Someday, you'll be in a new bode and you'll know it better than our old one. We'll build a new Thinking Circle and I will teach many Skywatchers, anyone who wants to learn. And you'll still have Dagan's and my faces." She stroked Esri's cheek.

"And you'll still stop me from being sad," Esri hugged the older woman. "I'm glad you're well again, Zura."

"And I'm glad to hear your songs again." Zura saw Dagan walking toward them, "It looks like Dagan has trapped something."

Dagan grinned at the two women and held up a brown rabbit, "She's not large but her meat will make us strong. We'll make a fire long enough to cook her."

The last night at their temporary site, they had a good story-telling and singing night. The relief of seeing Zura back into her old form made them happy and animated and with full stomachs from the rabbit, they all slept soundly through the night.

In the pre-dawn, Zura, Dagan and Esri awoke at that same time, likely from the same sound. A group of Others, hunting spears poised in their hands were standing a few feet away from them. Their faces were wild and angry.

WILLA

Joe gently shook Esri. "Hey, Esri, you've got to wake up. Time for school. You can't sleep in today. C'mon. We need to get going."

Esri gasped, looked up at Joe expecting to see a group of menacing Others. "What!?!?"

"I know you're tired, Es. But you've got to get moving. What's goin' on with you? Did you get to bed late?"

"I . . . don't . . . know." Esri could hardly get out any words.

"Well, your alarm was blaring away. Couldn't you hear it? You sure you're ok?"

"Uh, yeah."

"Well, don't fall back asleep. I've got to get going."

"Ok, yeah, I will, Dad." Esri sat up.

Joe left the room, calling over his shoulder, "Jilly's eating her cereal. See you at supper. Bye sweeties."

"Bye…"

What? Where am I? Thought Esri, staring at the room. Nope, no Zura or Dagan, no sleeping under animal skins, no scary people with spears. Were they Violent Ones? I - am - in – Toronto, Ontario, Canada. Ho-k, get ready for school, pack Jilly's lunch. Really need to talk to someone about these dreams.

It took Esri much longer than usual that day to shake off her dream. Even in her favourite ancient history class, Mr. Romero scolded her for not paying attention.

At least it was Friday. Ada and Luka would be waiting after school. Between the usual homework demands, family duties, work schedules, and Esri's participation in the city soccer tournament – the team finished third, not bad – the three friends had not been together for days. Esri wanted to tell them both in person about her job with Solithh, now Clea. Much to Esri's relief, when her Dad and Clea met, they really hit it off.

"Hey, spacey one, what were you off thinking about in Romero's class?" Luka came bouncing up to Esri.

Once again, Esri felt her throat close as she tried to say something about her dreams. She coughed, cleared her throat, and started again. "Oh my god. That was so embarrassing. I couldn't focus on the discussion. I didn't sleep too well again last night. I'm glad the weekend is here. But hey, I've got something to tell you and Ada."

They could see Ada walking toward them with a couple of her new friends from the computer club. The club was busy working on some computer game that they were sure would make them all rich. Ada broke away from the group and joined Luka and Esri.

"Hi, you two. Esri, are you okay? I've never seen you flummoxed like that in a history discussion." Ada, too, was in Mr. Romero's ancient history class.

"Yeah, I'm fine. I don't know what happened, so awkward. Anyway, I've been waiting for days to tell you guys about my new job. You'll never, ever guess who I'm working for?"

Ada guessed, "Sarah Lealand?" Esri's favourite singer. "The ROM?" The popular name for the Royal Ontario Museum, Esri's favourite.

"No, no something more local, very local, with someone we've wondered about for a long time and kind of been a little afraid of too."

Ada and Luka stared blankly at Esri. Then Ada said, "Solithh? I know you went to see her house last Saturday but a job too?"

"Yeah, that's right. I'm going to work for Clea. That's her real name. Just Saturdays for now. I'll help her around her house and yard and stuff. It's such an awesome place. She's great, and I can bring Jilly."

They were silent for a few seconds, then Luka spoke, "You are kidding me? Seriously, Esri?"

"Seriously, she's really nice, really. I'll bet you can come and visit sometime while I'm there. You'd like her."

Ada then said, "Wow, well, if you say so, Esri. You seem excited about it. Are you sure? What does your Dad say?"

"He went and talked to Clea a couple of days ago and he really liked her. She's got this amazing backyard with all these wild plants. You know how he loves stuff like that. It reminded him of his grandmother, I think."

Luka said, "I don't care how witchy she is, maybe now you'll be able to get your own phone and won't have to nag us to use ours all the time."

Ada punched Luka on the arm, "Stop it, Luka. It's no big deal, Esri. You know that."

"I know," said Esri. "It's just a pity that some of us lack a certain sensitivity to their dearest friends."

"Oh god. I'm cut to the quick. I'm so sorry, puppy," said Luka and gave Esri a hug and she tickled him hard under the arms.

■ ■ ■

Saturday morning, Esri and Jilly arrived at Clea's house promptly at 10. They knocked on the door and heard Clea's cheerful, "Come on in, you two."

Before they opened the door, a big, fluffy white cat came bounding out of the bushes with a mouse in her mouth. They jumped back, yelping. Clea stepped outside and closed the door.

"Ah, Willa, there you are, but you can't bring that inside. But you two can come in. We'll let Willa finish up her business outside. Despite her affliction, she is a remarkable hunter."

Esri and Jilly wondered what affliction Willa might have.

Clea chuckled, "She's been cross-eyed since she was a little wee kitten. I don't know how she does it. She must see two mice and then pounces in the middle. Whatever, she has learned to compensate most successfully," Clea paused, looked up, and mumbled something.

"Sorry, Clea, what did you say?"

"Ohhh, it's probably nothing. I caught a whiff of an odd smell, rather unpleasant."

Esri spoke carefully, "I smelled something odd, just before we ran into you last Saturday but nothing since then. And I don't smell anything now."

"Ah well, that's fine then. It's probably not as bad as I thought. I do tend to have a particularly sensitive nose."

TIED UP

Zura, Dagan, and Esri sat up slowly. Zura whispered, "Don't move unless I tell you. Watch me."

Zura looked up at the Others, nodded quietly with the smallest of smiles, and gradually moved her hand into one of the food pouches. She brought out a piece of root, took a bite and offered it to the largest and oldest of the four Others standing around them.

He stared at her in astonishment and brought up his spear. Zura did not flinch. She put her hand on Dagan's arm to keep him sitting and quiet as she could sense his aggression building. She said softly, "We wait."

The large Other did not hurl his spear but began gesturing with it, waving it up and down and saying something she couldn't understand.

"I think he wants us to stand. To look at us." Zura put the root down on the animal skins.

Cautiously, watching the movement of the Others, she, Dagan, and Esri stood up. Zura had the three of them turn slowly and open their robes so that the Others could see that they were People like them. Zura, Dagan, and Esri stood still, a little apart from each other, their hands at their sides.

Once they were standing, Dagan's great size and obvious strength became the center of attention for the Others. They stayed poised with their spears raised, except for the large, older Other. He lowered his spear and gazed at Zura, curious about this older woman who was clearly the leader of this little group of strangers. It was unusual to encounter someone so calm and fearless. Where had they come from? He wanted to know, but their words were different than his words and he could not make them understand what he was saying.

Zura patted her chest saying, "Zura, Zura." Then she touched Dagan's chest and said, "Dagan" and touched Esri and said, "Esri." And she repeated this again.

The large, older Other understood what she was doing, patted his own chest and said, "Tars." Zura nodded, gestured toward him with her hands and said "Tars."

Tars then pointed to a man about his age in his group and said, "Piram," Tars motioned to the young woman, "Riga" and finally the young man, "Kai." Zura knew then that they would not be killed, at least not instantly. These were the familiar beginning rituals when they traded with groups of Others.

But their safety was by no means assured. They needed to be careful. If these Others were Violent Ones, they might have decided not to strike immediately, though it would be to their advantage to do so.

Zura said, "It's good we are exchanging names. Stay quiet. I'm going to show them what we are carrying."

The Others were particularly interested in the carefully knapped points from Esri's pouch. Kai, the younger man, came over to examine them. He picked up several of the most precisely made points and her Huti stone and tucked them away in his pouch. Esri did not move.

Zura tried to indicate what direction they were traveling from and pointed at Esri's Sun-Man Stick to show how many days they had walked. It was doubtful that the Others grasped what she was trying to convey but Tars, especially, seemed to understand that Zura had a story to tell and he wanted to hear it. Perhaps she held knowledge that could explain the Ash Rain that had passed through and killed so many and why it was so cold.

Zura knew that their lives depended on every move they made and how it was interpreted. These were fearsome times and though Tars, the leader, appeared to be intelligent, she was sure he would not hesitate to strike them down if he felt they were a threat. What she did next surprised all of them.

She packed everything away again, had Dagan and Esri pick up their pouches, and ready themselves to walk. All of this was done deliberately and cautiously. Then she told Dagan, "Tie my hands."

"What?"

She pulled one of the strings of hide hanging from his belt. "Tight" she said.

Using her tied together hands, Zura pulled another string from Dagan's belt, handed it to Tars and motioned him to tie Dagan's hands together.

Zura held her breath as she knew how much she was asking of Dagan. Though he was always obedient to her, she had never asked this much of him before. Submitting his strength in this way went against every hunting instinct that was at the core of his being. She could sense his shallow breathing. For several moments, he kept standing with his hands at his side, not looking at her. Then he took a step forward and lifted up his crossed wrists to Tars.

Tars did not bind Dagan's wrists tightly.

Esri's wrists were also bound by Tars, not tightly. Tars motioned the group to start moving. They continued along the River of Life. All seven of them understood that they were taking a great risk. Zura and Tars understood it most of all. Those two also knew that it was potentially a greater risk if they stayed apart or began killing each other.

After a while, Tars spoke with Kai, the young man who took Esri's flints, and Kai took off running ahead of them.

Esri spoke to Zura, "Why do we have our hands tied? It makes it difficult to walk and you are still not well. You can't go like this for long."

"I don't think we have far to go. They're traveling light and now the young man, Kai, has run ahead, probably to let Others know we are coming," said Zura. "I don't think they are Violent Ones. Tars, the leader, has wisdom in his eyes. I wanted to let them know we are not Violent Ones."

"And now do we look too weak?" asked Esri.

"I can easily break my ties," said Dagan.

"I know," said Zura. "And Tars knows that too."

Zura was right. They soon came to a bodefire in front of a cave. Besides Kai, three Others were sitting around the fire, a young boy, a woman Zura's age who appeared unwell, and a younger woman who looked like the older woman, probably her daughter.

None of them could have imagined what an important moment that was and how what unfolded in those first minutes, days, weeks, and months would resonate down through time.

MORE WORK

Esri woke up Sunday morning. It was such a wonderful luxury to be able to sleep in and not have to worry about Jilly, getting up for school, or really anything.

Though Joe occasionally worked on Sundays, it was fairly rare. Often Sunday mornings he would get up to make pancakes and fashion pieces of fruit into silly faces in the pancakes. Jilly's giggles coming from the kitchen were proof that he had done so this morning.

Esri thought about last night's dream. The dreams were coming more frequently now, and they were increasingly lingering in Esri's awake time. Esri worried about what was happening to the people in the dreams, Zura and Dagan. They felt so real. Where on earth were the dreams coming from? Cave people! The dreams kept coming and unrolling in a continuous story, like episodes in a TV series but way more realistic with Esri right there in the middle. And, the biggest mystery of all was why was it not possible to talk to anyone about the dreams?

Esri lay in bed. In a little while, Joe peeked in. "Just wanted to see if you were awake. I'm taking Jilly over to Nasima's. Farhana got free tickets for the girls to go the Halloween Party at Casa Loma today. I'll be back soon and make some pancakes for you."

Esri laughed. "I hope Farhana takes pictures. I'm sure their costumes will be memorable."

"Yeah, probably so." Joe seemed a bit off to Esri, kind of down. "I'll be back in a few minutes."

"You ok, Dad?"

"Yeah, but something's come up. We'll talk when I'm back."

Esri got up and started making pancakes. She was putting them on her plate when Joe came back. "So, what's up, Dad?"

Joe poured a cup of coffee and joined Esri at the table. He sat quietly for a minute, looking off into the living room, gathering his thoughts. Esri knew something bad was coming and Joe was trying to figure out how best to talk to her about it. This made Esri imagine the worst possible thing, which would be that Joe had some kind of terminal disease.

"Walt cut my pay."

"What? I thought Walt was your friend? You've worked for him for years! You're always there whenever he needs you. You even work when you're sick. What a jerk!"

"Calm down, Esri. I'm not blaming Walt, well, trying not to. The kind of contracting work we do has gotten really competitive. People are underbidding each other. Walt's having to drop his prices to get work. So he can't pay people like he used to. He's also had a few people who stiffed him or partly stiffed him when the job was done. He even had to lay off a couple of the regular guys who have worked with us for a while. At least I still have a job but I'm going to make $2 an hour less and that's almost $100 less a week, which means over $400 less a month. We're going to feel that, Esri."

"But I'm earning money from Clea. I'll give you what I make."

"I really wanted you to keep it. Teenagers need money. I don't want you to feel like you can't do anything. I've relied on you so much to look after Jilly and you've done a great job. And there's so much you do here at home, cooking and cleaning. And you're doing well in school. You're a great kid. You deserve some rewards."

"And you're a great Dad. You deserve some rewards, too."

Joe couldn't help but smile. "I've got you and Jilly. I couldn't ask for more. Anyway, I'm thinking about looking for a part-time job that I could do on Sundays, but it would mean you'd be looking after Jilly. Right now, that's your only free time. I wanted to talk to you about it."

"That's not a big deal. You know I can do that. But what about you? Working seven days a week? That's crazy. You need to have some fun too."

"Lots of the people that live in this building work more than one job, six or seven days a week. Anyway, it won't be forever. But first I've got to find this Sunday job." Joe nodded to Esri. "Thanks for your support, kiddo."

"No problem."

"So, any big plans for today? You should get out and do something."

"Yeah, I'm going downtown with Ada and Luka. There's a concert thing happening at City Hall. One of the groups is from our school. You know Jerome's group."

"Ah right, the kid in the wheelchair who lives in our building. I hear he's pretty good. Sounds like fun."

Early afternoon, Ada and Luka came by and the three of them headed off to Nathan Phillips Square in front of City Hall. It was a crisp, bright day. Groups from various Toronto high schools were performing. The expansive square was packed, and the three friends hooked up with other classmates maneuvering as close as possible to the concert stage. They yelled and screamed when Jerome's group, Veracity, came on. While it wasn't a contest, everyone was clearly there to support the group from their school. Jerome's words and performance were mesmerizing. By the time Veracity finished, the whole crowd was in a frenzy.

Everyone who went to Esri's school knew Jerome. And most, like Esri, were in total awe of him. He lived in Esri's apartment building with his mother and younger sister, Brianna, who Esri knew from elementary school.

Esri usually gave Jerome a wide berth. He was a few years older and often with several other equally intimidating friends, not that Jerome or his friends ever said or did anything threatening. It was just that she was certain she would say something really dumb if they ever talked to her.

As well as being a brilliant rapper/singer/songwriter, Jerome was also an intense and riveting actor and at the centre of the school Drama Club, which is how Luka knew him.

The three friends were excited after Veracity's performance.

Luka bellowed, "Whoa, Jerome is incredible. And he's a really incandescent guy too."

"Luka, everyone and everything is incandescent to you. I think you need a new word," said Esri.

"Seriously, Esri. I know you find him scary, but you shouldn't run when you see him."

"I don't run."

"Oh yeah? Last week you slowed us down going into our building to avoid getting on the elevator with him."

"Yeah, well, now that you two are such good buds . . ."

"C'mon, let's go congratulate him," Luka said.

"Oh god, Luka, that's so embarrassing. He doesn't want to be congratulated by us."

"It'll only take a sec."

They made their way to the side of the stage. A lot of people were standing around Jerome but Luka maneuvered his way through, using his jokey manner to work open a pathway until he was right in front. Jerome was deep in conversation with some flashy looking promoter-type. Surely this was a bad time to butt in, thought Esri. As the promoter guy was talking, Jerome turned his head, saw Luka, and a huge grin spread across Jerome's face. "Hey, man."

"Hey Jerome, don't want to interrupt but just wanted to say that you were IN-CAN-DESCENT and that it was not only our school makin' noise. You had that whole crowd in the palm of your hand.'

"Hey, thanks, Luka. Thanks for coming over."

The promoter guy looked annoyed and started talking to Jerome again. Just then, the dead mouse smell, like at the donut shop, hit Esri. She started to slowly back away. The smell was coming from the promoter.

"Ada, are you smelling something gross, like something died?" Esri asked.

"Ah, no. Maybe you stepped on something?"

As in the donut shop, no one else appeared to notice the awful stink.

FLAT ROCKS

Like Esri's old bode, this bode also had a large, deep cave, which probably explained how they survived the Ash Rain. The cave was a distance above the River of Life. A well-worn path wound down from the cave to the river. At that point, the river widened out creating several shallow pools surrounded by large, flat rocks. As they soon found out, the bode was called Flat Rocks.

The unwell older woman, her daughter, and young boy who were sitting by the bodefire stared intently at Zura, Dagan, and Esri, especially at their bound hands and waited for Tars to explain. The little boy looked with round, wide eyes and sat close to the young woman.

Dagan said, "I don't see others in the cave. Maybe some are out looking for food. But I don't think so. They wouldn't leave those three alone for long."

Zura said, "I agree. I believe it is only those we see who live in this bode."

The seven in the bode were comprised of the four in Tars's scouting group plus the three sitting around the fire: four men and three women. The boy at the fire was the youngest. Tars and the unwell woman were the oldest.

Tars spoke for some time, showed the three sitting by the fire what Zura, Dagan, and Esri were carrying. Kai brought out Esri's points and passed them around. Zura heard her name mentioned several times.

The sickly older woman then spoke as did all the others in turn, even the little boy. Zura watched the sickly woman closely as it was to her that Tars and the others mainly addressed themselves.

Zura said, "The old woman has the dry cough from the Ash Rain. Perhaps the cough will not worsen and she can still be saved. I have plants for a tea that can help her, if they let me."

Though sickly, there was nothing soft about the woman and she sat tall, taking in every detail of the three strangers that Tars brought back to the bode. She gazed into Zura's eyes for a long time. Zura chanced a slight smile and a nod. The woman spoke to the young woman sitting next to her who then helped the old woman get to her feet and slowly she walked over to Zura.

The sickly woman patted Zura's chest and said, "Zura" and then patted her own chest and said, "Nagar." And repeated the names again. Then Zura, gestured to Nagar with her bound hands and said, "Nagar, untie."

Nagar took Zura's hands and unbound them. She kept holding on to Zura's hands and stared into Zura's eyes. Before she could stop herself, tears began to run down Zura's cheeks. The death of nearly everyone she knew at her bode, the weeks of walking, and the anxiety that maybe no other people were alive anywhere overcame her. She had not cried since she was a small child, not even during the Ash Rain, but now she could not stop the tears as her hands were held by this strange woman with the intense eyes.

Zura knew she should be projecting strength, not powerlessness but it was too late to pull back the tears.

Nagar continued to hold onto Zura with one hand. With the other hand, she gestured to the young woman who had helped her get up and said, "Saba," and then to the young boy and said "Fenti-Dumu."

Zura felt a calmness wash over her. There was something emanating from Nagar that felt comforting. Clearly, Nagar was a woman of unusual intelligence, and this reassured and excited Zura. Though Zura held a high stature among her people, she often felt lonely and isolated. Esri might be her equal one day, but she still had much to learn. No, this was something new. But would Nagar's intelligence be a threat to them or could they learn to trust each other? If Zura had only known that Nagar was having identical thoughts about Zura at that moment.

No one moved or spoke, as if they were all unsure what to do next. And then Esri began to sing. No doubt, an odd, possibly dangerous thing to do at this delicate, early stage of meeting these strangers, but it worked. She sang their journey song. At first the Others were startled, but her clear, lovely voice soon softened and calmed the group.

Nagar turned and spoke a few words to Tars who, in turn spoke to Kai and he went and untied both Esri's and Dagan's hands.

When Esri finished her song, Zura walked over to Esri and Dagan and said, "Learn their language. Make them happy. Appear mild – unless they harm us."

HUTI STONE

MAKING FRIENDS

The first days at Flat Rocks were difficult. The three newcomers struggled to understand the language of the others. Zura, Dagan, and Esri tried to appear non-threatening in all of their actions and yet not look too weak. Each group watched the other closely.

Several things happened that helped bring everyone together. Zura brewed some of her special healing tea, and after she, Dagan, and Esri drank some to prove that it was not harmful, Zura gave it to Nagar. After several days of drinking the tea, Nagar coughed less and not as deeply.

And Esri's singing. The first night around the fire, she started singing one of the songs from her bode, soon joined by Dagan and Zura. The young boy, Fenti-Dumu, stood by Esri and tried to imitate her singing.

After that, every night around the fire Fenti-Dumu went to Esri, patted her knee until she started to sing and he tried to join her. He was an engaging little boy who made them smile and Esri charmed them all.

But it was the innate trust of the two older women, Zura and Nagar, that solidified the bonds between the groups. The two women worked hard to learn each other's words and they, in turn, taught the rest of them to understand each other.

Gradually, Zura and Nagar exchanged stories of how they survived the Ash Rain. The stories were similar.

Zura told Nagar, "Like you at Flat Rocks, we had a cave with water at our bode. I tried to keep people deep in the cave, away from the Ash Rain that was making people sick. Only Dagan and Esri stayed with me far back in the cave. For days we only ate a few roots. Those that tried to hunt or gather plants sickened and died. Many of the people were afraid of the powerful spirits living in the cave and stayed near the opening but they were too near the Ash Rain and they also got sick and died."

Nagar asked, "Only Dagan and Esri stayed with you?"

"Yes," Zura shook her head. "In the end, it was only the three of us. Dagan and Esri are not my birth children, but they have been with me since they were small. Dagan and his birth mother got the scarring fever when he was starting to walk. She died. I took care of him and now he takes care of me."

"I see the marks on his face," said Nagar. "But he is not a weak man. You healed him well."

Zura laughed, "Yes, he has the strength of a buffalo, the speed of a big cat, and the eyes of a vulture."

"And stays silent like a large tree," Nagar smiled. "And Esri?"

"Esri's mother died giving birth to a boy who also died. And Esri came to live with me. Dagan and I call her Little Bird because she likes to sing. She stopped singing for a long time after the Ash Rain but started again on our walk."

"And now Femti-Dumu won't let her stop!" The two women laughed. The others sitting nearby couldn't yet understand much of each other's language and found the women's laughter bewildering.

"Why did you get the cough so badly, Nagar?" Zura asked.

"I went out and tried to convince people not to drink the river water and to come deep in the cave with us, but many did not want to listen to me."

"And they didn't make it."

"No, they didn't. Tars and I had the same mother. Saba is my child. They are close to me and listen to me."

"Yes, she looks like you and Tars. What about Fenti-Dumu and the others?"

"Fenti-Dumu is the son of Fenti. She died early on and I took him in. He does not yet have his own name. We will have a Naming for him soon, when he stops being a boy and we can understand who he is."

"And the others?"

"Piram is my sister's mate. He came from one of our trading groups. Riga is my sister's daughter and Kai is the son of Tars' mate. Riga and Kai's mothers are both dead."

"And that is all that is left of your group?"

"Yes"

"What about the Others you trade with?" asked Zura.

"They're all gone. We have not seen any of them. Tars took the scouting party to find Others but they were all dead or disappeared. Then he found you."

"Esri's Sun-Man Stick counts the days we walked. She marked the days when we found Others but they were all dead too." Zura spoke carefully. "Some looked like they had not died from the Ash Rain but were killed. What did Tars find?"

"The same. That is why we were frightened when we found you," Nagar gazed at Zura.

"Why didn't you kill us?"

"Piram thought we should, but Tars saw that there were just three of you. And though Dagan is powerful, you were the leader. They watched you, saw you were sick, and how Dagan and Esri took care of you and did not leave you to die."

"And, if we join you and not fight you, there are more of us. We are stronger together," said Zura.

"Yes, I believe that too."

The trust between Zura and Nagar grew rapidly and they spent much of their time together exchanging knowledge about their bodes and themselves.

Nagar was gifted in understanding the cycles of women and how to help women through what could be the difficult times of childbirth. She and Zura hoped that with the end of the Ash Rain and the Always Cloud becoming thinner, that life would return to normal and babies might come again.

Zura talked to Nagar about Thinking Circles and how Guideposts and Sky Bones could measure the wet and dry seasons, tracking cycles for finding plants and migrating animals. Nagar's group had similar counting ways but the Elders who were most knowledgeable about tracking the seasons all died in the Ash Rain before passing on their knowledge.

Both women knew many healing rituals from their mothers that they shared with each other.

Most importantly, they shared an urgency to find a way for their people to survive these terrible times. And to move beyond merely surviving and find a way for their little community to grow and flourish in this changed world.

Zura and Nagar knew that Nagar would not last much longer. Zura's teas made Nagar more comfortable and gave her a little more time, but there was no way to reverse the damage from the ash. Any further small illness would be difficult for Nagar to overcome.

Tars, Piram, and the younger people were more cautious about interacting but they gradually began to get to know each other. Curiosity got the better of some of their fears and seeing the growing warmth and friendship between Zura and Nagar did much to persuade the others to push aside their mistrust.

Esri was unhappy about Kai taking her points. They were chipped off of her flake stone that was now almost used up and she wasn't sure if she could find another in this new place.

But the worst was that Kai took the Huti stone. Esri worried what Kai would do with it. She liked holding the stone. It reminded her of her bode, now many days journey away and a place she would likely never see again.

Esri decided to explore among the rocks above and beyond the cave. Whenever she or Dagan went beyond the area close by the cave, one of the others followed. With Esri it was usually Riga, sometimes Saba. Today it was Kai. She did not like Kai because he had not returned her points and Huti stone.

"Don't follow me," she said to him.

"Where are you going?"

"I want to be alone."

"What are you doing?"

"Go away."

"Wait. Here," and Kai reached into his pouch and handed her the Huti stone and the small points he had taken from her.

Esri stopped and looked at his outstretched hand. She walked back and took the stones from his palm. She looked up at him and saw he was smiling at her and he asked her again, "Where are you going?"

"I want to find a flake stone."

"Like these are made of?"

"Yes."

"I'll take you to a place where you can find flake stones . . . if you show me how to make these." Kai smiled wider, "and if you sing a little."

Esri considered his offer. She carried a lot of anger toward him and was surprised that now it seemed to be slipping away with just a few smiles. She thought about Zura and her laughter with Nagar. Maybe Esri could be a little softer.

"Yes, I will show you how I make small flints if we find a flake stone this big," Esri showed him with her hands.

"And the song?"

"Maybe later."

MUSEUM ROCKS

"Hey, look at this incandescent mummy!"

"Ah yes, Luka. Though I wouldn't choose to describe the mummy as incandescent. It is exceptional," Mr. Romero laughed. "I encourage you all to take a careful look around before you decide which artifact you're going to research, and write about."

Mr. Romero had organized a field trip for the Grade 9 Ancient History class to look at ancient artifacts at the Royal Ontario Museum. "And remember, you can pick any object in these galleries for your project as long as it is something dated BCE, Before Common Era. Sometimes even very tiny pieces can tell interesting stories. When you've found your object, come see me and we'll talk about how to do further research. There are also museum volunteers here to help us. This is for your end-of-term project and presentation, so choose carefully."

The class spread out in the exhibits about ancient cultures. Luka was not to be distracted from the mummy. Esri and Ada decided to check out the Nubia gallery as most of the class headed in other directions.

Esri said, "It probably won't be as exciting as the ancient Egyptians, but maybe we'll find something interesting."

Many of the cases in the Nubia gallery were filled with artifacts from the height of the Kush empire.

Ada said, "Look at this, Esri. It says that in the Kush kingdom that some women rulers appeared to have equal status to the men rulers. They have a picture of a tomb here where the king and queen are portrayed as the same size, both fighting their enemies. Look, Queen Am-an-i-to-re, or however you say it. Jilly would love this."

"No kidding."

"Do you want to use this for your project?" Ada asked Esri.

"No, that's ok. You go ahead. There's lots of other stuff here." Esri walked to a display case in the middle of the gallery.

The case was filled with ordinary-looking rocks. Esri wondered what was so special about them. Then she saw that they were from a much older time than the Kush empire – more than 75,000 years ago – Middle Stone Age. The sign said that they were tools of some sort. She bent over the glass case trying to see what made them different from just regular rocks lying around. How would someone even know what they were?

As she peered down, she noticed that one of the rocks had a stripe running through it that reminded her of the Egyptian god they had studied, her favorite: Thoth, the ibis-headed man. Then it hit her like a thunderbolt. It was the Huti stone from her dreams, the one Kai returned to her. In her dream last night, she took it out of the palm of his hand.

Everything went black.

■ ■ ■

When Esri came to, Mr. Romero, Ada, Luka, and what seemed like the whole class and some museum staff were standing around her. Mr. Romero had his hand on her forehead, "Please, everyone, move away. Esri fainted. We're getting a nurse. She'll be fine. Give her some space."

Esri started to sit up. "No, Esri, lie still for now. Let's wait for the nurse."

"I'm fine. I just got a little dizzy." No way could she explain finding her Huti stone in the case with the Stone Age tools.

The nurse came, checked that Esri was okay, gave her some juice, and told her to sit for a while. Mr. Romero was not too concerned. He had past experience with fainting students, and given proper attention they usually recovered quickly.

Esri was mortified about doing something that drew so much attention to herself. Ada and Luka stayed with her until her color was better and Mr. Romero gave her the ok to get up and walk around. All Esri wanted to do was go back and look at the stone with the outline of the ibis. It was probably only similar. No way could it be the same rock.

The thing is, she knew the stone really well. She had held it and looked at it many times on the long walk with Zura and Dagan. Esri went back to the display case. It was definitely her stone, the Huti stone.

■ ■ ■

Esri was relieved that the next morning was Saturday and she could spend the day with Clea.

Esri brought down the bundles of herbs drying in Clea's attic. They took the herbs out of their paper bags, untied the bundles, and began removing the leaves.

Jilly jabbered away to the cornhusk dolls Clea had made for her. Jilly tried to get Willa engaged in her make-believe play, but the cat just swished her tail and stayed perched on a chair next to Esri.

"You're very quiet today. Anything on your mind?" asked Clea.

Anything on my mind? thought Esri. I'm only losing my mind. I feel like I'm living two lives. "I'm not sleeping so well these days. I guess I'm tired."

"Are you worried about something? Is it keeping you awake?"

"I'm sort of sleeping ok. It's just these weird dreams I'm having. They're hard to explain."

"Try me. I've had a weird dream or two in my lifetime."

"Well, I'm constantly dreaming about being with these cave people. And it feels so real. It's like I'm actually living with them. I eat and sleep with them, help get food, make things. And what is happening to us continues on from one dream to the next, almost every night." Esri was amazed that the words flowed out so easily. She wanted to tell her Dad and talk to Ada and Luka about the dreams, but for whatever reason, she couldn't. Her throat would close up. Now here with Clea it poured out. She couldn't imagine why that was, but what a relief.

She continued, "A lot of what happens in the dream is hard because bad things are going on. We're cold a lot. Food is hard to find. I'm aware in my dream that not long ago there was terrible pollution in the air for a long time, a thick ash that made many people sick and die. And there's a dense haze that's always hanging high in the air, blotting out the sun. Often we're scared. But the people I'm with are really nice."

"It sounds like you worry about these dream people."

"I do. Dumb, huh?"

"Not really. As I said, I've had a fair bit of experience with vivid dreams, some not unlike what you describe, a long, involved story. It can feel overwhelming. I learned to go along with it and if it feels real, let yourself get more involved. No harm. I believe that there are some people who dream deeper and sometimes there are big things your mind is trying to work out. Just let it happen."

They didn't discuss Esri's dreams anymore that day, but it made Esri feel better knowing that she could talk about them with Clea. Esri didn't tell Clea about the Huti stone. She needed more time to think about that.

NEW WAYS

Esri and Kai started spending more time together. He took her to his favorite spots for finding stones that flaked easily and hard hammer stones to strike off the flakes. They shared their knapping techniques with each other. Kai had long, strong graceful hands that could quickly shape the core flakes. Esri's hands were smaller but she was more gifted at coming up with new ideas for creating effective tools for hunting, scraping hides, preparing foods. They both took pride in their work and sometimes shaped the stones simply to make something beautiful.

The relationship between Dagan, Saba, and Riga was a little more complicated. As everyone became more comfortable with each other and could understand each other's words, it was clear that both of the young women were attracted to Dagan.

Riga was the more attractive and out-going of the two so she was usually more successful at getting his attention. But Saba had a quiet warmth that also drew Dagan. He admired her devotion to caring for Nagar and how Saba was always pleasant to everyone. Growing up with Zura, Dagan understood that kindness and caring were more important than physical beauty or strength.

Riga approached Dagan, "Dagan, come with us. We are going to look for Others. It would be good to have another strong man. We may be gone a long time."

It was the first time they had approached Dagan to be an equal member of a scouting party. He wanted to go but was worried, "What about the bode? Who will stay here with Zura and Nagar?"

"Tars, Piram, you, and I will go. Kai and the others will stay here."

Saba didn't like what Riga was suggesting and said, "Maybe Esri should go with you too."

"No, it's better if she stays. Nagar wants to plan Fenti-Dumu's Naming. She can help with that," said Riga.

Saba didn't know what to say. Tars and Piram would probably walk and hunt together on the trip, mostly leaving Riga alone with Dagan. They would be gone for days, maybe Dagan and Riga would even come back paired. Saba was sure that was what Riga had in mind. Dagan was so appealing to Saba. Among all the people she had known, including traders, she had never seen anyone like him who was both so strong and gentle. But she could not go and leave Nagar for so long.

Sometimes there were women who never mated. Until Dagan came, Saba thought she might be one of those and now he was going off to be almost alone with Riga for days. But what could she do?

Nagar, Zura, and Tars agreed that they should try again to find more people. The merging of their two little groups was working. Maybe there were more like them who had survived the Ash Rain. They just had to look harder. Though it was risky, they would be stronger if they were a larger group.

Tars, Piram, Riga, and Dagan left the next morning.

As they were leaving, Esri told Dagan, "I will keep a Sun-Man Stick until you return."

He leaned close to her, "Don't worry, Little Bird. I will always come back to you and Zura."

Zura tried not to appear so, but she too was anxious. The blending of their two groups was going well but it was still new. If something bad happened in the scouting party, it would be three against one. And though older, Tars and Piram were still strong and could probably take down Dagan.

Before they left, Tars showed Esri on one of her old counting sticks the number of days he thought they would be gone. It looked like a long time. She watched them leave and carved the first notch on her Sun-Man Stick.

Soon after the scouting party was out of sight, Nagar and Zura engaged those remaining in the plans for Fenti-Dumu's Naming.

Nagar pointed to the spot where Namings happened, "We will fix the Naming Place. We have not used it for a long time. Now that the Ash Rain is over and the Always Cloud is weaker, we can look to the heavens again. Zura is a Skywatcher. She can help us set the Guideposts."

Zura said, "As the plants and animals return, we need to watch closely what is happening in the heavens. We need new knowledge. Maybe some of the knowledge of the Ancients has changed. We will make the Naming Place a Thinking Circle like we had in our bode and use it to mark what is happening around us. When we are done and the scouting party returns, we'll have Fenti-Dumu's naming."

Esri, Kai, and Saba looked at each other. This was something new, to make changes to knowledge from the Ancients. How would they do this?

Zura saw their glances. "We'll keep many old ways but we have a new world and we're building a new bode. We need to learn new ways to survive."

Kai smiled, "Where do we start?"

Zura said, "Let's start with finding good stones for marking Moon-Woman's journeys so we'll know when she shines brightest and when she disappears." She held up a round, reddish rock. "Find me more stones that are the same size and color as this one."

Nagar said, "Saba, you go with Kai and Esri. I will be all right."

The three knew where to go. They walked to the cove of smooth rocks by the river, down from the cave.

Esri asked Saba, "How does the Naming happen?"

"I will tell you what we did before the Ash Rain came, but maybe this will change now. I hope so. The tradition is when the Elders see a child is starting to be more adult than child, they declare that it is time for the Naming. The child is taken by a group of Elders to the far hills and they're left there from sundown until sundown the next day. For most of the walk, the child's eyes are covered as they are led through the winding narrow pathways. It is a place where it's easy to get lost. The group of Elders comes for the child at the next sundown. While the child is alone, sometimes the big cats or scavenger animals come and the child dies. You're not supposed to talk about it but I crawled up into a tree as high as I could go."

"So did I!" said Kai.

Saba said, "Maybe that's what everyone does who survives, but we never talk about it. We're not supposed to. If the child is alive, the Elders decide on a name. It can come from something the child says or something the Elders saw. The Elders and the child come back to Flat Rocks. We make a big fire, tell stories, and the Elders reveal the child's name."

"Do children ever die?" Esri asked.

Saba was quiet and Kai said, "Nagar's son was killed by big cats. Nagar wanted the ritual to end and she never again took part as an Elder in a Naming."

"And no one listened to her?"

"Tars would have gone along with changing the way of Naming, but too many others did not. They were afraid the Ancients would get angry. I'm sure Nagar will make a different Naming for Fenti-Dumu," Kai said.

"Maybe these bad times are a sign from the Ancients not to always keep to the old ways if they are harming people. That's what Zura says, and we saw it in our bode - people dying who were afraid of the deep cave. It's because of her that Dagan and I are alive. Zura was right to leave our bode and find you," said Esri.

Saba said, "It's good you came. I was afraid at first, but everything is better. I remember the first time Nagar and Zura laughed together. I hadn't heard Nagar laugh in so long."

"And now even Esri smiles at me," teased Kai.

NICOLE AND BILLY

Saturday morning, Esri lounged in bed reading a little but mainly thinking about her dreams. Joe was at work and Jilly slept overnight at Nasima's.
Farhana said Esri could pick Jilly up after working at Clea's. Someone
rapped loudly at the front door of the apartment. Esri got out of bed and
peered through the front door eyehole. It was her neighbor, Nicole, with
her 6-month-old baby, Billy. Nicole was crying.

Esri opened the door, "Nicole, come in. Are you ok?"

"Oh, Esri. I'm sorry. Did I get you out of bed? Is Joe here? I tried my
girlfriend, Ashley but she wasn't home. I didn't know where else to turn."

"No, my Dad's at work. They're doing extra time to finish a job. Come
sit down."

"Oh, I was hoping he could help me and talk to Darren I don't know
what to do," Nicole's voice quavered.

"Can I help?"

"I don't think so, but can I stay here for a little while? I need to get out
of the apartment and . . . I don't know what. . ."

"Do you want something to drink? We have some apple juice."

"Yes, thank you, Esri. That would be nice."

"Go on, sit down, Nicole. It's fine. I'll be right back."

Esri came back with the juice, handed Nicole a box of tissues, picked
up Billy, and stood swaying with him in her arms.

"I so miss talking with your mother. She was such a good friend. She helped me a lot when I started working at the dental clinic and then your dad helped Darren get a job. I really need help." She started crying again.

Nicole dabbed her eyes and spoke between sobs, "You probably know Darren lost his job recently. We've been fighting – a lot. I want to go back to work at the clinic, and Darren could look after Billy. Just for a while until we figure out what to do. I don't know how else we can pay our rent or buy food. But oh no, he has his big, manly pride. He's not going to stoop to staying home looking after a baby. He's borrowing money. I know he borrowed from your dad to pay the rent. It's stupid. We can't go on like this, but he won't listen to me. We're having terrible fights. He . . . he does more than yell sometimes." Nicole looked down. "I was really frightened this morning. It's why I left. I'm so ashamed. I didn't know where else to go. I thought maybe Joe could talk to Darren."

Esri felt unsure what to do. "My dad won't be back until late this afternoon, but you're welcome to stay here. I have to go to my job soon and then I'll pick up Jilly. We should be back by 3 or so. Why not stay here, Nicole? We have lots of food. You can help yourself."

"I'm sorry to lay this on you. You're too young to have to hear all this. You're such a sweet girl - kind, like your parents."

"I wish I could help you, but maybe my dad will think of something. But really, hang out here for a while." Billy had fallen asleep in Esri's arms. She handed him back to Nicole.

"It's very kind of you. I think I may stay for a bit."

Esri left shortly to go to Clea's. She was so wrapped up thinking about Nicole that when she stepped off the elevator she nearly ran right into Jerome, who was waiting in the lobby.

Oh god, what could she say to him. "Uh, hi."

"Hey, hi, friend of Luka's, right?"

"Yeah"

"Well, I could use a little company. As usual, the wheelchair van is over an hour late, thanks to our brilliant mayor who decided to cut more money from the wheelchair van budget. You in a hurry, friend of Luka's?"

"I'm going to work, but I have a little time." Oh god, thought Esri.

"You're a singer too, aren't you?"

"No, not really."

"I thought I heard you singing at a school concert once, a few years ago. At my kid sister's school. Didn't you do a solo? I thought it was you."

"Oh, right. I did."

"You've got a great voice. You still singing?" Jerome grinned at Esri.

"No . . . I . . . uh . . . after my mom died. . ."

"Oh, I'm sorry, I didn't mean . . ."

"It's ok."

Just then the van pulled up.

"Ah, my ride at last. So what's your name, friend of Luka's?"

"Esri."

"Esri, nice talking to you. Start singing again – you've got a gift."

"Ok, thanks."

Holy, Esri was stunned that Jerome remembered hearing her sing. He was probably just being nice but still. Not so scary to talk to after all.

It was turning out to be an eventful morning. Esri's thoughts returned to Nicole's distressing situation. If only her dad had been home when Nicole came with Billy.

As soon as Clea saw Esri, she knew something was troubling her.

"Are you ok, dear?"

"Yes, no. Can I talk to you about something? It's pretty private but you won't tell anybody, will you?"

"No, no, of course not, you know that. Come, let's sit down, I've just made a nice pot of tea and pulled some muffins out of the oven."

They sat at the large kitchen table with the November sun streaming in the window and the warm smell of the fresh baked muffins in the air. Willa claimed a spot on Esri's lap, purring so loudly it made Esri laugh.

Clea laughed too, "She really likes you. I think even more than me though I'm the one who feeds her. Fickle cat. Now, what's on your mind?"

Esri told her the whole story about Nicole and the fights with Darren, how scared Nicole was, and how confused Esri felt about what to do.

Esri finished. Clea looked out the window and murmured, "That shouldn't be. We need a Mending."

"What do you mean? Mending?"

Clea looked back at Esri, patted her hand. "Oh, thinking about how you can help Nicole and Darren. It sounds like what you did was the right thing. It's always good when two people are having a heated argument that's going nowhere to separate them for a while. Let everyone cool down. If people are not agreeing and keep going at each other, back and forth, they can end up saying and doing things that are hurtful and sometimes harmful. Do you think your dad will be able to help?"

"I don't know. My Dad is worried about losing his job too. But he's a calmer guy than Darren. And I think that Darren would listen to my Dad but what can my Dad tell Darren? To be honest, I don't think Darren is the type of guy who could deal with looking after a baby."

"I'm sure with a little support, he could learn to enjoy being with his baby. It's the most important job there is, helping a small one flourish."

"I'm so angry with Darren. I want to yell at him and tell him not to be such a jerk but I know it won't do any good. He's freaked out about losing his job. I'm scared for Nicole and little Billy."

"Maybe your dad will be able to help, at least to get them to talk calmly with each other."

THINKING CIRCLE

Those remaining at the Flat Rocks bode worried about the scouting party. Each morning they gathered around Esri as she marked another notch on her Sun-Man Stick and then compared it to the place marked on the stick Tars had left that indicated how long he thought they would be gone.

Fenti-Dumu said what no one wanted to say out loud; "Maybe they're not coming back. They've been gone many days longer than Tars said they would be. I will never have a Naming. I will be Fenti-Dumu forever."

Nagar hugged him, "You will be named. And it will be a wonderful Naming in our new Thinking Circle. We have to be a little more patient. They'll be back soon."

Nagar knew her words sounded unconvincing.

Esri and Kai wanted to look for the scouting party but it was risky as it would leave those remaining at Flat Rocks too vulnerable.

The restoration of the Naming Place, now a Thinking Circle, provided some distraction from worrying about the scouting party. Zura used the new Thinking Circle to teach Skywatching knowledge to everyone at Flat Rocks, even Fenti-Dumu.

At various times in the night, many of those left at Flat Rocks joined Zura in the Thinking Circle. She showed them how to set Guideposts to make alignments with the bright orbs in the night sky and use small stones to mark the daily journeys.

Fenti-Dumu was especially keen on Skywatching, "Why are you the only Skywatcher?" he asked Zura.

"In our bode, only a few were given Skywatching knowledge and the Elders decided who that would be. Dagan and Esri were not chosen. When the Ash Rain came and everyone else died, I was the only Skywatcher left," said Zura.

Kai said, "It was the same at Flat Rocks. We were taught that only a few should receive the knowledge of the skies or great harm would come to us. We had two Skywatchers, as you call them and they both died in the Ash Rain."

Fenti-Dumu listened closely. "Will something happen to us if we are all Skywatchers?"

Zura replied, "No, it's better if we all learn. The Ash Rain showed us what happens if we don't share knowledge. I believe that's what the Ancients are telling us. I will teach you everything I know about Skywatching. Skywatching is like fire-building, finding roots, flint-making, hunting, helping mothers give birth, taking care of those who are sick, everything we do. Some people are especially good at these tasks but all should share the knowledge in case many people die quickly again."

Fenti-Dumu said, "Kai and Esri are good at making flints and Piram is good at finding big cats. I will be good at Skywatching, but I don't like doing some things. I don't like looking for roots."

Zura said, "Everything we do is important. Some tasks are simple, like digging for roots. It can make the difference of whether we live or die. But, I agree," she tousled his hair. "Skywatching is more enjoyable. Let's do both, Fenti-Dumu."

Mid-morning, Zura and Nagar spoke alone while the others went down to the river.

Nagar rested her hand on Zura's arm. "My friend, I could not have come through these times without you. What if Tars had not found you? We were nearing the end. Now your teas make me better. But much more than your teas, it is your wisdom and words that give me strength and hope."

"And you saved us, Nagar. As soon as I saw your eyes and how you looked at me, I knew that you were someone who saw deeper visions. Do you remember how I cried in your arms?"

"Yes, I wanted to be able to tell you not to fear us. Tars told me everything you did after he found you. I felt we should try to trust you. We've done well. We've found how to bring our two bodes together and take the best from each other. And we're learning not be afraid to try new paths."

"The Ancients could not have foreseen these hard times I'm no longer afraid to do things in a new way using the best of what we know. But I fear for the scouting party and what will happen if they don't return," said Zura.

"They'll return. I don't think they are dead. Tars is a cautious man. I think they had a reason to go farther or something slowed them down. Let's wait until after the Moon-Woman makes another journey before thinking they might not return."

"And if they find others . . . I know it is what we want, but I worry there are maybe too many and they may want to harm us," said Zura.

"I know. I share your worry and hope that they can find others like you, Dagan, and Esri."

The others came rushing up from the river, Kai and Esri leading. They ran in the cave, came out with their spears, and raced back toward the river. Saba and Fenti-Dumu were a little behind and came over to the older women.

FLINT-KNAPPING

Esri woke up, out of breath with her alarm blaring, and Jilly yelling, "Turn it off, turn if off!"

Esri slammed her hand on the alarm, shutting it off. She now dreamt about the cave-people every night. Often little happened in the dreams - just normal food gathering, talking and singing. But if something intense occurred like running to grab spears, she had a hard time coming out of the dream at the right time and needed the alarm to wake her up. Unfortunately, it meant that Jilly also got jolted awake.

Jilly came over to Esri and stood with her hands on her hips. "Do you have to make the radio so loud? And what's wrong with you? Why are you going huff, huff?"

"The alarm startled me. Shook me awake. I'm ok," said Esri.

Joe poked his head in, "You got everything under control? I need to get going."

"Yeah, we're fine, Dad. You go ahead."

Joe came in and gave each girl a hug and a kiss. "See you later 'gators." And he was gone.

"C'mon, Jills, let's get going. I want to get to school early today. I've got a big presentation in Mr. Romero's class, and I want to have time to review my notes at school."

This week they were doing their Royal Ontario Museum project presentations. Esri's was scheduled for today. Her presentation was about the Huti stone and the other stone tools with it in the display case.

The sign on the display said the stone tools dated from the Middle Stone Age and were found on terraces above the Blue Nile. One of the volunteers at the museum explained to her that the Middle Stone Age covered the time period from about 300,000 years ago until about 30,000 years ago, and that the tools were used by homo sapiens who, by that point in time, were not that different from us today - except with way less technology.

Esri read about how archeologists believe the stones were used and she found a survivalist group in Toronto who does flint-knapping – striking hand axes on pieces of obsidian to create arrowheads and spearheads. She e-mailed them and one of the members, Hank, invited her to come over and watch him.

One evening, Joe took Esri and Jilly to visit Hank. He showed Esri how to strike the obsidian and make a basic arrowhead. He sat her down with protective gear - goggles, and a leather pad for her lap and let her try her hand at it. As soon as Esri grasped the stones, she knew exactly what to do to shape a perfect point. She tried to pretend to be awkward about striking the stones but it was as familiar as tying her shoe.

"Well, aren't you sumthin'," Hank said. "I've been doing this for years and you just made a better point than I ever could. Hard to believe you've never done this before, Esri."

"Ah, I'm kind of a good mimic. I probably just had a few lucky strikes." Esri sensed that Hank felt something else was at play but he didn't press her any further. She was glad that Jilly and her dad were distracted exploring the odd and interesting tools and objects scattered around Hank's basement workshop.

For her class presentation, Esri gave a detailed description of the artifacts in the case and their likely use. She talked about her visit to the flint-knapper and showed the class the point she made with him, describing the process.

Esri reviewed what she gleaned from her research. Since experts can only speculate about what Stone Age lives were like and sometimes they disagree, Esri drew freely from her dream experiences, careful to couch her words with expressions like, "some paleoanthropologists believe that. . ." or "a few experts have suggested. . ."

She only slipped-up once when she said, "Kai likes using smaller hammerstones." Ooopsy. "I mean I liked using the smaller hammerstones, I mean hand axes, from when I tried it with Hank, the flint-knapper." Not a bad recovery, she thought, though she saw Ada and Luka exchange quizzical looks.

"I would pass around the point I made, but it's super sharp. See how easily it pokes through this piece of paper. Mr. Romero would kill me if one of you got cut. I keep it wrapped in this piece of leather." She showed the class.

When she finished, Mr. Romero paused and said, "Well, Esri, you certainly got quite absorbed in your research. You must have read a lot of sources to have gathered so many details."

"Let's hear it for Wilma Flintstone!" someone called out.

After class, Luka and Ada came up to her. "Jeez, Es, you were really into that," Luka said.

"I was really impressed, Esri. You must have spent a ton of time at the library. It was like you knew what it might have felt like to live then," said Ada.

Listening to them, Esri felt she had gone on for too long. She should have picked something else for her project and researched about the ibis/ Huti stone on her own. Even if she could start talking about her dreams to Ada and Luka, how could she do it now? They would think she was crazy. "I just found it really interesting. The more I read about those Stone Age people, the more I realized they were pretty much like us but without all our technology. If they dressed like us, we wouldn't know they were from tens of thousands of years ago. I found that kind of neat."

They jostled along the student-packed hallway to their next classes, weaving their way through the other students. When they got to the staircase, Ada and Luka went up and Esri continued on. Her next class was around the corner past the entrance to the cafeteria. The first lunch break was starting. Esri's lunch was on second shift today.

The usual clusters of kids were hanging around. Unlike the lower grades, now many cliques sorted themselves by race and ethnicity. It meant that Esri felt distant from some of her old friends. They weren't mean to her or anything - just not as available to hang out with anymore. She didn't begrudge them. In a big high school like Esri's, you do what you've got to do to fit in. With her mixed background from Joe and Sofie, Esri might have found a place in a few different groups but, so far, chose to navigate around them.

"Whoa, look out, there's cave woman!" someone called out from one of the groups. "You gonna let me grab your hair and pull you into my cave?" Much hooting laughter. Esri kept walking. Great.

After school, Esri detoured through Taylor Creek ravine. The first large snowfall of the season was underway. As the snow blanketed the trees and bushes, there was a hushed, magical feeling walking through the ravine. Few people were out. She mostly had the forested walk to herself. Esri decided to see if Clea was home.

Clea opened her front door. "Well, hello dear, come on in. Look at you. You look like you've been to the North Pole."

"Hi Clea. Is it okay if I come in for a little bit? I don't have to pick Jilly up for another hour."

"Sure, come in. We'll make some tea."

"I don't want to disturb you if you're busy. It's not that important."

"No, no. Come inside. Take off your wet things. We can dry them on the radiator. Ah look, here comes Willa. You're glad to see, Esri, aren't you?"

Esri dropped her wet outer clothes on the radiator in the hall and walked back to the kitchen. Clea had one of her revitalizing, flavorful teas steeping in the pot. As soon as Esri sat down, Willa jumped onto Esri's lap.

"What's on your mind?" Clea queried.

"You remember I told you about those dreams I'm having about cave-people?"

"Yes. Are you still having them?"

"Every night. I'm kind of used to them now, though sometimes I have a hard time waking up in the morning. It's like I'm more in my dream than in the real world. I know that sounds weird. I'm worried I'm kind of losing it. I don't want to see a shrink or anything but I wonder if there is any way to get them to stop."

"You want the dreams to stop?"

"I do and I don't. If they stopped, I would feel normal again. But . . . I don't know how to say this. I'm worried about the people in my dreams." Esri looked out the window. "I know how crazy that sounds."

Clea poured the tea. "Here, drink some of this."

Esri took a sip and looked back out the window. "I haven't been able to talk to my dad or even Ada or Luka about the dreams. Just you. And now, even if I could start talking to any of them, what would they think? Do you think I am having some sort of mental breakdown? I'm worried. And I'm scared." Her voice dropped.

Clea watched Esri, waited until she turned back to face her, "First, Esri, you are not crazy. Not even a little bit. I want you to get that notion right out of your head. In fact, you're quite the opposite."

"How do you know?" asked Esri.

"I've spent enough time around you to know that you are a kind, caring person. And very bright. I know you more than you might think."

"What about the dreams?"

"Tell me about them. Do you remember them?"

"Oh yes, I remember everything. It may take a while."

"Go ahead." And Esri described everything that had happened with Zura and Dagan, meeting Nagar, Tars, Kai, and the rest, the Huti stone, seeing it at the museum, up until when the alarm woke her this morning. When she described finding the Huti stone at the ROM, Clea laughed and shook her head.

When Esri was finished Clea said, "Well, that's quite something, Esri."

"Why did you laugh when I talked about the Huti stone?"

"Oh, just enjoying how clever and amusing they can be."

"They? What do you mean? They."

"Did I say 'they'? Um, well . . . Oh dear, now look at the time. You mustn't be late for Jilly. It sounds like so far the people in your dreams are managing all right. They trust each other and are good to each other. I wouldn't worry about it, Esri, but please drop by more often. I'm usually here. And tell me all about your dreams. It might make you feel better."

"I do feel better. It felt good to talk about it all. Thanks for listening, Clea. I guess it's a phase I'm going through." Esri shrugged.

"Yes, probably so. We'll keep talking about it."

Esri bundled up in her nearly dried out clothes, picked up Jilly, and went home to start supper. Joe left a message on the phone that he was going to be late. When he got home, he was grinning. "I have a Sunday job. And I think it will work out well. The pay is decent, hours are not bad, 6 to 11 am, and it's down by Harbourfront. It's janitorial work and restocking at one of the big lakeside clubs. I'm thinking that you and Jilly could meet me sometimes when I'm done work and we could go skating at the outdoor rink."

"That's great, Dad. I guess, I'm still worried about you working too much. How did you find it?" asked Esri.

"Well, it was kind of lucky. This morning I saw an ad posted at the bus stop and I called right away and made an appointment to talk to the manager after I was done with work. I guess she liked me all right because she hired me on the spot. Said she'd try me for a few weeks and see how it goes. She was worried about getting someone hired for this weekend."

"Everybody in the whole world likes you, Daddy, because you're the nicest Daddy in the whole world," said Jilly.

"And that's because the world's nicest Daddy, lives with the world's nicest daughters," said Joe. He hugged Esri, kissing the top of her head, and sat and pulled Jilly onto his lap and wrapped his arms around her.

ON THE HUNT

Nagar and Zura were alarmed. What was happening? Was someone attacking them? Zura stood up. Saba held up her hand, "No, it's all right. We found antelope tracks! Kai and Esri are going after them."

This was indeed hopeful news if the large animals were coming back. They would have better supplies of meat and bone marrow again. They were trapping some small animals but they only provided meager amounts of meat.

Fenti-Dumu was anxious to go, "I want to hunt too!"

Nagar told him, "Not this time, Fenti-Dumu. Your time will come. If the large animals are back, the hunters will start taking you and show you what to do."

Kai and Esri were experienced hunters. And though the two had never hunted large animals together, they often talked about it and practiced using their spears and working together should the opportunity ever come. And now, here it was. They could not contain their excitement. If they could start finding and killing large animals again, it would make everyone stronger and happy to have bigger, satisfying meals once more.

It would be difficult to make a quick kill with just the two of them. They could possibly run down one of the antelope, but that might take days and bring them too far away from Flat Rocks. They worked out their plan as they ran back to where they saw the antelope tracks. They followed their traces. It appeared to be 4 or 5 antelope feeding on some of the new plant shoots growing by the river. The small herd would likely be following the river for a while. Esri and Kai split up. Kai circled away from the river and ran as fast as he could. Esri kept moving behind the tracks.

Their best opportunity would occur if Kai could get ahead of the herd to the large tree that hung over one of the well-worn animal paths coming up from the river. The tree was a favorite hunting spot from the days before the Ash Rain. The track was narrow and rugged at the point where it passed beside the tree. Even an agile antelope needed to slow slightly, allowing a skilled hunter hiding in the branches of the tree the opportunity to thrust a spear into a fatal spot.

Kai raced to position himself in the tree and wait for the antelope to navigate the track underneath and, hopefully, be able to thrust his spear into one of them as they ran by. Coming up behind, Esri's job was to encourage the herd to go in the direction of the tree and be there to finish off the kill if need be.

The tracks were fresh and if the herd moved quickly, it would be difficult for Kai to get far enough ahead of them. Hopefully, the antelope would continue to stop and feed. Esri moved swiftly and silently. She needed to come close enough to spot them, follow them, and, at the right moment, startle them up the narrow path, running under the tree where Kai was perched. The antelope could easily decide to move off in many directions that she would not be able to control. This would be far easier with a larger hunting party.

Esri slipped over the next rise and stayed low. There below stood the herd. Four antelope, two adults and two calves, were grazing near the river. They looked small and underfed but, still, far bigger than any animal she had seen in a long time. She was sure Kai would try for one of the adults if she could steer them up the path. The wind was in her favor. The herd did not notice her and kept eating.

On several of their pretend hunts, Kai had shown her the tree over the path. Esri knew exactly where it was and how long it would take him to get there. If only the antelope would keep eating a little longer.

The adults took turns looking around. One started to move away from Esri. They didn't seem alarmed, just wanting to move along. She watched them go up and over the next rise before she moved away from her cover. If she startled them now, they might take off in the wrong direction. Creeping along, she was relieved to spot them again when she crested the next hill. A little farther and they would have few options but to go up the path by the tree. The herd moved on, still ambling. When they turned away from her, she moved quietly from one bush to the next, making her way closer to the river.

Esri took a small stick and broke it. The antelopes' heads and ears went up and they began trotting along faster. She wanted to keep them in sight. It was time to make her move. If Kai had not tripped or fallen, he should be up in the tree by now and the herd was very close. Esri no longer tried to conceal herself and came up from the river toward them.

The antelope went on high alert and began racing off. Esri could hardly breathe watching them go. The first adult sprang up the path followed by the other three. Esri was pumping her legs as she scrambled up the hill after them. She looked up and saw Kai poised in the tree. The herd was nearly under him. She gasped, as he let the first adult go by, but then realized the other adult was bringing up the rear and would have to slow down for the two young antelope ahead of her. Kai hurled his spear and managed to thrust it deep into the back haunch of the last antelope. He and Esri were both yelling. Kai jumped down and Esri kept coming as the antelope struggled to get away.

The antelope stumbled. Esri thrust another spear into the mid-section and Kai pulled up the antelope's head and ran a sharp flint across her neck. It was over quickly. Kai and Esri looked at each other, gasping and laughing. They were dirty and bloody. They looked at the motionless antelope and placed their hands on the still-warm body.

Kai said, "Let us thank this beautiful antelope for sacrificing herself for us. Do you have a song, Esri?"

"Yes, I do. This is what we used to sing for the animals we killed who gave themselves to us," and she began to sing.

They did what they could to prepare the antelope. She wasn't large. Esri carried one of the hind quarters and Kai hoisted the rest of the body onto his back and they walked back to the bode. Esri sang all the way. The others heard her, and Zura knew from the song that the hunt was successful.

Everyone at the Flat Rocks bode worked on the antelope, skinning, carving meat, extracting marrow from the bones. They roasted some of the meat, and used some of Esri's finely wrought sharp flints to cut thin strips to be dried and eaten later. There was almost no waste, even the bones were cleaned to be used for tools or objects carved for the Thinking Circle. By late afternoon, they were nearly done with the most urgent tasks, preserving the meat, and finishing the most satisfying meal they had had in a long time.

Fenti-Dumu wanted Kai and Esri to show him where and how the kill happened. He was urging them to go by standing on top of one of the ledges above the cave when he started to yell, "They're back! They're back! And they're bringing many others."

Kai and Esri rushed up to Fenti-Dumu. Saba helped Nagar get to her feet. Zura stood and the three women joined the others on the ledge. Coming from the far-away hills, they could see a line of people walking straight towards them. They were moving slowly. It looked like Tars was leading, then Piram, and after them it looked like strangers. From the angle they were looking, they couldn't see everyone in the line. Hopefully, Dagan and Riga were bringing up the rear.

Nagar, whose eyesight was the worst said, "How many are there?"

Kai responded, "It looks like as many as the fingers on my hands." Ten.

Nagar said, "Go get your spears."

Kai went back to the cave and brought spears for Esri, Saba, and himself.

Fenti-Dumu asked, "Why are we getting spears? Can't I run to Tars and see who he has brought?"

Nagar told him, "Let's wait. It was different when Zura, Dagan, and Esri came. There were only three of them, the scouting party was not gone for so long, and Kai came ahead and told us they had made gestures of peace, offering to bind their hands. We do not know who these new people are and if they too are coming in peace or what has happened to them. We will keep watching."

The six of them, even Fenti-Dumu, stood quietly as the line approached. There was a dip in the trail and when the scouting party re-emerged they were closer and walking at more of an angle. As they appeared one at a time over the rise, Nagar and the others could see the rest of the individuals following Tars and Piram. First came a young woman who looked to be pregnant, nearly at term, then a young man and woman, and another young man, who appeared to be carrying someone, it looked like a child, and then an older man. Finally, Riga and at the very end came Dagan who was smiling broadly.

When they saw Dagan, everyone at the Flat Rocks bode relaxed. With a woman close to giving birth and perhaps a sick child it would explain why they were moving slowly. Nagar was about to tell Fenti-Dumu that he could run and meet them when she saw Zura half-running toward the group with her arms spread wide. "Barsa, Barsa," she repeated over and over.

The older man broke away from the group and came toward Zura. He grabbed her and hugged her, then pulled back looking into her face and began laughing. "Zura, my shining sister, I have missed you so much."

She hugged him tightly, "And I have missed you, loving brother."

BARSA'S BODE

Seeing Barsa in the group of newcomers, Zura knew they had nothing to fear from them. She and the others at Flat Rocks worked at welcoming them. They built up the fire, set-up places to sit, brought food and teas. The young man carrying the child, a girl close to Fenti-Dunu's age, kept her in his arms. Barsa convinced the young man to let Zura give the child tea, apply a salve to her chest, and feed her a little bone marrow.

The other newcomers were anxious and frequently spoke to Barsa for reassurance. Barsa, meanwhile, could not stop smiling.

It was quite a gathering that night at Flat Rocks. So many stories to tell, Zura and Barsa's reunion, the scouting party's journey, the newcomers' stories, and the events at Flat Rocks – building the Thinking Circle, Skywatching, and the successful antelope hunt.

It was confusing as not everyone could understand each other. Those who could, helped with translation. The scouting party and the newcomers had spent enough time together that they understood the basics of each other's languages. Though he had not used it for many years, Barsa remembered his first language from growing up with Zura. On their long walk, he worked diligently with Dagan to learn the language of Flat Rocks.

All of the excited voices created a wall of sound. Finally, Nagar and Zura, with Barsa's help translating, convinced everyone to quiet down. They would go around the circle, one at a time, helping each other with translation. The bounty from the antelope meant that there was plenty to eat for all. Though the scouting party and newcomers were tired from their long walk, few people around the fire went to sleep before Sun-Man rose.

Nagar suggested, "Let's begin with Zura and Barsa's story, and then the story of the newcomers and how they survived the Ash Rain."

Zura began, "My mother had three children. I came first, then Barsa and finally, a little sister who died of a sickness when she was younger than Fenti-Dumu. Our mother was a wise woman, an elder, a Skywatcher, a healer and a skilled hunter. She knew how to read the tracks and signs of the animals and the cycles of the plants. Her mate was also knowledgeable of many things. They taught Barsa and me everything they knew until their End Days came.

"Barsa and I were as one for many years. When we were old enough, we began to go to the trading places and meet Others. I did not go as often but preferred staying at our bode, Skywatching in the Thinking Circle and healing when it was needed. Barsa liked to go trading, seeing new places, and meeting new people, learning their words. He started going farther and farther away, but he always came back. Then he met a young woman. He came back but could not forget her and so he left and we never saw him again. We heard that her family moved farther away and he went with them. That was a long time ago, but I think about him every day. And now he has come to live with me again at Flat Rocks. This is truly a welcome sign from the Ancients."

She spoke in the language of Flat Rocks, Barsa understood enough and knew the story well enough to translate to the newcomers. When Zura was done, the newcomers started talking amongst themselves.

Barsa spoke, "Not everyone wants to stay. We came to get help from you, Zura, for the little girl, Dara, and we understand there's a woman here who knows much about helping mothers when babies come."

Zura asked, "Did you leave others behind?"

"No, everyone else is dead."

"Then stay with us here. These are good people. But we're too few to survive easily. And you are too few alone."

"You're right. As always," and he smiled at her. "But some are not sure. Let us stay here for a while, wait until Wilki's baby is born. Maybe little Dara will get better and then we'll see what happens."

"Yes, and you are right too," Zura put her hand on his arm. "Let them decide. Please tell them that they can stay as long as they want and are free to go whenever they want."

He did and the newcomers relaxed a little. Seeing how Zura and Barsa were together gave them comfort. Watching the two side-by-side, the similarities were remarkable, even some of their hand gestures were the same. It was easy to see why Dagan had recognized Barsa at once.

Barsa began talking about his little group and what happened at their bode. Zura and Dagan translated his words for the Flat Rocks people, "We're all that is left of our bode. This is Wilki. She is pregnant with her first child. She is a healthy young woman who carries the hope of our future in her womb. There's no one left of our people who knows well how to care for women during childbirth. We heard that there was such a woman here," and he gestured to Nagar. "It was one of the reasons we decided to come."

"This is Grayla and Jolam. They are mated. Jolam came from a trading people and he joined us before the Ash Rain came. Grayla and Jolam, they say little and work as one," Barsa smiled. "They find things for us to eat when no one else can."

"And this is Nat, son of my mate. She died shortly after she gave birth to him. Nat is the bravest and strongest of all men," Barsa said proudly. "The girl, Dara, is the daughter of Nat's mate. She died not long before your scouting party came. She was kind and gentle and could no longer breathe. She was called to the Ancients. I'm afraid that little Dara will follow her soon, but Nat does not want her to leave him. I'm hoping that my sister, Zura, can help Dara, though it may be too late. It is the other reason we came."

Zura asked, "Brother, how did you survive the Ash Rain?"

"Our bode was growing and Nat and I began to look for another cave nearby where some of us could live. We found a narrow opening that went deep into the hill and using a fire stick, we walked in and saw that it opened into a much larger space. It had a spring far back inside. We worked to make the opening larger.

"Those you see here are those that were living in this new cave. When the Ash Rain blew hardest, we stayed deep in the cave. All of the people in our old bode died soon from the Ash Rain. We could not get to them until the worst was over and then it was too late. No one was left alive.

"Since the Ash Rain ended, we are starting to find more food again and, except for Dara, are stronger. Before Tars' scouting party came, we were deciding what to do. Should we try to find Others? But where should we go? I wanted to find you, Zura, and see if anyone was still alive from my old bode but thought it would be too far for Wilki and Dara."

He stopped then and let them think about what he had said. He turned to Tars, and asked him to continue the story about when the scouting party came.

"We found other bodes but it was always the same. No one was alive anymore. And like the other times we went looking, sometimes there were signs that the End Days for people came at the hands of Violent Ones. It made us afraid and it made us careful. Still we thought we might find other people like we found Zura, Dagan, and Esri. We decided to continue for a few more days and then go back to Flat Rocks. On our way back, we walked farther away from the River of Life to see new places.

"The first day we began on our return walk to Flat Rocks, we saw footprints from people. We found a place to hide and sent Dagan to follow the tracks. He found the cave Barsa described. We watched before showing ourselves to see if the people were Violent Ones. When Dagan saw Barsa, Dagan was certain that Barsa was the brother you often spoke of, Zura. He looks so much like you. Dagan convinced us that we should make contact soon."

Dagan continued, "And the next morning I saw Barsa and Nat walking by themselves. I made noise coming up behind them. They turned and I stopped. I knew they might be afraid and might attack me. I yelled in the words of our old bode – 'Barsa, brother of Zura. She wants to see you!' and Barsa grabbed Nat's arm and stared at me like I was a river spirit." Dagan laughed.

Barsa jumped in, "'Who are you?' I cried. I could not believe what Dagan was saying. I had not heard anyone say your name in so many years, Zura. I wanted to run to Dagan and touch him and feel like I was touching you, but Nat was worried it was a trick."

Dagan said, "We talked for a long time before we moved closer to each other. It was like talking to Zura. I told Barsa everything. How Zura raised me and raised Esri. How Zura, Esri, and I came to the Flat Rocks bode, the people at Flat Rocks, and, now, our scouting party to find others. And Barsa told me his story."

Barsa said, "Our groups met several times. In the end, it was Dara and Wilki who convinced us to go and not wait. The trip here was long and difficult. It was good we didn't know how far it was but now that we are here, I feel it was wise."

Nat spoke gruffly to Barsa, "It's good for Wilki but Dara is now weaker and when her End Days come she will not be near the final place of her mother. After Wilki's baby comes and Wilki is ready to travel, I'll go back to our bode with Wilki and take Dara either as she is or her bones to be with her mother. Others can come with me or not as they choose." Barsa did not translate Nat's words to the Flat Rocks people.

Esri stood and motioned Fenti-Dumu to stand beside her, "Fenti-Dumu and I made a song for when you returned. We will sing it for you."

Esri and Fenti-Dumu worried they might never be able to sing their song to the scouting party. What if they had never returned? Seeing everyone around the bodefire again and Zura's brother with the newcomers, it was the happy occasion they hoped it would be and they sang with joy.

Kai began tapping a log with a stick as they sang, others joined him. By the time they ended, everyone was smiling. Even little Dara opened her eyes and lifted her head to smile at the two singers.

The talking went on about the Thinking Circle, the antelope hunt, and then moved to quiet conversations while some people slept. Tars made certain that at least one person among the Flat Rocks people was always awake to watch the newcomers, and the newcomers also made sure one of them was awake to keep watch. While Zura and Barsa's relationship made it easier for people to start trusting each other, it would take time before the trust was complete.

All through the stories, Saba watched Dagan and Riga. When she first saw Dagan walking back to Flat Rocks with the huge smile on his face, she assumed that it meant he was paired with Riga. But she saw that his happiness was for the reunion of Barsa and Zura, and she continued to wonder what had happened with Riga.

Dagan and Riga sat next to each other and exchanged comments during the stories. Riga often put her hand on Dagan's arm but he never reached out to Riga and often looked over at Saba.

In Saba's experience, with newly paired people, the touching happened both ways. While Dagan was quiet, he was not shy. If he was paired with Riga, Saba felt it would be obvious. But maybe she was imagining that the pairing had not happened because that is what she wanted so badly. As people started going to their sleeping spots, Dagan came over to her and put his hands on her shoulders and said, "It's nice to see your face again."

WINTER ACTIVITIES

After a few weeks of doing the Sunday bar clean-up, the manager told Joe that the job would continue to be his as long as the quality of his work stayed the same. The next Sunday, the first weekend of the Christmas holidays, Joe arranged for Esri and Jilly to meet him at the Harbourfront skating rink after he finished work.

Esri and Jilly each got their first pair of used skates as soon as they were able to walk. Sundays in the winter the family often skated on one of Toronto's outdoor rinks. Before Sofie got sick, Joe cobbled together enough used equipment for Esri to play in the girls' hockey league at an arena near their apartment. Esri was good enough to play on select teams but there was no way they could afford the higher fees so she stayed with the house league. But once Sofie could not work, even the house league was no longer affordable.

Esri was glad that Joe's new Sunday job still allowed them to go skating. It was one of the few activities where Joe was all theirs. Joe grew up playing hockey in his small community on the Prairies and he enjoyed showing off for them, teaching them to move confidently across the ice.

When the girls arrived at the Harbourfront rink, Joe was finishing lacing up his skates in the change room. He helped Jilly with her skates. They put their boots in a locker and got on the ice. It was busy but not too crowded. The rink sat by Lake Ontario. A short distance across the lake they could see the snowy crescent of the low-lying Toronto Islands. It was sunny and cold but not biting. Piles of glistening snow edged the skating rink. Everyone on the ice was smiling.

Joe, Esri, and Jilly did several laps, holding hands, taking turns with Joe twirling them around. An attractive young woman at the side waved at them and Joe stopped and skated over to her. "Esri, Jills, come here. There's someone I want you to meet. This is my boss, Randi. And these are my daughters, Esri and Jilly".

"They're lovely, Joe. You three make quite the trio out there, the way you all can skate."

"You sure are pretty and you smell good too!" said Jilly.

"Jilly," Joe shushed her.

Randi laughed. She had a beautiful smile complimented by perfect make-up and stylish clothes. "That's very sweet of you, Jilly. I'm so impressed with how well you skate. I wish I could skate half as well."

"My Daddy can teach you. He's the best skater in the whole world."

"Well, he may be the best skater in the whole world, but I'm the worst skater. A few of my friends have tried to teach me before, but I'm hopeless."

"I'm happy to try, Randi. If you have time. Why don't you rent some skates?" said Joe.

"Oh, I don't want to interrupt your time with your daughters."

"Please, please, Randi. Let Daddy teach you." Jilly bounced up and down. "I know he can. I know he can." And she twirled around.

Joe smiled, "I think you'd better try. Once Jilly gets fixated on something, it's hard to change her mind."

"Ok, but I won't stay for long and you girls have to promise not to laugh at me." Randi rented some skates and brought them outside. Joe helped her lace them up. Jilly kept up a continuous flow of chatter. To her, Randi looked like someone out of a fashion magazine.

Jilly was smitten; Esri less so. As much as she encouraged Joe to get out and start dating again, the reality was something different. Seeing him bend over tying Randi's skates and helping her get on her feet was like a stab in the gut. What if he did bring a strange woman into their lives? She would hate it. It felt like such a betrayal to her mom.

Joe held onto to Randi's hands and began slowly skating backwards, gently pulling her along, his soothing voice encouraging her to relax, bend her knees, and glide, just like he had taught Esri and Jilly.

Randi managed a couple of laps and then said she had to get to work. She only stayed skating for a short while, but it was long enough for plenty of opportunities for her to cling to Joe, and Joe to grasp onto her when it looked like she might fall. Esri wondered why someone as high-class looking as Randi would want to go skating with her Sunday morning janitor. Skating behind them, Esri tried watching Joe as if she was not his daughter and there was no denying he was a good-looking man, and his laughing confidence on the ice made him even more attractive.

Randi said, "I'll let you three carry on without me to slow you down. But you were right, Jilly, your dad is a good teacher. I've never done that well before on skates. Thank you for that."

"Come skating again with us!"

"Well, maybe, Jilly."

Joe said, "Sure, Randi, you're welcome to join us wherever. You'd be surprised how quickly you'll gain confidence skating if you keep at it."

"Thank you. I'll definitely think about it. It was very nice to meet you girls. You've got a great dad."

"I already know that."

"Jilly!"

"It's ok, Joe, she's proud of you. I'll see you next Sunday and, who knows, maybe I'll see all of you. Anyway, carry on, I'll watch you skate while I put on my boots."

After Randi left Joe said, "Es, you ok? You're awfully quiet."

"Yeah, I'm fine. She was sure coming onto you, Dad. Don't you think that was a bit weird, being your boss and all?"

"She's just friendly. I wouldn't read too much into it."

■ ■ ■

Esri was relieved that the two-week holiday break had finally arrived. At least for a while she was out from under the tyranny of the morning alarm clock. Maybe it would give her time to work the cave-people dreams out of her system.

Joe, Esri, and Jilly put up a few Christmas decorations and bought a small tree. Joe took a couple of days off work, but mainly the girls were left on their own.

Shortly before Christmas, the family went to a Handel "Messiah" sing-a-long. It was something Sofie had enjoyed doing, and Joe and Esri wanted to keep the tradition going in her memory. By now, Joe and Esri were familiar with the music and were able participants. The past few years, with Jilly still so young, they left early but this year she made it through the entire program.

The three exchanged gifts on Christmas morning. Small things. Esri and Jilly made their gifts. Joe got Esri new soccer cleats, and Jilly a princess castle. They followed the present opening with strawberry pancakes and, on Clea's invitation, went to her house for Christmas dinner. Esri hoped that this too might become a tradition. Clea had come to feel almost like family. Esri wondered that Clea didn't have anyone else to be with at Christmas. She was such a warm, interesting woman.

On Boxing Day, Esri and Jilly met Luka and Ada and Ada's two little brothers at the big sledding hill. Several inches of fresh snow had fallen overnight and the dense snowfall continued, adding to the accumulation. They screamed and laughed as their sliding carpets and flying saucers took repeated runs through the fluffy, thick snow.

Luka waved enthusiastically at someone on the sidewalk at the top of the hill. Esri turned and saw that it was Jerome with his younger sister, Brianna. "Yo, Jerome, Bri!"

Jerome waved back. "C'mon, let's go see them," said Luka. Brianna was also in Grade 9. In the lower grades, Esri, Ada and Luka often played with Brianna but since high school Brianna didn't associate much with them anymore. She was usually with one of the groups that hung out in front of the cafeteria at school.

Jerome and Luka laughed and joked. Esri, Ada, and Brianna watched them. Jilly and Ada's brothers were anxious to start sledding again.

"Your tribe is getting restless to go sledding. The snow looks amazing," said Jerome.

"It's perfect, like sailing through cotton candy – but it's not sticky. Do you want to try?" said Luka

"What are you saying?" Brianna glared at Luka. Esri and Ada looked at each other.

"Why not? We've got a big saucer. Jerome and I can go down together," said Luka.

"And how is he going to get back up to the top?" said Brianna.

Jerome said, "Whoa, whoa, whoa, Bri. Let's look at this. There's a lot of us here. Maybe we can work something out."

Esri said, "I have an idea that might work. We could take Jerome's chair down below to where the sidewalk loops over to the parking lot. It's not that far from the bottom of the hill. We could pull the saucer over to his chair from down there."

Jerome lifted his eyebrows and looked at Brianna. "It should work. What is the worst that could happen?"

"You break a leg."

"So, I've already got a wheelchair. Anyway, I won't break a leg."

Brianna scowled, "I don't know why you're even talking to me. You're going to do this. OK, but promise me you'll go down where it's not so steep. You know we're going to be late meeting with that guy."

"If he thinks he can make money off of me, he won't mind. That's how he works." Jerome looked at Luka, "Let's do it, man."

"All right!" Luka and Jerome high-fived.

Knowing Luka was generally long on enthusiasm but short on practicalities, Esri stepped in to ensure the saucer was secure before transferring Jerome. Jerome and Brianna directed the others on how best to move him onto the saucer. Once Jerome was settled, Luka squeezed in behind.

Esri said, "Brianna, if you want to ride down too, on the other saucer, I can take Jerome's chair down to the bottom. Ada can handle the kids."

"Ya, sure, why not, I haven't been sledding in ages," said Brianna.

"Ok, here we go," said Esri and stepped away from in front of Jerome and Luka's saucer. Ada gave them a push and away they went. They could hear them laughing and yelling all the way down. Brianna followed closely after, Esri ran down the path with Jerome's wheelchair, and Ada and the kids ran and tumbled down to the bottom of the hill.

When Esri got to the bottom with the wheelchair, Luka and Brianna had already pulled Jerome over to the sidewalk. Coordinating together, they hoisted him back up in his chair.

"Whoa, that was amazing!" said Jerome.

"You're a crazy fool. Now can we go?" said Brianna. She turned to the rest of them, "You know what? That was ok, thanks."

THE NAMING

ELDERS COUNCIL

Nagar sought out the pregnant Wilki who was equally anxious to get to know Nagar. Communication was difficult at first but both women were motivated to understand each other before Wilki's labor began which would be soon. Saba supported Nagar and Wilki however she could. The three women eagerly planned for the birth of the baby.

Nagar told Wilki, "I want you to eat a little of the antelope meat each day as long as the smoked pieces last. It will help make you strong. Let us hope we can kill more. I'll do everything I can to help you when the baby starts to come and in the days after."

Wilki said, "Will the baby be all right? Will I have a lot of pain?"

"You are a strong young woman but the long walk was hard on you. Zura has tea that will help you and the baby inside you to sleep better in the days ahead. I think the baby will come soon. I can feel that it is moving into position with its head pointing to the ground. This is good."

Wilki was grateful to be in the hands of these two women. Nagar had seen many babies into the world. Wilki was a little intimidated by her and also worried about Nagar's health. But with Saba also there, who was such a kind and caring woman, Wilki felt she had made the right choice taking the long walk. Still, she was determined to go back to her old bode after the baby came.

Nagar said, "Why don't you think about staying with us? We all will be safer if there are more of us. We have good shelter and water here, and some of the animals are returning."

"Yes, but it's better to go back to my own bode," Wilki murmured.

Nagar was puzzled by Wilki's reluctance to stay as she seemed eager to learn the ways of Flat Rocks and enjoyed spending time with Saba and, recently, Esri.

One day Esri asked Nagar if she could speak with her alone, "Zura told me to come talk to you. Wilki is afraid of Piram. That's why she wants to go back after the baby comes. Piram told her that because he found her, she had to be with him as his mate and she doesn't want to be with him. She doesn't want to create trouble and thinks it best to return to her bode. Others would go with her."

"Does Barsa know?" Nagar asked.

"He knows that some want to go back but thinks it has more to do with Nat and that they are missing their bode. Wilki has not talked to Barsa about Piram. She cares for Barsa and is afraid he would fight Piram and get hurt or even killed."

"Too often Piram acts in ways that only serve him and no one else. He was not always kind to my sister," Nagar said.

"Did he hurt your sister? And what about Riga? Her daughter?"

"My sister and Riga were with Saba and me much of the time. Piram knew that Tars and I were watching him so he was careful not to go too far, but I worried and wondered how he might be if we weren't around. Before the Ash Rain and so many died, there were more who were like Piram. They used their strength to make others afraid and sometimes forced them to do things they didn't want to do."

"Did anyone try to stop them from doing bad things?" asked Esri.

"The Elders would try. We would speak with the person and tell them to stop hurting others. Some we sent away from the bode for a while, and sometimes we never saw them again."

Esri nodded, "It was like that in our bode. Zura was an Elder like you who tried to stop those who hurt others. What happened at Flat Rocks if an Elder did something bad?"

"Sometimes nothing happened." Nagar sighed, "I would speak about it, but nothing happened."

Esri spoke vehemently, "That is something we can change. Wilki should not be forced to be with Piram if she doesn't want to be with him."

"I agree, Esri, and we should begin now. In these times, with so many who have died, we're starting again and that's hard, but maybe some things we can do differently and better."

Esri smiled. "I think that you and Zura are like sisters, the way you both talk."

Nagar laughed, "Yes, she often says exactly what I am thinking. She helps me feel stronger. What we need to do is form an Elders Council and decide about Piram."

"What about Barsa? What will happen?"

"First, I'll speak with Zura about how we can do this so that Wilki feels safe and Piram doesn't end up fighting someone," said Nagar.

"And what about getting Piram to change?"

"Yes, that's the hardest. It won't be easy but maybe there is some way we can start. One thing, in these uncertain times, Piram would know how risky it would be for him if he was told to leave Flat Rocks even for one Moon-Woman journey."

"And that might make him change? I hope so."

Nagar put her hand on Esri, "You have a gift, Esri. People feel comfortable speaking to you. They trust you. Take care of that gift."

"Sometimes I don't know what to do, how to help them," said Esri.

"You will learn. What is important is that you want to help. As you get older, you'll understand more. Keep listening to the good people around you."

That evening, Nagar had a proposal for the bode. Earlier, she and Zura discussed what to do and they, in turn, spoke with Tars and Barsa to help shape their proposal and inform the two men about what was going on between Piram and Wilki. Barsa understood then, that besides Nat's longing to return to his mate's grave, Piram's claim on Wilki was another reason his group wanted to return to their bode. He found Piram to be gruff and forceful and could understand why Wilki would not want to be Piram's mate.

Nagar said to the Flat Rocks group, "We are now more people at Flat Rocks and want to grow bigger. We hope to find more who survived the Ash Rain and look forward to having the babies come again." She nodded at Wilki. "We need to be able to decide things as a group so that we can live well together. And, we need to have a way to fix things so that we don't fight and hurt each other."

Kai said, "But things are good now. Why change?"

Tars spoke, "It may not always be that way. Now that the animals might be back, what if everyone wants to hunt and no one is gathering roots and plants? Or what if Others join our group and they decide to take over your sleeping place? How would we fix these things?"

Kai looked at Tars and Nagar, "What are you saying? We go back to how everything used to be at Flat Rocks? Elders Council, and only a few learning the ways of Skywatchers and the rest?"

"And what if our ways are different?" asked Nat.

Nagar said, "No, I don't think everything should be as before. And, yes, I think we should look at different ways of doing things." She looked at each of the faces circling the bodefire. "Let me tell you what I think. Listen to everything I say and then we will talk. And we'll talk again tomorrow night. And again, if people want to talk more."

She continued. "I think we should begin by talking about what is done and not done in our bodes. It will be easier if we know how we are the same and how we are different. We know a lot of this already, but there is much still to learn about each other.

"In some of the ways we are different it doesn't matter: how we make spear points, prepare antelope meat, sing our Moon-Woman songs. Many things we can each keep doing as we want or have always done.

"In other things, how we decide on mates, who goes on hunts, who learns the ways of Skywatching, it does matter and we need to agree. For those, we will decide as a bode, what is the best way. We want to hear from everyone, even the youngest if they want to speak. I ask each of you to think about what is the best way, which may not be your old way. This will be hard for many. We may not be able to agree on some things. When this happens, we'll have the Elders Council decide. And if you disagree with their decision, and do not want to live by their decision, then you should not live in the Flat Rocks bode."

Piram asked, "Who will be on the Elders Council?"

Nagar said, "We'll begin with the older members of our group: Zura, Tars, Barsa, me, and you, Piram." He looked surprised, but pleased.

Nat said, "Because people are old does not mean they're wise."

"That's true, Nat, but often they know more than someone young because they have lived longer," said Esri. Nat looked unconvinced. Esri knew that he was worried that giving Piram more power could make things more difficult for Wilki. Esri trusted all of the others on the Council and saw that including Piram might be a way to influence him to change his ways.

"What if we also have a young person on the Council?" asked Esri.

"I think that's a good idea," said Barsa.

"Let's talk about all of this," said Zura.

The discussion went long into the night and for many nights after. They found that their bodes did have many similar traditions around sharing food, hunting, gathering plants, forbidding people to hurt or harm each other, respecting family units. They agreed on how work would be divided, arranging it so that people might specialize in tasks if they wished, while some tasks would be shared by all or nearly all depending on someone's age or health.

In the end, they agreed that the Elders Council would also include Saba as someone younger. She would want to come anyway, to help Nagar if needed, and her calm, thoughtful demeanor made her a comfortable choice.

Saba knew she could not say no to the honor but sitting on the Elders Council made her nervous and a little afraid to be given such a role in the bode. She took Esri aside. "It should be you, Esri. You're not afraid to speak to the Elders."

"I think you're the right person, Saba."

Saba said, "Soon Nagar will want to talk about how we decide on mates. She wants to stop Piram from bothering Wilki. I'm worried what he might do. We cannot let him have his way. I'm afraid there will be a big fight, and Wilki and the other new people will leave. I want them to stay with us."

"I want them to stay too. Why don't we talk about what you will say at the Council. I'll pretend to be Piram."

Saba laughed, "You will have to be twice as big and stop making me laugh."

CHOOSING MATES

Nagar waited until the Elders Council met a few times and found agreement on several issues before bringing up how family units would be formed.

"Before the Ash Rain, our young people would look to the trading groups for mates or they would find someone in Flat Rocks who was not of their family. If the union was with someone in a trading group, we would seek two unions. One of our young people would go to the trading group and someone from the trading group would come to Flat Rocks. If both people were at Flat Rocks, they came together to the Elders Council and declared that they wanted to be mates. As long as both wanted to be paired and the Elders saw that the two were not from the same family, they would approve the union. I propose we continue with this tradition."

"But things are different now," said Piram. "The trading groups are all gone and we are few. We need to form new families. You say this often, Nagar. I no longer have a mate. Yes, I am an Elder, but I am not yet an old man. I should have a woman who sleeps with me and stays with me. We have women who are not from Flat Rocks who do not have mates. It's not right."

Zura spoke, "Are you saying that you would pick one, and they would have to be with you?"

"You do not need to worry, Zura. You are too old and Esri is still too young. I can take Wilki, and she and her baby can be my family," Piram smirked.

Barsa said, "Have you spoken to Wilki? What does she say?"

"What does it matter what she says? She needs to be mated again, and it should be with me."

"What does Wilki say?" Barsa repeated. He did not like Piram's tone.

Zura put her hand on Barsa to calm him and said, "Let's ask her."

"She will not agree," Piram said. "But I have a right to have a mate."

Nagar said, "What we need to do is decide if in our bode both people have to agree to be mated, or can one person pick a mate and the other has no choice."

"And what if two people pick the same person to be their mate?" said Zura.

"The man who is oldest or maybe strongest gets to choose," said Piram.

Zura asked Piram, "If Tars wanted Wilki, you would go along with that? Or what if it was two women who both wanted the same man?"

Piram did not respond to Zura and she continued, "I believe both people have to agree on being mated. It is best. Let's hear from everyone on the Elders Council."

Everyone but Piram agreed with Zura. The Council continued to discuss the issue for some time as they did not want Piram to walk away angry and continue to harass Wilki. Even though she would not have to mate with him, this would not be a good outcome. They agreed, that soon after Wilki's baby came and Fenti-Dumu's naming, another scouting party would go out to try to find more people, which might produce a new choice of mate for Piram.

The more delicate matter was that, unless Piram became less stubborn and aggressive, it was likely that the same problem would arise again. No one had yet broached this.

Finally Saba said, "I want to say something. I hope it will be all right." She turned to Piram, "Piram, I have known you all my life. You are a good hunter and a strong man. Sometimes I am a little frightened of you because you get angry at the people around you. I think this makes people scared of you and try to stay away from you. I know I'm only a young woman who does not have years of wisdom. I want to tell you this because, maybe, if you could be less angry, it would be easier for someone to want to be your mate."

They waited to see Piram's reaction. He stared into the fire for some time and finally said, "You're right, Saba. You are only a young woman who has no experience with being a mate or a mother. But I will think about what you said."

They were quiet. Most doubted that Piram would change his ways. Yet it was unusual that he did not react with anger to Saba's words. Perhaps it was because the words came from Saba, who rarely spoke and never raised her voice in anger, or perhaps something of what she said managed to get through to him.

The next morning, Saba took Esri aside and told her about what happened at the Elders Council. "Esri, I was so scared when I spoke, but I thought about what you told me, that I needed to say what I was feeling. Thank you for helping me put the words together to speak."

Piram did not suddenly become a nice, gentle person, but he did stop bothering Wilki and talking about how she would be his mate after the baby came. With the entire Elders Council supporting Wilki, Piram restrained himself – for now - and did not risk being banished from Flat Rocks.

PUNCHING EGGS

"Wake up, Esri. I'm hungry," Jilly said inches from Esri's ear.

Esri opened her eyes and stared at Jilly.

Jilly whined, "You sleep and sleep all the time and I'm hungry. I tried to make my breakfast but I have many, many problems."

"You have many, many problems? What kind of problems?" Esri sat up. She didn't smell anything. That was a good sign. She was sleeping a lot. So much was happening at Flat Rocks: killing the antelope; the scouting party going for so long; finding Zura's brother, Barsa, and the other new people; the Elders Council. Things were getting complicated, but at least the scouting party was back and the new people seemed all right. It was amazing that they found Barsa.

"Esri, come on. Stop looking like a zombie."

Esri turned to Jilly. "Yes, ok, I'm here, Jills. Let's see about your many, many problems."

"I tried to make pancakes but I can't punch out the eggs."

"Jilly, you know you're never, never to touch the stove."

"Don't get so mad. I didn't touch the dumb stove. I was making pancake stuff."

Esri walked into the kitchen. It looked like Jilly had tried to "punch out" quite a few eggs before she gave up. Broken shells and raw eggs were strewn across the kitchen table and dripping down the legs. One egg must have dropped on the way out of the refrigerator. Some had made it in the bowl along with their shells and a small mountain of pancake mix.

"Yes, many, many problems. Let's see what we can do." Esri cleaned up the floor and table and carefully scooped out as much of the pancake mix as she could salvage that was still dry and put it back in the box. She picked egg shells out of the batter and added milk to bring it to the right consistency. There would be enough batter to last them for several days.

"Next time, wait until I'm up. I'll show you how to crack the eggs and how to mix and measure everything, but we should do it together," Esri said.

"But you sleep and sleep and sleep, and get mad when I wake you up."

"I'll tell you what. I promise not to get angry if you have to wake me up, if you promise me not to wake me by yelling in my ear. Okay?"

"Okay. Don't get all huffy again. Am I going to Nasima's today?"

"Yup, Farhana's not working today, and tomorrow I'll take you and Nasima to Jenny's birthday party and pick you up after."

After Esri came back from taking Jilly to Nasima's, she plopped on the couch. It was great not to have to go back to school for a few more days. She had no plans for the rest of the day. It was appealing to do nothing but lie and stare at the ceiling until her Dad came home. Doing nothing in the here and now, that is. Her head was full of the activities at Flat Rocks and she struggled to process what was happening in her dreams. She decided to go see Clea.

In the elevator she ran into Nicole with Billy, surrounded by a large suitcase and several bags. Nicole glanced at Esri and quickly looked aside, but Esri had already seen the fresh bruise on the side of Nicole's face.

"Nicole, what happened?"

"Esri, I'm glad it's you. I'm leaving Darren. He's gone out but I don't know for how long. Can you help me get these things on the bus?"

"Sure. Where are you going? Let me come with you."

The elevator reached the lobby. "We need to hurry. I'm afraid of what Darren will do if he sees me. I don't have much money. I have to take a bus, if only it comes soon. Can you help me get my things to the next stop, away from the building? We have to move quickly, in case he comes back."

"No problem. I can come with you wherever you're going. Jilly's at a friend's."

"Oh Esri, I don't want to involve you, and they told me not to tell anyone who knows Darren where I'm going," Nicole said.

"You're going to a women's shelter? He did that to you didn't he?"

"Please, Esri, let's move. I don't want to talk about it now."

They hurried along with Nicole's belongings to the bus stop a few streets away from the apartment building. Nicole carried Billy and a bag, and Esri rolled the suitcase and lugged the other bags. They scanned the streets for Darren, hoping he wouldn't appear. The bus stop was on a busy street, which meant there were taxis. Esri flagged one down.

"What are you doing?" said Nicole.

"Here," Esri shoved several bills into Nicole's hand. "I have cash from my job. You can pay me back whenever. You need to get away and be safe. Go to the shelter. Nicole, let us know if you need anything. Anything at all. Don't worry. I won't say anything to Darren."

"Esri, thank you. Thank god I ran into you when I did. I'm so afraid. I don't know what will happen to me and Billy." They loaded the bags and suitcase into the trunk of the taxi. Esri hugged Nicole and Billy and they drove off. Esri hated Darren. She walked back to the apartment building and decided not to go see Clea. She wanted to talk to her Dad as soon as he got home. Back in her apartment, Esri started watching a movie but couldn't concentrate and found it annoying.

There was a knock on the door. She assumed it was Ada or Luka. Maybe one of them got off work early. It was probably Ada because Luka usually yelled something goofy. She opened the door and Darren came barging in, "Well, Esri, where's Nicole?"

Dumb. She should have known he'd come looking for Nicole. Esri was scared, and angry.

"She's not here."

"Well, I wonder now, Esri. I know how Nicole likes to play little games," he grinned.

Esri backed up. Joe wouldn't be home for a while. "She's not here. You can look around."

"Maybe I will look around. I know how you girls stick together." He winked at her and took a quick look around the apartment. "You know, Esri, I love Nicole, but she does get a little over-emotional at times and makes stuff up. You shouldn't believe what she says about me."

Esri was trying to think what to do. She wanted to scream at him for what he did to Nicole but was terrified about enraging him. "Did . . . something happen?"

Darren spoke calmly, "Did something happen? Why would you ask that? No, nothing happened. I expected to find her home but she and Billy are not there, and I think maybe you know something." He walked toward her.

"I have to go pick up Jilly. If I see Nicole, I'll let her know you're looking for her," Esri moved toward the door.

Darren dropped his smiling, winking facade and grabbed her arm, "You better deal straight with me. If I find out you know where Nicole is . . ."

"I have to go. I'm late," Esri wrenched away from him and stood outside the front door waiting for him to leave. As soon as he was out, she shut the door and ran to the stairs, taking them two at a time to Farhana's floor. It was too early to pick up Jilly, but Esri wasn't sure what to do. She decided to go back to the stairwell and gradually walk all the way to the top floor of the apartment building and slowly back down to kill time. From now on, she would look before opening the door to anyone.

Even with her slow climb up and down the stairs, Esri was still early picking up Jilly, who was miffed. "We haven't finished playing!" Jilly whined.

"You'll have lots of time tomorrow. Dad will be home in a while. You can help me get supper ready in a little bit."

"Can I punch out some eggs?"

Back at their apartment, Esri fretted about what to say to her Dad. She would tell him that Nicole left Darren and about seeing her bruised face, but probably not about Darren threatening her. She would just tell him that she had seen Darren and he was looking for Nicole. Joe was a peaceful, calm guy but hugely protective of his daughters. Esri worried what might happen if Joe did or said something that set-off Darren's hair-trigger anger.

Too much was piling up. Esri felt desperate to unload to Clea about her dreams. And now there was this business with Nicole and Darren.

Esri waited until Jilly went to bed before speaking with Joe about what had happened. And after, he went to talk with Darren. Esri waited up for him to return.

"You found him? You didn't tell Darren about my seeing Nicole, did you?" Esri asked.

"No, no honey. Don't worry. I said you told me he was looking for Nicole, and then I let him talk for a while."

"What did he say?"

"He was pretty upset. First angry, saying how Nicole blew stuff out of proportion, and then admitting that maybe he'd gone a little too far. And, if I could convince her to come back, he'd never let it happen again. I mainly listened. He's guessed she might be at a shelter because no one seems to know where she is. Don't worry, Esri, I didn't say anything about where she might be. I told him he needed to get some help getting his anger under control. He didn't take that very well, and asked me several times what you told him. Is there something you haven't told me? "

Joe waited. Esri started to cry. Joe said, "Did he do something to you?"

"Don't do anything, Dad. I didn't want to tell you. It really wasn't that bad. I was worried you'd yell at him and he'd lose it and hit you and something bad would happen. He just grabbed my arm and said I'd better tell him anything I knew about Nicole."

"Where did it happen? Where did you talk to Darren?"

"Here," Esri said softly.

"Here, inside the apartment? You let him come in?"

"Yeah…"

"Oh Esri, why did you let him into the apartment after you saw what he did to Nicole?" Joe frowned.

"I didn't look before I opened the door. I thought it was probably Ada."

"Oh honey, how many times do I have to tell you? Never, never, open the door when you're here alone or it's just you and Jilly. It takes one second to see who is there. Please, you know how I rely on you to look after yourself and Jilly when I'm not here."

"I know, Dad, believe me. I won't forget."

"And, please, don't ever keep anything like this away from me again. I promise you. I won't do anything foolish. I've known a lot of guys like Darren and I know how they function. If your Mom and Nicole hadn't been such good friends, I probably wouldn't have gotten friendly with him. But life isn't that simple, and Nicole needs our help. Frankly, Darren needs help too."

"I hate him."

"I'm going to keep talking to him about getting some help, even though he doesn't want to hear it. Promise me you'll have nothing to do with him. Don't open the door to him. If he calls, say you have to go. Walk away if you see him. And if something happens, please tell me everything. I don't trust him, especially if he's been drinking."

"Don't worry, I'll be careful. It's Nicole and Billy I'm really worried about. What will happen to them?"

"I don't know. I don't know what we can do for them. We'll figure it out. I'm glad you were there to help her get away. I'm sorry if I sound angry. I worry about how much you have to hold down the fort here. I love you so much, Esri," Joe said.

"I know, Dad. Me too."

"Let's go to bed. It's late."

CHASING ELAND

Nat continued his vigil over Dara. When they first arrived at Flat Rocks, she seemed to get stronger thanks to Zura's teas and ministrations. Esri took two of the bones from the antelope and carved a little face at the end of each and gave them to Fenti-Dumu to give to Dara. On days when Dara felt better, she and Fenti-Dumu played with the bones. They pretended the bones were people and made up stories with them. Esri often joined the children, singing little songs about the bone people that made Dara and Fenti-Dumu laugh. But soon, most days, Dara mainly slept, only waking to eat. She kept the bone dolls nearby, within reach of her fingers.

Nat was consumed with grief for his mate, Marim. Though Barsa tried, he found nothing that could diminish Nat's sadness. Nat hardly mixed with the people at Flat Rocks. Sometimes he spoke at the bodefire, but his words tended to be unfriendly and distant. This was not the Nat that Barsa knew, the robust, joyful boy, then young man, who for so long was Barsa's shadow. Barsa understood how Nat felt. When Barsa's mate, Nat's mother, died, Barsa wanted to end his days and be with her but Nat needed him. And then Barsa saw that others needed him too and, in time, Barsa understood that though his life was not the same, he could still find joy and feel contentment. All that Nat could see was Dara's little ailing face. Barsa could not bear the thought of losing Nat.

The Flat Rocks bode was again relying on plants and roots to eat. Though some combination of hunters went out each day, since Kai and Esri's antelope kill, no one had managed to take down any large game. A few times they spotted tracks, but the animals were elusive.

One day Grayla and Jolam, the quiet couple from Barsa's group, came running into Flat Rocks with news that they saw eland tracks that looked recent. This time, Flat Rocks would make a hunting party as large as possible, spread themselves widely, and gradually corral the animals to a place where they could easily be taken down.

Esri ran over to Nat. "Come, hunt with us this time. Dara is sleeping and Zura and Wilki will look after her. She'll be fine."

"I can't leave her," Nat said.

"We need you on the hunt. Barsa told me you are a good hunter and we need everyone. If we kill an eland, it will mean better food for Dara too. Come, get your spear." She held out her hand.

"I can't leave her for a long time."

"You can come back if we are not lucky soon."

Nat was torn. He did want to go on the hunt. He tried not to admit it to himself, but he felt restless spending so much time in the bode. Before all the misery that happened to him, he was usually the first one up and out most mornings and often the last to lay down at night. He saw that the others from his bode now talked and laughed with the Flat Rocks people. It annoyed him initially as it felt like a betrayal, but lately he realized how much he missed the camaraderie of a tight-knit bode.

He promised Marim that he would always return to her. He couldn't allow himself to become too attached to Flat Rocks, yet these were good people here. He looked at Esri. He had never known anyone who made people smile as much as she did. He didn't take her hand but stood up. "Yes, I will come."

Barsa was pleased and relieved to see Nat join the hunt.

The hunting party gathered. The only people left at Flat Rocks were Zura looking after Dara, Nagar with the pregnant Wilki, and Saba, who stayed to help Nagar and also to be a runner to the hunting party in case anything happened. Fenti-Dumu was thrilled to be a part of his first big animal hunt and promised to be as quiet as Dagan, which made everyone laugh.

Tars organized the hunting group, putting the fastest at the far ends to quickly expand the line out and forward. Fenti-Dumu stayed near Tars, as he would have the best chance of keeping the excited boy from making too much noise.

They moved out rapidly and quietly, spreading apart as widely as possible while still keeping the person next to them within sight. Except for Nat, the others had talked about and practiced how they would hunt together, and Nat quickly fell into place. Esri started out between Kai and Nat, with Kai at the far end. Soon after they were underway, she had Nat switch with her as she saw the agility with which he moved. Next time, he should be an end runner.

They picked up the eland tracks and kept moving ahead with the end runners angling forward. Esri heard Nat whistle. He pointed far off in the distance. His eyes were zeroing in on something not yet in her range of vision. Then Kai whistled. Nat indicated to Esri that the hunting line needed to alter its direction, shifting more toward their end of the line. Esri communicated this to Piram on the other side of her and she could feel the shift of the hunting line. Kai and Nat raced further out and forward, and she followed their movements. Before long, she spotted the eland. There were about ten dispersed along the savannah, slowly grazing.

Dagan was the end-runner at the opposite end of the line. By now he had spotted the herd and was racing to get his end into position. Moving silently was of utmost importance now. Esri hoped that Tars would be able to contain Fenti-Dumu's exuberance.

The eland herd was nearly surrounded by the hunting line. As Kai and Dagan began closing the circle, they crept toward the herd to nudge them toward Tars and Piram without putting the eland into full flight. Piram and Tars, with Fenti-Dumu next to him, positioned themselves behind some shrubs and would make the first spear throws when the eland were close.

Sensing the movement and smells of Kai and Dagan, the herd nervously shifted their movements back toward the middle of the hunting line where Piram and Tars were positioned. The eland did not linger. The largest one sensed something was amiss and began running. The herd scattered and ran off in all directions.

Tars shouted, "Take them!" and spears were hurled. In the end two eland came down, two of the smaller ones. The herd bolted before the hunting circle could tighten up, allowing most to dart away in the gaps. Dagan's and Nat's spears dealt the crippling blows to the two that were killed.

Fenti-Dumu glowed with excitement. Esri hugged him for doing so well his first time on a hunting line.

Nat looked up and saw Saba running toward them. He raced to meet her and she called out to him, "You must come back, Dara . . ."

"Is she dead?"

"No, but Zura thinks it will be soon."

Before leaving, Nat spoke with Kai for a few minutes and pointed to a spot slightly away from where the hunting line had circled in. Then Nat hurried back to Flat Rocks. Saba and Barsa followed him. Nat was soon far ahead. The rest of the hunting party carved up the eland and prepared them to be taken back to Flat Rocks.

Running back, Nat anguished about leaving Dara to go on the hunt. He pushed himself to his limits and arrived gasping for air. Zura held Dara, gently rocking and singing to her.

"I will take her now. I should not have left," Nat said.

"She never woke up after you left. Her breathing changed and that is when Saba went to get you. We were always with her, holding her. Nothing would have been different if you had stayed here, Nat."

Nat sat still heaving for air, holding Dara in his arms. He could not imagine ever forgiving himself for leaving her when he did. Why did he agree to go on the hunt? Not only had he taken Dara to this strange bode, now he left Dara with these strangers while she was dying. He looked down at Dara's waxen face and heard her labored breathing. Barsa and Saba arrived and sat by Nat and Dara.

Holding Dara close, Nat's heavy breathing roused her and her eyes fluttered open. He brought her face close to his, "Dara," he said, and she murmured, "I want to sleep." Then she closed her eyes again and in a short while her breathing stopped. Her body began to cool. Dara was dead.

They wept. Nat continued rocking Dara, his face a mask of grief, his anger palpable when he spoke. "I should never have come here. Dara and I should have stayed and died beside Marim's grave."

A long, powerful moan came from the opposite side of Flat Rocks. No one was alarmed. They knew what was happening. Wilki was in labor.

DEATH AND BIRTH

Zura spoke first, "Barsa, stay with Nat and Dara. Saba and I will go to Wilki and help Nagar. Let's hope the others will be back soon. We need many hands right now. Send Esri to me as soon as you see her."

Saba and Zura found Nagar encouraging Wilki to breathe slowly. The women helped Wilki walk to the birthing place they made near the river. Birthings went better when there was water close by to wash mothers, babies, and birth-helpers, and make teas.

Nagar gathered the salves and teas that she and Zura had prepared to help Wilki. They knew their preparations would provide only small comforts for the birthing and hoped that Wilki's labor would not last long and that there would be no complications. Saba would provide most of the assistance to Wilki while Nagar explained what was happening, and who should do what and when.

Nagar was disappointed that the others had not yet returned. As with Skywatching, she wanted to share her birthing knowledge with many, men as well as women. And right now she could use extra hands to support Wilki, tend the fire, warm water, and sing songs for the new life coming into the world.

The women made Wilki as comfortable as possible in the birthing place. The contractions were powerful but still spaced far enough apart that Nagar knew the birth was not imminent. She showed Saba how to feel the position of the baby, what to look for in the dilation. They kept talking to Wilki, assuring her that all was normal. Between contractions and moans, they encouraged Wilki to join their birthing chanting and singing.

And then the contractions picked up their pace. Wilki squatted while Nagar and Zura held Wilki's arms on either side. Saba positioned herself in front of Wilki. They rocked and chanted with each contraction. Nagar kept repeating, "Slowly, slowly, little mother, let the little one come." She didn't want Wilki to push too quickly, trying to prevent her from tearing badly. A large tear could take a long time to heal, and sometimes it didn't heal well and the mother died.

Just then the hunting party returned to the camp and saw and heard that Wilki's labor had begun. They hurried down to the birthing place. Nagar was relieved to see them and started giving orders. "Jolam and Grayla, come take Wilki's arms. You are stronger and can give her better support. Dagan, look after the fire. We need some good coals. Riga, make tea from these leaves. Kai, use the coals from the fire to warm water in these bowls. Wilki and her little one are working hard. We will do everything to help her. The baby is well positioned but needs a little more time."

Zura took Esri aside. "You must go to Nat. Dara died."

"Oh no, poor little Dara. Poor Nat."

"Barsa is with Nat. They are grieving for Dara. And Barsa is worried that Nat will now go back to Marim's grave and give up wanting to live. You need to help them."

"What can I do?" asked Esri.

"Nat listens to you. He went on the hunt."

"Not because of me," Esri said. "You should have seen him, Zura. He sees so far and moves like the big cats. Nat and Dagan's spears brought down the eland. Nat was the first to see the eland. Without him, we would not have made a kill."

Zura said, "Go now. We need Nat to stay at Flat Rocks and he needs us, but he can't move beyond his grief with Dara gone. He may be lost unless something keeps him here. Dara was still alive when he returned. She died in his arms."

"I will go. I don't know what I can do, but I can help prepare Dara."

Esri found Nat still holding onto Dara with Barsa at his side. Barsa was singing quietly. Nat's face was filled with pain and sorrow. He said to Esri, "I shouldn't have gone on the hunt."

Esri knelt down by him and put her hands on Dara. "You made the hunt successful and helped the whole bode, and you were with Dara for her last breath."

"Maybe if I stayed she would still be alive."

"Do you really believe that?" Esri looked at Nat.

He looked at her and his face crumbled. "No, she was hardly awake anymore, and hardly ate. Feel how little she weighs," and he placed Dara in Esri's arms. "She opened her eyes right at the end. I almost wasn't here."

"But you were here. And if you hadn't made it back, Zura was with Dara and you know how much Dara loved being with Zura. I don't know anyone who is more caring than Zura. But you were here with Dara at the end and so it was meant to be, as it was meant to be that you would hunt with us."

"Perhaps," Nat said softly.

"Should we prepare Dara?"

"Yes. Can you help me? In time, I want to take her back to Marim. If we bury Dara, after a few journeys of Moon-Woman Dara's bones will be ready to take back and lie with Marim."

Barsa said, "Or Dara can stay here, Nat."

"I'm going back. I said I would and I will," Nat spoke gruffly.

Esri handed Dara back to Nat. "I want to get a few things to prepare Dara for burial. I'll be back soon." She returned with Zura and the two women took Dara. They tucked the bone dolls into her hands and wrapped Dara in a skin left from the time before the Ash Rain. Esri began singing. Now and then Barsa and Zura joined her. Nat stared at the little enshrouded body. They would wait until Wilki's delivery was over and then gather the bode.

At the birthing place, Wilki was now in the final stages. Nagar urged Wilki to push and the baby's head slowly emerged. Saba helped Wilki nudge out first one of the baby's shoulders, then the other, and suddenly, there he was. A new little life, the first in so long. No babies had survived since the Ash Rain began. After the death of so many, they needed to start having children. Maybe this one would make it. He was beautiful.

Nagar explained how to wait for the afterbirth and when it came they buried it beside the birthing place.

Everyone was smiling. The delivery went well. The baby looked healthy. Wilki beamed at the little boy and said, "I will follow your ways and call him Wilki-Dumu until his naming. I was afraid of the birthing. I worried on the long walk here what would happen, but now I know it was the right thing to do." She smiled at Nagar and Saba and looked for Esri and Zura, then turned to Kai.

"Where are Esri and Zura, Kai?"

"They are with Nat. And Dara."

"What is happening?"

"Dara died, Wilki. Zura said Dara died in Nat's arms. Dara opened her eyes at the end and Nat's face was the last thing she saw. Esri and Zura are preparing her to be buried," said Kai.

"We should be with them."

Saba said, "And you should rest."

"I can rest later. I want to see Dara before she is buried."

Nagar said to the group, "Come, with many you can carry Wilki and Wilki-Dumu to Nat. She should not walk until the bleeding is less but she needs to say good-bye to Dara."

Saba drew Dagan aside, "Let the others do this. I need you to help me with Nagar. The birthing took all of her strength. It will be hard for her to climb to the cave."

He nodded, "Of course."

Kai organized the rest of the group at the birthing. They moved Wilki onto a large antelope skin, tucked Wilki-Dumu against her, and grabbing corners and edges, carried them both back up to Nat.

Nagar sat down, her breath coming in shallow gasps. Saba knelt beside Nagar holding her. Dagan stooped down, picked up Nagar, and carried her back to her sleeping spot. She wanted to join the others but Saba held Nagar's hands and told her she had done enough for the day. Saba sat by Nagar until she fell asleep.

The group from the birthing placed Wilki and Wilki-Dumu near Nat and joined Esri and others in singing songs for Dara. Nat sat without moving, as if he was also dead. Wilki-Dumu started to cry. Nat looked over, surprised to see Wilki.

"I have a little boy, Nat. He wanted to say goodbye to Dara." She held up Wilki-Dumu.

Nat turned to them and traced his fingers along Wilki-Dumu's cheek and stroked his arm. "I remember the day Dara was born."

Esri looked at Kai who nodded to Riga and Fenti-Dumu. The three went over to Nat. Kai spoke, "Our mothers are buried on the hill beside Turtle Rock. It would please us if you buried Dara near them. It's a special place for us and a good place for Dara."

"You would allow that? We are strangers and, in time, I will take Dara's bones back to Marim. Maybe it's not right to bury her with your mothers if I take her later. But what you're offering is a great honor for Dara, to rest with your mothers."

Esri said, "You're not strangers. Bury Dara near the mothers, Nat. You don't know when you might go or if something would happen to you. This is a good place for Dara to be right now."

Nat agreed it was good to bury Dara beside Kai, Riga, and Fenti-Dumu's mothers. That evening he carried her to Turtle Rock. Others went ahead and prepared a place for her body. He laid her in a shallow grave and each member of the bode brought rocks to cover her. Nat kept a vigil by Dara's grave throughout the night. Someone was always with him.

CLEA STARTS TALKING

Talking to her Dad last night eased some of Esri's worry about Nicole and Darren, though it was hard to see how things could get fixed. At least, for now, Nicole and Billy were safe.

Today, nothing would stop Esri from going to Clea's. Last night, again, so much happened at Flat Rocks. Clea remained the only person Esri could talk to about the cave-people dreams. It puzzled Esri but at least, thank god, she had Clea, who didn't find the bizarre, intense dreams at all odd.

When they talked about the dreams. Clea encouraged Esri to describe everything in as much detail as Esri could recall, every nuance of the conversations and the dynamics between the people at Flat Rocks. That was helpful, but Esri wanted Clea to do more than listen. This cave-people dream business was not normal, and Esri sensed that Clea knew something more about the dreams. Otherwise, why was Clea the only person Esri could talk to about them?

Esri knocked on Clea's door, opened it, and called in, "It's Esri. I'll leave my coat and boots by the door."

Clea called back, "I'm in the kitchen."

Esri came down the hallway. Clea said, "I was hoping you might stop by. You enjoying your holiday break? Where's Jilly today?"

"She's at a birthday party this afternoon. I was wondering if you'd have time to talk? If you had a phone, I'd call ahead of time."

"Don't need a phone. Yes, yes, come on in. I have lots of time, and you know you're always welcome. I'll make some tea. I'm thinking, it's the dreams again?"

"Yes, it's the dreams. I want to talk about the dreams, but I also want you to tell me what you think they mean. I believe you when you say that I'm not going crazy. But the dreams aren't normal, are they, Clea? And I think you might be able to tell me something about them."

Clea sighed, "Yes, I can. I've been thinking that it might be time to begin."

"Begin what?"

"Here, I've got some fresh muffins. Ah, and there's Willa at the back door. She'll want to hear this too. We'll all get comfortable and then let's get caught up on your cave-people."

"So you do know something more about these dreams than you've been telling me?"

"Yes, I do and I promise you, Esri, I will tell you certain things, but first I want to hear everything you've dreamt about since the last time we talked."

Once again, Esri walked Clea through all that had happened to her and the others at Flat Rocks since they last spoke about the dreams. Clea asked many questions. It took a long time but Esri made sure that she finished with plenty of time left to probe Clea about what her dreams meant.

Esri said, "That's it. That's everything I've dreamt up until this morning. So what does this all mean? You said when I came today that it was 'time to begin.'"

"Yes, umm, time to begin. Where to begin?" Clea paused. "Well, I'll begin by telling you that you have a special calling, and that's why you're having these dreams."

"What? You make it sound like I'm supposed to be a nun or something."

Clea laughed, "No, no. Nothing like that. It's something much rarer. It usually starts when you're a little older and begins more gradually. But I think it's because certain things are veering too rapidly in the wrong direction. Your Mending time needed to be sped up. Which is unfortunate, because it makes it harder for you, but it must be done."

"Ah, Clea, you're not making any sense. I have no idea what you're talking about."

"I know. I know. It will take some time and it will take some getting used to. We'll just begin today and I need to tell you, that I don't know everything. I'm much like you, only I've lived longer and had a lifetime to try to come to terms with being a Mender," Clea said.

"A Mender?"

"You and I are Menders, Esri. And I'm your Guide for the beginning of your Mending Years. When I was a little older than you, I also began to have vivid dreams and shortly after, I met my Guide who stayed close to me for many years."

"I . . . I really don't get what you're saying. What's a Mender?"

"Esri, I know this will be hard for you to accept right away," Clea leaned forward, looked intently at Esri. "As Menders, we get sent back in time to fix things. Things that are hurting the rhythm of life."

Esri pulled back and sputtered, "What?? No. No. That's not possible."

"You are already going back in time. Those are not dreams you're having." Clea waited for Esri to take in what she was saying. "You're actually there, living in that time."

Esri shook her head. "No, Clea. That's too crazy. I don't believe that." Willa jumped on Esri's lap and settled in.

"I know. I felt the same when my Guide first told me what was happening. But, it's true. Over time you'll understand more and grow used to the idea." Clea spoke calmly.

"Stuff like this doesn't happen. But just say this is true, then explain to me how does it work?" Esri demanded. "How come I was picked to be a Mender? Who decided? And what's the deal with the cave-people? What am I supposed to be changing? And, anyway, if you change stuff back a long time ago, that messes up everything."

"I don't have answers for all of that. What I know is mostly from my Guide, and from my dreams. There is a life spirit that is the heartbeat of our planet and beyond. We see it in the great cycles of birth, growth, death, and regeneration that are all around us, though it's not so obvious to many these days. As humans evolved, an evil force came into being that threatens the steady rhythm that drives these cycles. As Menders, we've tried to control the evil. But it's getting more aggressive, like a cancer that we can't contain."

"Soooo, this life spirit decides who is a Mender and what they should do?"

"The life spirit is not an entity with a physical shape, and there's no specific god or goddess. It's more a feeling or pulse. My dreams told me that I needed to wait for you and find you."

"And how was I chosen? How were you chosen?"

"It's who we are from birth and who we become. Like everyone, you were born with basic human goodness. We all start with that but it needs to be fostered and stoked as we grow up until, hopefully, it sort of takes on a life of its own. Unfortunately, sometimes it gets smothered."

"I know a few of those types."

"And then each of us has something extra, our gift, what's special about us. And what you need to be a Mender is courage."

Esri stared at Clea. "Well, that counts me out. I'm an insecure mess most of the time."

"Ah but Esri, courage is not about being fearless. Courage is about knowing your fears and making your way through them. I'll bet you're someone who sort of plows ahead, right?"

"Blunders is more like it. Are there lots of Menders? Are you and I related?"

"We might be related far back in time. I don't know. The only Menders I've known are my Guide and he had a Guide, and me and now you. I don't know if there is more than one of us that does Mending at a time, or how far back the Mending goes. But I do know it goes back a long time. My Guide told me."

"Still, why me? I'm a pretty ordinary kid. In fact, I think I'm sort of sub-par in many ways." Willa stood up, circled around Esri's lap and lay back down, purring.

"You're anything but ordinary. You're still discovering who you are. What you've been doing in your dreams and how you've been balancing that with your life here shows that you're more than up to the task." Clea topped up Esri's tea.

"And what is my task? If you change something back in time, it would have a huge ripple effect on everything that happened since then. It would be chaos."

"The ripples don't start appearing until the present time you're living, and they start small."

"And my task? Why am I with cave-people? Why them and why that time?"

"None of that is clear to me yet, nor what it is you need to mend, which is why I want to keep going over your dreams in detail. Having you find the Huti stone in the museum was a clever way to give us a time marker. We need to learn whatever we can about what was happening then."

"I did a bunch of reading for my school project, but there isn't a lot that's known. It was so long ago and long before there were any written records."

"Where did you do research? What about the big reference library downtown? They have lots of rare resources in their stacks," asked Clea.

"No, I've never been there. I mainly read stuff on-line and from the school library and the library by the park. I like reading about that kind of stuff."

"Well then, you'll definitely love the reference library. Since it seems I can still leave my house, why don't we go there on Saturday and see what more we can find out about your cave-people? We might find something useful in the stacks. We'll bring something to keep Jilly occupied and quiet, hopefully – at least for a little while!" Clea smiled.

"Dad said he's not working on Saturday. He was planning on being with Jilly anyway, so she'll be with him. That sounds great, Clea. I'd love to learn more about cave-people and whatever helps explain my dreams. But what do you mean about leaving your house? I've noticed you don't go out much, do you? Are you okay?"

"Yes, I'm fine. It's . . . ah, it's not a big issue - yet. We'll talk about it another day. Really, I'm fine. But now it is getting late. You don't want to be late picking up Jilly. "

"You know this all still seems pretty crazy and unbelievable," Esri stroked Willa.

"I know, it's a lot to take in, but we'll keep talking. It will make more sense over time."

"One thing I do know is that the dreams are not normal, not at all. They feel so so real. I could almost believe you that I'm actually back there living with Zura and Dagan and everyone at Flat Rocks. And the Huti stone. That was totally freaky. And the way I felt when I was doing the flint-knapping. I knew exactly what to do." Esri said. "Next time, I want to hear about what you went to mend and when, was it also with cave-people?"

"No, it wasn't with cave-people. Someday I'll tell you all about it. But right now we need to concentrate on your Mending and there is much to do and learn."

CATS COME BACK

The birth of Wilki's baby and Dara's death and burial delayed discussion about the big hunt. When the mourning songs ended and normal activities began, Kai spoke to the bode. "Nat saw signs on the hunt we should talk about. We were making the final run to trap the eland. He saw footprints made by a big cat. He told me where they were and I went back and looked. The tracks are faint, but I think he's right. This is good news. It could mean more animals are back, but it also means there is more danger again when we go out. We should always have watchers, even on short walks to get roots."

Piram said, "Perhaps, but I've not seen any signs of big cats. Let's not worry too much yet."

"A few of us will go to where Nat and Kai saw the tracks and see what we can find," said Tars. "What else did you see, Nat?"

"In the eland herd, there was a doe that escaped early. She had a bloody tear on her back leg that happened recently. It looked like it came from a spearhead grazing the leg. None of us had thrown spears yet and I did not hear of anyone recently wounding an eland. This means there are other people someplace not far away."

"I didn't see that. Did anyone else?" asked Piram. No one had seen it.

"Nat has eyes like Huti, the big white river bird. He saw the eland long before anyone else," said Esri.

Tars said, "We must pay attention to every sign and explore what it might mean. It's like the big cat tracks. If Others are near, it can be both good and dangerous for us."

Kai and Nat took Piram to where they spotted the big cat tracks. Piram was skeptical that there could be a big cat around and he wouldn't have seen the signs. The two younger men showed Piram the spot and stood quietly while Piram surveyed the area. He knew the ways of big cats. He walked some distance from Kai and Nat, and let out a shout, "Come here!" He found more tracks and these were unmistakable. "Now the fight begins again. I've missed the big cats." He offered one of his rare smiles.

LIBRARY VISIT

Saturday Clea and Esri made an early start and arrived at the reference library shortly after the doors opened. Standing in the central atrium, Esri gaped at the size. Surely here they would uncover something interesting about her cave-people. They rode the glass elevator to one of the upper floors and found an empty table near some windows. She was astounded at the endless shelves of materials and spaces to study. Even at this early hour it was alive with people pouring over materials, writing, using computers. Spacious and light-filled. "Could I live here for a while?"

Clea laughed, "Well, I don't know about that. And there is even more back in the stacks that the librarians will retrieve for us, some of the older rarer resources. Come, I'll take you to the computers we can use to search. I usually ask a librarian to help me. I'm not very good with computers but I'm sure you're a whiz and will know what to do."

They went to the computer terminals. Clea continued, "We know from the Huti stone that it was likely used 50,000 to 150,000 years ago, and your cave people are probably in eastern Africa, given where the stone was found. If the stone continued to hold special meaning, it might have moved around some, but it's doubtful that it would have gone any great distance. Let's focus our research using those clues."

They made a good team. Esri worked the library computers while Clea guided the scope of their searches to hone in on the most promising materials. They accumulated a large pile of books, papers, and periodicals from the stacks. Hours sped by as they skimmed the resources, making notes and investigating further threads of inquiry that arose from their reading.

"I have to eat something," said Clea. "Let's leave our coats and go down and get something to eat in the coffee shop – my treat. No one will disturb our materials. We won't be gone long. Have you found anything?"

"Lots! I'm hungry too, but there's so much interesting stuff here, I don't want to stop."

In the coffee shop Clea said, "I've found some things that might have a bearing on why you're going back to that time period. What have you found?"

"Oh my god, so much. I could spend tons of days here. I've been looking for stuff about how people might have lived around 100,000 years ago. They don't know a lot but believe that people were a lot like we are today – same brain size, probably in much better physical shape, which is certainly true for the people at Flat Rocks. They're super fit. Clea, I saw pictures of spear points, some small ones, like I've made in my dreams. Even remains of places like Zura's Thinking Circle. And I looked at a book about hunter-gatherers in Africa and how they lived just 50 years ago. So similar to Flat Rocks - it's incredible! I'm kind of overwhelmed. What about you?"

"I've been reading about the DNA work they've done tracing the migration of homo sapiens out of Africa. They believe that the first wave was 50,000 to 70,000 years ago. Not that long ago when you think about the evolution of humans. And that led me to read about population bottlenecks."

"What's that?"

"It's when there are huge shrinkages in the populations of humans or other animals. It sometimes ends in extinction. There is DNA evidence that there was a population bottleneck of homo sapiens – us – possibly around the time period of the Huti stone. That the human population got down to a few thousand, some even speculate a few hundred people."

"Wow, you mean humans were almost extinct?"

"It appears so. It happened to the Neanderthals."

"That's crazy. Do you think it was the Ash Rain and Always Cloud, whatever they were?" Esri finished her sandwich. "Can we still stay for a while?"

"Sure, we can do a couple more hours. And you can come again some time."

They finished eating and went back to their table in the library. After about an hour, Esri gasped, "This is it!"

Clea looked up and nodded, "The Toba volcano eruption? I just found that too."

"Yes! It explains so much: why so many died, where the Ash Rain and Always Cloud came from, why it's cold. That must be it, but it still doesn't explain what I'm supposed to do."

"No, not yet, but we have a lot to think about and consider now. What if the group of people who left Africa and ended up populating the rest of the world are some of those at Flat Rocks? What might that mean?" Clea said.

Esri scrunched up her face.

Clea said, "What's wrong?"

"I smell something really bad."

"Oh yes, I smell it now too. Oh god, we must leave. Hurry, grab your things. Go, run, push the button for the elevator. Don't let anyone else get on. I'll come as quickly as I can."

"What?"

"No questions, just go, run."

When Clea got to the elevator, Esri was holding open the doors and explaining to some students that she couldn't let them on. Her grandmother needed to go down and she was mentally unstable and couldn't be on the elevator with others. The students gave Clea a wide berth as she made her way into the elevator.

"I didn't know what else to say," Esri whispered to Clea.

"Don't worry. You did fine. It's my fault. I had some signs. I should have sent you here alone."

"What are you talking about?"

"I'll explain later. When we get down, you run out and get a cab. Make sure he smells all right."

"But that will cost a small fortune."

"I have money."

"There's the Tall Man!" Esri yelped.

"What tall man?"

"Look, the one running toward the stairs," Esri pointed through the glass wall at the back of the elevator at a tall man racing toward the wide spiral staircase on the opposite side of the atrium. "I've seen him before."

The elevator began its downward descent. They watched the man rush down the stairs. Though the elevator made no stops on the way down, at the pace that the man was moving and with Clea's hampered gait, he would catch up to them before they could get into a taxi.

"I must get back to my house," said Clea. The elevator doors opened and Esri ran out.

By the time Clea reached the sidewalk, Esri was waiting beside a taxi and helped Clea get inside. As they were driving away, Clea looked back at the library entrance and was surprised to see no sign of the man they saw on the staircase. What she didn't know was that the man's descent was delayed by tripping over the cane of an elderly man whose books and papers got strewn across the stairs.

Clea pointed to the taxi driver and wrote a note to Esri – 'We'll talk when we get home.'

Clea sat back in the cab and closed her eyes until they arrived at her house. She gave Esri money for the taxi and walked slowly up the sidewalk. Clea went back to the kitchen, sat leaning her head against her hand and stared into the backyard. "Esri, would you put some water on for tea?"

"Sure, Clea. Are you all right?"

"I feel a headache coming on. But I'll be all right. I'm glad to be home. I'll have some tea and then lie down for a while, but there are a few things I need to tell you."

"Is there anything else I can do for you? I can stay with you for a while." Esri hovered over Clea.

"Thank you dear. You were marvelous at the library. It would be best if I didn't leave my house and yard for a while. It will mean I need to rely on you even more for errands. I'm not sure how long it will last. It could be months."

"Why, what's happening? Is it the Tall Man?"

"You said you had seen him before. Where?"

"I saw him in the donut shop the day Jilly and I ran into you out front. There was also that terrible dead mouse smell that day, and he was staring at us in a really creepy way."

"Oh dear, he was already around. I wish you had told me about him, but then, why would you? I thought I had noticed an odor that day, but I was too busy pulling out the cotter pin on my buggy."

"You did that on purpose?" Esri was stunned.

"Yes, yes, of course. My dreams were telling me that it was becoming urgent to make contact with you."

"How did you know I was the one, the Mender?"

"I could smell you. Faintly when you were little, the first time when you came trick or treating. I wasn't sure if it was you or one of your friends, though I thought it was you by the way you carried yourself. When my dreams became more intense, I started following you around to make sure."

"I remember that. We started seeing you more and thought that was weird. So what do I smell like?"

"Sweet grass," Clea smiled.

"Sweet grass? Like they make into braids? We burned one in class once."

"Yes, here, and in Europe it has a long tradition as well. It has a soothing smell."

"But only you can smell me?"

"I imagine another Mender would smell you. And the Disruptors."

"Disruptors? Ok, what now? The dead mouse smell? The Tall Man running down the stairs? Is he a Disruptor?" Esri sounded skeptical.

"Yes, I'm sure he is. I was hoping to avoid talking about them for a while. I don't want to pile too much on you. It's a lot to take in. How are you doing?"

"I'm fine, Clea. Tell me, who the Disruptors are and why you were so frightened?"

"The Disruptors have been around for a long time. They disturb the heartbeat and rhythms of our life and are growing stronger year after year, century after century. Many thousands of years ago when there were fewer humans, the Disruptors had a limited affect. But now that we've become so many, they're starting to dislocate the cycles of most living things."

"There must be a lot of Disruptors," said Esri.

"Perhaps not. The way Disruptors work is by convincing people who convince other people who convince others, gradually affecting huge masses."

"What do they do?"

"Convince people to take, not give; harm, not heal. And it's escalating. We're heading to chaos, large-scale deprivation, increasing extinctions, including people." Clea spoke sadly.

"Why are the Disruptors doing this?"

"I don't know. I wish I did. I can only think that there is a larger conflict at play that is beyond our realm of understanding. What I do know is that this round piece of rock we live on thrums with magical life-giving rhythms, all held in a delicate balance. And that you and I, as Menders, must not allow that balance to be disrupted." Clea closed her eyes. Her head sank.

"Clea, you need to lie down. We can talk more later. Let me help you." Esri got up and helped Clea move to the single bed tucked into a corner of the study off of the kitchen.

"Thank you, dear, and you should go. Your Dad will be wondering where you are." Clea laid down. Esri covered her with an afghan and sat beside Clea on the bed.

"Are you going to be all right? What if the Disruptor finds you?"

"I'm safe in my house and in my yard. You needn't worry. And Esri, watch out for them. They can't harm you, but they will try to stop your dreams."

NAT MAKES FRIENDS

Nat visited Dara's grave often. He was waiting for the completion of enough moon cycles so that he could dig up her bones and carry them back to Marim's grave. In those weeks, Nat's wall of grief started to come down. He was thankful for how welcoming and good the Flat Rocks bode was to Dara while she was sick and dying and, like Wilki, he now felt they had done the right thing by making the long walk from their bode. He realized that Dara's last days were better at Flat Rocks than if he had tried to nurse her alone. And he would never forget the day she died: how there was always someone with him throughout his all-night vigil by Dara's grave. Some came who he hardly knew.

He wanted to show his gratitude to the bode before he left, so he worked hard, gathering food, hunting, helping Wilki with her baby, and pretty much any projects that needed doing. He continued to keep himself somewhat apart, rarely joining in with any of the laughter or singing.

Riga made several flirtatious attempts to interest Nat, to no avail. She had given up on Dagan, who seemed more interested in Saba, though with Dagan and Saba's shy ways, theirs was a slow-moving courtship.

It was only when hunting with Kai and Esri that Nat seemed to enjoy himself. Several times the three of them tracked the now more-common eland herds, hiving off the oldest and literally running it to death. While eland could run more quickly in short spurts, they needed to rest more often and, unlike the hunters, the eland had no means of carrying water. The three found if they could keep an eland moving, not giving it a chance to stop for water, eventually, it would collapse.

It could take a long time. Esri, Kai and Nat worked out systems for storing caches of water and carrying water with them. Usually Esri and Kai left it to Nat to make the solo run at the end of the hunt to bring the eland to complete exhaustion. Esri and Kai were skilled trackers, but Nat was exceptional. They also saw a more joyful person emerging on those hunts, and hoped the hunting trips would persuade Nat to stay at Flat Rocks.

Before Nat came, Dagan usually hunted with Kai and Esri. Esri spoke with Dagan about taking Nat with them to help shake Nat out of his sadness. Dagan understood and did not mind staying close to the bode as he worried about the big cat signs near Flat Rocks and was anxious to look out for the more vulnerable people: Wilki with her baby, Zura and Nagar, and Fenti-Dumu. And this meant more time with Saba, as she was usually near Nagar.

The hunts were not always successful. Sometimes even Nat's keen eyes lost sight of the track, and the lucky eland managed to live another day. At the end of one long and unsuccessful day, they trudged back to Flat Rocks. Saba, Riga, Wilki and her baby were sitting by the fire. The returning hunters were tired but not unhappy. They had a successful hunt not long ago, and just to be out again with the possibility of finding game was still exciting.

The three women sitting by the fire noticed that Nat was even smiling. Kai and Esri were teasing him about losing track of the old eland they were chasing. He started teasing them back, saying, "I think that you two want to get rid of me and be alone to mate."

Saba and Riga looked at each other and started laughing. Riga said, "I doubt that."

"Why do you say that?" said Nat.

Wilki wondered too what was going on. She glanced at Kai and Esri, and then it slowly dawned on her, "Ah, could it be that maybe Kai doesn't want to couple with women?"

Kai smiled, "You're right, Wilki. I do like women and I really like Esri, but I dream of men."

"Ah yes, we too had men who mated with men and women with women," she said. "You and Esri confuse me because you are often together but sleep on opposite sides of the bode."

"We're few at Flat Rocks. It's hard to find mates, but maybe we'll find more people and there will be others like me. I hope so," Kai said. "And now that we all know about me," he looked around the group, "I think everyone else should tell me about their special dreams."

They laughed but no one volunteered any more personal thoughts, and they went back to talking about the hunt and playing with Wilki-Dumu. Unlike other times, Nat stayed around, even adding a comment now and then. It was a revealing insight for him, discovering that Esri and Kai were not life-mates or wanting to become life-mates. He felt dumb for misreading what was going on between Esri and Kai, and remembered how Marim used to tease him that he was better at understanding animals than people. Nat was aware that thinking about Marim was not as painful as it used to be.

RUMINATING

After the visit to the Reference Library, Esri began stopping by Clea's once or twice during the week to see if she needed anything. Clea told her to not bother knocking, to just come in and find her. And yes, she was perfectly safe.

During the week, Esri couldn't linger for long, and for the next several Saturdays she always had to bring Jilly to Clea's. There were no opportunities for extended conversations about Menders and Disruptors, and even if there had been, Clea wasn't herself. She hardly spoke. She was distracted and looked tired.

When they did have brief opportunities to speak, Clea only wanted details of what was happening in the dreams. How were the people at Flat Rocks treating each other? Were any bad things happening? Esri assured her that though the living was still hard, food scarce, and it remained cold, there was laughter and singing, and excitement and joy about Wilki's baby. And Piram was still a jerk but he was leaving Wilki alone.

Esri felt both better and worse about the dreams. It was a relief to be able to share everything that was going on at Flat Rocks with someone. She was consumed with reading as much as she could find about the Stone Age times of the Huti stone, and became increasingly convinced that it was the Toba volcano eruption that caused the Ash Rain and persistent cold from the Always Cloud.

What Clea told her about the Menders and Disruptors helped make sense out of the intensity and persistence of the dreams and the odd smells and the Tall Man. But - and this was a huge but, what if Clea was completely batty? Maybe she regularly lured unsuspecting children into her sphere and made-up a bunch of weird stories. It was all so far-fetched. Was Clea dangerous? Maybe Esri should walk away and find someone else to run errands for Clea. Wouldn't that be the wise thing to do?

And yet, and yet, what if it were all true? What if she, Esri, was a Mender and there was something really important she needed to do? What harm was there in at least playing along for a while? And she couldn't bear thinking about not visiting Clea. Clea made Esri feel good about herself, something she hadn't felt in a long time. Clea was a kind, gentle, and wise sounding board for everything that was going on with Esri and not only the dreams. Her Dad was wonderful but he was gone so much and had enough worries of his own.

NEW NAME

Nagar asked the Elders Council to meet. "It's time to have Fenti-Dumu's naming. Wilki's baby has come, we have a good store of food, and we have our Thinking Circle in place. I want to talk about how we will do the Naming. We are from different bodes with different Naming ceremonies and should agree on what we want to do."

Piram said, "Fenti-Dumu is from Flat Rocks. We should do what we have always done."

Tars said, "I want to hear how others do Naming. Our Namings sometimes harmed the child. We are so few. I don't want to do anything that might risk hurting Fenti-Dumu."

"But he has to prove himself. If he's weak, he's no good to us," said Piram.

"I think we should give him a good name and make a path for him to follow to become strong and able to take care of himself and others," said Tars. "I would have him hunt with you, Piram. Now that it seems the big cats are back, he should learn how to understand their movements. No one knows that better than you, Piram. You have much you can teach him."

"For Fenti-Dumu's Naming let's make songs to say the things we're talking about and tell the stories of Flat Rocks especially after the Always

Cloud came. Esri already has some. We need a good way to remember these things," said Zura.

"And what about his name?" said Saba.

Nagar said, "Well, I had a dream about Fenti-Dumu. He was singing to Wilki-Dumu. They were sitting in the Thinking Circle and there were yellow birds sitting around them on the stones. It came to me that Grilu would be a good name for him. It's the sound of the yellow bird and like the yellow bird, I think that Fenti-Dumu will be a singer and a hunter."

They all agreed that it was a good name and decided that the Naming would happen in a few days on the night of the next half Moon-Woman. The Elders decided what each of their stories or songs would say to Fenti-Dumu. Nagar asked Tars to be last and give Fenti-Dumu his name. She wanted the Naming to be powerful and knew she no longer had the strength. There would also be singing and dancing from the others in the bode that would last throughout the night.

Fenti-Dumu was thrilled that his Naming was finally happening and could hardly contain himself. Riga and Saba worked on a new cape for him made from eland skin. Esri composed a song about Fenti-Dumu. Kai and Dagan sought out some hollow logs for drumming dance rhythms. Everyone worked at something, gathering wood for a big bodefire inside the Thinking Circle and preparing food. Each day they watched Zura move the Moon-Woman cycle stones in the Thinking Circle, marking the days until the half-moon. Finally the day came and as evening fell the bode gathered in the Thinking Circle. Kai began a slow, soft cadence on a log.

Nat was missing. Barsa walked to Turtle Rock to find him. Nat was lying on top of Dara's grave. He was silent, but shaking, tears streaming from his eyes.

"Come, Nat. We're starting the Naming. People want you to come. There's nothing you can do for Dara. She's in a good place here." Barsa sat and placed his hands on Nat.

Nat took a deep breath and sat up, clasping his arms on Barsa's, "You've always been good to me, Barsa. I've been lost in my grief for so long. I came to tell Dara that I want to stay at Flat Rocks. Sit with me for a while and then we'll go down to the Naming."

Esri started singing and many others soon joined her. Some drummed on logs. Others stood swaying and shuffling around the fire. Fenti-Dumu sat proudly on a rock near the fire with the Elders on either side. Esri tried to focus on Fenti-Dumu and the Naming but couldn't help glancing up the path leading to Turtle Rock where Barsa had gone.

Nagar signaled that they should begin the Elders' words and songs for Fenti-Dumu. She spoke first and in a sing-song voice, talked about Fenti-Dumu's mother, how Fenti had kept Fenti-Dumu far back in the cave to stay away from the Ash Rain, and when she was dying, asked Nagar and Saba to look after him. Nagar sang/spoke about the hard and terrible times of the Ash Rain and the joy that Fenti-Dumu brought them in the sad times. He kept them from giving up.

She spoke of Fenti-Dumu's important duty to the bode, which was to remind those coming after him of what happened when the Ash Rain came and what they did to survive. People must understand that the world around them may change, and the old ways may not keep working. She finished with, "Remember what is said at your Naming today and carry it with you always. My End Days will come before you are a man but know my spirit will be with you even after I am buried at Turtle Rock."

Everyone was quiet. Esri looked up and saw that Nat and Barsa were standing just outside the Thinking Circle. They waited until Nagar finished before joining the group. Nagar nodded to Esri who began singing.

Through the night, the Elders took turns sharing stories, with singing and dancing in between. Piram spoke about teaching Fenti-Dumu to hunt and learning the ways of the big cat. Saba sang about looking after babies and children to keep them safe and guide them on a path to become good Elders.

Barsa had stories about when he was a young man, how he enjoyed visiting many bodes, trading with them, and learning their ways. The stories talked about strangers meeting and building trust and no one was harmed. He also told stories of others who used force and that this would not be the way of Flat Rocks. Barsa spoke about showing peace without showing weakness, but cautioned that building respect and trust with people who enslave and deal cruelly with others can be difficult.

Zura spoke to Fenti-Dumu about watching and listening to the rhythms of the world: the Travelers, Sun-Man, Moon-Woman, River of Life, people, animals, plants, and everything around them. She talked about Skywatching and marking the seasons and passage of time. She said to him, "Learn from those older than you who carry the knowledge of the Ancients and pass along their wisdom to those who come after you. Keep watch, stay alert to changes, learn from others, and learn from the earth."

After Zura finished speaking, the original people from Flat Rocks: Tars, Piram, Riga, Kai, and Saba sang and danced their Naming song, the tradition of generations at Flat Rocks. Nagar did not join them. Saba prepared a bed for Nagar at the edge of the Thinking Circle so she could rest nearby.

It was now well into the night. Tars stood and brought Fenti-Dumu to stand in front of him by the fire. Saba woke-up Nagar and helped her move closer, near Tars and Fenti-Dumu. Nagar knew that Tars' words would be what Fenti-Dumu would remember most from this night, and what he would carry forward throughout his life.

Would making a new way of Naming anger the Ancients? Nagar thought back to that day long ago when the two Elders brought her the mangled remains of her son, killed by a big cat during his Naming night. She vowed to put an end to risking the lives of children, and at last it was done. They would make Namings about starting children on a path to not only help them survive but help their bode survive.

Tars began to speak, "Fenti-Dumu. This is the last time anyone will call you by that name. As the Travelers make their way across the heavens, so too do we make our way through our time on earth. Our journey has many stages, beginning when we are babies coming out of our mother's womb. For many the journey is short. We strive for our journeys to last until the days when we reach the wisdom of Elders.

"You have now passed through the days when you were small and weak and could not survive alone. Tonight marks the beginning of the days when you are half man and half child. You will keep learning and you will start to carry responsibilities that are yours alone. This will take time. How quickly you become a man depends on you.

"In your short life, Flat Rocks has experienced much sorrow and many difficulties. It is still difficult. If we are going to survive, we must stay strong. And that means each of us becoming as strong as we can and working together.

"There are times in life's journey when you need to help others, like the very young or very old or sick. And there will be times when it is you who need help. The strong today become the weak tomorrow, and the weak today become the strong. It is part of life's journey.

"Use the days ahead to learn everything you can from those around you. You will find something that is your special gift to Flat Rocks. Do not forget what is said tonight. These are the stories that have brought us together and will carry us forward.

"Tonight you receive a name that is yours for the rest of your days. The Ancients came to Nagar in a dream to give you your name - Grilu. It's like the sound of the hunting bird. It's a good name, Grilu."

Grilu smiled. Tars was right. It was a good name.

GRILU'S CAT

ALL MADE UP

"I'm seven! I'm seven! I'm seven!"

"Jilly, stop yelling and calm down!"

"I've been quiet for hours and hours and let you sleep like Daddy told me."

"What time is it?"

"The clock says 9 – 0 - 2. You have to get up now. We have to get ready for my party."

"When did you get up?"

"7 – 1 – 5"

"Almost 2 hours. What have you been doing?"

"Watching TV and I got a bowl of cereal all by myself, like you showed me. I'm seven now. I can do everything."

"Okay, I guess that's okay. Here, let me give the birthday girl a hug."

Esri was impressed. Not too much of a mess in the kitchen, only a little spilled milk. Joe was at his Sunday cleaning job. It was Jilly's birthday today and this afternoon four of Jilly's friends were coming over for a party. Jilly wanted to invite more, but Joe and Esri convinced her that it would be too crowded in their little apartment. Joe promised a big surprise for Jilly's party. Esri didn't know what he had planned. He was even taking care of the cake. He asked Esri to pick up ice cream and organize treat bags for the guests.

Esri expected to see her dad by noon. The party was starting at one. 12:30 and still no Joe. At 12:45 he arrived – with Randi decked out as usual in trendy clothes, perfect make-up, in a cloud of expensive-smelling perfume. Joe was carrying a large box that looked like it came from a fancy bakery. Randi carried an overnight-sized bag.

"Randi! Randi! Randi!" Jilly yelled.

"Happy birthday, Jilly. I'm glad you're so happy to see me."

"Randi wanted to keep it as a surprise," said Joe.

Esri was surprised. Shocked was more like it. They had seen Randi a few times skating at Harbourfront but coming to their apartment? For Jilly's birthday? That was getting more familiar than Esri was comfortable with. No wonder Joe and Randi wanted it to be a surprise. If Joe had asked her ahead of time, Esri would not have agreed. This was treading too far into their family.

Joe looked at Esri and raised his eyebrows. "Randi's got a fun plan for the party."

Esri nodded. She'd try to be nice to Randi, if having her at the party made Joe and Jilly happy.

In a few minutes the four party guests arrived. Randi gathered Jilly and the other little girls in a circle and brought out her bag, which was filled with make-up. Her treat was showing the girls how to put on make-up. She started with Jilly, helped her pick eyeshadow, lipstick colors, then paired off the girls and they practiced putting make-up on each other.

Randi also brought a curling iron and several different hair pieces and extensions to create an array of hair-styles. She took pictures of the girls and promised to print off colored copies for them that she'd give to Joe and he could pass them on.

"Esri, what about you? Let Randi fix you up," said Jilly.

"Ah, no, that's okay."

"Come on, pretty please. It's my birthday. You look so plain."

Randi said, "We won't force her, Jilly. She looks lovely just as she is. Though I would be happy to make you up, Esri. I'll be quick. You might be surprised how nice it looks."

Joe looked at Esri. "Okay, but not too much," said Esri. She didn't like standing so close to Randi. God, that perfume.

Randi worked quickly applying make-up, and using a couple of strategically placed combs, swept Esri's hair up on one side.

"You look great, Es," said Joe. He leaned close to her. "I'll go get the cake ready." There was a knock on the door. "Can you get that?"

It was Luka - with Jerome. Oh great.

"Oh my god, Esri! What happened to you?" Luka bellowed.

"Shut up, Luka. We're just goofing around for Jilly's party." Esri was mortified.

Jerome smiled. "Well, that's kinda perfect for what we want to talk to you about. But it sounds like you're busy."

"Yeah, it's Jilly's birthday party. We're about to do the cake. Do you want to come in?" Though Esri really didn't want them to stay as she felt that she probably looked ridiculous.

"Thanks, but I've got some people I need to see. Luka, maybe you can stay and explain what's up," said Jerome.

Luka laughed, "I think I'll take a pass too. I'm not that good at that princess talk. I'll come back in a little while."

"They'll be gone in a couple of hours. Come by after supper, Luka." God, she was embarrassed. She was relieved when they left, but wondered what they had come to talk to her about.

Joe came out of the kitchen with the cake, also Randi's doing. Esri had never seen such a fancy birthday cake. It must have cost a bundle, Esri thought. Jilly was over the moon about everything Randi did. Thankfully, Randi also showed the girls how to remove most of the make-up. Esri was worried what their parents would think when they picked their daughters up if they were painted up like little beauty queens.

Before Esri wiped her make-up off, she went to look at herself in the mirror. Yes, she looked like a lot of the popular girls at school, but she still hated it. She was relieved to wipe it off and relieved when the party ended and that Randi did not hang around after Jilly's friends left.

"Randi, please, please stay. That was the best party ever. Thank you!" Jilly gave Randi a big hug.

"I do have to get going. I'm glad you enjoyed everything, Jilly. It was my pleasure. I'll see you next Sunday, Joe," Randi touched his arm. Joe walked her to the door. He briefly put his hand on her shoulder as she left.

The phone rang. "God, is that Luka already? I'll get it," said Esri. "Hello"

"Hey, hot babe."

"Luka, please. Don't start. What do you want?"

"Okay, okay, you don't have to get so angry. I'm calling about something extremely cool, and it will make you and me a bunch of money."

"What?"

"This promoter guy who thinks Jerome is the next big thing wants to use one of his songs in a commercial and thought it would be cool to have a bunch of kids from Jerome's 'hood in it – give it an 'authentic' feel as he says. It involves some singing so I suggested you, and Jerome thought that was totally great. And we'll get paid! And, this is so cool - it's for Dragon Garb and we'll probably be able to keep some of the clothes after."

"Whoa, ok, yeah, that does sound pretty cool. And, Dragon Garb, that's a big deal. Jerome must be psyched. But I'll have to check with my Dad. When? And what about Ada? Though it's probably not her thing."

"I asked her but, you're right. She's not that comfortable performing in front of people, and also thinks her folks would probably say no. You know they're pretty strict. But you'll do it, won't you?"

"If you're sure that it's ok with Jerome and everyone else who'll be there. Is Brianna going to do it?"

"I assume so. Look, if Jerome's cool with you, then the rest of them will be too."

"And am I going to have to get all made up and wear something dumb?" asked Esri.

"Like a tight little skirt? I dunno, maybe, maybe not, 'cause part of the idea is to have a bunch of different looks, and anyway it's really good money."

"And when?"

"They want to shoot the commercial next weekend. It could take a chunk of Saturday and Sunday."

"I'm usually at Clea's but I'm sure I can figure something out with her."

SCAVENGING

Piram was anxious to look for the cat. If the big cats were back, the bode should know what territory they were taking over, both for the protection of Flat Rocks and to take advantage of scavenging the remains of the cats' kills.

Piram wanted to take Grilu with him and asked Dagan to join them. Piram was more at ease with Dagan's amiable, quiet ways than some of the other younger adults, who often challenged his opinions.

They got up early the next day, before sunrise. Esri rose with them. Before they started off, Esri pulled Dagan aside. "Watch over Grilu. I worry that Piram will push him to do something dangerous."

"It will be all right, Esri. Piram is a good tracker, and Grilu is anxious to learn the ways of the big cats. You know I'll be careful."

Esri helped them pack extra water and bundles of smoked meat. Magenta clouds illuminated the morning sky as they walked away. She stood for a long time on top of the cave, watching them clear the next ridge.

It took them until nearly midday to locate big cat tracks. Sometimes the tracks disappeared for long stretches. Whenever they did, Piram and Dagan conferred over the most likely direction the cats would go. Grilu paid rapt attention to these conversations. He still had his little boy spark and enthusiasm, but since the Naming, he restrained his exuberance and was eager to prove himself as a great hunter.

While Piram no longer had the vitality of a young man, he had years of experience studying the wily ways of the big cats. He and Dagan usually agreed about which direction to take when the tracks disappeared. Whenever they didn't agree, they followed Piram's instincts.

That night they built a small shelter out of branches and grasses and rationed their supply of smoked meat and water. Grilu slept soundly, with a child's confidence that the adults would keep him safe. Piram and Dagan took turns staying alert throughout the night to any potentially threatening noises. The next morning, Dagan rose first and noticed several vultures circling in the distance. He pointed them out to Piram and they quickly broke camp and set out in that direction.

It might be a recent big cat kill that they could scavenge, with care. They needed to move cautiously, determine the location of any big cats, and time their attempts at scavenging until after the big cats took their share. There would be other animals who would want to scavenge the kill but if there weren't too many, they could hold them off until they carved off some portions to take back to Flat Rocks. Maybe the kill would provide a good haul of meat and offer Grilu a lesson on how tracking big cats could yield easy food.

When they came close to the circling vultures, they saw a large eland lying on the ground, half of its side torn away. Piram and Dagan split up circling around the kill in opposite directions. Grilu went with Piram. The men used bird whistles to signal if they sighted any big cats or other animals. Piram said to Grilu, "Look, the vultures are starting to feed on the eland. That means the big cats are probably not close anymore."

Piram had Grilu climb a tree until Piram was certain there were no powerful predators nearby. Grilu was light enough that he could reach the higher, smaller branches that would keep him safe. Piram proceeded alone. Grilu watched from high in the tree, eager to be taking part in the scavenging.

Piram continued walking, scanning the area for signs of big cats. He moved a distance from where he left Grilu and saw Dagan on the opposite side of the kill. Dagan looked over toward Piram and began shouting and waving his arms and running. Piram spun around in the direction Dagan was gesturing and saw Grilu racing toward the kill, his small flint spear held high, yelling at the vultures, intent on claiming a piece of the eland for himself. Grilu didn't realize that one small boy would do little to scare away the vultures and he was putting himself in danger. Piram also began running and yelling and waving his arms.

One of the vultures attacked Grilu. At the same time a huge white cat came charging out of the underbrush. Grilu screamed and fell behind the eland. Piram and Dagan lost sight of him. The cat pounced where Grilu went down and the vulture flew off. The men knew that the big cat could easily kill the boy before they could reach him. When Dagan and Piram got to Grilu, the cat had one large paw on the boy's chest with her face inches away from Grilu's. She looked up at the two men, turned, and vanished into the bush as quickly as she appeared.

The two men were horrified when they looked at the little boy. Piram said, "Oh, no, his face. Is he dead?"

Grilu began crying and screaming, "I can't see. I can't see."

The side of Grilu's face was horribly slashed either by the vulture's beak or the cat's claws or both. Grilu's right eye was bleeding badly and his right cheek was in ribbons. Dagan knelt down and cradled Grilu, trying to calm him and determine where he was hurt.

Piram said, "I need to find the big cat and make sure she doesn't attack us again. Carry Grilu far enough away from the kill that he is safe."

"I think she is a Ghost Cat. She's so large and all white with strange eyes. I don't know if you will find her."

"I must try," Piram took several steps toward where the big cat ran off and stopped. "These tracks are like none we have seen. They're very large. This is not the cat that made this kill. Maybe you are right, but what is a Ghost Cat doing here?"

"We must get Grilu back to Flat Rocks. Zura can do more for him than we can. We'll talk to the Elders about the Ghost Cat."

They moved Grilu away from the kill and took care of him as best as they could. His left eye was clogged with blood from the other wounds but not damaged otherwise. Once the blood was cleaned off, he could see again from that eye. This helped to calm him. Dagan used a small piece of hide and two pieces of sinew as a sort of bandage around Grilu's cheek to close up the lacerations. He covered the damaged right eye with moss he had brought. They began walking and walked through the night, arriving at Flat Rocks early the next morning.

Esri spotted them first and went running out to them. Piram carried Grilu. Dagan pulled Esri aside and said, "Don't get angry at Piram right now." He and Piram were exhausted. By now, everyone at Flat Rocks was up.

Esri helped Zura tend to Grilu. Zura asked that it only be Esri. Zura knew that it was critical to keep Grilu quiet while he healed, and it would be difficult if people were constantly coming around.

Esri quickly made up a soft bed for Grilu. Zura examined him from top to bottom for injuries and determined he was not hurt beyond his face. She delicately undid the bandage Dagan had wrapped around Grilu's check and removed the moss from his right eye. She was horrified by what she saw but kept her face calm and spoke soothingly to him. The less he was upset about what happened to him, the better he would heal. She spoke to him, "I know you're scared and in much pain. You're safe now and we'll help you heal. It's important that you lie quietly. I'm going to make a drink that will help you sleep. Close your eyes. I'll be back soon. Esri is also here. We will take care of you."

Zura did not want Esri to look at Grilu until she had spoken to her. When Zura was sure Grilu could not overhear, she said, "He is badly hurt. His face will always be scarred and he lost one eye."

Esri gasped, "Will he die?"

"No, he won't if he heals well. We need to remove the poisons from the attack. This will be painful. And if he does not lie still for many days, the skin will not bind together well. But as important as the healing is what he believes inside. If Grilu feels he cannot overcome what happened to him, he could die. I have seen this happen. You need to prepare yourself. When you look at his face, you will feel a huge sadness. You must not let him see this."

"But if he is changed, others will say something."

"Yes, but in a few days he will not look as bad as he does now. And we will talk to him about being different. I wanted to prepare you for when you first looked at his face."

Zura went back to Grilu with a strong brew of tea. His injuries made it difficult for him to drink but he managed to swallow enough to feel drowsy.

Zura said, "Grilu, Esri and I are going to clean away the poisons from the attack. We'll do this with warm water and move softly. You'll feel pain at times but it will help you to heal. Every day going forward, you will have less pain."

Though she was warned, Esri was barely able to stop herself from crying out when she first saw Grilu's damaged face. The beautiful little boy was gone.

Esri did what she frequently did when she was overwhelmed or at a loss of what to do. She started to sing. It was the little song she taught Grilu that first night she, Zura, and Dagan sat around the bodefire at Flat Rocks and Grilu came over and tapped her arm and tried to sing with her. Grilu opened his one good eye and managed a small smile when he heard Esri singing.

Zura and Esri took turns cleaning away the blood and dirt. Zura believed that when animals attacked, they left their poisons behind and if you didn't wash them away, they would kill you. It was heartbreaking work hovering over his little face. There was nothing to be done for the right eye. The beak of the vulture pierced too deeply.

Kai came and told them, "We're meeting to talk about what happened on the hunt. Can you come?"

Zura said, "Esri, you go. You can tell them how Grilu is doing. I know you're angry with Piram, but listen to what he and Dagan have to say before you speak."

"Esri," Grilu called faintly.

Esri leaned down close to him. "Grilu, I'm here. Don't talk now. Lie quietly."

"The big cat saved me. Don't let them hunt the big cat."

"The big cat saved you?"

"Yes, she hit the vulture away from me. Then I felt her paw on my chest. Her claws were inside. She did not hurt me. She did nothing to me. She saved me."

Esri looked again at his chest and there were indeed no claw marks from a big cat.

He went on, "I disobeyed Piram. Don't be mad at him."

Esri smiled down at Grilu. "Don't worry. I will take your words to the meeting. Promise me that you will lie quietly. You need to not speak for a few days so that your cheek can heal. I promise not to get angry, if you promise to be quiet. All right?"

"Yes. But remember, don't hunt the big cat," and he closed his eyes.

Esri and Kai went up to the bodefire. Everyone was gathered and wanted to hear how Grilu was, how badly he was hurt. No one spoke to Piram and Dagan, who sat glumly to the side. Tars asked everyone to be quiet and let Piram and Dagan describe what happened. Piram went first, and to Esri's surprise, did not blame Grilu for disobeying him as she thought he would. The tone of the group changed when they heard how Piram took care to make sure Grilu was safe. Then Dagan spoke, confirming everything Piram said. He spoke at greater length about the mysterious big cat.

Tars said, "We can't be sure it's a Ghost Cat. If she's not, we need to kill her for what she did to Grilu."

Esri spoke, "Grilu told me the big cat saved him. That she hit the vulture so it flew away and then sat with her paw on his chest and did nothing. She didn't bring out her claws. He has no marks at all on him from the big cat."

Piram said, "We thought Grilu was hurt by the cat. When we reached him, she was standing with one paw on his chest. Her face was this close to his," and he demonstrated with his hand an inch away from his face. "But it's true. We did not see the cat harm Grilu. She ran off as soon as we came near without making any threatening sounds or movement toward us."

"She looked at us before disappearing and had eyes like this," and Dagan crossed his eyes. Several people gasped.

"Her tracks were like none we have yet seen. There were this big," said Piram and used both of his hands to show the size of the tracks.

Esri said, "If she saved Grilu, we should not hunt her."

Nagar said, "And if she is a Ghost Cat, we probably can't find her anyway."

The discussion about what had happened and whether or not to hunt the big cat went on for some time. Esri described Grilu's injuries and what Zura was doing to help him heal, why it was important to keep Grilu quiet and not talking until the skin started to bind together again.

They decided to have a few of them go and follow the tracks of the Ghost Cat. If they did find her, they would not harm her but watch and see where she was living and hunting and how many others were in her family. Big cats never lived alone.

Many volunteered to go. Finally, it was decided that it would be Piram, Dagan, Grayla, and Jolam. They might be gone for some time, depending on how far the tracks led them. And, if they did find the big cat family, they would stay and watch them for a while. They left the next day. Before they left, Dagan talked to Grilu, told him what they were doing, and reassured him that they would not harm the big cat.

DRAGON GARB

Esri woke, upset and anxious about Grilu. She looked around. Where was Jilly? She wasn't in her bed. Where was she? It was too quiet. Had something happened?

Now that Jilly was seven, Joe was more relaxed about her puttering around in the apartment on her own and letting Esri sleep in longer on the weekends. But after what happened to Grilu, Esri panicked. He's probably Jilly's age. Oh my god, it was horrible, his beautiful face. Children need to be watched every second. What if something happened to Jilly that forever transformed her? Esri would never forgive herself. Look at Jerome, his life changed in a split second. Esri ran out of the bedroom and screamed, "Jilly! Jilly!"

"Jeez, Esri, I'm right here. Stop yelling. You're always yelling at me."

"Are you okay? Have you been awake a long time? What have you been doing?"

"I'm fine. I'm watching cartoons like I always do and eating cereal. What's the big deal?"

Esri hugged her. "I'm sorry. I worry about you. I don't want you to get hurt, ever."

"Esri, stop it. You're acting weird. Let me watch cartoons."

Jerome's clothing commercial shoot was starting at ten today and might go late. Jilly was staying with Luka's mother until after lunch when she went to work. Ada was on the early morning shift at the donut shop, so she could look after Jilly along with Ada's younger brothers in the afternoon until Joe got home. Shortly before Ersi expected Luka, the phone rang.

"Hello?"

"Esri, is that you? It's Nicole."

"Hey, Nicole. How are you doing? How's Billy?"

"We're okay. I wanted to let you know we're okay. And . . . and to hear a familiar voice."

"Is there anything we can do to help? Have you figured out what you're going to do?"

"No, not yet. The staff here are really nice and very helpful. It's just hard. I know we're safe but it's kind of crowded. Everyone living here is pretty stressed, so I spend a lot of time with Billy in our room."

"People are mean to you?"

"No, no, not really. I think it's that people are anxious and then little things blow up. We take turns cooking and all. I'm just feeling kind of lost and alone."

"How long will you stay there?"

"I don't know. We're working on finding some good, affordable day-care for Billy, and I'm on a waiting list for a subsidized apartment. And then, if I can get back on at the dental clinic . . . But that's a lot to work out and sometimes I don't know how far I want to go with this."

"Gosh, Nicole. That's pretty big."

"Do you ever see Darren? I'm still so frightened of him, more for Billy than me. I don't want Billy to grow up with that kind of anger in his home. But I miss my life when Darren had a job. He was a little intense at times, but he mostly kept it in check. I miss being a family. I don't know what to do."

There was a knock at the door. That would be Luka and his mother. "Nicole, I'm really, really sorry but I've got to go. Luka and his mom are at the door – Jills, can you let them in – Luka and I have a job to go to."

"Oh, sorry, Esri. I've gone on. I'll let you go."

"It's okay, really. Call again, Nicole. Usually this is a good time. Let me know if there's anything we can do. Give Billy a hug for me."

"I will. Thanks for listening. Bye."

"Was that Nicole from upstairs?" asked Luka.

"Ah ya, it's . . . a . . . kind of private."

"Luka, you don't have to poke your nose in everyone's business," his mom said.

"Yo, ma, I get it. You don't have to remind me. You ready, Esri?"

"Not really. I haven't got Jilly organized yet. I need a few minutes."

Luka's mom said, "Don't worry, honey. I'll fix her up and pull the door closed when we leave. I'm looking forward to spending some one-on-one time with my favorite little girl. And tomorrow morning too." She squatted down and Jilly hugged her.

Esri and Luka arrived at the studio where the commercial shoot was taking place. As soon as Esri opened the door. The dead-mouse smell accosted her.

"I don't know if I can do this, Luka."

"What do you mean? You have to. You promised me."

"You don't smell anything?"

"No, I don't smell anything. What's with you? Come on, we're already late."

Esri didn't know what to do. She couldn't disappoint Luka, and Jerome, and Brianna, who wasn't so cliquish anymore. But that smell. It meant a Disruptor. Clea said they wouldn't harm Esri, just stop her dreams. Maybe if she just avoided whoever smelled like a dead mouse and stayed close to Luka, it would be all right.

The smell made Esri nauseous, but she pushed herself to ignore it as much as possible. There were about a dozen of them working on the commercial. Esri knew nearly everyone, at least by sight. Some of the coolest kids from school were here. She felt self-conscious and intimidated, but Luka was at ease and always nearby. And though Jerome was busy and in the center of things, he still found moments to convey an encouraging word or nod in her direction. Esri gradually relaxed, and she and Brianna clicked on singing background vocals. Jerome even had them do a small duet.

The dead mouse smell seemed linked to the promoter, the same one Esri saw talking to Jerome in front of City Hall in the fall. Esri thought the promoter stared at her a lot, but she was probably imagining it. When the promoter left for several hours in the afternoon, the smell receded. Esri almost didn't notice it anymore but it unnerved her when he came back and the sickening odor hit her again with full force. What if Clea was right?

Fortunately, the promoter wasn't around at all on Sunday. The dead mouse smell lingered but faintly. Before she left home, Esri found a perfume sample that Randi left after Jilly's party and dabbed some around her nose. That helped, but it also reminded her of Randi.

At the end of the shoot on Sunday, Luka and Esri headed back to the apartment building together, "God, Es, was that ever beyond incandescent or what? I can't wait to see it on TV. We'll be famous. And, we made a ton of money and these clothes. I definitely know what I want to do when I grow up. Hell, from here on out. And that promoter guy really seemed interested in you. You're going to follow-up with him, aren't you?"

"I don't know, Luka. You're right. It was exciting and I can definitely use the money. And singing, that was super fun. Jerome's song is amazing."

"But, I hear a 'but' there in your voice."

"The promoter guy made me uneasy. He's kind of a sleaze-ball."

"Yeah, so? Who cares, if he can line up gigs like this."

"Yeah, maybe. I'll have to think about it."

That night Esri didn't dream about Flat Rocks, nor did she for the rest of the week. She kept telling herself she should be relieved, but it made her anxious. What was happening to Grilu? Was he healing? What if he died? Would that be her fault? It doesn't matter, she told herself. They're just dreams. As much as she kept repeating that to herself she knew that wasn't true. As inexplicable and fantastic as the whole idea of being a Mender seemed, deep down she felt the truth of it.

For the first time, Esri dreaded going to Clea's on Saturday. She wondered what Clea would say or do when she heard that Esri's dreams about the cave-people had stopped.

THOMAS

"Oh goody, going to Clea's today. She promised we'd make cookies. Can we go soon?"

"Hang on, Jilly. It's too early. I'm still eating breakfast." The phone rang. Esri wondered if that might be Nicole calling again.

"Hello?"

"Hey, go turn on your TV to the news channel!"

"Luka? What's up?"

"Just turn it on. I'll stay on the phone." Esri turned on the TV and flipped to the all-news station. There were pictures of a massive fire. The words on the screen said it was in Bangladesh. Esri thought immediately of Jilly's friend, Nasima, and her mother, Farhana, who came with her husband from Bangladesh shortly before Nasima was born.

"I've got the TV on. Looks like a big fire in Bangladesh. I'm thinking about Farhana. What happened?"

"Esri, they locked people into the building. They don't know how many died. They think hundreds. But the thing is. All the clothes they made were for Dragon Garb."

"What!!?"

"The news is saying that Dragon Garb has one of the worst reputations in the clothing industry."

"I feel sick. Why didn't we know that?" said Esri.

"Because we're just stupid kids."

"Can't we stop them showing the commercial? I don't want to be a part of it."

"We all signed those waivers and everything. There's nothing we can do unless you have a bunch of money to hire a lawyer, which I'm sure you don't."

"Well, one thing I'm not going to do is use any of the money I made from the commercial. I'll give it away. Maybe to the people hurt in the fire or their families. Farhana might know. Oh god, she'll think I'm such a horrible person. And I am."

"I've already spent a lot of mine. But I feel like crap. I wonder what Jerome thinks."

"I don't know, but I've gotta go, Luka. Clea's expecting us. Let's talk later. I just don't get why people are so awful . . ."

"Yeah. Well, it's all about money. That's totally that promoter guy. You smelled something there all along, Esri. I'm sorry I got you into this."

Smelled is right, thought Esri, "Luka, it's not your fault. We'll figure something out. I'll be home by three. Come by before you go to work this evening."

"K."

Esri knew this would send Luka into a tailspin. It sent her into a tailspin. She listened to more of the newscast. Many of the people locked in the factory were girls her age and younger. Why did these things happen?

"What's happening on the TV? Why did Luka call?" asked Jilly.

"Something very sad happened, Jilly. A lot of people died in a fire, and he wanted to talk about it. C'mon, let's go make some cookies with Clea."

Esri had been feeling uncomfortable about going to Clea's. With the cave people dreams seemingly over, she thought maybe there was nothing to them and Clea was just some eccentric old lady. But maybe the dreams ended because the promoter was a Disruptor.

"Clea, we're here to make cookies," Jilly yelled when they walked into Clea's house.

"Don't worry, Clea, I'm also here to do some real work for you," called Esri.

"Come on back, girls, there's someone I want you to meet." This was new. Clea never had company. The girls took off their coats and walked back to the kitchen. An old man sat at the table. Ancient would be more like it. Clea appeared youthful by comparison. He sat crumped in his chair with a cane leaning between his legs. Yet there was nothing old or dim about his eyes.

"Ah, so here she is," he said.

"Yes, this is Esri and the cookie maker is Jilly," said Clea. "Girls, I want you to meet my oldest friend and teacher, Thomas. I haven't seen him for many years."

Jilly hung back, uncharacteristically shy. She had never seen anyone who looked so old. Esri said, "Nice to meet you, Mr. . . ."

"Just, Thomas," said Thomas. "And likewise Esri. I've been looking forward to meeting you for a very long time."

Clea said, "Jilly, we'll make the cookies after lunch. Come," she took Jilly by the hand, "I set up something special for you in the dining room. It's something I played with when I was a little girl, a fairyland forest. You'll like it. Ah, and look, there's Willa sitting on the table to keep you company."

When they left the room, Esri said, "Thomas, um, this may sound odd but are you Clea's Mending Guide?"

He raised his eyebrows and smiled at her. "What makes you ask that?"

"There's something about you. You kind of remind me of Clea. And I've never seen anyone else at her house. I just thought you might be."

"Well, Esri, you are a forthright one. I won't deny it. You're right. I am Clea's Mending Guide. I have been since she was in her mid-20's. I don't get out much anymore but, strangely, I started Mending Creams again. It's been years since I had them. And though I can't do much, I've been watching Clea and checking in on her." He smiled at Clea as she walked back into the kitchen and said to her, "Well that didn't take her long to figure out."

"Who you are?" Clea smiled. "She's good at reading people."

"Unfortunately, not always," said Esri, "Is Jilly okay?"

"Yes, that will keep her occupied for a little while. I've told Willa to keep Jilly company. Jilly will like that but we'll see. It's important that we talk. Thomas is going to stay with me for a while. I'm thinking that perhaps he can help us understand your Mending. I've told him all about what's happening in your dreams. Now, tell us what you've dreamt since we last spoke."

Esri paused before she spoke, "I haven't had any dreams for the last week. Not since Friday night."

"Oh my," Clea's expression became grim.

"This is most troubling. What happened to you since then?" asked Thomas.

Esri took a deep breath and told them everything: her ongoing doubts about Menders and Disruptors, doing the commercial, the dead-mouse smell around the promoter, and this morning's news about the horrible fire. She told them how she and Luka wish they hadn't done the commercial, and how terrible they felt about what happened to the people in the fire. Clea and Thomas let her talk it out.

"Oh child, it's been too much, too fast, and you're still so young. Those people dying in the fire are not your fault but, you're right, those things should not happen. There is no justification for it. None. But we've evolved a way of living that allows it," said Clea.

"I think that's why your Mending is taking you so far back in time," said Thomas, "and why the Disruptors are so active, and, possibly why they've brought me back out of retirement as it were."

"But if I've stopped dreaming, then I can't do any Mending, can I?" said Esri.

"But hopefully, it will be temporary. What are you planning on doing?" said Clea.

"I don't know what I can do. I haven't spent any of the money I made doing the commercial. I was saving it. I want to return it or give it away. Luka and I are going to ask Farhana what she thinks."

"Your idea of talking to Farhana is a good one. Also, read as much as you can about the fire, and understand what happened and why," said Clea.

"Esri, you're still feeling unsure about being a Mender, aren't you?" said Thomas.

"Yes, I have to be honest, I am, but less so. I'm sorry Clea has been wonderful. I can talk to her about anything and Jilly and I love coming here, though I don't feel I always do enough work. But the Mender and Disruptor business is so 'out there' and crazy. Can you understand why I have some doubts?"

"Yes, it does sound fantastical when you first hear about it. I was older than you and my Mending revealed itself more slowly, though still, it was difficult to take in," said Thomas.

"The same was true for me. You remember?" Clea nodded to Thomas. "For you, Esri, keep talking to me about everything, including all your doubts. We'll continue to go a step at a time and let things unfold. You've had such a strong – and worthy - reaction to what the Disruptor got you involved in. Perhaps when you give away the money your dreams will start again. But be on guard for the Disruptors. If you ever encounter the Disruptor smell again, walk away and come see me as soon as you can. "

"I will, Clea. I feel better already having talked to you and Thomas. It's funny, I kind of like myself better in the dreams. I seem braver and more confident, and happier too," said Esri.

"You are brave here too. And you will become braver and more confident as you get older. And I hope happier. You're a good person, Esri," said Clea.

"That's nice of you to say. We'll see. You help me a lot. But what about you, Clea? Are you in danger?"

"I'm all right as long as I stay here. And it's good that Thomas is going to move in with me. It will make it safer for both of us," said Clea.

Jilly stood in the doorway holding the cat, "What's going on? I'm hungry and so is Willa."

"Hey, Jills, how long have you been there?" said Esri.

"I heard you say Clea is in danger. What danger?"

"Oh, it's just that she can't really go out and about in the wintertime with all the ice and snow. She could fall so easily. And speaking of going out, I should get some shopping done for you, Clea. Do you want me to make some sandwiches first for lunch?" said Esri.

"Yes, yes, that would be perfect. Let's eat, and while you're out shopping, Jilly and I can start on those cookies."

Willa jumped out of Jilly's arms and wound around Esri's legs.

After finishing at Clea's, the girls returned to their apartment. Esri phoned Luka and the three of them went to see Farhana. She didn't have any immediate family hurt in the fire, but it happened not far from where she and her husband grew up.

Farhana was touched by Esri and Luka's concern and their desire not to make any profit from Dragon Garb. Because of all of the media surrounding the factory fire, she hoped there would be enough pressure on Dragon Garb to adequately compensate the families. She would find out what was being done and how to best channel donations to the families affected by the fire. Farhana worried that there were so many other factories with lax safety and underpaid employees and had another suggestion for Esri and Luka.

Farhana said, "My cousin runs a school for girls from poor families in the community where the factory fire happened. The classes are scheduled at times when the girls are not at work. It helps them move into better paying, safer jobs. She runs the school on very little. I try to send her money when I can to help pay the teachers and buy supplies. I'm sure she would be grateful to receive support from you."

Esri talked with her Dad when he got home from work, and he agreed that supporting Farhana's cousin's school would be a good thing to do. Luka did the same with the money he had not spent from the commercial, plus adding extra from his regular job.

Farhana coordinated the money transfer for them and within a few days, she received an email from her cousin to pass along to Esri and Luka with excited thanks and pictures of some of the girls at the school. For Esri and Luka, it felt good to be rid of the money from the commercial shoot, and the connection with Farhana's cousin touched them deeply.

It also pried open a worldview neither had thought about a whole lot before. Growing up in the apartment building, they knew many people from other countries who sent money back to family members. Ada's family did this too. But understanding that buying cheap clothes in the mall might mean someone their age getting paid poverty wages to work long hours, locked into a poorly constructed building, this sunk in in a way it had never done before.

■ ■ ■

Despite Esri's heartfelt gesture to return the money she made from the commercial, the Flat Rocks dreams did not come back. Maybe that was it. Maybe they were done. She could tell that Clea and Thomas were worried, though their dreams were telling them that the Disruptors were still active.

At the end of school on Thursday, Luka found Esri.

"Hey, Jerome wants to get together at his place tonight with all of us who did the Dragon Garb shoot. I told him about what we did with Farhana and he thought that was way good. Can you come?"

"Sure, I guess. You know how that group kind of intimidates me. But I will since you're going."

Not everyone from the shoot showed up, and several who were there couldn't see what the big deal was and had no interest in returning the money they had made. They felt the fire was terrible and all, but their donating money was not going to do much except superficially make them feel better. Esri was uncomfortable and wanted to leave. But she was frustrated with some of the attitudes and thought about how she was in the cave-people dreams and tried to be braver.

When there was a lull in the discussion, Esri said, "Jerome? What if you wrote a song about the fire and we did a video of that and, uh, we pushed it on social media?"

It was the first time Esri spoke. Everyone turned and stared at her, some smirked and looked over at Jerome.

Jerome's mom, tidying the kitchen, came out and said, "Who said that?'

"I did," said Esri.

"Well, that's the first sensible thing I've heard any of you say. You know, Jerome, I keep out of your business but this is a disturbing situation, and if you have aspirations of making money on your god-given talent, you need to find a path that is. . .'"

Jerome held up his hand, "Ma, you don't have to say anything more. I hear you and I hear Esri. Let me see what I can do. I think it's not a bad idea."

Some of the kids still thought it was kind of lame to think they could do anything to affect something that happened half a world away, but they respected Jerome and the idea of making another video was appealing. The school had equipment, and likely there would be teachers keen to help.

Esri accepted that anything they did would be a small act and it wasn't a magic wand that could instantly create a fair world for everyone, but she believed that doing something rather than nothing was important. A lot of somethings could become a magic wand. She slept soundly for the first time in many nights.

SELA AND MUNI

Either Zura or Esri were always near Grilu, and others from the bode took turns helping them. They sang to Grilu and told him stories. Fortunately for Grilu, Zura was adamant about cleaning away the vulture poisons twice a day until she could see that the healing was going well.

Nat told Grilu the story of a wise man he knew as a little boy and how this man lost an eye and still went hunting and was a respected Elder in his bode. And others did what they could to lift the spirits of the boy who was forever changed.

Nagar's words did the most to encourage Grilu to accept his fate and be patient with the healing when she told him, "The big cat spared you for a reason. She saw a special destiny for you."

Within a week, Grilu was moving around, becoming accustomed to navigating the world with one eye. Zura insisted that he continue to keep his face as motionless as possible until the next big round Moon-Woman, and she showed him how to mark the days in the Thinking Circle. Bit by bit, he went farther afield, learning more about plants and roots and set-ting traps and snares for small animals. He particularly enjoyed spending time with Zura in the Thinking Circle, as she guided him through the meaning of the stars in the night sky.

The bode eagerly awaited the return of Piram, Dagar, Grayla, and Jolam from searching for the big cat. Almost two weeks after they left,

Riga, Esri, and Grilu were out checking their animal snares when Riga spotted the returning group. "Look, there's Piram and the others, and they found two more people. They're small. They must be children."

"Run back to Flat Rocks and tell the others. I'll walk to meet them with Grilu," said Esri.

"I want to meet them," said Riga.

"All right, but don't run to them. It's still too soon for Grilu to start running," said Esri, and she headed back to Flat Rocks.

Riga and Grilu walked forward to meet the returning group. Piram went running over to them when he saw it was Grilu. It was still a shock to see what had happened to Grilu, but he looked much better than when Piram left. Piram put his hands on Grilu's shoulders. "You are strong again, and the healing is going well."

Riga jumped in. "We're not letting him talk much yet. Zura said he should try to stay quiet until the next big round Moon-Woman. Who have you brought with you?"

"We think they are sister and brother from a place many days' walk away. We don't know their story. They only talk to each other, and only a few words sound like ours. They're hungry. We found them breaking open bones from a kill where all the meat was gone, looking for the food inside the bones."

Riga and Grilu studied the gaunt and wary boy and girl standing between Dagan and Grayla. The girl was older than the boy and both looked older than Grilu. They stared at Grilu, no doubt wondering what happened to his face.

Dagan said, "We're hoping that maybe Barsa, who visited so many communities as a young man, might be able to understand more of their words. We tried to be gentle with them, but they're frightened of us. I think they've seen some bad things."

Grilu reached into his pouch and pulled out some of the nuts he had gathered, and then held them out to the children. He gave them a small smile and said, "Here, for you." The two stared at Grilu. First the girl, then the boy ate the nuts. Grilu understood that his face was causing them distress and wanted to show them that they did not have to be afraid of him.

Dagan stroked Grilu's head. Grilu had come a long way in healing and accepting what had happened to him in the two weeks Dagan was gone. Dagan patted Grilu's chest, looked at the children and repeated, "Grilu, Grilu," several times and then patted himself and said, "Dagan." He gestured toward the children but they remained mute.

Piram said, "Come, let's go. The others at Flat Rocks will be anxious to hear our stories."

The people were busy at Flat Rocks, organizing foods and seating around the bodefire, eager to hear about the trip and meet the two young people. Though the travelers were tired, they would talk and eat first before resting. Dagan and Grayla sat so that the children could be between them, the girl beside Grayla and the boy beside Dagan. Dagan explained the little he knew about them and tried again to get them to speak or at least say their names, yet they stayed silent.

Zura said, "Tell us the story of your trip. The young ones you found will need some time to learn to trust us."

Piram began, "We returned to the site of the kill where Grilu was attacked by the vulture and found the tracks of the big cat. We followed her for all of the next day and then the tracks ended. We never saw her joining other tracks of big cats, or any places where she slept. She kept moving alone. It was not normal. I've never followed a big cat who behaved that way.

"We walked for a day in the direction she seemed to be moving but didn't find her tracks again. We went back and tried another direction she might have gone. Still nothing. And then we tried one more time in a different direction. This time we did find big cat tracks, but not hers. Then we found the children, who were trying to use stones to break open the bones of a kill.

"We approached them. They cried and tried to run away, but they were so weak they could hardly stand, and the boy fell over. Dagan picked him up, and the girl began clawing at Dagan and tried to bite him. We had to hold her back. She fought but was soon exhausted. We made a small camp and gave them some water and food."

Dagan continued the story. "It was difficult to bring them back. They would eat and drink and get a little strength and run off. We could have easily caught them, but we knew they would soon be thirsty and hungry again. I thought that if we didn't chase them, they might start to trust us. It sort of worked because here we are, but we still can't get them to even tell us their names. They're frightened. I think something very bad happened to them, or they saw something very bad."

All eyes were on the girl and boy. They started talking to each other. Barsa walked over to them and sat down in front of them, speaking softly. They both began to cry and speak rapidly to Barsa. He listened until they finished and said, "I understand a little of what they're saying. They come from a river valley that is many days' walk toward where the sun sets. I visited there when I was young but did not stay for long. They were peaceful people, but in the next valley over were others who were known to act violently, killing and stealing people to be their slaves. I did not want to stay there."

Zura said, "Did they tell you what happened to them?"

Barsa said, "I think they're the only ones left of their bode. But whether everyone else died from the Ash Rain or were killed, I'm not certain. I've told them that no one will harm them here."

Dagan said, "And their names?"

Barsa and the children spoke for several minutes. He said, "Their names are Sela and Muni and they are sister and brother. They want to see everyone who lives here to see if any of the bad people are here."

One by one, everyone at Flat Rocks came over to Sela and Muni. Barsa told the children everyone's name, their relationship to others, and explained how some of them came from other bodes. When they met Wilki and her baby they even smiled. Wilki showed them how to tickle Wilki-Dumu, and he laughed and gurgled for them. They could see that no one was a slave at Flat Rocks and that made them feel much safer than they had in a long time.

Grayla asked Barsa to ask them if they wanted to share a sleeping spot with her and Jolam. While Muni had grown attached to Dagan, he wanted to go wherever Sela went. The children agreed they would like this arrangement.

In the first week, Sela and Muni ran off a few times but no one chased after them. Grayla or Jolam kept a distant watch on the children to make sure no harm came to them. They never went far and as it grew dark, always returned to Flat Rocks and their sleeping place with Grayla and Jolam. Gradually Sela and Muni came to trust the people in their new home and learned how to speak with the people at Flat Rocks.

Over time, they told their story. Like everyone at Flat Rocks, Sela and Muni's bode lost many in the Ash Rain. The adults tried to protect the children as much as possible, keeping them sheltered inside a cave. They were fortunate to have an underground spring nearby that provided them with fresh water. But only Sela and Muni, three other children and two adults survived the Ash Rain. They were having a hard time finding food, but were afraid to move and lose their source of water.

Three men attacked their bode. They were from one of the groups their bode sometimes traded with, but they feared them and stayed away from them as much as possible because they were a violent people who took others as slaves.

The two adults tried to protect the children but were killed immediately by the Violent Ones. The children screamed and cried and tried to run away, but the Violent Ones grabbed them and beat them and bound them with sinew so they couldn't escape. The Violent Ones released one child to wait on them, fetching water and all the food that was available. When there was nothing left to eat, the children were forced to start walking to the Violent Ones' bode. The smallest child died on the way.

Sela and Muni managed to escape one night. They set off in one direction for a while, then carefully covered their tracks and changed course hoping that the Violent Ones would not try hard to find them. Before their mother died from the Ash Rain, she told Sela and Muni to find the River of Life and then walk toward where the Sun-Man came up and stay near the River until they found people who did not have slaves.

There were details of the horrors they experienced that Sela and Muni never spoke about, not even to each other, until they marked their days as Elders. As the days passed, the memory of what they went through dimmed, and the people of Flat Rocks folded them into their bode.

GIRLFRIEND

Jerome wrote a brilliant song that the time had come to call out the business bullies of the world. It was clever and catchy, not preachy. Making the video ended up being a big project at the school, with a number of the teachers and students participating. The video started to gain traction online and attracted some media.

The night Esri made the suggestion at Jerome's apartment to do the video, she began to dream about Flat Rocks again. The dreams didn't come every night right away. That took a few weeks.

Esri was haunted by the factory fire in Bangladesh. Previous tragedies reported in the news had not affected her so deeply. She would feel sad for a little while but it wouldn't last long as Esri felt she had enough to handle in her own day-to-day life. This time, she became obsessed reading about the girls her age and younger who worked long hours for little pay, and no opportunity to go to school and how many were also forced into prostitution. Why? Why did people treat each other so badly? She talked to her Dad, who didn't try to sugar coat anything yet worried how intense Esri was becoming.

"It all comes down to people wanting more money, doesn't it, Dad?"

"Yeah, a lot does. There're many, many people who don't have enough to eat or stay warm and healthy. That would make anyone feel desperate. And then there are others who have a lot of money yet never seem to have enough and keep grabbing for more, cheating and short-changing others however they can."

"What about us?"

"Well, things are definitely tight for us right now. It's hard to find good, decent-paying work, and the price of everything keeps going up. We don't own a car. We don't go out much to movies or do things that cost money. But we manage to pay rent and have enough to eat, and we're fortunate to live in a country with decent education and healthcare. And, Esri, we have each other and all the good people we know, many in this apartment building. You and I haven't talked a lot about your Mom dying. I still struggle so much thinking about her," he paused. "Losing her was so big. I thought I would never be able to move beyond always feeling sad. But you know, sweetie, it also made me hold on to moments when things are good and not take them for granted. And those moments come from people, especially you and Jilly, not things we buy."

"I wish you didn't have to work so much."

"Yeah, me too, but maybe in time that will change." He hesitated. "There's something I've been wanting to talk to you about."

"Randi?"

"Yeah, I guess you've noticed I've been coming home later on Sundays. Randi and I've been going out for coffee, getting to know each other. I know you don't seem to like her that much. She's kind of stayed away since Jilly's birthday. She could tell you weren't so happy about having her here. But if you got to know her better, you'd feel more comfortable around her. I want to have her over every so often, maybe for supper sometimes. She usually doesn't start working until late. Esri, no one will ever replace your Mom, ever. But I miss being in a relationship. I'm not saying that Randi is going to be a permanent part of our lives, but I'd like to see where it might go. Jilly sure likes her."

"I'll try, Dad. It's hard seeing you with someone, though I know I have to get over it. I don't want you to be alone the rest of your life or anything. So sure, bring her for supper sometimes, but can you promise me that she won't be a part of our birthday celebration? At least this time?" Esri and Joe were born on the same day and their birthdays were coming up.

"Ok, I'm all right with that. Now, let's go to bed. I'm really proud of you, Esri, and how you're thinking about what's going on in the world. Not many kids do that, or adults either for that matter. We get so caught up in ourselves. Good for you, kiddo. Keep it up, but don't let it overwhelm you either." He gave her a hug.

AGREEMENTS

PLEDGING SMILES

Finding Sela and Muni spurred a desire in Flat Rocks to send out more scouting parties to search for survivors of the Ash Rain, and find and free anyone who was enslaved. Many opinions were voiced and options discussed about what to do. Should they look for survivors and try to avoid Violent Ones, or try to kill any Violent Ones they found and get rid of them?

Nagar, as much as her health would allow her, and Zura spoke passionately against violence, that it would only bring on more violence. They wanted Flat Rocks to continue to be a place where doing violence to others was not tolerated. Even those most in favour of killing Violent Ones had to agree that what they had at Flat Rocks was a good way to live.

The stories and songs told and sung around the bode fire every night were an inspiring reminder of what they had all been through, how they came together, and the ways of the new bode that they were forming. Though they had only lived together a short time, they already had a sizable repertoire of stories and encouraged new additions. They talked and sang about Tars finding Zura, Dagan, and Esri; finding Barsa and the group's long walk to Flat Rocks; the birth of Wilki-Dumu; Grilu's naming; and the first big, successful eland hunt, which generally prompted an extended retelling with many participants.

Some stories were repeated often and some more rarely, depending on the mood of the teller or the mood of the listeners. Some nights the stories were funny – Kai and Esri were particularly gifted at playing off of each other and giving animated, comical twists to their interactions, such as Kai taking and returning Esri's Huti stone, and their first antelope sighting and successful hunt.

Sometimes the bode spoke of the sad times, such as Dara's death and honoring others who had died and how they came back in dreams to visit. Zura encouraged remembering what gifts those people left behind. It might be knowledge, an object they made, or a story or song that was theirs.

Grilu began telling the story of losing his eye. At first he only spoke a few sentences. As he listened to others' stories, and thought about everything that had happened to him and what it might mean, the story grew longer and more elaborate. In time, it became a favorite at the bode fire. Hearing how Grilu's ghost cat saved his life enthralled listeners. It was a story Grilu would tell until he was old and in his End Days, and then it was retold by others long after he was gone.

Everyone was encouraged to start a new story or song, even the children and the newest to join the bode. One night, Sela spoke. "I want to tell a story."

She and Muni didn't run away anymore but they remained withdrawn and, since their first days at Flat Rocks, never spoke further about what they experienced with the Violent Ones.

Sela held Muni's hand. "I want to tell the story of how Muni and I ran away from the Violent Ones." Like Grilu, the first night she spoke, her story was short. But those first sentences were not about frightened children. It was a story of bravery and gave a glimpse of the spunky girl who, up until now, had been hiding from them.

The bodefire stories and songs spun the story of Flat Rocks. A bode where neither violence nor slavery were tolerated. All of the people had passed through difficult times, losing many loved ones. The bode they were rebuilding out of the remnants of the Ash Rain gave them hope. Living was difficult but less fearful and more joyful. It was a new start.

In some ways, living was even better than before the Ash Rain. No one wanted to lose that. And most understood how much they owed to Zura and Nagar for how they began forging together their different bodes.

The bode decided that killing people, even Violent Ones, would not happen. They would look for other survivors, and free any they found who were enslaved. In particular, they wanted to find the two children who were taken from Sela and Muni's bode. But how to deal with Violent Ones? How do you stop people who only know violence?

During one of the discussions Esri said, "We all think slavery is not right. If we find more survivors, we should tell them how we live together, the things we said to Grilu at his Naming. No one is allowed to harm another, even if they are Elders. In my old community, we had some people who were allowed to treat others cruelly because they were keepers of knowledge or were bigger and stronger."

Nagar said, "That was also true at Flat Rocks."

Esri said, "It's better how we are living here now. I don't want that to change."

Barsa said, "The bode I came from was peaceful when I first lived there. It was one of the reasons I stopped my roaming when I was a young man."

Wilki said, "But it was starting to change."

Barsa said, "Yes, that's true. When I first came, there was a Council of three powerful Elders. Their word controlled what happened, and they fixed problems that came up. They did not allow weapons to be used against people, only for hunting. If two people had an argument, the Elders listened to both sides and decided what should happen. They were wise and respected. They did not use their power to acquire more than others or to favor those close to them or make people fearful."

Nat continued, "But, before the Ash Rain came, two of the Elders died and two new Elders were added to the Council. The new Elders were not wise like the old ones, and they began to demand larger portions of food gathered or hunted and decided arguments in favor of those closest to them. It was part of the reason we looked for a new living site. Of course, now they are all gone."

Barsa said, "But, it was good in the bode when the wise ones were alive. I think we now have wise ones on our Elders Council at Flat Rocks." He laughed. "I know that includes me, but I'm thinking about the others. Saba is still young but the rest of us are not. What will happen when we are gone?"

Nagar nodded, "I have been thinking about this. We want to bring more people into Flat Rocks, but we don't want to lose the peace we've found."

Tars said, "Things could have been very different if Zura, Dagan, and Esri had fought us when we found them, or if Dagan had not recognized Barsa and we had fought because we were too frightened to trust each other."

Zura said, "I believe that the Ancients helped us because we needed to find each other in order to survive. But I have no more roaming brothers." She smiled at Barsa. "It might be very different if we find another group of survivors."

Saba spoke, "I want to talk more about what Esri said about a kind of Naming for new people coming into Flat Rocks. Not that we give them a new name, but that we tell them how we live together and what we expect of them."

Barsa said, "And what we expect of each other and our Elders."

Kai said, "And if people don't agree?"

"Then they cannot stay," said Tars.

"If people see how we live, I think that even Violent Ones can change," said Nagar.

Piram said, "You can't change a Violent Ones' bode."

"I agree with Piram," said Tars. "If we find many Violent Ones, it will be difficult."

Nagar looked at Piram. "But not all those living in a Violent Ones' bode may want to stay with violent ways."

Esri noticed Piram make the slightest of nods as Nagar spoke.

Zura said, "We can put Guideposts in the Thinking Circle to show how we live at Flat Rocks, and use those Guideposts when we bring new people into the bode. We need to agree on what the Guideposts should mean. I know what is important to me but I want to hear from all of you." People began calling out many things from having no slaves to deciding who gets to sleep where.

Zura laughed, "So many things! Let's decide which are the most important to us. New people may have different ways of hunting or singing or many other things. If their ways of living don't harm anyone, they can keep doing them. But some things do harm others, like making people slaves or not sharing roots with someone who cannot gather for themselves."

The discussion lasted a long time. People talked for many days. One day, Nagar and Zura sat huddled together and that evening presented the following agreements to the bode:

- All knowledge is for all
- All provide food and warmth
- Those too young, old, or sick to provide will receive food and warmth
- Different ways of living are accepted if none are harmed

Nagar said, "These are the things we talked about the most, that people feel most strongly about. In time, there may be other Agreements we want to add."

Zura repeated the Agreements several times. People were quiet and listened closely. Everyone wanted assurance that what was most important to them was included.

Tars said, "These are good. If we live by these Agreements, the Flat Rocks bode will be a safe place for people."

Grilu pouted. "Safe, maybe, but what about singing? And, and stories?"

They looked at Grilu, many nodded. Nagar smiled, "Do we need another agreement?"

Esri sat next to Grilu. She cupped his head in her hands and said to him, "Not everyone sings or tells stories, Grilu, but what if we make an agreement about bringing smiles to others? Like you do. This could happen in many ways."

Grilu turned to Nagar. "Can we have an agreement that everyone brings smiles to the bode?"

Nagar looked around the group. Smiles turned to laughter and all agreed to include Grilu's agreement about bringing smiles to the bode.

When the group quieted, Nat spoke, "The Agreements are good, but I still worry if later we have bad Elders."

"Yes, you're right. We need to all watch that this doesn't happen," Nagar said.

Zura said, "I will put a marker in the Thinking Circle for each Agreement. Grilu, Sela, and Muni, as the youngest, you will live with the Agreements the longest. You can help me find good stones to mark our Agreements. We'll use them as Guideposts to tell new people about how we live at Flat Rocks and to receive their pledge to live by the Agreements."

Barsa said, "I want each of us to give our pledge too. We need to be strong together."

The next day they made a special feast and one-by-one, everyone vowed to follow the Agreements. While Wilki-Dumu couldn't promise he did burble and say "Mama" as Wilki made her pledge. His time would come with his Naming. They told stories, sang, and laughed well into the night.

BIRTHDAYS

Real-time Toronto life was trundling along. Soccer practice for the spring season was in full swing. When time and weather allowed, Esri took long runs in the Taylor Creek ravine with Jilly pedalling on a bike Joe had refurbished from a yard sale. School no longer felt like this big, scary place, and some of the kids didn't seem so cliquish anymore. Randi came for supper a few times but didn't hang around a lot when Esri was there. Jerome's video to banish business bullies turned out great, though Esri heard from Brianna that the sleazy promoter guy dropped Jerome and was spreading rumors about Jerome to give him a bad reputation.

Dream-time Flat Rocks life was going better. Esri frequently woke up excited and inspired after her nights of dreaming about the conversations happening at Flat Rocks. The day-to-day life at the bode remained a struggle, but everyone - even cranky Piram, aloof Nat, and the children - were engaged in creating the Agreements. After the dream where everyone pledged to support the Agreements, Esri couldn't wait to tell Clea and Thomas. She went to visit them that evening after supper.

As usual, Esri gave a detailed description of everything that had happened in her dreams since the last time she spoke with them earlier in the week.

"It feels really special to be a part of deciding the Agreements, and Zura and Nagar are so amazing. They keep reminding people that being different is ok as long as it doesn't hurt anyone. God, I wish some of the kids at school would pledge to those Agreements. They get so judgmental."

"This is very interesting. Amazing to think what the world would be like if we were all still abiding by those Agreements today," said Clea.

"I believe this is significant, Esri," said Thomas. "What is happening at Flat Rocks right now is key to your Mending."

"How do you mean?"

"The purpose of Mendings are to, well, nudge people to behave better to each other and the world around them. I think your Mending is about finding a way to have the Agreements carry forward so that they continue to be a part of everyone's lives today. Many religions and belief systems have made attempts, yet there's still so much greed and violence in our world. So many suffer," said Thomas.

Esri shook her head, "Whoa, hold on. That's insane. Do you seriously think I could make that happen? I am half believing about being a Mender; otherwise, how to explain these dreams? But to affect everyone around the world is too much."

"Maybe it's not that 'insane,'" said Clea. "We know there was a population bottleneck at the time of your Flat Rocks people. If there were only a very few people left and those Agreements got firmly imbedded in their culture, it could keep resonating forward. It's fascinating how Zura and Nagar, in particular, have used the catastrophe of the Ash Rain to encourage more openness and question some long-standing traditions."

"I'm only playing a small, supporting role in all this, Zura and Nagar are definitely the big drivers," said Esri.

"That's not surprising," said Clea. "It was similar in my Mending. It's often those in supporting roles that make the difference when groups of people are working to build and establish something positive in a larger context. And often the best leaders start by taking on supporting roles and learning from strong role-models. You're undervaluing the contribution you're making."

"Well, I don't know about my role, but I'm glad that Zura and Nagar are supported by pretty much everyone at Flat Rocks," said Esri.

"Yes, it's critical that they're so respected. I can't help but think how things would be turning out if the majority of the survivors at Flat Rocks were more like Piram or the people he came from, or worse," said Clea.

"You must stay watchful of the Violent Ones, Esri. Who knows how many of them there may be and what damage they might bring. What Sela and Muni experienced is terrible. But you're right. What's happening at Flat Rocks is inspiring," said Thomas.

■ ■ ■

Esri and Joe's birthday was on Sunday, St. Patrick's Day. Though hardly Irish, they always celebrated by going all out green: their clothes, green icing on the cake, a birthday meal of spinach pasta with broccoli and green beans, garden salad and green lemonade. It was something Sofie started when Esri was little. On Sofie's last St. Patrick's Day, though terribly sick, she insisted that they celebrate all green as usual.

Jilly, who seemed to have inherited Sofie's sense of celebration at any excuse, spent Sunday morning festooning the apartment with green crepe-paper streamers – even in the bathroom.

Joe had a good laugh at the streamers when he arrived home from his cleaning job. He sorted it out with Randi about the birthday celebration. Esri didn't know or care what he told Randi, as long as she didn't come. He told Esri that Randi totally understood and that she wanted to contribute something to the party and gave Joe eight movie tickets and concession stand vouchers that Randi got from one of the bar's suppliers. Esri felt guilty but happily took the vouchers. She'd keep working on her feelings toward Randi.

Joe, Esri, and Jilly ate their green meal at lunch, then Esri and seven of her friends went off to the movies and came back for green cake and pistachio ice cream at the apartment.

SEARCHING FOR OTHERS

After everyone pledged to keep the Agreements, Flat Rocks sent out small scouting parties of three or four to look for more Ash Rain survivors. The scouting parties went in different directions and with great caution, staying alert at all times for the Violent Ones who had taken Sela and Muni.

With every scouting group, Zura told them, "Only rescue slaves if you can do so without getting captured yourself. If there are too many Violent Ones, come back to Flat Rocks and we will make a bigger group." She knew how much everyone wanted to find the children from Sela and Muni's bode, and worried that some might move too quickly and put themselves at risk of being killed or captured.

If they could find a few more people, the bode would be a normal size again.

The scouting parties came back empty-handed. Several went back to where Sela and Muni were found, but the tracks of the Violent Ones ended at a stream bed. Though they followed the stream for some distance in both directions, they were not able to pick up the tracks of the Violent Ones and the children.

After several moon cycles, Dagan, Esri, and Kai's scouting party returned with news of finding survivors.

Kai described the group, "We saw a man, a woman, and two girls. The children are Grilu's size. The woman and man are mates. There were no signs of anyone else. They're not Violent Ones. We should bring them to Flat Rocks where they will be safer."

Dagan said, "They'll be frightened when we approach them and fight us. We don't want to harm them."

Esri said, "If Barsa comes, maybe he can speak with them. And we could take Sela too. If they see a little girl they might feel less threatened. What do you think, Grayla? If you went with us, would Sela go?"

Grayla nodded, "Let me speak with her."

It was decided, Dagan, Esri, and Kai would return, and be joined by Barsa, Grayla, and Sela. It was the first time that Sela and Muni were separated since coming to Flat Rocks. Sela was excited to be asked to go with Grayla but worried about leaving Muni. However, he was perfectly happy to stay with Jolam, who promised to take Muni and Grilu on some small hunting expeditions.

With their larger numbers, the scouting group would appear strong, but hopefully Sela's presence would not make them look like a warring party.

It took them several days to walk back to the survivors. The scouting party decided to approach the survivors as Tars did with Zura, Dagan, and Esri, shortly before Sun-Man's arrival. The scouting party was barely in place in front of the cave where the survivors slept when the family awoke and all four of them grabbed flints and spears and began fighting as if their lives depended on it.

Grayla pulled Sela away from the melee. Grayla would keep Sela safe and only join in if she was needed.

Dagan and Kai dove for the man's legs, brought him down, and tied him up with the lengths of stout vines they brought.

The woman threw a spear at Esri and Barsa. Barsa ducked. Esri jumped away but she was unable to completely avoid the sharp edge. The flint cut into her upper left arm and Esri paused. The woman used the opportunity to grab one of the little girls and run away from the cave. Barsa grabbed the other child.

Esri's arm throbbed. Blood oozed out of the cut. She hoped it wasn't too deep. Barsa said, "When they finish with the man, let Dagan and Kai go after the others. They won't go far. Come, help me with this little one. She is frightened. You can sing to her."

Kai and Dagan finished immobilizing the man and only then saw the bleeding gash on Esri's arm. They ran to her and she waved them away. "I'll be fine. Go on. Get the other two. They ran that way,' Esri pointed.

Soon they were back. The woman's hands were tied. She looked terrified and frequently stumbled. She shrugged off Kai's attempts to support her. Dagan carried the little girl who stared fearfully around at everyone but didn't struggle. Either she understood she had no hope of getting free or perhaps something told her that the big man holding her would not harm her.

Kai said, "They were hiding behind the bushes over there, not far. The woman did not fight us."

It was all too much for Sela. Seeing the fear and panic of the people, especially the little girls, she began to sob and clung to Grayla.

The survivors stared at Sela, not certain how to interpret what was happening. Barsa let go of the little girl he held. She ran to the woman.

The scouting party looked at each other, unsure what to do next.

"We should untie them. Show them we're not going to hurt them," said Esri.

Kai said, "No, they should stay tied up. Look what she did to your arm."

Barsa said, "I agree. Let's wait to untie them. We'll bring them together and let them sit for a while. Then I will try to speak with them, and help them understand we will not harm them." They carried the man out of the cave and sat him within a few feet of the woman.

Dagan said, "Esri, let me take care of your arm. Zura will be angry at me if I don't look after you. She gave me some of her healing moss before we left."

Esri smiled at Dagan, "She also gave me moss."

The survivors followed this exchange. They couldn't understand what Dagan and Esri were saying but could see the warmth between Dagan and Esri in their actions and facial expressions.

When Barsa sensed a subtle shift in the survivors from fright to wariness, he sat close to them and began by saying his name and pointing and saying the names of the others in the scouting party, then gestured to the survivors. The woman spoke for some time. Barsa listened closely. A few words sounded familiar but he couldn't put together the gist of what she was saying. He started again with names, then began naming objects. The woman and man spoke to each other and then were quiet for a long time. Then the woman spoke again, this time, giving Barsa their names.

This tentative back and forth carried on for a while. Once the survivors began to repeat the names of the scouting party, Barsa said, "Let's untie them, but first gather by the spears and flints. We still need to be careful."

The survivors did not move and began an animated discussion.

It was a long, exhausting day. The scouting party, mainly Barsa and Esri, worked at communicating with the survivors but it was a tiring process. Bit by bit, they started some simple conversations. Though the survivors sat quietly and had no sharp weapons, there was still a risk they might try to fight again. The scouting party ensured that someone kept close watch throughout the night.

END OF DOUBTS

"Esri, wake-up. What happened to your arm? You're bleeding all over your sheets." Joe's anxious face loomed over Esri. She stared blankly at him for several seconds. Her mind was still with the scouting party and the survivors.

To Joe, it looked like Esri didn't even know who he was, "Es, honey, what is it? It's me."

Esri looked at the bleeding gash on her arm, up at her Dad and again at her arm and again at her Dad. She saw Jilly sitting on the edge of her bed, staring wide-eyed at Esri. Esri struggled to wake up, "Aา, Dad. Sorry, I was sound asleep. Weird dream."

"But your arm. What did you do?"

"Ahhh, I cut it. It was an accident. I guess . . . it's deeper than I thought." Esri's mind raced. The cut was where the woman's spear sliced into Esri's arm. Clea never mentioned that what happened to Esri in the dreams could carry over into her real life. "I, ah, think it's from . . . that thorn bush in Clea's yard. I brushed against it yesterday. Um really hard."

"It was still pretty cold out yesterday. Why weren't you wearing a jacket?"

"I was cleaning up some stuff in Clea's yard and got hot."

"This is a pretty deep cut, Esri, didn't Clea see it? I'm surprised she didn't do anything. You need to go to the clinic and get it looked at." Joe shook his head. "Esri, what you're telling me doesn't entirely make sense. Why didn't you say anything last night? Is there something you're not telling me?"

"I didn't realize it was that deep and didn't show it to Clea. I didn't want her to start fussing. It's not her fault. It seemed ok last night. It's just bleeding a little." Esri got out of bed. She didn't want to keep talking to her Dad. "I'll go right away to the clinic, as soon as I drop Jilly off. Write me a note for school. I'll be fine, really, Dad." She called over her shoulder and quickly got into the shower before her Dad could interrogate her any further. She knew he needed to leave for work.

After her Dad's reaction to the thorn bush story, Esri thought she needed a better story for the clinic. She told them that the cut came from a sharp piece of metal sticking out of a school locker. The doctor assumed from looking at the cut that it had just happened. Esri mumbled something about a meeting in school before class and not paying attention to what she was doing. Esri was desperate to talk to Clea.

Esri rushed to Clea's after school. "Why didn't you tell me this could happen?" Esri pulled off her jacket, pushed up her sleeve, and pointed to her bandaged arm.

"Oh my dear. What happened to your arm?" said Clea.

"Clea! It happened in my dream last night. We found more Ash Rain survivors. They were frightened of us and one on them threw a spear at me and cut my arm. When I woke up this morning, the cut was still there and there was blood on my sheets. My Dad and Jilly were freaking out and, of course I couldn't explain. I didn't know what to say. It's deep enough that the doctor put stitches in at the clinic." Esri's voice was strained and shaking when she finished.

Clea shook her head, rubbing her hand on her leg. She sighed. "Oh dear. Please sit, Esri. Tell me what happened. Is it painful?"

Esri sat and spoke angrily to Clea. "I'm fine. You need to talk to me. You hurt your leg in your Mending, didn't you? Why didn't you tell me? What if something really bad happens to me in my dreams? What if I die? Will my Dad and Jilly find my dead body in bed one morning? You need to tell me everything that happened to you."

Clea looked distraught. "You're right. I should have told you about my leg. Thomas and I talked about whether to say anything to you, at least at this point. I didn't want to frighten you unnecessarily. You're having to deal with so much. And since your dreams started again, and the wonderful Agreements at Flat Rocks, I thought everything was back on track with your Mending."

Thomas said, "You were still having some doubts that your Mending is real, weren't you?"

"Yes, a few, but just small ones," said Esri.

"And do you have any doubts now?"

"No. None. None at all."

Clea looked down at her folded hands, "I know how you feel, Esri. Being a Mender can feel overwhelming. Why me? You're thinking." She looked at Esri. "But it's also an honor. You were chosen for the courage inside you and it will see you through. Never lose faith in that. The life spirit, whatever it is that drives this, needs your unwavering belief in The Mending. I'm so sorry about your arm, Esri. What a terrible day you've had. What did the doctor say?"

"It's just a little sore. I'll probably have a faint scar but if I'm careful for the next little while it should heal fine," Esri's tone softened. "I'm sorry I sounded angry, Clea. If I could only talk to my Dad or Ada or Luka about it. I'm not being honest with them and I don't like that. It's not who I am."

"I understand. One of the hardest parts of the Mending is that you can't talk about it to the people closest to you."

Thomas said, "Esri, you won't die in your dreams. You will need to guide the next Mender. The life spirit will ensure you get through your Mending."

Esri spoke longer with Clea and Thomas and told them everything that was happening in her dreams.

After Esri left, Clea said, "Are we sure that Esri is safe? What if the Disruptors have become so strong that the life spirit can't protect her anymore?"

Thomas said, "I don't believe that could happen. But if that ever becomes the case, then we are all lost."

VICTORIA DAY FIREWORKS

As the doctor promised, the cut on Esri's arm left only a thin scar.

During the long Victoria Day weekend in May, Esri spent every day working in Clea's garden. She didn't mind. She was grateful to earn the extra money, and it meant avoiding outings with her Dad, Jilly, and Randi. They would have a better time without her anyway.

It hardly felt like work. Esri loved being in Clea's yard and learning about all the plants, how to take care of them, and being outdoors was wonderful.

Clea planted a vegetable garden in her backyard in the open area near the house. Beyond were several perennial beds, with many herbs and medicinal plants, various berries, wandering paths, and seating spots in shady nooks. Most of the back half of the yard Clea left as a natural forest merging into the ravine park. As the wild springtime flowers appeared in the forest – bloodroot, trillium and others - Clea took Esri and Jilly to see the plants' short-lived flower displays in hidden areas of the woods.

Weeks earlier, Clea and Esri had started a variety of vegetable plants indoors. Most were ready to start planting in the garden. Under Clea's guidance, Esri prepared the soil in the vegetable plot and they discussed what they would plant where. Thomas sat outside, a light blanket over his legs, reading a book. Willa napped contently on his lap.

"You like this work, don't you Esri?" said Clea.

"I do. I never thought I would like gardening. I thought it would be boring but it's not, at least not with you. I guess with all that dreaming about living in Flat Rocks, I'm used to being outdoors." They all laughed. It was a relief for Esri when she could spend time alone with Clea and Thomas and speak freely about life at Flat Rocks.

"And, how are you feeling about Randi these days?" asked Clea.

"Oh, I don't know. My Dad and Jilly like her so I'm trying not to say much, but she bugs me. I don't trust something about her but maybe it's just that she's so different from my Mom. I don't understand why my Dad is attracted to her. She's really pretty and all, but she's so into being made-up and fancy clothes. My Dad is a good-looking, super nice guy but we're poor, I'd think Randi'd want to latch onto some rich guy. I'm sure she could."

"Well, you never know. Maybe there are things missing in her life that aren't the things you can buy with money," said Clea.

"I guess. But I'm not sure she's the greatest influence on Jilly. She's always buying her lots of stuff. Jilly just has to mention something she saw on TV, and Randi gets it for her."

"Does she buy things for you too?"

"Oh god no. She did at first, but I told her not to and I told Dad to tell her not to, and she finally took the hint and stopped. My Mom was really big on living simply and not relying on owning things to be happy. I guess I'm more like her. My Mom would have done well at Flat Rocks." Esri smiled faintly.

"Are you and your friends still planning on watching the fireworks at Ashbridge's Bay tonight?" asked Clea.

"Yup, that's the plan. Even Ada's parents agreed to let her go."

■ ■ ■

That evening, the wide beach along Lake Ontario was jammed with people who had come to watch the city's largest Victoria Day fireworks display. Esri, Ada, and Luka met up with other friends from school and they gathered on blankets spread out on the sand. The fireworks didn't start until 10:00 p.m., when the sky was good and dark. After they were over, Esri said to Ada and Luka, "C'mon, let's walk by the lake away from the lights and look at the stars. The buses will be jammed now anyway."

The three walked farther into the park and sat on a bench overlooking the lake. They snuggled together under the blanket Luka brought. He sat in the middle, his long arms encircling the two girls, pulling them all close together.

"Everyone cozy?" he said. "Okay? What now?"

Esri looked across the lake and up at the sky. She knew the stars would not look like they did at Flat Rocks, still, much was familiar. How many pre-dawn hours had she spent with Zura, watching the seasonal march of Angry Snake and the other Travelers?

"Okay, see this tree trunk?" she pointed at a tall white pine toward the left of them. "Just to the right is a bright star, down low, near the horizon."

"Right, yes, I see it," Ada said.

"Me too," said Luka.

"Ok, now hold up your hand and measure the position of the star compared to the tree trunk and remember that," Esri demonstrated. "For me, when I hold my hand out like this, it's about the width from my little finger to my thumb."

Ada and Luka positioned their hands in front of themselves like Esri had done. "Got it," Luka said. "What next?"

"We wait a little and look at the other stars," Esri said. "I think I can find the North Star." They looked up, found the few constellations they knew and followed the blinking lights of airplanes but mainly they sat quietly gazing at the sky.

Luka murmured, "You know, I'm pretty sure I'm going to pass all of my classes. My mom's like so amazed. I just want you two to know that when I'm a famous Hollywood actor, I won't forget you. I'll mention you in my Oscar acceptance speech."

Esri and Ada laughed. Luka said, "No seriously. I know I joke around a lot, but you two have done some serious butt-saving for me. I just want to say thanks." The girls said in unison, "Aw, Luka!"

They were quiet again for a while and Ada spoke, "I want to say thanks too. I never would have had the nerve to join the computer club if you two hadn't pushed me to. I assumed it would be all nerdy guys who would make fun of a nerdy girl who looks like she belongs in Grade 5."

Esri said, "Oh Ada. You're so totally amazing! And now they're always hanging around you. You're like the queen bee of the computer club."

Ada said, "Well, I don't know about that, but you two mean a lot to me."

Luka said, "What about you, Es? You're so, so sensible and good at a lot of stuff. Probably would be perfectly fine without us."

"Oh, don't be ridiculous. I would fall apart without you two. I heard someone say recently how important it is to bring people smiles and that's exactly what you two do, every time I see you." Esri stuck her hand out toward the pine tree trunk and spread her fingers, "Look, how far our star has moved!"

Ada and Luka likewise measured the star's movement with their hands. Luka said, "Wow, while we've been sitting here our little star has really been putting on some miles."

Ada said, "Amazing to think about that. All of that universe out there is moving along. I've never felt it like this before. Is this what you wanted us to see, Esri?"

"Yeah, exactly. I think it's exciting to see how there are these movements and rhythms happening around us that are so way bigger than we are, but we kind of don't notice them a lot of the time."

They sat a little longer and Ada said, "We should probably go. I'll let my parents know we're on our way. Do you want to phone your dad, Esri?"

"Sure, when you're done, thanks."

MAKING PEACE

Several days passed while the scouting party struggled to communicate with the survivors and keep careful watch of their movements. They shared food and gradually everyone relaxed. Esri made up a song for Sela and the little girls, rhyming their names and combining simple expressions from all of their dialects.

Dagan and Kai managed to kill an antelope which they divvied out among everyone. The survivors were delighted with this, indicating that it was the first large animal that they had eaten in a long time. With so few of them and the two little girls, it was difficult to hunt the larger game. They all took part in preparing the leftover antelope for drying and smoking, though the scouting party did all of the cutting as they continued to control the sharp tools.

Finally, there was enough shared understanding among the two groups that the scouting party was able to explain that they wanted the survivors to join them at Flat Rocks and that they would not be slaves. Esri showed on her Sun-Man Stick how many days the walk would take and that the spears and flints would be returned once they began walking to Flat Rocks.

The woman and man spoke intensely. They seemed to be arguing. The scouting party gathered that the woman wanted to go but not the man.

"We must leave tomorrow," Barsa told the survivors He knew that the people back at Flat Rocks would be getting worried about the scouting party.

"We stay," said the man.

"But you're too few. It's dangerous," said Esri.

"You did not hurt us, but we don't know about the others at Flat Rocks."

Barsa turned to Esri, "We can't force them. We need to get back. They'll be worrying. We can come back in a little while and try again."

Esri knew he was right. They needed to get back and it might take a long time to convince the man to come. She was disappointed that they had not won his trust. As she had done for Dara, she had taken bones from the antelope and carved little faces on them. She had planned on giving them to the girls while they were on the long walk to Flat Rocks. Since the survivors were not joining them, the next morning Esri gave the small bone carvings to Sela and told her to give one to each of the girls who were delighted, and hugged Sela.

Esri and Grayla then returned the spears and flints. And the scouting party left. As they walked away, they heard the little girls singing Esri's song.

It was disheartening. Though the beginning of the encounter with the survivors was rough, by the time the scouting party left some mutual affection had developed between the two groups. The scouting party knew that it would be difficult for the group of four to survive for long on their own, and worried what they might find when they returned.

Esri said, "I keep thinking about what we could have done differently so that they would have come with us."

Barsa said, "They had every reason to fear us and fight us when we first went to them. They are cautious and they should be. This is not yet ended, you'll see. For now, let's not walk too quickly. My old bones are tired."

At Barsa's request, the scouting party stopped early that day. The next morning he reminded them, "We need to keep watching carefully all around us."

Kai was the first to spot them. The survivors were following them. Barsa's request to slow up was not because of his 'old bones,' but because he had a hunch that the four might follow them. With the two little girls, it would be difficult for them to move quickly.

The walk to Flat Rocks took several days and the two groups continued walking separately, usually within sight of each other. After a few days, Kai and Grayla walked back to the survivors and gave them food and told them where they could find water, but did not attempt to bring them closer.

Meanwhile at Flat Rocks, they were anxious about how long the scouting party was gone, particularly. Muni, Saba, and Nat. Muni had never been separated from his sister for so long. First it felt kind of adventuresome and he could have Jolam all to himself, but now he was scared something had happened to Sela.

Saba fretted for Dagan. They were now a couple. He shared a sleeping space with her, Nagar, and Grilu. Dagan and Saba's union, like Grilu's Naming, was yet another sign of a more normal life returning to Flat Rocks. Seeing these two kind, gentle people together made everyone feel good. Even Riga, who was rejected by Dagan, was glad for Saba's happiness.

Nat and Esri's situation was more muddled. It was obvious how much Nat admired Esri. His eyes were always on her when she was around. And Esri was attracted to Nat, but she felt he was still mourning his mate and that he enjoyed Esri's company but nothing more. They were both a little proud and a little uncertain, and hadn't yet managed to talk about their feelings to each other.

Nat wanted to go with the scouting party but Tars asked him to stay, as there were already many going and it would leave Flat Rocks too vulnerable if Nat also went. As the days stretched on, each morning Nat went to the high ridge nearly an hour's run in the direction the scouting party had gone. He would scan the horizon for a while and then return to Flat Rocks, checking and resetting snares on his way back. Finally, one morning he saw tiny figures far off in the distance. He knew he should first make sure who it was and hurry back to Flat Rocks to let others know, but he couldn't contain himself, and began to run. He needed to know if it was the scouting party, if they were all right, and to see Esri.

She was the first to spot the lone figure running toward them and knew immediately from the loping gate that it was Nat. "Look, it's Nat!"

He ran up to the scouting party and was alarmed to see the fresh cut on Esri's arm, "What happened, Esri?" She explained and described how Dagan did a good job of taking care of her, that it was healing well. She told Nat about the survivors and pointed to where they were, following the scouting party.

Nat hurried back to Flat Rocks to tell them that the scouting party would be there soon and everyone was fine. It was a day of celebration and relief to have them back. The scouting party took turns relating everything that happened in their encounter with the survivors. Muni sat nearly on top of Sela, comforted to have her back at Flat Rocks and in awe that she was part of such an important undertaking. The survivors camped a distance away from Flat Rocks. They were left alone for the night.

The next morning, Kai and Barsa took Muni and Sela and visited the survivors, bringing them food and inviting them to move closer. Though the adults tried to contain them, as soon as the little girls saw Sela, they went running to her waving their carved antelope bones. Muni was delighted to meet more children. The four of them were soon all giggling and running about.

The woman and man survivors remained cautious. Barsa visited them every day, bringing different people from Flat Rocks, usually with Sela and Muni. He was worried how the group might react when they saw Grilu's face, if they would take that as a sign of people doing violence at Flat Rocks. But Sela and Muni talked about Grilu and the story of his Ghost Cat so much that soon even the adults were asking to meet him. The day Barsa brought Grilu, the Flat Rocks group stayed the night with the survivors. Grilu told the story of losing his eye and the Ghost Cat, now a well-polished tale.

The survivors moved into Flat Rocks and before long were fully a part of the bode, adding their stories and songs to the evening bodefire. The woman became a member of the Elders Council. She was an intelligent strong woman who brought a cautious, thoughtful approach to the deliberations of the Council.

SUMMER DAYS

End of Grade 9 – Luka's mother brought home a cake from the bakery at her work and had a small party for Luka, Esri, Ada, and their families to celebrate the successful completion of the friends' first year in high school.

"I know, it's only one year of high school, but I'm so proud of you three," she said. "When I was your age, I was already in big trouble, missing lots of classes, barely passing, and dropped out in Grade 10 – biggest mistake of my life."

As usual, Esri and Ada did somewhat better than Luka, but his marks were not bad. He passed all his courses and only ended up in the principal's office a few times for acting out in class. His passion for the Drama Club provided a strong motivation to keep doing well in school.

It had been a while since Esri, Ada, and Luka's families had gotten together, not like when the children were little and the adults were helping each other with child-minding. It was difficult to find time to socialize with everyone so busy, working long hours. While some juggled more than one job. Esri thought it was very sweet of Luka's mom to organize the get-together. Though their families came from different backgrounds, they shared a fierce loyalty and concern for their children and, by extension held a shared warmth and trust of each other. It felt good to Esri to be amongst them again. She was relieved that Randi wasn't there.

Esri was grateful to have a job this summer, one that was so enjoyable and where she could bring Jilly with her. Finances were tight and Joe was already worried about how they would manage schooling for Esri after high school.

This summer they couldn't afford to pay for Esri to play recreational soccer. The fees had increased considerably because the city and schools were charging more to use the soccer fields. Esri didn't say much about it. She didn't want Joe to feel bad, but he knew she missed it. She had played in the league since she was little. He knew if he mentioned it to Randi she'd probably insist on paying the fees, but also knew that Esri would not want that.

Esri and usually Jilly spent nearly every day at Clea's. When Ada and Luka weren't working they often came as well, occasionally with Ada's younger brothers, and Jilly sometimes brought Nasima. Clea enjoyed having all the young people about. She had an endless trove of imaginative projects for the younger ones if they tired of their own games. Ada and Luka usually helped Esri in the garden. Clea showed the three friends a place in her yard where they could build a secluded sitting area for themselves to sit and talk if they wanted. They scavenged materials to create a small circle of seats.

Thomas didn't interact with the young people too much. He usually sat in the sheltered area by the kitchen door, reading and snoozing. He saved his talkative times for when he, Clea, and Esri discussed Esri's dreams. As Jilly was usually around, Clea and Esri devised a variety of play projects that kept Jilly in sight but out of earshot. If Willa, who Jilly adored, could be persuaded to keep Jilly company, it guaranteed their having ample time to discuss the latest Flat Rocks developments.

"Young Esri, now that Willa has the ever animated Jilly occupied in a game of hide and seek, tell us the latest that's happened with our friends at Flat Rocks," said Thomas.

"Both a lot and not much. It's amazing how much the bode has grown and that we've found even more survivors from the Ash Rain of the Toba volcano. It's good we kept looking. Those little groups of people couldn't have survived well on their own. With so many people, the Agreements are really important. A few people have been banished by the Elders Council for things like hitting someone or not sharing after a hunt, but they've come around after a little while. They get it pretty quickly that Flat Rocks is a good place to be. Mostly the people who have come into the bode blend in fairly well once they're comfortable with the language and see that people are peaceful."

"That's quite remarkable, really. I guess I carry the stereotype that our cave people ancestors were all a bunch of brutish thugs," laughed Thomas.

"No, they most definitely are not. It's such a relief for them to feel safer after the Ash Rain. And Zura and Nagar really pound into all of us to make newcomers feel comfortable. There is, for sure, tension at times, but overall things are pretty good and on the right track. I'm not sure that 'Mending' is needed."

"Something is going to change because you're still at Flat Rocks. Every night, right?" said Clea.

"Yes, every night," said Esri.

"And Clea and I are still having disturbing dreams and we continue to sense the threats around us," said Thomas. "It's most odd that I got resurrected, brought out of retirement, or whatever you want to call it. It must mean this is building to something bigger."

"That's why I'm having you expand and deepen the sweet grass verges around the property," said Clea.

"I wondered if it was somehow related to keeping your place safe. Are you stuck here forever?" asked Esri.

"No. I'm fairly certain that once your Mending is complete, we'll be safe to move about again freely," said Clea.

"What would happen if you did leave your yard? Would the Disruptors attack you?" said Esri.

"We might be safe for a little while. It's hard to say. I sense that the Disruptors are staying nearby but they don't want to draw attention to themselves. Anything that happened to us would look like an 'accident,'" said Clea.

"And you're sure I'm safe from them? Why wouldn't they make me try to have an 'accident'?"

"The life spirit is focusing its energy on protecting you during your Mending. With that protection, the most the Disruptors can do is to try to get you out of the dreams, like with the Dragon Garb video," said Thomas. "Just stay clear of them."

"If you smell that awful smell of theirs, walk away. Don't engage with them," said Clea. "And that's where having a Guide helps," Clea placed her hand on Thomas' shoulder.

"You've certainly helped me, Clea," said Esri. "And, you too, Thomas."

Thomas said, "I don't know how much I can do for you, Esri, but my dreams tell me there is a little more I need to do for Clea."

Sometimes heading home from Clea's, Esri convinced Jilly to take the long way through the ravine. In the summertime, the trees created a green tunnel of fluttering leaves, with dense branches arching far overhead. The foliage hid any signs of houses or buildings perched on the steep hills overlooking the ravine and muffled most of the city noises. Ducks paddled in the creek running beside the path.

Esri and Jilly played a sort of game with the park benches that dotted the ravine path. Jilly would run ahead to the next park bench and sit and wait for Esri, and as soon as Esri touched the bench, Jilly raced to the next bench while Esri counted slowly to 20. Jilly enjoyed running ahead on her own, though Esri was never more than a 20 second interval behind her. Halfway between two benches, Jilly suddenly stopped, crouched down, and motioned Esri to come quietly.

"What's up?" Esri whispered when she got near Jilly.

"Look, it's Willa. I think she's hunting. What is she doing so far from Clea's?" Jilly pointed to where the cat was creeping slowing in the underbrush.

"Oh, wow, yes. Look how quietly she's moving. We might not be that far away from Clea's. I've never figured out exactly where her backyard connects to the ravine. Maybe it's right up there." The girls strained to see if they could spot anything familiar on top of the bluff, but the foliage was too dense. "We need to look more carefully in the winter when the leaves are all gone."

"I can stand in Clea's yard and wave a little flag and you can stand down in the ravine and see where I am," said Jilly.

"Not a bad idea, we'll need to remember to do that. Look, there goes Willa. She's caught something and is heading straight up the hill. It must be the back of Clea's house."

They ran into Farhana and Nasima on their way home. Farhana invited Jilly to join them for supper. When Esri got to the apartment building, Jerome was sitting in the lobby. She was less intimidated by him after doing the videos and gave him a big grin. "Ah, waiting for the van?"

"You got it. Keep me company?" Jerome was friendly but not his usual upbeat self.

"Sure. What's the latest on the business bullies video? How many hits? I heard from Bri that there are some issues with it?"

"Ah, well. That's a curious story. The file keeps getting corrupted and taken down so people aren't watching it so much or passing it around."

"How does that happen?"

"I don't know and I've given up trying to sort out what's going on. Right now, I'm concentrating on getting my schooling lined up for the fall."

"I thought you had a scholarship to study music at that fancy school."

"Well, there's another interesting story. The scholarship got pulled. They'd give me a loan but there's no way I can handle going into so much debt, so I'm looking at something where I can live at home, and a program that's shorter and cheaper."

"What? You're kidding? What happened?"

"I can't prove it but I think that guy we did the Dragon Garb video for has something to do with this all."

"I'm really sorry, I feel. . ."

"Don't say it, Esri, it's not your fault. I'm really proud of the business bullies video. Nobody made me do it. I knew it might have ramifications, but I was naïve about how big they might be. Now I know."

"So, what are you going to do?"

"I'm looking at a 2-year program doing music production. Maybe that will give me a better handle on how I can work more independently. Anyway," he smiled, "my Mom has been super happy with me ever since we made the business bullies video. She's constantly talking to her friends about it. So if she's happy, it makes me happy. I'm pissed off about what's happened, for sure, but taking it a day at a time."

"You're so talented. I'm sure something will work out." That sounded kind of lame but it was all Esri could think of to say.

"Anyway, here's my ride. Ah, that's nice, my favorite driver. Thanks for the company, Es. See you around," and as he headed out the door he said, "Esri. You promise me you'll keep singing, ok? "

"Yeah, sure."

Nicole called that evening and told them that she had been meeting with Darren. They were trying to work things out. Both Esri and Joe talked to her.

"What do you think about what Nicole said, Dad?"

"Well, if Darren behaves . . ."

"But you don't sound so sure. I'm worried for her and Billy, but she's really lonely too."

"Yeah, I know. Darren's getting some work here and there, but a lot of the stuff that was causing problems are all still there or right under the surface. I'm not a counsellor. I can listen to him but he gets angry if I try to suggest anything. So, to be honest, I've been avoiding him and, anyway, I'm pretty busy. I'm sorry, Esri. You're too young for all this."

"I'm ok. But I feel sorry for Nicole."

SHELL BEAD PEOPLE

GRADE 10

First day, their second year in high school, Esri, Ada, and Luka walked to school together.

"This really feels different than a year ago. Remember how nervous we were about starting high school?" said Ada.

Luka said, "You and Esri were nervous. Me, I knew I'd be luminous."

"What? New school year, new word, Luka? Is everyone now going to be luminous instead of incandescent?" Ada nudged him. "Anyway, you were a wreck a year ago. You babbled all the way to school."

"That's what I do, and you'd miss it if I didn't, right? Right, Esri? Hello, you with us here?"

Esri had fallen behind them, absorbed in her own thoughts.

Ada turned around, "Es, you ok?"

Esri looked at Ada and Luka who had stopped in front of her. "Ah, sure. I'm just worried about some stuff."

"Like what? We're early. We can take our time getting to school. Is it about your Dad and Randi?" asked Ada.

"Boy, she is one hot babe," said Luka.

"Luka, not helpful," said Ada. "What is it Esri?"

"Yeah, that's part of it, a big part of it. He's staying overnight at her condo sometimes. So I guess that they're having sex. I'm kind of freaked out about it. It feels like such a betrayal of my Mom, though I don't think my Dad should be alone his whole life. I don't know what to think, but maybe I'd feel ok if it wasn't Randi. I don't like her. I've tried. I don't hate her, I guess. I dunno. Maybe I'd feel this way about anyone my Dad was with."

Luka said, "I know what that's like. I hate it when my mom is dating someone. Our life doesn't feel normal. She gets all excited and happy at first. Then something happens and the guy acts like a jerk. And they treat me like I'm some kind of alien being and could I please make myself scarce. There was one guy, Milo. He was great, but ended up moving to BC for work. I think she's kind of given up."

"Jilly likes being around Randi, but I think it's because Randi buys her lots of stuff. God, she's even started buying clothes for my Dad. I feel like she's trying to make him over. It's like you said, Luka. It doesn't seem like our normal life anymore and I miss it. I keep hoping my Dad and Randi will decide they're too different, but that's not happening."

"Have you talked to your Dad?" asked Ada.

"A little. He knows I don't like Randi too much and is always telling me how nice she is, that she's hurt that I don't hang around when she's there, and how she'd like to get to know me. Blah, blah, blah."

"Is there anything else, Esri? You made it sound like there was more stuff bothering you," said Ada.

"I found out last night that Nicole has decided to move back in with Darren," said Esri.

"Eesh, that guy's a walking time bomb. That can't be good," said Luka.

"I know," sighed Esri.

■ ■ ■

After not playing in the summer soccer rec league, Esri was looking forward to the fall soccer season at school. The previous year, even though she was only in Grade 9, she was one of the starting midfielders in the spring. With some of the top players graduating, she felt confident about her position on the team.

The first practice was a bit rough. Though Esri spent the summer doing lots of physical work in Clea's garden and took long runs regularly through the ravines, she felt out of sync with the team. Many of them had played together in the summer league, including some of the new, Grade 9's trying out for the team.

"You ok, Esri?" asked the coach after a couple of practices. "Your timing's kind of off and sometimes you look distracted."

"Ah. I didn't have a chance to play much soccer over the summer, but I did run a lot. I'm in good shape. I'll be fine."

"Think about keeping your head in the game. Your role is key out there."

With everything that was happening in both her awake and sleeping life, Esri felt she didn't have a lot of control over her head anymore. She was easily distracted. And the soccer team felt different this year. Last year's captain, who graduated in the spring, had been super welcoming. The girl who was named captain this year had obvious favorites and Esri definitely wasn't one of them.

The coach started Esri in the first match. She had a lousy game, made several sloppy plays, and was berated loudly by the captain. The coach replaced Esri in the second half.

After the game the coach said, "I'm sorry, Esri. I'm going to switch you to sub for the next few games. Keep working hard in practice and we'll see how it goes about putting you back to starting."

Esri was close to tears. She quickly changed out of her cleats and left the field. She avoided talking to anyone. The game was at another high school. Esri walked for a while before getting on a bus to go home. She didn't have to worry about Jilly. Her Dad was picking Jilly up at Farhana's. Esri wanted to compose herself before she got home. She forgot until she opened the door to the apartment that Randi was coming for supper.

"Not her," Esri said softly when she saw Randi, who looked straight at her. Randi probably heard her and read her lips. Randi, Joe, and Jilly looked like an ad for "hip Toronto family enjoys an evening at home," all decked out in their Randi-purchased clothes. God.

"Hey Es, we were getting a little worried about you. Aren't you kind of late? How was the game?" asked Joe.

Esri didn't want to talk about it but she knew she had to as it was eating away at her. "We won. But I had a lousy game. I'm thinking maybe I should quit the team. I don't think I'm good enough anymore."

"What are you talking about? You're great at soccer, Esri. Probably just had an off day. Don't give up so easily. It doesn't sound like you," said Joe. He came over and put his arm around her. "Go take your shower and we'll talk about it some more. We've got some of your favorite Thai takeout for supper."

By the time Esri got out of the shower she felt she had her emotions in check and was no longer on the verge of tears. "Dad, I'm okay. I don't really want to talk about it."

"But you're not still thinking about quitting, are you?" said Joe.

"I don't know. The coach is switching me to sub, so that feels really, shitty, okay, Dad?" said Esri.

"Esri, you do not use that kind of language. Not in front of your sister, not in front of Randi, and not in front of me," said Joe.

"Whatever," Esri retorted.

"Whatever? You can go to your room. We're going to go ahead and eat, and when I come and get you, I expect a decent apology from you for me, Randi, and Jilly. And change your t-shirt. That one has holes. It's a rag. You have decent clothes. Wear them."

Joe was angry. Randi raised her eyebrows. Jilly was wide-eyed. Esri and her Dad rarely fought. Jilly had never heard them sound so mean to each other.

Esri went to her room. Joe knocked on the door a half hour later. Esri had put herself to bed and pretended to be asleep. Later, after Randi left and Joe tucked Jilly into bed, he came and leaned over Esri and said, "Come on kiddo, let's talk."

Esri got up, joined him in the living room, and then she did cry, hard. Joe heated up the leftovers and insisted she eat something. She described the game to him and the dynamic with the new captain, but she didn't say anything about how not playing in the summer rec league might have influenced her position on the school team.

"You still like to play, don't you?" asked Joe.

"I do, but it doesn't feel good like it did last year."

"Well, try to see what you can do to make it more like it was last year. A lot of what's fun about sports is the tone of the team. From what you've said about the new captain, I'll bet there are others on the team who feel left out like you do. You keep being nice to everyone, even the girls who are maybe not being so nice to you right now. It might take a while, but things will change. And let's keep talking. That was pretty unfair the way you bit my head off."

"I know, Dad. But can we talk when it's just you and me?"

"Sure. Promise you'll not give up on soccer? At least commit to finishing the fall season."

"Ok, Dad, I will. Thanks for talking and making me supper. I love you, you know. I'm sorry."

"Me too. Love you and I'm sorry. Now off to bed."

ANGRY SNAKE RETURNS

Over the next few months, more survivors were found and Flat Rocks now had close to 30 people. Some people transitioned in easily, others took more time. Those who were at first leery about pledging to The Agreements eventually came around as they experienced life at Flat Rocks. After the devastation of the Ash Rain, the bode offered a rare refuge of safety, comfort, and acceptance. As with many things at Flat Rocks, the stories and songs around the bodefire at night were a mixture of new and old from the survivors' bodes.

Esri was now also on the Elders Council. Most of the disagreements that came to the Council were minor and easily dealt with. There were a few violent incidents that resulted in people being banished from Flat Rocks for periods of time. The Council worked to find a resolution to whatever had caused the violence. So far, in every case, those banished had returned making a renewed commitment to The Agreements. The Council acknowledged that this might become more difficult as the effects of the Ash Rain diminished and living outside of Flat Rocks felt safer.

One evening Zura sat with Grilu and Sela in the Thinking Circle. Those two were the keenest of the children to learn the workings of the Circle, what the Guideposts meant, and how to set the markers. Esri came to join them, "Is tonight the night, Zura?"

"That's what the Sky Bones tell me. You'll watch with me tonight?" asked Zura.

"Of course. So much has happened since the last time we waited for her. The Always Cloud is so much weaker. How little we knew," said Esri. "I wonder what changes will come this next time around?"

"What? Who are you talking about? Who is coming?" Grilu piped up.

Sela said, "They're talking about Angry Snake. Is she coming back? You said she would. When can I see her? What will happen? You're not going to leave the bode when she comes, are you?"

Zura laughed, "No, no, we're not leaving Flat Rocks. And yes, Sela and Grilu, the Sky Bones are saying that before Sun-Man returns in the morning. Angry Snake will begin her journey across the sky. Esri and I will once again greet her."

Grilu yelled, "And Sela and I will too!"

Esri smiled, "Yes, of course, if you want. I'll come get you when it's time."

Sela said, "When you talk about Angry Snake, you say she brings change. What will happen? I don't want anything to change. Why does Angry Snake make things change?"

Zura said, "She doesn't make change, but she reminds us that nothing stays the same and we need to be watchful what is happening around us and keep seeking what I call - harmony."

"Har-mo-ny? What's that, Zura?" asked Grilu.

Esri laughed, "It's one of those Zura words. It's when things feel calm and steady, when we have plenty of food, no one is hurt, no one is angry, no one is scared. You know those times when everyone in the bode is happy."

Sela said, "We have harmony at Flat Rocks now. Everything needs to stay the same. Can't we tell Angry Snake we don't want change? What if bad change comes?"

Zura shook her head, "We can't stop change. Babies are born, people die. Or terrible things happen like the Ash Rain. What we can do is to keep seeking harmony, even if the change is bad. That's the lesson of Angry Snake and what she is coming around to remind us of."

Grilu asked, "Is that why you and Nagar made the Agreements? To seek harmony?"

"Yes. With people coming to live together from different bodes, we needed some things clear, like the Guideposts we use for the night sky, to help us find harmony among strangers," said Zura.

Sela said, "I like the Agreements. They mean no one will hurt me or Muni or you, Grilu. That is, no person will hurt you! I never want to leave Flat Rocks."

Zura said, "There will come a time soon when there are too many at Flat Rocks and some will go to start a new bode. But they will also have the Agreements. And it will be a good bode too, like Flat Rocks."

Sela said, "I'll stay here."

■ ■ ■

One afternoon, Esri, Nat, and Dagan were out looking for eland tracks.

"Look, over there," Nat said and pointed off in the distance. "Who's that?"

"More survivors? They're coming from the direction where we found Sela and Muni," said Dagan.

"We must be careful. What if they're Violent Ones?" said Esri.

"It looks like a group with no children. They're walking quickly and not trying to hide. They're not afraid," said Nat.

"We should meet them, but there should be many of us so they won't hurt us. We must get others," said Esri.

"They haven't seen us. We're hidden here. I'll stay and watch them. You and Dagan get more people," said Nat.

Esri and Dagan hurried and came back with a larger group from Flat Rocks.

"It's all men in the group," said Nat.

"Let's make ourselves visible and walk forward slowly. But be ready," said Barsa. There were five men in the group of strangers All were carrying spears and looked to be in good health. Two were around Barsa's age and the other three younger, like Nat. Barsa and Piram quickly chose who should fight whom if it came to that. The Flat Rocks people carried strands of sinew to tie up the strangers if necessary. Though they outnumbered the strangers, with five strong men, if the strangers did fight, it would be difficult to subdue them.

"I wonder why there're no women with them?" said Esri.

"In the past, I met some people who did not let women hunt big animals. Maybe they're like that," said Barsa

"They're not moving like they're hunting," said Piram.

"You're right. It's like they want to be seen. Let's walk like we have no fear," said Barsa.

Gradually the two groups moved toward each other. When they were near enough to read the expressions on each other's faces, one of the strangers began waving what looked to be a belt strung with shells and started speaking loudly.

"I think they want to trade," said Esri. "He's using some words like Sela and Muni's. I know from some of the early songs we made together."

"Esri and I will go forward and speak with them. Stay a little behind us but move immediately if anything happens," said Barsa.

Esri and Barsa worked out that trade was what they strangers wanted. The strangers brought out some finely cured, soft antelope skins and necklaces and bracelets of sinew strung with small shell beads. The strangers indicated that they wanted to trade for some flints and pieces of obsidian, as there was little obsidian where they came from.

The two groups sat together under some large trees. Esri and Barsa did most of the talking for the Flat Rocks people. Barsa had some familiarity of the strangers' language from his travels and Esri from spending a lot of time with Sela and Muni in their early days at Flat Rocks.

Though this sort of trading meeting should have felt normal, like what used to happen in the days before the Ash Rain, it did not. There was an undertone that made the Flat Rocks people uneasy. The strangers snarled and laughed at times in a way that felt unsettling.

The Shell Bead People were clearly interested in the women from Flat Rocks. Only Riga gave some response to a flirtatious gesture from the one of the young men, the largest, most handsome of the group. Esri tried asking them about their women. The strangers either didn't understand or chose not to respond.

After a few hours, Barsa said to the Shell Bead People, "We'll go now and come tomorrow and bring things to trade." He gestured with his hands and used a stick to draw pictures on the ground to further illustrate his words. "You stay here."

One of the older strangers who appeared to be the leader said, "I am Ulun. We'll stay and trade tomorrow."

The Flat Rocks people walked back home. Once they were a short distance from the strangers, Piram said, "Kai and I will hide nearby and watch the strangers tonight. I don't trust them."

"Nor I, Piram," said Barsa.

"I worry that they're here for some reason other than trading," said Esri.

"Or maybe that is all they are here for. It would be good if we could begin trading again," said Riga.

They went back the next day with some obsidian, flints, and carved bowls in exchange for some of the pieces the Shell Bead People brought. They wouldn't say who had done the work. It was agreed that the two groups would meet again in the same place at the next full moon.

The Shell Bead People were vague about the location of their bode but left the impression that it was not more than two days' walk which meant that they must have moved there recently. The Flat Rocks scouting parties had not encountered the Shell Bead People in their broad searches for Ash Rain survivors.

Over the next months, the trading continued somewhat regularly. A few times the Shell Bead People brought an older woman who was the mate of the leader, Ulun, and the mother of the handsome young man Riga spoke with, Hanu, and one of the other young men, Otom.

Riga always wanted to go to the trading, each time getting a little more familiar with the handsome one, Hanu. No one was too surprised when Riga announced she was going to stay with Hanu and start living with the Shell Bead People. Esri tried to dissuade her, "You don't know how they live together. What if they have harsh ways? We should get to know them better."

"It's time that I had a mate and Hanu is strong and handsome. You don't like it that he picked me and not you," said Riga.

"No, no, that's not true. I don't want any harm to come to you," said Esri. "Promise me you'll come to the tradings often."

Riga left with the Shell Bead People and came to the next trading. She was wearing a beautiful, soft cape of antelope skin and an elaborate bead belt. "You should see my wonderful bode and the nice things I have, and Hanu is a great hunter. We have lots to eat."

"Your cape is beautiful. It must have been hard work to make it so soft. How did you do it?" asked Esri.

"Oh, I didn't make it. Others did. They made it for me. Hanu is a respected man in the bode," said Riga.

"And you are happy, Riga? Is it like Flat Rocks?" asked Esri.

"Of course, I'm happy with Hanu. He takes good care of me. I don't go hunting for antelope anymore, but I don't need to so it doesn't matter. Things are decided better than at Flat Rocks. Everyone knows their place, less talking about everything," said Riga.

TALL MAN

Esri and Ada stood in the upstairs hallway of the high school waiting outside of Luka's last class of the day. City funding cuts meant that their local library branch closed down, so when the three had no after school activities, they usually went to Clea's for an hour or so to study around her large kitchen table. Esri and Ada held Luka to the same strict regimen that they had at the library: "we're here to study, not talk."

Esri looked out the window at the students milling around outside the school. She gasped. Could it be? The Tall Man from the donut shop and the reference library? Talking to a couple of students? A Disruptor? What was he doing?

"What's the matter?" said Ada.

"That guy there. Do you know him? I've seen him around some. He's so creepy."

"The tall man talking to Brad the loudmouth in my English class? No, I don't know him, but so what? I don't think he's that creepy looking. Maybe he's Brad's dad or something," Ada sighed. "Brad is such a jerk. It wouldn't surprise me if his dad was a jerk."

"Does Brad bother you?"

"Sometimes, but I ignore him."

"Hey lovely, luminous ladies! You here to carry me off to the study torture chamber?" Luka came bursting out of the classroom.

Esri laughed, "Right, some torture chamber. Homemade muffins, cozy kitchen, garden view, cute cat."

Though it made her nervous, Esri wanted to verify if the man talking to Brad was indeed a Disruptor and hurried Luka and Ada along.

By the time they got downstairs and outside the school, the man was gone, but Brad and his friends were still standing around.

"Esri, don't go over there. I don't want to walk by Brad," said Ada.

"You and Luka go that way, I want to check something out. I'll catch up with you," said Esri.

"Why?"

"Just go. It'll only take me a sec."

Luka and Ada circled away from Brad and his friends and didn't question Esri any further. Over the last year or so, Esri sometimes did odd things, with little explanation.

Esri walked right in front of Brad. He said, "You almost smacked me with your pack. Watch where you're going." Esri kept walking. It was faint, but whiffs of the dead mouse smell still hung in the air. She looked around. The Tall Man was nowhere in sight. She ran and caught up with Luka and Ada.

At least neither Brad nor any of the kids around him were Disruptors. The dead mouse smell would have been stronger. Esri wanted to ask Brad what the Tall Man said but knew that would go nowhere. It made her uneasy.

When they opened Clea's front door, they were greeted by the smell of fresh-baked banana-bread.

"Clea, I want to marry you and we'll live happily ever after," Luka called out. He usually proposed marriage as soon as they walked in the door. Clea laughed. She enjoyed having the three friends and the excuse to do some baking. She made extra for them to take home. Once they were settled in, she and Thomas left them alone and sat in the living room reading, talking, and listening to music.

As the three friends were leaving Clea's, Esri said, "Go on ahead . . ."

Luka cut in, "I know. You'll catch up in a sec – you always have these little secrets to tell Clea. Someday Ada and I will stay and listen."

When Ada and Luka were out of earshot, Esri said, "Clea, I saw the Tall Man, the Disruptor from the reference library, outside the school today talking to some kids."

"Oh, that can't be good. Stay alert to anything unusual going on. Make note of everything. We'll talk it through when you come on Saturday. What about Flat Rocks?"

"Well, that's it. Those Shell Bead People, I don't trust them at all and now Riga's gone off to live with them. She acts all superior, but something's not right."

"We need to be very careful. All these signs are troubling."

■ ■ ■

Next day, Esri had a soccer game. She was still only a sub. She played most games, usually coming in sometime in the middle of the second half. She realized that her status would likely not change this season unless someone was injured. The starting line-up had gelled and they were winning most of their games. No reason to change things.

Joe kept a close eye on the game schedule to ensure that he had time alone with Esri after every game to talk over what happened and how she was feeling. The debriefs with Joe helped Esri regain some confidence. During games and practices, she kept her emotions in check and tried to stay positive about the other team members, even those who regularly snubbed her. She had to admit, in a tiny way, it seemed to be working. At least she wasn't dreading going to practices like after that first disastrous game of the season.

Esri loved her Dad for the support he gave her around the soccer team but as his relationship with Randi intensified so too did Esri's feeling of alienation from her family. Joe now stayed with Randi several nights a week, mostly weekend nights but occasionally even during the week. Randi often joined them for supper, usually bringing take-out from the bar she managed. On Sunday afternoons Joe and Randi took Jilly out. Esri begged off as much as she could. If Randi was around, Esri would go to her room saying she had to study or she went to Clea's.

Since today Esri had a soccer game, Randi wouldn't be around this evening, and once Jilly was in bed, Esri would have her Dad's undivided attention.

"Hey, Dad, Jills," said Esri as she walked in the door.

"Good game, kiddo?" said Jilly. "That's what Dad always says, so I thought I'd say it first."

Esri laughed. "Yeah, it was not too bad. I played for a good chunk of the second half and had a few good plays. Even Miss Stuck-up captain said, 'Good play, Esri.' That was new."

Joe said, "I'm anxious to hear all about it Es, but you better call Ada or go see her. She called a little while ago and sounded pretty upset."

"Oh? Really? That's weird. She was fine when I saw her at lunch. I hope it's not something wrong with someone in her family," said Esri.

Esri called Ada. "Hey, Ada, Dad said you called. What's up?"

"I'm so glad you're home. Can I come down? Is there someplace we can talk?"

"Sure. We can go to my room, at least until Jilly goes to bed."

Joe agreed to keep Jilly occupied until bedtime. "But you let me know if there is anything I can do, and encourage her to talk to her parents about whatever it is."

Ada arrived a few minutes later, and she and Esri went to the bedroom, "Ada, what is it?"

Ada started to cry. "I'm so angry. That jerk, Brad, started going on about how people like my parents and their families are murdering people."

"What? That's stupid. Why is he saying that?"

"It's all that stuff in the news about where we came from. They're finding mass graves and fire-bombing people's homes. It's why my parents left. And now, the latest killings are happening by people supposedly of our religion, but they're not. They're some kind of sick fanatics."

"Of course, Ada. No one would think otherwise."

"Yesterday Brad and some of his friends started calling me and my family 'murderers' and 'baby-killers' and, I can't even say it all . . ." she started to cry.

"But that's so ridiculous. Didn't your teacher say anything?"

"They made sure the teacher didn't hear. It happened between classes. I said I was going to the principal and they laughed and said they'd start going after my little brothers. A lot of other kids overheard them and no one took my side. They just looked at me like I was something nasty."

"Did you tell your parents?"

"No, they're so upset about what's going on. We have cousins who are still there. My parents have been trying to get in touch with them but can't. The last thing my parents need is more stuff to worry about. It's not like Brad and his friends are going to kill me or anything. But if they get kids to taunt my little brothers . . . it's so unfair. I don't want to go to school."

"Ada, you should go talk to the principal. I'll come with you. You can't let it go on."

"Maybe. I'll see what happens tomorrow. Maybe Brad will move onto something else. Even for him, this is extreme. I don't know I'm worried if I go to the principal it will stir Brad up even more."

"Ok, see what happens but, at the very least, Ada, let's make sure you're not having to deal with Brad and his friends alone. For the classes we don't have together, Luka or I will meet up with you between classes and find you so you're never alone. We'll work out a schedule for the next few days. I'll make up some excuse to leave my classes a little early if I need to. I'll talk to Luka and we'll figure something out. "

Esri and Luka made sure that one or the other, or both of them were always with Ada unless she was in a classroom with a teacher. Ada's English class with Brad met every other day, and up until the class met again, Ada managed to avoid Brad. Both Esri and Luka planned on meeting up with Ada after her English class, but neither was in a class nearby. Ten minutes before Esri's class was scheduled to end. She told the teacher that she had a stomach ache, implying it was diarrhea and urgent.

Esri flew down the hallway. Unfortunately, Ada's class got out a few minutes early. When Esri reached Ada, Brad and another boy had cornered her in the nearby stairwell. They were smirking and making lewd and suggestive remarks and gestures at Ada, Brad was whispering in Ada's ear.

"What's going on here?" said Esri.

"Hey, look at this, friend of the baby-killer," said Brad.

"Stop it," said Esri.

"What are you goin' to do?" said Brad.

"I'm going to tell you to shut your mouth," it was Luka. He grabbed Brad's arm and spun him around. Brad raised his fist but before he could connect, Luka hit him in the stomach, knocking the wind out of him.

Brad's friend, a large boy nearly twice the size of Ada, pushed her against the wall with one large hand and started grabbing one of her breasts with the other. "I'll teach you baby-killer."

Esri was enraged, seeing him assault good, gentle Ada, like a sister to her. Esri had her hand in the pocket of her jacket and felt the leather-wrapped flint she had carried around like a talisman since her presentation last year in Mr. Romero's class. She dug out the flint and scraped it across the boy's arm that was pressed against Ada. The boy howled and pulled back from Ada. Blood dripped from the gash in his arm.

TROUBLES

Ada's English teacher and another teacher from a nearby classroom came running out to the stairwell in time to see the large boy holding his arm, blood dripping on the floor and Esri holding the bloody flint. Brad and his friend saw the teachers first and immediately stopped fighting. Esri and Luka, with their backs to the teachers, continued to flail and kick at the boys until the teachers grabbed them from behind.

"Drop that weapon. We're calling the police," said one of the teachers. Esri dropped the flint. It shattered into several pieces. "Meanwhile all you kids are going to the office."

Brad said, "You saw. We were just standing there and they started pounding on us. They're a bunch of psychos. You should expel them."

Ada's English teacher said, "Save it for the principal, and the police. You three," pointing to Ada, Esri, and Luka, "and you two," pointing to Brad and his friend, "come with us. The rest of you, go on about your business," he said to the large crowd of students that had gathered. He turned to the boy with the cut arm. "We'll get someone to take you to emerg to get that looked after."

A short time after they arrived at the principal's office, two police officers came, a man and a woman. One of the vice-principals drove the injured boy to the hospital. They put Esri, Ada, and Luka in a room separate from Brad. The principal and the woman officer interviewed the students one at a time starting with Brad. The other police officer ensured that there was no further trouble.

Ada was devastated. She could hardly speak, choking on her tears. "I'm so frightened and now you are in terrible trouble . . . and my family."

Luka was completely wound up. Esri tried to comfort Ada, and calm down Luka, all the while horrified by what she had done. The boy was a complete jerk but she had stabbed him. That was beyond overreacting. She should have tried to push him away until the teachers came, but seeing what he was doing to Ada and the look on her face, what was Esri supposed to do? She would certainly be charged by the police, probably kicked out of school. Oh God, her Dad.

And Flat Rocks, her dreams would stop she was sure. The Disruptors did their job. How could she be so stupid, so impulsive? Whoever chose her to be a Mender chose poorly.

Esri was the last to be called into the principal's office. Before she went in, she turned to Luka and Ada and said, "You two go on. Don't wait for me. Luka, if I'm not home by 5, pick up Jilly at Farhana's. Please don't say anything, just that I was delayed at school. My Dad will be home by six. I'll try to talk to him as soon as I can."

Once seated in the office, the Officer Calvino spoke first. "Young lady, you could be charged with aggravated assault with a weapon and I could haul you out right now, book you, and put you in a detention center pending your trial. Your principal here tells me you've never been in any trouble before, are a good student, and, if anything, tend to be a peacemaker. She thinks we should be lenient with you. I want to hear what you have to say."

Esri took a deep breath. She thought about Clea. Not that Clea would ever stab somebody, but how Clea would expect Esri to face up to what she had done, and what she could try to do to fix this mess.

"I did a terrible thing. I want to tell you what happened and why I did it. I know that doesn't make it right or excuse what I did. It's really hard to do nothing when you see someone you care about, who's been good to you your whole life, who's one of the best people you've ever known being hurt and threatened. But what I did was wrong. I know that." Esri struggled not to cry.

The principal's phone rang. "Let me get that. It's probably my VP phoning from the hospital," she said. "Hello. Ian? Tell me about the boy . . . no stitches? . . . that's good. How is he?"

Officer Calvino cut in, "I want to talk to the boy. What's his name?"

"Hang on, Ian. Officer Calvino wants to talk to Troy. Can you put him on?"

"Troy. This is Officer Calvino. I'm glad to hear you're doing ok. I'm sitting in Principal Wong's office. We've been talking to everyone involved in what happened today and I wanted to hear what you have to say. Why do you think the girl cut you with that sharp stone? . . . If I asked the kids standing on the stairwell what you were doing, would they say? . . . And if someone caught it on video on their phone? . . . Ok, you go on home. And Troy, you promise me not to get any big retaliation ideas. Tomorrow morning when you come to school, go straight to the principal's office. Got that? Ok. You can give the phone back to the vice-principal."

Officer Calvino handed the phone to Principal Wong, "Troy did admit he grabbed Ada's breast, claimed it was an 'accident' but was starting to waffle on that." They turned to Esri.

"Esri? That's your name, right? Can you tell me what the heck you were doing carrying around a razor sharp spearhead or whatever that was? And where did you get it? I must admit that's a new one on me," said Officer Calvino.

"I made it. I did some research for a school project on cave people and talked to a guy that does flint-knapping - that's what it's called - and he showed me how to make it. I guess I liked it and I've been carrying it around ever since. I never had any intention of using it, but yeah, dumb of me to have it because it's super sharp. It's broken now anyway. It's just that boy was so big and Ada's so small and I'm not that big either. I was scared for her. . . I didn't think."

Principal Wong spoke. "Esri, I can't even begin to tell you how shocked and disappointed I am in you about what happened. I know you're a good kid. We've talked a few times when you've met Luka here after he got into trouble. You're a loyal friend and I know you were involved with Jerome's video last year. And, I pulled up your file – your marks are good. You don't skip class. I'm frankly baffled. The thing is, we simply cannot tolerate this kind of behavior at our school. This is very serious. Effective immediately, I'm suspending you from school for a week. It's up to you to stay on top of your school work. But there will be further ramifications. You should be prepared. I'm going to call your home this evening. Will your parents be in?"

Esri nodded, "Yeah, my Dad should be home by six." She walked out of the office and was surprised to see Mr. Romero, her last year's ancient history teacher, waiting for her. She wanted a hole to open up and swallow her. It was almost as bad as facing her dad.

"Esri, I heard about what happened. Do you have time to talk? This is so out of character for you. I want to hear from you what happened and if I can help you in any way."

They went to his classroom. The school was largely empty now. Esri still had time until her dad got home. She borrowed Mr. Romero's cellphone to call Luka and make sure Jilly was okay. Esri described the incident in the stairwell, and after some gentle prodding from Mr. Romero, told him about the baby-killer bullying and the threats to harass Ada's younger brothers and parents. She told him she felt bad about cutting Troy, and was worried that Brad and his friends would retaliate.

Mr. Romero said, "I find it odd that Brad and Troy and the others would pick on Ada. We have lots of kids from many different backgrounds, and sometimes political strife happening overseas does have ripple effects in our school. But in this case, given what I know about the perpetrators, I'm surprised they would get so riled and then to target Ada of all people. It puzzles me. What do you think is going on?"

"I don't know. Maybe Brad has family who are affected by what's happening. I don't know Brad very well, but he seems to enjoy bullying people and maybe saw Ada as an easy target."

"Well, I have two concerns. One is to make sure that you don't get derailed by this and that you stay in school and stay on track."

"Mr. Romero, you don't have to worry on that account. I know I really screwed up. I'm really worried that I'll get kicked out of school. The officer said I could end up in a detention center. I am terrified of that. Even if they want to send me to another school, I'd hate it, but I'd deal with it."

"Esri, you're a good kid. I know that. You should go to university. You've got such a keen interest in learning and a great mind. Just know, I'll do what I can to support your coming back to school here. You can reach out to me whenever you need. My other big concern is how to stop Brad and his friends from retaliating and escalating the situation."

"I know. I'm terrified for Ada, and Luka too. I don't know what to do."

"I'm going to talk to Principal Wong about seeing if we could bring in someone to try doing mediation between you all, but I wanted to talk to you first before going to her. And you should know, she may not agree. Some of the school counselors are trained mediators but their time is limited. Mrs. Wong has a lot of issues she's dealing with in a school this size and may think, perhaps rightly, that someone like Brad is not a good candidate for mediation as he may be too entrenched in his attitudes."

"I'm not sure I know exactly what mediation is. Do we all get in a room together and come to an agreement? I don't know if that would work so well, but I'm certainly willing to try."

"There's a fairly structured process where the participants agree on the steps of the mediation, terms of confidentiality, desired outcomes. It's something we should use more often. I've heard of schools where they even train students to be mediators. Anyway, here are a few links to websites about it. I'll pursue it on my end and see what we can do. Now, you should be getting home. What about your folks?"

"It's just my Dad. He's going to be really upset," Esri struggled not to cry. "He's a super Dad. He works so hard. He'll want to hear everything, but this is by far the worst thing I've ever done. He's going to be so disappointed in me." The tears rolled down.

"I don't think you need to worry. The key, Esri, is to soldier through this. Do the best you can to set things right, and there will come a time when you can look back and say, Yeah, that was a bad time but I learned from it and I'm ok now." Mr. Romero gave a crinkled grin "And, young lady, no more flintknapping, ok?"

Esri managed a small smile, "Not in this lifetime, anyway. Thanks for this, Mr. Romero."

Esri picked up Jilly at Luka's and got home shortly before Joe arrived. Randi was with him. Now what? Esri knew she had to plunge ahead and talk about what happened because Principal Wong might be calling any minute. She wanted to include Jilly in the conversation as Jilly already knew some of what happened from Luka and would hear more tomorrow from people in the apartment building and kids at school. And, trying to exclude Randi would be awkward and create more problems.

"Dad, I did something very bad today at school and I need to tell you about it. Principal Wong will be calling you soon. Jilly knows some of what happened, and she should hear the whole story."

"Do you want me to leave?" Randi asked.

"No, stay," said Esri. "Dad will want to talk to you about it anyway." Esri told them much the same as she had explained to Mr. Romero, talking more in depth about the taunting and her conversation with Mr. Romero. She was almost finished when the phone range. It was Principal Wong. Joe spoke with her for several minutes, mainly listening. He got off the phone.

"I hardly know what to say, Esri. I never imagined that you would do something to get yourself suspended from school and perhaps even expelled. They're still deciding what to do. You've been distant lately. Is something going on that I don't know about?"

Yes, she thought, I'm leading a double life that I can't talk to you about and I can't stand your girlfriend. Esri said, "I wish I had a good explanation for you, but I don't. But you know Ada, how nice she is, quiet, smart, and funny. She never says anything mean or gossipy about anyone. If you had seen that horrible Troy grabbing her breast and hurting her – I . . . I couldn't stand by and do nothing."

Randi put her hand on Joe's arm. "Sometimes you have to get aggressive with thugs. That's how you keep them in line."

Joe looked at Randi. "I don't really agree, Randi. I worry that it only escalates matters."

"I know, Dad. Mr. Romero talked about that too. He talked to me about maybe trying mediation to sort this out. Do you know how that works?"

"Your principal mentioned Mr. Romero talking to her about a mediation process. I'm a little familiar with it, but your Principal seems to feel that in this case it won't work. She's quite worried about what may happen next. For now, Luka and the one boy are each suspended for 3 days and you and the boy you cut, who witnesses have confirmed was hurting Ada, are both suspended for 6 days each. But it's not over. It may still mean you'll be sent to another school to avoid further problems."

Randi spoke, "I'm wondering, too, Esri, if you spent more time with your Dad and Jilly. You spend a lot of time at that old lady's house. Clea, that's her name? I'll be honest, it seems a little odd that you would prefer being with her over your friends and family."

Why bring Clea into this? Esri thought, but stopped herself from making a snide retort. She was in enough trouble already.

MEDIATION

Over the next days, there were many conversations between the three friends, their parents, and the school. Esri worked extra hard to keep up with her assignments. She was to report to Mrs. Wong after her six-day suspension and would find out then if she was being transferred or continuing on a probationary basis or what. Not only would Esri hate starting in a new school in the middle of the year where she didn't know anybody. It could create big problems for looking after Jilly, especially in the mornings if Esri was facing a long commute. She worried about Ada and Luka, and how Brad and his friends would continue their reign of terror.

And the dreams stopped again. She had a bad feeling about the Shell Bead People Riga had gone to, and now there was nothing she could do about it. But Esri had to do something. If Brad and Troy were open and willing to take part in a mediation process, maybe, just maybe, things could get fixed.

Esri found out where Troy lived. Fortunately it was in an apartment building not too far from hers. On the fourth day of her suspension when Brad was back in school but Troy was still out, Esri found a coffee shop where she could watch the entrance to Troy's apartment building. She worried that he might stay inside all day. Around one, she saw him leave the building. She quickly gathered her things together while keeping an eye on him. Good grief, he was heading for the coffee shop. She sat back down. It might be easier to get him to sit and talk with her there than confront him on the street. She waited.

After Troy placed his order at the counter, Esri went up to him. "Troy, uh, hi. Please, can you give me a minute? I'm really sorry about your arm. I just want to talk to you."

"What the . . . ?"

Esri reached down deep and turned on every ounce of charm she could sqeeze out. She focused on channeling Clea's calm warmth and told herself she would persist no matter what. Troy was reluctant and unpleasant to begin with, but he did sit with her. It was better than hanging around home watching TV all day, and he was frankly curious.

Esri felt she never worked as hard at anything in her life. Troy was the kind of kid she normally avoided. Too loud, too aggressive. She wanted to get him to agree to the mediation but knew she couldn't just spring it on him. She also knew that it would never work unless he entered into it willingly and understood it would mean laying aside some of his bravado. And even harder, he'd have to convince Brad to do the same.

Looking back on it later, Esri was amazed. Who knew she had it in her to be such a talker and persuader, especially with someone like Troy? Every time she felt unsure of how to proceed or Troy started disengaging, she thought about Clea and how Clea got people to open up about themselves. Clea did it with Esri, and Esri watched Clea do it with Esri's dad, Ada, and Luka – through gentle probing and lots of smiles.

Esri and Troy talked for most of the afternoon. At first, Esri struggled to stay neutral and coax the conversation toward topics where they could find common ground. Little by little, Troy softened, dropped some of his swagger. They started sharing family stories. He lived with his mom and older brother in an apartment building much like Esri's. At one point, after they spoke for a couple of hours Troy paused, looked out the window, and said quietly, "I am sorry I grabbed your friend, Ada." He turned back to Esri.

Esri took that as her opening. "I came to talk to you because Mr. Romero gave me an idea about something, how maybe we can get out of this mess."

Troy laughed, "That would sure make my mom happy. She's about ready to kick me out of the house. I almost don't know what happened, how Brad got us going about Ada and her family. He was pretty whipped up about it, but now it almost doesn't make sense. Anyway, what's Mr. Romero's big idea?"

Esri explained to him what she knew about mediation, but warned him that the principal was not that keen. Principal Wong worried that they wouldn't be sincere about it, and there would be on-going retaliation. She was leaning to dividing them up and sending them to other schools to get rid of the problem. "Even if we agree to do mediation, I'm not sure how we can convince her."

Troy sighed, "Yeah, she's got a low bullshit threshold. I've, ah, had a few dealings with her."

"Maybe we can get Mr. Romero to help us."

"Sure, but we need something more. I have an idea. I don't know how you'd feel about it. What if next Tuesday, when we have to check in with Principal Wong, you and I meet up and walk to school together, comfortable-like. Let the kids and teachers see us and go walking into her office looking like we're old friends. What do you think?" Troy grinned.

"Um, sure, if you're ok with that, I'm ok. I'll have to let Ada and Luka know. They might be a little shocked, but not when I explain everything. What about Brad?"

"I dunno. He hates to back down on anything. But you know what would help? You're tight with Jerome, aren't you? Brad would love to be in one of Jerome's videos. Is that something you could set up?"

"Oh, I don't know. I'm not that tight with Jerome. I could certainly make the introductions but only if we get through this and Brad stops being a jerk. I don't want to make any big promises."

"That's cool. I'll talk to Brad. Should we meet up here say on Monday, lunchtime again, plan our Tuesday morning entrance?"

"Sure. Sounds good. And thanks for hearing me out, Troy."

"You're one funny kid, Esri. I imagine it took some nerve for you to find me. The UN should hire you to do peace negotiations."

On Tuesday morning, as planned, Esri and Troy met up several blocks away from school. They sauntered along, talking and laughing past gaping students and staring teachers to Principal Wong's office. They kept up their easy chatter as they sat in the waiting room outside her office. And it was that image of two friendly students that Principal Wong confronted when she went to call them in. Esri and Troy decided that Troy should talk first about the mediation as, of the two, Principal Wong would assume he would be the least likely to be accommodating about the process.

Principal Wong did agree to go ahead with the mediation, which included Esri, Luka, Ada, Brad, and Troy. The process was not without its hiccups but eventually there was an agreement and everyone was allowed to stay at the school with the understanding that even a tiny misstep would bring expulsion to another school.

Esri was relieved when the dreams started again once the mediation process was underway. After the mediation concluded there was a mutually understood truce, and Brad and Troy had little to do with Esri, Ada, and Luka - with one exception, Esri and Troy. They didn't hang out together, but the two would talk every now and again.

Throughout all of the bullying stairwell incident, suspension, and mediation, Esri continued her close contact with Clea. During Esri's suspension, she spent many hours at Clea's house. Thomas usually joined their conversations. He was particularly helpful preparing for the talk with Troy, even roll-playing how Troy would likely react. Esri was amazed how closely Thomas nailed what Troy said when she confronted him at the coffee shop.

At home, things were not so good. Joe didn't ground her for long, but he was constantly asking Esri for a detailed accounting of everything she did or was planning to do. It felt like he had lost trust in her. And Jilly seemed intent on being annoying in any way she could manage. She was picky about what she ate, what she wanted to do, what she wanted to wear, what she wanted Esri to wear, how she wanted Esri to act toward her. Unless they were at Clea's. Somehow Clea, usually with Willa's help, could bring back the sunny little girl.

One positive by-product of the school suspension was that several times Esri witnessed her Dad getting annoyed with Randi. He shushed Randi when she got off on rants about how great it was that Esri showed moxie fighting those boys with that arrowhead thing. Esri could only hope this might be opening up a crack in Joe and Randi's relationship.

TRUE NATURE REVEALED

Riga didn't come to the next trading and at the one after she was more subdued. Esri approached her. "I missed seeing you at the last trading. I was thinking maybe some of us could come and visit some time."

Riga hesitated. "Not yet, Esri. I haven't been at Hanu's bode for long and Ulun would have to agree. He did want me to ask you if he and a small group could come and visit Flat Rocks. Can you speak at the Elders Council about it? I'm hoping that I can come with them."

"Why wouldn't you come?" asked Esri.

"Sometimes they leave some things just to the men and other things just to the women. It's easier."

Esri didn't argue with Riga, but life with the Shell Bead People didn't sound so appealing. Though Riga still claimed she was very happy, Esri was not convinced and worried about Riga and what else might be happening at the Shell Bead People's bode. Perhaps it would be good to exchange visits to each other's bodes. Ulun spoke with Barsa about arranging a visit to Flat Rocks at the next trading. Barsa agreed to speak with the other Elders.

When the Elders Council met, Zura said, "I find it interesting that as well as speaking with Barsa about visiting us, Ulun also had Riga speak with Esri."

"Ulun watches closely what happens at our tradings. He sees that when Riga comes, that Esri spends time talking to her. He's using their relationship to get what he wants," said Barsa.

"He's a sly one, that Ulun. We must be careful," said Piram. "I remember men like him from my days as a boy with my old bode."

"If by having the Shell Bead People come to Flat Rocks, then some of us can visit their bode, then we should go ahead," said Zura.

Nagar was lying down near the Elders Council and partially raised herself up. "We need to find out if they are Violent Ones or if they keep slaves. A visit to their bode would tell us a lot, even if they try to make it look like they don't have slaves. It will be difficult for them to hide the truth." And she laid back down.

"I keep thinking about those children with Sela and Muni, and what might have happened to them," said Saba.

"We all do. If the Shell Bead People come to visit, they must not see Sela and Muni," said Zura.

"But it would be good if Sela and Muni could look at the Shell Bead People and see if any of them are those that kidnapped and hurt them," said Tars.

Saba said, "I haven't gone to any of the tradings. When the Shell Bead People come to visit, they won't notice if I am not here. I can take Sela and Muni to the ledge above the cave behind the bushes. We can look down on them without them seeing us."

"We should welcome the Shell Bead People like they are friends, feed them well, tell them about our Agreements, but be organized to fight them swiftly if need be. Extend one arm with a well-roasted piece of antelope, while holding a sharp flint behind our backs," said Tars.

They nodded in agreement. Nagar spoke again, "If they do attack, first bring them down and tie them up. Do not kill them."

Tars said, "We might not have a choice, Nagar."

The woman whose spear cut Esri's arm said, "We must give them a choice. And give them time to understand how we live at Flat Rocks." She looked at Esri. "This finally worked for me."

"Yes, but you did not keep slaves or harm others. You were only protecting your people," said Piram.

Barsa said, "In my old bode, a young man who grew up in a bode that had slaves came to live with a woman in our bode. I never saw or heard of him doing anything bad to another person. Once, when the two of us went on a long hunt together he talked to me about what they did at his old bode and the bad things he had done because that was all he knew as a boy. If people want to, they can change."

Tars said, "Yes, but if many are violent, they see violence as a way to have power and will fight to keep that power. Before the Ash Rain, we traded with some people who spoke of Violent Ones who stole others, particularly women and children, to make slaves and thought nothing of killing those who tried to stop them. When we look for survivors, sometimes we find a bode where it looks like people died violently, not just from the Ash Rain."

Zura said, "Yes, we do not know yet who these Shell Bead People are, but we need to find out."

The Elders Council agreed to go ahead with the Shell Bead People visit. Plans were made about what would be discussed and shown - the Agreements and Flat Rocks ways of living together. And those things they would not discuss - how many able-bodied people lived at Flat Rocks. They would give the appearance of being many more by creating extra sleeping shelters and talking about some people being away on hunting and gathering expeditions. They wanted to leave the Shell Bead People with the impression that Flat Rocks was a large, healthy, strong bode that welcomed many survivors of the Ash Rain.

The Shell Bead People's visit to Flat Rocks happened with the next trading. Only the five men who regularly traded came to take part in the visit. Esri was disappointed not to see Riga. "Where is Riga, Hanu?"

"She wanted to stay with the women," said Hanu and walked away from her.

It was nearly dark when the two trading groups reached Flat Rocks. The Shell Bead People camped a short distance away at a spot that was laid out for them with wood for a fire and food to eat. It was understood that the formal visit would begin the next morning. Nat and Kai spent the night out of sight near the Shell Bead People. Early the next morning, when it was still dark, Saba went to Grayla and Jolam's sleeping place and woke-up Sela and Muni. The three of them climbed up above the cave. Dagan made a comfortable hiding place for them to peer down at the Shell Bead People when they arrived.

The Flat Rocks bode was tense and nervous about the Shell Bead People coming. The Elders Council, minus Saba, would do most of the talking and were conscious of trying not to appear anxious about the visitors. The Shell Bead People would spend the day at Flat Rocks, sleep again at the campsite of the night before, and then be on their way.

The worst part of the day came right at the beginning. As soon as Sela and Muni saw the Shell Bead People they recognized their kidnappers as Hanu and his brother Otom. Though the children were warned that they must not make a sound no matter what, Muni let out a sobbing cry. Ulun jerked his head toward the noise and saw a shrieking Grilu jumping up on Esri at the mouth of the cave. Esri worried that it might be difficult for Sela and Muni to stay quiet if they saw their kidnappers and worked out a diversion with Grilu ahead of time. Saba moved the children farther away from Flat Rocks where they would spend the day until the visitors were gone.

Word spread quickly and quietly through Flat Rocks that Sela and Muni had recognized their kidnappers. The Elders remained cordial but they made certain that the visit would not be prolonged and that the movement of the Shell Bead People in Flat Rocks would stay as confined as possible.

There was no doubt now that the Shell Bead People came to spy on the Flat Rocks bode, assessing the size, layout, strengths and weaknesses of the community.

What most befuddled the visitors was determining who was the leader at Flat Rocks. The visitors spoke with and saw an array of women and men, some old, some young, all of whom spoke and acted with some authority. Ulun asked many questions about who was in charge of the hunting parties, who divided the food, who spoke for the Ancients. He received a variety of responses.

The Flat Rocks people sang songs and told stories of their Agreements to share food and knowledge, and not have slaves nor do violence to one another.

In response, the Shell Bead People told stories of the great hunting prowess of their men and the beauty of their women. Hanu made the slip of saying that the five strong men they saw before them did all of the hunting of big animals. Ulun did not want to leave the impression that their bode was so small and quickly stepped in to say that they had many strong men but that the five of them were the strongest.

Esri stayed near the group for most of their visit. She focused her attention on Ulun, not only what he was asking and telling them but also his eye movements. And he, in turn, was aware of her scrutiny and noted the role she played at Flat Rocks. Though she was young and a woman, her words and actions held sway with others. He had seen this too at the tradings.

As night fell, many of the Flat Rocks people went with the Shell Bead People to their nearby campsite and stayed late, singing songs and exchanging stories. Nat and Kai again kept a hidden vigil nearby through the night and followed the Shell Bead People group at a distance the next morning.

STRESSES

"Wake up! You're making creepy noises," Jilly yelled in Esri's ear.

Esri jerked awake. Oh, god, the Shell Bead People were the Violent Ones. She feared as much and now they knew it for certain. Jilly started pushing at Esri, "Stop ignoring me!"

Esri lurched mentally back to her apartment in Toronto and yelled at Jilly, "And you stop yelling in my ear. I've told you a million times. That's a terrible thing to do to someone when they're sleeping."

"I want my own room!"

"Oh, stop acting like a spoiled brat. Believe me, I'd love to not share a room with you."

Jilly started wailing. "You're not nice. You're always mean to me."

Joe came into the bedroom, "What did you do now, Esri?"

"It's not always my fault, you know."

"Well then, why is Jilly the one crying? What happened?"

"Oh forget it. I told Clea I'd be there early today. I've got to get going," Esri strode by her Dad.

"Don't you walk away from me."

Esri kept walking to the bathroom. Joe did not follow her. He went over to Jilly, "You ok?"

"Yeah, Daddy, don't yell at Esri. I don't think she likes me anymore." She cried harder.

"Don't be silly, Jills. Esri loves you very much. Nothing will ever change that. She's just going through a rough time."

Esri concentrated on breathing deeply and slowly while she was in the shower as Clea told her to do when Esri felt angry or stressed. After she dressed, Esri found Jilly and Joe eating breakfast with Randi. Randi must have spent the night again. She was all made-up and enveloped in her perfume cloud. Randi must have been up for ages already. No doubt she heard the whole argument.

"Jilly, Dad, I'm really, really sorry. I know I make weird noises sometimes when I'm asleep and it freaks Jilly out. I've told her to wake me up, but Jills, can you be a little more gentle? Maybe we can practice. I'll show you how." Esri smiled at Jilly and stroked Jilly's head. "Admit it. You'd miss me if you had a room to yourself."

"I guess."

The phone rang. Esri said, "I'm up, I'll get it."

"Hello . . . Nicole? What happened? Are you all right? . . . What? . . . Oh, god. . .And Billy?. . .How can we help?. . .OK. . . Yes, I'll tell my Dad . .We'll see you soon. . .We love you too, Nicole. Bye."

Esri put down the phone. She looked distraught. Joe got up and put his arm around Esri. "Nicole? Is she all right?"

Jilly looked at them, "What? What's going on?"

Esri said, "It was Nicole. She's fine. She's moved again. Jilly, why don't you go ahead and get dressed. We'll leave for Clea's soon. Maybe Randi could help you create a fashion statement."

"Yay! C'mon, Randi."

Randi shot Esri an unhappy look but quickly smiled up at Joe when he turned to her. "Sure Jills, let's go."

When they were alone, Joe said to Esri, "Tell me what happened."

"Nicole and Billy are back at the shelter. She was pretty upset on the phone, but she and Billy are all right. Darren was drinking last night and started pushing her around. She got him calmed down and left with Billy after Darren fell asleep."

Joe said, "Did she get hurt?"

"She said she's ok, but I don't know. I think she's worried about us being too involved and what Darren might do."

"I wish I knew better how we could help. I'm glad she's back at the shelter. I don't want Jilly to hear about all of this."

Randi and Jilly came back. Joe said, "Hey, Jills, you look terrific." They all laughed because she did. You had to hand it to Randi. She did have an artistic flair and had helped Jilly put together a wonderful ensemble. Esri knew Clea and Thomas would enjoy it too. Jilly piped up, "I'm so pretty! I'm going to pack up my princess dollies to take to Clea's today." And she ran back to her room.

Randi said, "Joe, this would be a good time to mention my offer to Esri."

"Ah, sure, yeah. Um, Esri. Randi and I, that is, I've, been thinking, you know I'm very fond of Clea and all, but she is kind of an odd old duck and I worry that maybe you're spending a little too much time with her." Esri stiffened.

Joe continued, "Hear me out, Esri, before you say anything. I've been thinking about this a lot. I'm worried that all the time and stuff you do with Clea has become kind of distracting for you. I've even wondered if it might have affected your demotion on the soccer team, you know, not being able to keep your head in the game as much as you used to. I know Clea gets you involved in doing all sorts of interesting things, but you must admit it's kind of unusual for a kid your age to spend so much time with someone like that.

"And, it also coincides with your recent troubles in school. What you did was so out of character for you. Anyway, Randi has made a very generous offer for you to do some work at her restaurant for decent pay and working at hours that fit in with our schedules. So what do you think?"

Esri stared up at her Dad. Breathe deep, don't get angry.

Randi jumped in, "Joe, you should mention that this needs to happen soon. I can't keep the offer open indefinitely. You felt pretty firmly about what Esri should do."

Joe placed his hand on Randi's shoulder, "I know you're anxious to move ahead with this, Randi. But let's give Esri a little time to think this over."

Esri looked back and forth between her Dad and Randi. Esri said to Randi, "Have you met Clea?"

"No, but your Dad certainly has told me a lot about her. You should listen to your Dad, Esri. He only wants the best for you, you know."

"I know. And I do appreciate your offer, Randi." Esri turned to her Dad. Stay calm, she told herself. Don't get angry. Talk reasonably. "Dad, I know we haven't talked a lot recently. And . . . and I want to change that. But I really don't think that Clea is to blame for anything that's happened. In fact, if it weren't for her, I don't think that the mediation would have happened. She really helped me a lot to understand what I could do and say to try to fix things.

"And I'm ok about soccer. Things got better toward the end of the fall season and I'll try hard again when spring season comes. You really helped me work through that. Let's not change anything with Clea. Why don't you come and visit her? You haven't for a while. She'd like that, and bring Randi." Esri stopped and held her breathe.

Jilly came bouncing out. "Ready? I can't wait to see Clea and Thomas and show them what I'm wearing."

Esri said, "They'll love it for sure. Dad, I should get going. I can eat breakfast at Clea's. Can we keep everything the same for a little while? See how things go? I'll be really good, I promise. And, Randi, thank you so much for trying to help out. It means a lot." Esri tried to sound as sincere as she could muster. It clearly wasn't enough as Randi glared at her, but not that Joe noticed.

"Ok, Esri. Let's see how things are when the school term ends at Christmas. You know, kiddo, that school suspension really knocked me for a loop. I just want to make sure you stay on track."

"I will, Dad, I promise. That was really, really stupid what happened. I know that."

"Ok, sounds good. And let's talk tonight again about what we can do for Nicole."

"Later, Dad, love you."

NABBING

As soon as the Shell Bead People left Flat Rocks, Jolam and Grayla went to get Saba, Sela, and Muni and bring them back to the bode.

"What if they sneak up on us in the night and kill everyone?" asked Sela.

Muni asked, "Are the other children from our bode dead?"

"We are many more than they are. Someone at Flat Rocks is always watching. They will not attack us," said Jolam,

"What about the children? And Riga? Why didn't Riga come?" said Sela.

Saba said, "I don't know, Sela. I'm worried too. We need to make a plan. You can help us because you can tell us things about them."

Grayla put her arms around the children, "You and Muni are safe with us. We will not let them harm you."

The next day, after Nat and Kai returned. People gathered to discuss what to do about the Shell Bead People who they now called the Violent Ones.

"We need to attack them before they attack us," said Piram. "Now that they have seen where we live and how many we are, they're making plans to come in and kill the strong ones and make the weak and little ones slaves. We have all seen what people like this can do. We must move quickly."

"If we attack them, many of us will be killed. It will bring sorrow and anger and then we become killers and Violent Ones like them." said Nagar – gasping and coughing.

"But Piram is right. We can't just sit here. And what about the children and Riga?" said Tars.

Zura said, "Listen to what Nagar is saying. If we kill them, we're saying that killing people is right. Our Agreements say it is not right. She is not saying we do nothing, but we need to find a way to help the slaves that is not by killing."

"A few of us can go and watch them. See where they live, how many are in their bode," said Nat.

Esri said, "It might be possible to get slaves away from them during the night."

Barsa said, "Maybe some of the Violent Ones want to leave. Last night at their campfire, the young man, Geslo, who doesn't say much in the tradings, sat with me away from the others. He asked me many questions about our Agreements and how we live. Some of his questions were curious. He asked me if we laughed a lot and if everyone laughed a lot, not just the Elders."

"You're saying they're not all Violent Ones?" said Esri.

Barsa shrugged, "Perhaps not."

It was agreed that Kai and Nat would scout the Violent Ones' bode and they left the next morning. It would be several days before they returned as it was nearly a two-day walk.

The people at Flat Rocks felt unsettled and anxious. They made sure that a number of them were always keeping watch. When people took children any distance from the bode, they did so with several adults for protection. A few days after Kai and Nat left, Grayla, Jolam, Sela, Muni, Grilu, Wilki, and Wilki-Dumu decided to go down to the river and gather mussels. Wilki said, "Esri, come with us. You've hardly left the bode in days."

Esri said, "No Wilki, I want to stay. If Nat and Kai come back early, I want to be here. Anyway, I have a bone carving I'm working on."

"I'm going to stay too with Esri," said Sela. "Can I work with you?"

"Of course, here, I have another bone. I'll show you how to make Muni's face." She turned to Wilki. "Be careful."

"Don't worry. We're a big group and we're not going far."

Esri was working on replicating Zura's Sky Bones with marks for noting the new rhythms of the plants and animals that they were noticing. Before she started on her work, she gave Sela a thigh bone from an antelope and showed her how to etch it with a flint, being careful to cover the flint edge resting in Sela's hand with a small piece of skin so she wouldn't cut herself.

Esri picked up one of her Sky Bones and compared it to one that Zura brought from their old bode. The work was tedious and exacting. Esri was glad to have something to absorb her thoughts and pass the time. She was impatient for Kai and Nat's return.

In a little while Esri said, "Sela, let me see what you've done."

"It's not very good, not like what you make. I've ruined the face. It doesn't look at all like Muni."

Esri laughed. "It's pretty good for your first try. I think it looks a little like Tars."

Sela crinkled her face. "I doubt he would want it."

"You might be surprised. Here, I'll show you how you can make his ears."

Shouts and screams came up from the river followed closely by the running figures of Jolam and Grayla pulling along Grilu and Muni. "They're here! The Violent Ones! They've come back! They're after us!"

The people of Flat Rocks gathered around Jolam and Grayla. "Where's Wilki?" asked Esri.

"She came with us," said Grayla. "She was yelling 'Run, run to Flat Rocks.' What happened to her? No, no! She was right behind us."

Esri took off for the river.

"Wait, Esri," said Tars. "Don't go by yourself."

"I'll go with her!" nearly everyone shouted.

"Quiet," said Tars. "How many Violent Ones were there?"

"Three," Grayla and Jolam said.

"Grayla, Jolam, Esri, and Piram, you go. The rest stay here. There may be other Violent Ones around waiting to come into Flat Rocks," said Tars.

When they reached the river, they could see signs of a struggle from traces on the ground.

"I thought she was running fast, even with Wilki-Dumu in his sling. Wilki is a strong woman," said Grayla.

"She fell," said Piram. "You can see she ran and then fell."

"And then they would have grabbed her," said Esri, "but they can't be far."

"They are far," said Jolam. "Look." And he pointed down the river. There were some people sitting on what looked like several logs lashed together moving rapidly away from Flat Rocks. As they watched, the raft went around a bend of the river.

"They must have built that and waited for someone to appear by the river," said Piram.

They kept staring at the point where Wilki disappeared. By the time they could build something similar to float down the river, the Violent Ones, Wilki and Wilki-Dumu would be long gone.

"I should have gone with you. She wanted me to," said Esri.

"We never thought they would come so close to Flat Rocks. They were waiting for us," said Jolam.

They walked back to Flat Rocks and told the others what happened.

"We need to go get Wilki and Wilki-Dumu," said Esri.

Zura said, "Yes, but it would help us greatly to hear what Kai and Nat have found out. We need to know how many live in the Violent Ones' bode and there may be others who need our help. Yet, we can't wait for long."

"Tomorrow morning, if they haven't yet returned, a few of us can find Kai and Nat, bring them back and then we can make a good plan," said Tars.

Nagar was resting in her usual spot. "Tars is right. I am worried about Wilki, but we don't want a massacre. They're not going to kill her. They would have done it right away."

"They want her as a slave or a partner for someone. And they'll want Wilki-Dumu to add to their bode," said Barsa.

When darkness fell, half of Moon-Woman shone above the cave. When most of Flat Rocks was asleep, Esri slipped away. She avoided the night-time watchers and began walking near the river in the direction where the Violent Ones took Wilki. Esri walked for hours and found the place where they left the raft and went on by foot. In a sheltered spot nearby, Esri slept for a few hours and walked and ran for all of the next day following the tracks.

As night fell again and she got closer to the Violent Ones' bode, she knew she needed to concentrate on stealth more than speed. She heard the panting noises of a big cat nearby and clambered up a tall tree, listening and watching in the light of the half moon. She saw no movement from big cats nor heard any further noise. After some time, hearing only the small night noises, Esri lowered herself to the ground. Immediately a large hand closed over her mouth.

VIOLENT ONES

RESCUE

Esri tried biting the hand covering her mouth and struggled to get away.

"Stop, Esri, it's me," whispered Dagan.

"What are you doing?"

"Zura saw you were gone. She came and got me. I should have realized you would go and try to get Wilki and her baby. You think it's your fault she was taken, don't you? It's not. Come back to Flat Rocks. We will get Kai and Nat and go with a big group. You can't do this alone, Esri."

"I'll find a way. Something terrible could happen if we wait."

"I knew you wouldn't agree to come back. Then I'm coming with you, but we will not kill. Zura and Nagar are right. If we start killing then we are no better than the Violent Ones. We'll watch. When it's dark, maybe then we'll have a chance. If we have to fight, try only to wound them, hurt their legs or arms."

"All right."

"Promise me this with your complete spirit."

Esri placed her hands on Dagan's chest, "I promise you, Dagan, with every part of me that I will not become a killer like the Violent Ones."

Dagan smiled at Esri, "All right, little songbird. We'll go find Wilki and Wilki-Dumu. Let's rest for the remainder of the night. Who knows how long it might be before we can sleep again."

The first light of day was breaking across the eastern sky. They walked for several hours, moving cautiously, alert to any sounds or movements, staying hidden as much as possible. They used hand signals to communicate. Mid-day, Dagan gestured to Esri to drop flat to the ground and motioned a distance away from them. Otom was standing relieving himself. They must be close to the Violent Ones' bode.

Esri and Dagan circled away from Otom and waited to see where he went after he was done. They advanced slowly in the direction he took, remaining hidden. Soon, they spotted the Violent Ones' bode and made their way to a stand of thorn bushes that provided a vantage point. Using their flints, they quietly cut away some of the lower branches and tunneled their way in, silently dealing with the painful scratches from the thorns.

The bode was smaller than Flat Rocks but the features looked much the same. There were a few caves and a few shelters made of sticks and skins. Small clusters of people - men, women, and children - were moving about, starting the day. A large central area had a low fire going in the middle. They saw Riga emerge from one of the caves and sit in the central area. She spoke to a young woman who brought Riga something to eat.

A woman's voice began yelling and Ulun came out of the largest cave, his arm wrapped around Wilki, pulling her hair. She was crying, trying to struggle while holding onto to Wilki-Dumu. Everyone at the bode came over to watch what was happening but no one did anything to help Wilki. Ulun said something, but Esri and Dagan were too far away to hear what it was. Otom grabbed Wilki from behind. At the same time, Ulun wrenched Wilki-Dumu away from Wilki. He held the baby above his head and began to laugh. Wilki screamed, "No, no, no!"

Esri gripped Dagan's arm, "Ulun is going to hurt Wilki-Dumu. We must save him."

"We'll drop down to those bushes," Dagan pointed below. "And then run in yelling. I'll fight off Ulun and take Wilki-Dumu. You free Wilki and then take her and the baby away. Run as fast as you can. Do not look back. Do not wait for me. I will hold them off."

The people in the bode were preoccupied with watching Ulun dance around with Wilki-Dumu over his head. They did not notice Esri and Dagan approaching.

When the two were close, at Dagan's signal, they came running and yelling. Ulun spun around. He looked like he might throw Wilki-Dumu. Riga rushed up to him and took the baby. Ulun yelled, "Kill them, kill them!"

Several of the Violent Ones grabbed spears and hurled them at Dagan and Esri. They barely managed to duck away from the sharp edges.

Dagan bellowed. "Get them and run. Run Esri!" He was now close enough to slash at Ulun's legs with the long, sharp flint at the end of his spear and the large man toppled over.

At the same time, Esri's spear cut into Otom's shoulder. He bellowed, dropped his cut arm and Esri wrenched Wilki away from him. Esri took the baby from Riga. They exchanged a brief look and Riga said, "Go."

Dagan continued to roar and slash wildly, fending off the ones in the bode who were fighting them. "Run, Esri," he raged again, and again.

"Follow me, Wilki," Esri shouted as she started running, holding Wilki-Dumu, with Wilki close behind. Though Dagan had told her not to, Esri glanced back and saw a flint cut deeply into Dagan's arm. She stumbled and nearly fell with Wilki-Dumu. She needed to save that baby. She needed to run away. Two men from the bode broke away from the fight with Dagan and chased after Esri, Wilki, and Wilki-Dumu.

Wilki and Esri, carrying Wilki-Dumu, topped the ridge overlooking the bode and came face-to-face with a huge snarling cat. Now they were trapped.

She was a large, white cat with strange wandering eyes. Grilu's cat. The big cat streaked by Esri, Wilki and the baby and raced toward the two men who were chasing them. When the men saw the cat they turned and ran back toward their bode. Esri and Wilki stood stunned by what they had seen.

"We must keep moving before more come after us," said Esri. Wilki-Dumu was sobbing in Esri's arms, "Give me your sling, Wilki. I'll keep carrying Wilki-Dumu. Are you all right to travel? Did they hurt you?"

"They did, but I can walk. They are horrible people. Ulun was going to kill Wilki-Dumu. He was mad because I kept fighting them. But Dagan, where is he? How can he fight them all?"

"He can't."

"What do we do, Esri?"

"They will kill us if we go back."

The women held each other. Wilki-Dumu quieted down and went to sleep. He was a healthy baby, starting to walk. His birth brought such joy and promise of a new beginning after the devastation of the Ash Rain. They looked at him and knew that no matter what, they needed to bring him safely back to Flat Rocks.

They walked steadily until night fell, continually looking back to see if anyone was following them, but it didn't appear so. They found a sheltered place to spend the night. The two women took turns staying awake but they were so exhausted that when morning came they were both sound asleep. Esri woke first and sat up when she saw Wilki sleeping. A short distance away sat Grilu's cat, head up, calmly gazing around. The huge cat turned, looked at Esri, yawned, stood up, and padded away.

They had at least another day's walk ahead of them. Taking turns carrying Wilki-Dumu, they concentrated on moving quickly. They were less anxious about staying concealed. Grilu's cat appeared to be protecting them. Around mid-day they could see a large group of people off in the distance and not long after, Nat stepped out of some bushes ahead of them. He was scouting ahead of the group.

Nat said, "Why are you walking out in the open? They could easily find you. Where is Dagan?"

Esri dropped to her knees sobbing. Nat looked at Wilki who shook her head. Nat went to Esri and wrapped his arms around her.

DISTRAUGHT

Joe sat on Esri's bed. With his right hand he gently tried to rouse her. His left arm was wrapped around Jilly, who was sitting on his lap. They watched anxiously as Esri sobbed and thrashed around, gasping, "Dagan, Dagan, oh my god. No, no. Dagan, Dagan."

"C'mon, honey. It's ok. It's ok. I'm here. It's only a dream."

"He's dead. He's dead. I know he's dead." Esri was over-wrought.

"Es, wake up. No one is dead," Joe spoke louder. She seemed not to hear him.

Jilly said, "Daddy, I'm scared. Why won't Esri wake up. Who is dead?"

"She's having a really bad dream. She'll be all right in a few minutes." Though Joe wasn't so sure. Esri had been having some intense dreams in the last while, but she'd never been like this. He spoke more firmly and loudly, leaning close to her, "You're only dreaming. Open your eyes. C'mon now. Open your eyes, Esri."

Esri opened her eyes and stared at Joe and Jilly. Her shuddering sobbing continued. "Where's Nat?"

"Esri, it's me, honey, Dad. And Jilly's right here too."

Esri looked at them and began to grasp that she was back in her apartment in Toronto. Oh god, she couldn't bear it, thinking about Dagan. She had to talk to Clea.

Joe smiled at her, "Are you awake now, sweetie? It sounds like you had a terrible, terrible nightmare. Everything's ok. Do you want to talk about it?"

No, everything was not ok but there was no way she could tell him. "Dad, I'm not feeling too good. I want to stay home today.'

"You are all sweaty." He felt her forehead and cheeks. She did seem warm. "Sure, but I don't like leaving you alone all day. Do you want me to find someone to look in on you?"

"No, no, please don't, Dad. I'll be fine, really. And if I feel a lot worse, I'll call Luka's mom. I promise. She's home. She's working evenings this week."

"Ok, I'll try to get home early. Jilly, you get dressed. I'll call Farhana and take you to their place and they can walk you to school. Want some juice, Es?"

"Sure, Dad, that would great."

Esri waited until ten, then dressed quickly and ran over to Clea's.

"Esri, what are you doing here. Isn't it a school day?"

"Oh Clea," the anguish washed over Esri, "Dagan is dead, and it's all my fault."

"Oh dear, no, no, come here. I'm sure it's not your fault. Please, come in, come in. We'll make a nice pot of tea and talk this through. I'll get Thomas." Clea put her arm around Esri's waist and they walked back to the kitchen. "Thomas," she called out. "It's Esri. She's come through a terrible time. Dagan has died. Come join us in the kitchen.'

The three of them sat around the kitchen table for the rest of the morning. Willa perched on Esri's lap as she went over everything that had transpired over the last few days at Flat Rocks. Reliving the whole sequence of events was difficult. As Esri described the choices she made to Clea and Thomas, she kept trying to think of what she could have done differently, but every choice seemed to bring tragedy.

"Oh Esri," Clea's voice quavered, "I'm so sad about Dagan. You did a brave thing to go after Wilki and her baby. One or both might have been killed if you hadn't. And if Dagan hadn't come, what might have happened to you? His destiny was to ensure that no harm came to you. It is very difficult to deal with people who are violent without then becoming like them. Look at the world around us. Poor Dagan. In order to save you, he was left with no choice."

Esri sighed, "If only everyone was like the people at Flat Rocks, it would be a pretty peaceful world."

"How is it that Flat Rocks stays peaceful?" asked Thomas.

Esri thought, "Well, for one. The people who are respected the most like Zura, Nagar, Tars, Dagan, Barsa. . ." she smiled, "Ok, pretty much everyone. They believe that killing or hurting others is just plain wrong. It's something deep inside them, like a moral code. It's what's so hard about the way Dagan died, being backed into a corner where he felt his only option was to hurt others in order to save us." Tears sprang back into Esri's eyes. She dipped her head down, lightly stroking Willa's back.

Thomas probed, "But some don't share that deep, moral code?"

Esri looked up, "No, certainly Piram didn't when Zura, Dagan, and I first came to Flat Rocks. But somehow now he's not such a jerk. He still annoys me, but he's not done anything bad for a long time, and he really backed off hassling Wilki."

"Why do you think that is?" asked Thomas.

"I'm not sure, but I think putting him on the Elders Council was a big deal for him. I get the impression from Kai that before the Ash Rain, Piram was treated like an outsider by many in the bode even though he'd lived there for a long time."

"So what changed?"

"I think he feels more respected. But respected for being good, not respected for being bad. That's the difference between Flat Rocks and the Violent Ones, isn't it?"

Clea nodded. "And I believe this is key to your Mending."

"What? To change the ways of the Violent Ones? Keep steering them to live by The Agreements and eventually, poof, the Violent Ones will disappear? That's a good fantasy." Esri looked grim.

"Or maybe it's not a fantasy. Maybe that's your Mending."

Esri said, "Seriously? That's all pretty huge. I'm just one measly person, you know."

Clea said, "Yes, but you're a capable, caring young woman who people listen to who has been chosen to go back to the moment in time after the Toba volcano eruption when there were very few people left on earth. And you're surrounded by many good people at Flat Rocks."

"Yes, but what about the Violent Ones?"

"A few bad apples," said Thomas. "I know, some very, very bad apples. But it appears that the numbers are on your side at this point in history. So it's thinking about how to stop their violence and how to change them. Not easy, granted." He shrugged.

Clea added, "The Mending picks turning points in human history where a small group of people or even one person has the potential to readjust human behavior. Thomas and I were a part of turning points in our Mendings that resulted in change, but Disruptors managed to stifle the momentum of the changes. There needs to be a Mending that will do more. I'm hoping it will be yours."

"It still seems crazy that sending back one puny person like me would make a difference."

"Think of it more like a drop in the ocean that starts creating bigger and bigger waves until there's a tsunami of change. You're starting a peace tsunami," laughed Thomas.

"Except the changes won't start manifesting themselves until the time we're living in right now. But we will see them," said Clea.

"It's kind of fragile," said Esri.

"It is," said Clea. "Even the Disruptors can only do so much. Right now, you're at your peak of power and they're swirling around you. You can keep the Disruptors at bay, though it takes some work as we have seen."

"But what about you and Thomas, staying cooped up in this house?"

"Really, it's about saving our energy for you. We're much weaker now than when we were Mending, so it's better to be in a protected place like I've built up around this house."

"You mean the sweet grass?"

"Well, yes that, but there is much more. I'll explain it to you when your Mending is complete. You'll need to know for when your time comes to be a Guide."

"What if I don't want to be a Guide?"

Clea and Thomas said in unison, "You will."

"Well, if you say so. Anyway, I don't know about being able to change the course of all humankind to be more sharing and stop being violent, but I do know that I want to deal with the Violent Ones in a way that honors Dagan. He's one of the best people I've ever known. What do you think I can do?"

The three talked through lunch. Clea and Thomas were a fountain of information about non-violent cultures, societies, and practices.

Thomas said, "Esri, there is no perfect utopian society. People need latitude to express themselves and, at the same time, accept responsibility for taking care of each other. And above all, treating each other fairly." His voice softened, "And when we do make mistakes, or get a little wobbly with our moral compass, we need to help each other get back on track."

Clea said, "Mending is about harmony between ourselves and the rhythms of our world."

"Ho boy, now you're freaking me out again. It's kind of overwhelming," said Esri.

Clea placed her hand on Esri's arm, "Your Mending is planting a small seed and staying around to nurture it for a little while. Then it grows on its own."

"You've given me a lot to think about. I have to get going. My Dad will phone soon. But one more thing. What's the deal with Grilu's cat?"

Clea and Thomas smiled at each other. Thomas said, "Ah yes, the Welcome Disruptor. That's what Clea called hers. We all need them at times, don't we? As you've seen, the big cat is there not only for Grilu. Let the big cat come and go as she pleases. She won't harm you or those who you care about, but don't think that you can befriend her or control her in any way."

"Did you have a Welcome Disruptor too, Thomas?"

"Oh, yes indeed I did. I'll tell you all about him some day."

"I wish I had a Welcome Disruptor in today's world," Esri said. "I could use one."

After Esri left. Clea said to Thomas, "This Mending is different than yours or mine, Thomas, bigger, harder."

"I've thought that since my dreams started again." He chuckled. "I assumed that I had been long ago put out to pasture. So much we still don't know about the Mending after all these years, isn't there, Clea? It strikes me that things are pretty desperate if they had to bring back such an old has-been like me. Scraping the bottom of the barrel, as it were."

"I don't think you're the bottom of the barrel. But I agree, it's curious that your dreams started again. I'm so grateful you're here, Thomas. I hope it still holds true about the Disruptors, that they can't harm Esri directly. I worry."

CONFRONTATION

It took a long time for Esri to stop crying. She haltingly told Nat the story of Wilki and Wilki-Dumu's rescue, Grilu's cat, and likely what had happened to Dagan. As she was ending, the rest of the group from Flat Rocks joined them. Nat rose to his feet and quickly repeated Esri's story.

Saba was with the Flat Rocks group. Esri stayed seated on the ground, her head down. She couldn't look at Saba. Saba came and sat beside her and said. "We're both in pain, Esri. It will be easier if we share it." Esri took Saba's hands and held them. Losing Dagan felt unbearable to Esri. She had seen so many die, many who were close to her, but Dagan was so solid and strong she thought that he would always be there until they were both old.

Wilki added more details about the rescue, including Riga's role in taking Wilki-Dumu from Ulun. She wanted them to understand that she and her baby would now be dead if Esri and Dagan had not intervened when they did.

Nat said, "If Kai and I had stayed longer watching the Violent Ones, we would have seen them bring you, Wilki. But we were walking back to Flat Rocks." He shook his head. "We could have come for you."

"It is not what the fates wanted," said Tars. "You and Kai told us that if we tie up the five men who come trading, we can control the bode and free their slaves. It will take many of us to do this quickly. The Violent Ones will fight hard."

Piram said, "And without Grilu's cat, Esri, Wilki and her baby would now be dead too."

Esri stood up, "I want to go with you. Who can walk back to Flat Rocks with Wilki?"

The survivor woman who had slashed Esri's arm with her spear, stepped forward. "I'll go back with Wilki." The woman still felt badly about hurting Esri, even though Esri repeatedly told her she understood why it happened. By nightfall the two women and baby would be back at Flat Rocks.

The larger group continued walking toward the Violent Ones' bode. Hearing about what happened to Dagan increased their urgency. They still had a long walk ahead of them.

Their plan was to gain control of the bode by tying up those who fought, talk to everyone about the Agreements, and welcome any to come to Flat Rocks who wanted to live by the Agreements.

No one assumed it would be easy. Even those who were slaves might behave violently, as they would be afraid and uncertain about the strangers coming into their bode.

The Flat Rocks group hoped that Riga would help them and want to return with them, but that was by no means certain. It was why Saba came. If anyone could convince Riga to help them and return to Flat Rocks, it would be Saba.

Tars knew that if the Violent Ones killed Dagan, it would be difficult to hold Flat Rocks people back from exacting revenge. He was glad to have Esri come with them because she had a talent for breaking through the fears and anxieties of newcomers, but he worried that she would desire to seek vengeance for Dagan's killing and influence others to join her.

The group stopped for the night, spreading out with no fires and little conversation. The scouts went out before the sun was up and came back and met up with the rest of the group at mid-morning.

Nat said, "They're moving supplies into their large cave. The men are painting their bodies like they are preparing for a fight. I think they will fight us in their bode. Once they pull back into the cave, it will be hard to take them. We must move quickly."

Esri said, "They probably think they have more time. They don't know that we were already planning on coming before Wilki was taken."

Barsa said, "Though they saw the size of Flat Rocks, they'll be surprised how many we are. They don't think of women as hunters."

"We'll use our speed and size to surprise and overpower them," said Tars.

The Flat Rocks group was comfortable with Tars assuming the role of commander. He divided them into smaller groups, designating a leader for each. Every group and every person had a target. Tars repeated several times, "You all know your tasks. Move quickly and surely. Do not kill. Try not to draw blood, but if we must, pierce a leg or arm. Protect each other. Follow your group leader."

Flat Rocks moved silently to the bode and swooped in. They had the advantages of surprise and size, but the Violent Ones were on their home ground and their way of living meant they had no hesitancy to murder and maim.

The difficulty for the Flat Rocks people arose when they saw Dagan's inert body laid out in the middle of the bode. He was riddled with countless stab wounds, though they had not defiled him in any way by hacking apart his body. The Flat Rocks group went into disarray. Esri and Saba cried out and ran to Dagan. Nat, Piram, and others began yelling, "avenge Dagan," "kill them," and other words of retribution. A bloody slaughter seemed imminent.

FAMILIAR SMELL

"I love you, Esri, oh yes I do. I love you, Esri, oh yes I do," Jilly sang into Esri's ear as she snuggled up against her. "And please don't yell at me," Jilly kept on in her sing-song voice.

Esri opened her eyes. Her heart was racing. Oh god, why did she have to wake up right then? She felt Jilly's warm little body wrapped tightly around her. They had made up the little song together for Jilly to sing when Esri was thrashing about in her sleep and having a hard time waking up.

Breathe deeply, Esri told herself. Unless a Disruptor got her off course, and she was determined not to have that happen again, she would be back in her dream tonight, picking up right where it left off. "Thanks, Jills, I guess I was noisy again, wasn't I? It's pretty early but that was a perfect wake-up. You could hire yourself out as a personal alarm clock."

"What?"

"Just teasing you," Esri sat up, Jilly half wrapped around her. "Oh shoot. I promised Mr. Romero I'd come in early today and I forgot to tell Dad. He'll be mad I didn't make arrangements for you. It's still early. We'll figure something out. You can stay in bed a little longer if you want. I'll go talk to Dad."

Esri walked down the hallway to Joe's bedroom. She hoped Randi wasn't in there with him. Sometimes she came after the girls were in bed.

Esri slowly turned the knob. She didn't like the idea of seeing her Dad and Randi in bed together but didn't feel like she had a choice. If Randi was there and came in late, maybe she would be sound asleep and Esri could quietly get her Dad out into the hall. Esri inched open the door. So far so good. No noise.

Then it hit her. The dead mouse smell. Esri gagged, barely managing to silently close the door. She stood panicking in the hall. Oh god.

Randi was a Disruptor. Of course. Why hadn't Esri realized it before? It now seemed obvious: how easily Joe found a good-paying Sunday's-only job; why someone like Randi who was so hung up on looks, clothes and buying stuff would stay hooked up with a poor family like theirs; and that cloud of perfume she moved around in.

What was Randi planning to do? Stop her dreams? For sure. But Randi was definitely playing it cool so far, or was she? She had successfully insinuated herself into their lives. What had she already done to her Dad and Jilly? Clea and Thomas said the Disruptors wouldn't actually harm Esri, just influence her to do bad things but what about her Dad and Jilly? Esri was afraid. She needed to be cautious, but foremost, she needed to get Randi out of their lives.

Esri knocked softly on the bedroom door and whispered, "Dad, sorry, I have to talk to you. Can you come out?" No sound. She knocked louder and repeated her words then heard rustling noises and her Dad saying, "What are you doing?" and Randi mumbled something.

Joe opened the door a little and stepped into the hall, closing the door behind him. Esri smelled Randi's cloying perfume. She must have sprayed around herself before Joe opened the door.

"What is it, Esri?"

Now was not the time to confront her Dad. "I'm really sorry Dad. I forgot to tell you last night. Mr. Romero arranged a training session on mediation this morning before school starts and it's really important that I go. I'm sure Ada or Luka or someone can take Jilly to school. Do you mind sorting it out? I need to leave right away or I'll be late. I'm really, really sorry."

"God, Esri, I need you to do a better job of staying on top of things," Joe said, but then stopped himself from saying more. "I'll take care of Jilly.

You go ahead. Listen, I might have some good news tonight, maybe a new job that pays better and no work on the weekends."

"Randi?"

"Yeah, nothing's firm yet but I should know later today." He lowered his voice, "I know you have mixed feelings about her, but she's been awfully good to us. She's very generous."

"Dad, can you and I talk alone tonight? Like we used to do when you were helping me get through being demoted on the soccer team?"

"Sure, honey. We'll talk after Jilly goes to bed."

"I know you always make good decisions about what's right for our family, but can you not do anything drastic before we talk tonight? Promise?"

"Yeah, I guess, you know how sometimes Randi needs to make fast decisions with her business, but sure. We'll talk tonight. You ok?"

"Yeah. I've got to go. It'll look bad if I'm late. I love you, Dad." She gave him a hug and ran to get dressed and off to school.

Esri worried all day about what she could say to her Dad about Randi. She had no opportunity to talk to Clea and Thomas beforehand. Esri and Joe hardly spoke during supper, each preoccupied in their own thoughts. Finally, Jilly said, "Why is everyone unhappy?"

Joe smiled at her. "I'm not unhappy, just thinking."

"Me too, Jills," said Esri. "Let's do your bath and go ahead and get you ready for bed." Joe started tidying up the kitchen.

"But I don't want to go to bed."

Esri said, "Just get ready. We can read a long, long story tonight. You woke up super early this morning. I'll bet you're tired even if you don't think so."

Jilly fell fast asleep after a few pages. When Esri walked in the living room, Joe was sitting on the couch staring at their poster of the Canadian Rockies on the opposite wall. "Your Mom and I always wanted to take you and Jilly there." He gestured to the wall.

"We'll go sometime, Dad."

"Maybe when I'm old and grey. Come sit. So, who wants to go first? I think we both have important things we want to talk about"

"I'd like to go first, Dad. I . . . I . . . have something to ask you. It's something really, really big I want you to do, something you won't like, but it's more important than anything I've ever asked you to do. Please don't get angry and don't just say 'no.' I think our family is in danger." Esri's voice quivered.

"Jeez, Esri, it's ok. Take it slow. I promise I won't just say, 'no.' Go ahead, honey."

"I want you to stop seeing Randi. I don't think she's good for us - not just me, but you and Jilly too. I know she's helped us a lot financially, but we can make it without her. I think she's a really bad influence on Jilly, and she's changing you too. Sometimes I feel I don't know you anymore. And, it's not just that Randi's not like Mom. I know no one will ever be and that I'll always miss her terribly and that I have a hard time seeing you with someone else. But it's not just that. It's Randi. It's like she's cast some magic spell on you. You're not you around her, and I worry what will happen to you and Jilly and me if she stays in our lives. I can't live with her. I just really can't."

Joe put his head in his hands. "She's offered me an assistant manager's job at her club for almost twice what I make now. I'd have to work nights but it would be only 40 hours a week."

"Why is she doing this? Seriously, is she really that in love with you? I mean, she should be, but she doesn't really act like it a lot of the time."

"I don't know, Esri. I really don't know. But there's something else. She told me that she was so worried about you and your abnormal attachment to Clea that she had a private investigator friend check into Clea. She found out that a number of years ago Clea was accused of child molestation. All very hushed over. The charges were withdrawn, probably some kind of out of court settlement."

"That's a complete lie, Dad, and you know it!"

"Es, Es."

"What? You don't actually believe that, do you?"

"You know what, I don't believe it. I've dropped in on Clea many times unannounced. She's always welcoming. My god, she leaves her front door open half the time. She's not hiding anything. And you and Jilly are always happy and talking non-stop about the times you spend with her and her old friend Thomas. You know, Sofie always said you had one of the best radar systems about people's characters. And I think that's true."

"Randi hasn't even met, Clea, has she?"

"No, and that makes it really odd that she would be so obsessed about her. And, um, Randi came to the job site this afternoon. She was pretty revved up. Wanted me to quit right there and then and take the assistant manager's job, said it couldn't wait. Walt was not happy, but I took the afternoon off to talk with Randi."

"You took her job?"

"No, no, I didn't. And as much as anything, it was that whole business about Clea. Something is definitely off with Randi. And, Es, I don't love her, not at all. I'll admit I was really flattered that she seemed to find me attractive. She's a beautiful woman for sure. Funny, it's like you said, she did almost cast a spell on me."

"So Dad, are you saying it's done with Randi?"

"Oh yeah. But I'm afraid there will be some consequences; no Sunday job and I owe her some money I borrowed to give to Darren and Nicole to help them with rent and such after they got back together. This is hard, but I think we have to move into a 1-bedroom apartment. It will save us a couple hundred a month and we really need that. You and Jills can share the bedroom and I can sleep on the couch. I talked with the super. There's a decent 1-bedroom coming up down the hall. Hopefully, it will only be for a little while."

"But I've got the money I've been saving from working for Clea, for my school fund. Maybe with that we can stay here."

"Well, the thing is, I feel terrible about asking you this, but I'd like to use your money to pay off Randi. I think I can get an advance on my pay and then take care of what I owe her. I don't want to feel I owe her anything. She was kind of talking crazy this afternoon. Among other things, kept asking me if you made comments about her smell? Seriously, it got weird. I really don't want her around us anymore."

"That is weird."

"I do kind of feel like a veil's been lifted. I'm sorry about so much. You're right. Randi wasn't right for us, but it was a relief for a while not to worry so much about money."

Esri hugged her Dad. "We'll be ok."

"I hope so. We'll figure it out. Now, off to bed with you. And let me tell Jilly about Randi. I'm only working tomorrow afternoon, so I'll tell her in the morning. You're at Clea's, right?" Esri nodded, "I'll walk Jilly over when I head off to work."

Esri was enormously relieved, not only thinking that the Disruptors were maybe not so strong after all, but also that her Dad was indeed the good guy she had always known. Tonight's dreams were bound to be intense, but at least she had less to worry about in this time zone!

DAGAN'S GOLDEN ROCK

Tars thundered, "Tie them, do it now!" He and his team rushed to Ulun. Kai launched a spear, purposely only grazing Ulun's shoulder but enough to distract him while Tars came at Ulun from the other side. Tars swung the thick shaft of his spear against Ulun's legs, toppling him over. Four people jumped on Ulun, rapidly tying fast his arms and legs

At the same time, Esri stood over Dagan's body and shouted, "Do not kill. For Dagan. Do not kill!"

Spears flashed and flew, bodies crashed into each other, hands grabbed for arms, feet entangled legs. The struggle was fearsome but short-lived. Once the five men who regularly came trading were immobilized, no one else fought, only pleaded for their lives. There was lots of yelling, but eventually everyone quieted down. The people who were tied up were kept apart from everyone else. The rest, including Riga, huddled together. Riga sat mutely in their midst, avoiding eye contact. Saba took Riga aside.

Grayla and Jolam found the two children from Sela and Muni's bode. The children were shaking and crying, then stared at Grayla and Jolam and gasped when they heard Sela and Muni's names. Grayla and Jolam gave the children food and coaxed them to start walking to Flat Rocks and find Sela and Muni.

Esri and Barsa tried as best as they could to speak with the rest who were not tied up and sort out the relationships. There were five women, two children, and one old man. From the tradings, Esri and Barsa picked up some of the language of the Violent Ones, but the people were reluctant to speak. Most were weeping, the two children clung to their mothers.

Esri went over to Saba and Riga. Saba faintly shook her head and shrugged. Riga stared at the ground. Esri put her hand on Riga's shoulder, "Riga, have they treated you like a slave?"

"No."

"Has Hanu been good to you?"

Riga looked at Esri. "He's a better man than you think."

"Has Hanu been good to you?"

Riga looked back at the ground. "He's good to me when I do the right things."

"Some are slaves here."

"Yes."

"Tell me about the people who live in the bode."

"What will happen to me and Hanu? Will you kill us?"

Esri reassured Riga. "We're not going to kill anyone. We know that some here are slaves and we want to free them. Anyone who wants to live by the Agreements can come back with us to Flat Rocks. You can come back, Riga."

"Can Hanu come?"

"If he lives by the Agreements."

"And what about Dagan?" Riga began to cry.

Esri sat down by her, "I don't know. I don't know how I can live with those who killed him, but we want there to be no killing anymore. It's hard. I have such hatred. I understand that more killing will not bring him back. But what do we do to someone who kills?"

Riga said, "Ulun did not harm Dagan's body after he fell. He was going to bury Dagan so no animals would take his body. He admired how bravely Dagan fought with so many at one time."

Riga explained the relationship of the people at the Violent Ones' bode. Of the nine who were not tied up - she and Carthan, Ulun's mate and the mother of Hanu and Otom - were not slaves but the other seven were. The man and two older women had been with the Violent Ones for a long time. The two younger women each had a small child. They were taken more recently and had not attempted to escape as the Violent Ones threatened to harm their children if the women were caught trying to run away.

Esri took aside the two young slave women with their children. And Barsa spoke with the older slaves, the man and two women. Those three might be more reluctant about joining the Flat Rocks bode.

Esri brought Kai over to sit with her and the young slave women and their children. She remembered how Kai's infectious smile and light manner broke through her fears when she came to Flat Rocks. Maybe he could work his magic on them as well.

The other Flat Rocks people watched over the five men who were securely tied up and largely quiet.

And Dagan's body lying in the middle of the bode bore witness to all that was transpiring. His death brought rage and desire for retribution and, at the same time, there could hardly be a more powerful symbol of why there should be no violence.

Once the atmosphere calmed, Esri and Saba went to Tars.

"We must take care of Dagan's body," said Saba.

"We can't bury him near this place of such evil," said Esri.

"I know, I've been thinking about what to do to honour him," said Tars.

Piram joined them. "We can carry him away from here. He was a large man but there are enough of us. I want to mark the place we bury him so I can always find it." Esri stared at Piram and thought about how Dagan, better than anyone, even Tars, had been able to penetrate through Piram's crustiness and frequent insensitivity.

She realized that Piram had changed in the last while - not a lot, but he had changed. He didn't bother Wilki anymore and was less likely to behave gruffly or make curt comments. No doubt Dagan had a hand in this. They would all miss Dagan, even the most disagreeable among them. And how fortunate she was to grow up with Dagan and have him so close. Esri sank down beside his body. "Piram is right. Let's carry him out of here."

Nat said, "On our way here, we saw the large golden rock on the other side of the River of LIfe. We could bury him there. Dagan could face the Sun-Man when he leaves the sky."

They agreed it was a good spot. There would be plenty of stones around to build a large cairn over Dagan's body.

Esri said, "I can carve a picture of the big buffalo in the golden rock. We have not seen any buffalo since the Ash Rain, but maybe we will again someday. Dagan was like the big buffalo and he loved to hunt them."

Tars picked the strongest to carry Dagan's body to the golden rock and bury him. He knew many wanted to go, but they could not risk having too many gone.

Esri went to Tars. "Saba should go too. I'll sit with Riga until they're back." And he agreed. Esri would spend time with Dagan's grave later, when she could be alone.

Esri blamed herself for Dagan's death. How could she live with that? And how could she face Zura? The only thing she could think to do is end the ways of the Violent Ones as Dagan would have wished.

It did not take long before the two young slave women asked to join the Flat Rocks bode. They saw the grief the Flat Rocks people felt over Dagan's death and were astonished that no further blood was shed in revenge. Watching the interplay between the Flat Rocks people, assured them that they were nothing like the Violent Ones. When Dagan's burial party returned, a small group started back to Flat Rocks, including the two young former slave women and their children.

Now there were ten left from the Violent Ones' bode: the five who were tied up, Riga, the three older slaves, and Ulun's mate, Carthan. They were told repeatedly that if they pledged to live by the Agreements, then they could join the Flat Rocks bode. Ulun and Otom scoffed at the idea. The others were mute. None stepped forward to join Flat Rocks, not even the older slaves or Riga.

The discussions continued for days. Realizing how committed the Flat Rocks people were to avoiding bloodshed and violence, the Violent Ones decided to wait and see what would happen.

Watching over the Violent Ones became increasingly tedious for the Flat Rocks group. They decided to leave. One morning Tars said to the Violent Ones, "We're returning to Flat Rocks. We'll leave your spears and cutting tools on top of that hill." He pointed. "You can join Flat Rocks if you pledge to live by our Agreements. We don't want to fight you, but we will if you harm anyone at Flat Rocks."

Esri continued, "And we'll watch you and free any you take by force. And the trading is ended. We have a good life at Flat Rocks and we'll protect our bode and do everything we can to stop you from harming others."

Barsa said, "Think carefully about the way of living you have chosen."

And with that, the entire Flat Rocks group walked away, back to their bode. Though the Violent Ones understood the Flat Rocks people were trying to end things peacefully, still they were astonished at this outcome.

A few of the Violent Ones were ready to take up their spears and sharp flints and attack Flat Rocks to pay them back for this humiliation. Ulun stayed their anger. "They are many more than we are. It would be foolish to go after them. We'll find another way to remake our bode."

When the Flat Rocks group returned to their bode, Esri went immediately to Zura. "Dagan is dead because of me. He came after me and saved me."

DEBRIEFING

Esri was grateful that it was Saturday and she could spend the day with Clea and Thomas. And since Joe wasn't bringing Jilly until lunchtime, Esri would have a few hours alone with Clea and Thomas to tell them about Randi and get caught up on life at Flat Rocks.

As was their usual way, Clea and Thomas listened closely to Esri, only asking a few questions to clarify or provide more details. There were fewer questions, as Esri had become adept at providing them with the full scope of what was said, who said it, how they said it, and people's facial expressions. Even when she was conveying serious activities, sometimes they couldn't help laughing as Esri attempted to mimic the mannerisms and intonations of the people at Flat Rocks.

Clea said, "Oh my, these are difficult times at Flat Rocks. I know you're worried about Zura. You need to be forthright with her and tell her everything that happened with Dagan and the Violent Ones. She may find it difficult to give you the comfort you want from her right now."

"I know, and I will tell her everything. I think about when I lost my Mom. My Dad and I had a hard time comforting each other. We were each feeling so sad that we didn't have space to take on more sadness from the other person. I think that's what you're talking out."

"And how are you and your Dad now?"

"We're better."

Thomas said, "Despite everything that's going on at Flat Rocks and what happened to Dagan, you seem more at peace today, Esri. Is it knowing that Randi is out of your life?"

"Oh, for sure, Thomas, for sure. I'm worried she may try something, who knows what, but I feel I have my Dad back. But even once we get completely rid of her, I guess that's not the end of the Disruptors, is it?"

"I doubt it."

Esri said, "I worry how my Mending will end. The Violent Ones are much fewer but they can still do a lot of harm. I wish that more from their bode had wanted to join us at Flat Rocks. With the Ash Rain survivors, it took time for them to trust us but they were peaceful already, so there was no threat. This is different."

Thomas said, "Yes, this is different. You're asking people to give up ways of living that they've always known. For Ulun and his family, they would have to give up power and control. And this might also be true for the oldest slaves if they have wielded power over newer slaves."

"Now that many of the slaves are freed, some at Flat Rocks feel we should go back and kill everyone at the Violent Ones bode and get rid of them. But, of course, that would mean Riga too, and hardly anyone is comfortable with that. And if she is spared, why not some of the others?" said Esri.

Clea said, "Do you think there is any chance that will happen? Is is possible that some from Flat Rocks might go and kill everyone?"

"No, I don't think it will happen, because there's also a lot of talk that if the attack had been a slaughter, it's certain that innocent people, likely some of the children, would have died or been badly hurt. And, of course Piram, who would normally be leading the charge on being forceful, does not want any harm to come to Riga, so for now, he's in favor of waiting and watching them closely."

"Anybody home?" It was Joe calling from the front door. 'I've brought a fairy godmother." He and Jilly came walking into the kitchen and Jilly went running to Clea and gave her a big hug. Joe smiled and winked at Esri. "I only have to take care of a few things this afternoon. I shouldn't be back too late, Esri. And, great news, I heard the City Hall ice rink is already open. I thought we could go tomorrow."

"Yay, yay, yay," Jilly danced around.

"Sounds, great, dad," said Esri.

HEALING TALK

Esri forced herself not to cry. She did not want Zura to feel sorry for her.

"Did you kill Dagan?" demanded Zura.

"No, but if I had not gone by myself to get Wilki and her baby, he would still be alive."

"If you stayed here, would Wilki and Wilki-Dumu be alive?"

"Probably not."

"Did you force Dagan to fight the Violent Ones?"

"No, but it was because of me that he did."

"And because of Wilki?"

"Yes, yes, of course. But I can't stop thinking that he would still be here if it weren't for me." Esri's voice broke.

"There are consequences to all of our actions. Sometimes they are both good and bad. Am I angry about Dagan? Yes. I have such deep sorrow. I can't bear to think he's no longer with us. I've never known a better man. There is a part of my life that will be forever empty. But you need to stop saying you killed him. You did not, the Violent Ones did."

"What could I have done differently?"

"I don't know. Sometimes we have to make terrible choices. It's why the Agreements are so important. It's why we need to do everything we can to not hurt each other. We should try to live so that we do not have to face such choices. If you and Dagan had not gone and had waited to go with the others, Wilki and Wilki-Dumu would probably be dead. That too would have been terrible to live with."

Though Zura did not offer any easy answers or even as much sympathy as Esri might have hoped for, talking with her did help Esri to start moving beyond her deep anguish about Dagan's death. For a while, Esri felt so much guilt when she saw Saba that she avoided spending time with her. Zura saw this and told Esri, "Reach out to Saba. She needs you. Don't let her mourn alone." From then on, the two young women went frequently to where Dagan was buried and together worked on carving a large bull buffalo into the rock above his grave.

On one of their visits to the golden rock, Esri said, "I think when Great Bull Traveler comes again that Dagan will go with him."

Saba grasped Esri's hand, "And then we will see him each time Great Bull returns. When my End Days come, I'll wait for Great Bull and go with them."

The newcomers from the Violent Ones' bode folded into life at Flat Rocks. The two children from Sela and Muni's former bode were taken in by Grayla and Jolam. They shared their sleeping spot with the children and Sela and Muni. The children were anxious and frequently had nightmares. Sela took on a role as their little mother and protector. She made it her project to acquaint them with everyone at Flat Rocks, beginning with Grilu. Though initially they were startled by his appearance, he soon had them laughing and singing with him.

The two young former slave women with the two children settled into a sleeping spot by themselves. They did not stay isolated. So many at Flat Rocks had once been newcomers and remembered what it was like and went out of their way to interact with them. In a short time, the women and their children spent less time huddled together, their heads no longer down, and gradually started to smile and laugh with others.

Once the newcomers started to relax and became comfortable communicating, the Elders Council planned a large Agreements pledging ceremony. The newcomers were invited to contribute songs or stories from their past if they wished. Sela and Grilu asked Esri to help them make a special song that all the children, including the new ones, could sing together.

The Flat Rocks bode was proud of liberating the slaves from the Violent Ones and went all out both welcoming them and integrating them into the daily rhythms of the bode. However, nothing could remove the shadow of anxiety that hung over Flat Rocks with the Violent Ones still at large. All of the food collection happened in large groups with several people designated to act as guards and lookouts. There was considerable discussion about taking some kind of further action against the Violent Ones, though no agreement on what that might be.

Shortly before the Agreements pledging day, Geslo, the young man from the Violent Ones who had asked Barsa about laughter at Flat Rocks, walked into the bode. "I want to live here in Flat Rocks. You said I could live here if I pledged to live by the Agreements. I want to do that."

Barsa said, "Do you understand the Agreements - that we never make people slaves nor do violence to each other, and that we each help provide for all in the bode?"

"Yes, I understand. Living with the Violent Ones I'm often afraid, and I don't want to be afraid anymore. I don't want to hurt others. They're talking about walking toward the land of the Rising Sun far away from Flat Rocks and building a large bode again with many slaves. I don't want to go with them and live like that."

Zura asked, "They're all leaving?"

"Yes, soon. Flat Rocks is too big and powerful."

Many at Flat Rocks were relieved when they heard this. Kai said, "That's good, if we don't have to worry about the Violent Ones anymore."

Esri said, "But what if they find other people and make them slaves?"

Nat shrugged, "If they are far away, there is nothing we can do. Better that they go. You've seen how they are."

The Elders Council agreed that Geslo could join Flat Rocks as long as he pledged to the Agreements and lived by them. He took part in the pledging ceremony with the other newcomers. Though he seemed sincere, people avoided him. He did his part in hunting and gathering food, but even in a group, people kept their distance. He slept alone and usually ate alone. Everyone knew that he participated in killing Dagan and in kidnapping and slavery activities in the Violent Ones' bode. How could they ever allow him to be fully a part of Flat Rocks?

The Elders Council talked about what should be done.

Tars said, "We've created a difficult situation. If we keep pushing Geslo away, he may decide to leave Flat Rocks and go back to the Violent Ones. Yet how do we ask those who were slaves to live with him and not be afraid?"

Barsa said, "Geslo told me that he never knew there was another way to live in a bode until he came to visit Flat Rocks. He grew up afraid he would be killed if he didn't always do what Ulun said."

Esri asked, "How does he feel about what he has done?"

"Confused and sad, I think, but we should ask him."

Zura said, "We should also hear from those who were slaves with the Violent Ones and have them speak about what they need to feel comfortable with Geslo."

Saba said, "Perhaps they never will."

Piram said, "Even if Geslo wants to live here, he will find it difficult to change quickly to our ways."

Tars asked, "What should we do?"

Barsa said, "We need a Healing Talk."

"What is that?" Tars asked.

Zura smiled and nodded, "Yes, it's something we used to do in our bode long ago. I wish we had done it more. Our Mother was good at Healing Talks. It's using words to heal. When someone's body is cut or hurt, we try to fix the wound with different medicines. But there are also wounds inside that need to be healed - wounds of anger or fear or sorrow."

Piram said, "But you can't make anger or fear go away just by talking."

Zura said, "True, nothing can completely take away horrible things of the past. Even if you can't see them, the wounds inside will still have scars. But there is healing that can be done, and we can look for ways to make things better in the days ahead. It's not easy. It means going deep inside, and this can take time and can cause pain of a different kind than a wound on the outside of a person."

The Elders Council decided to make a Healing Talk. They began by talking one-on-one or in small groups with those who were taken as slaves by the Violent Ones, and speaking with Geslo. The former slaves wanted to feel safe and hear directly from Geslo that he would never hurt them again and that he knew it was wrong what he had done.

Flat Rocks came together. All the Elders spoke, Geslo spoke, and many others. It took a while for Geslo and those captured as slaves to speak openly about what had happened, what Geslo had done or not done. When he was with the Violent Ones, he showed compassion to the slaves by sometimes secretly bringing them extra food, yet he did not defend them from many of the brutalities they had endured.

It was a long and difficult discussion. Emotions were intense but Geslo's remorse felt genuine. He pledged again to keep the ways of Flat Rock. He went to every person and asked their forgiveness, promising never to bring harm to them again.

As Zura said, the Healing Talk did not erase the past, but Geslo's heart-felt words helped calm those who had been taken by the Violent Ones and reassured the Flat Rock's bode that Geslo would not cause harm. A few days after the Healing Talk, Kai came to Esri and said, "Come, let's ask Geslo to go with the two of us and look for eland. We will try to help the Healing."

■ ■ ■

Nagar no longer took part in the Elders Council. She rarely left her sleeping spot anymore. Saba and Zura took turns watching over her and taking care of her. Many others at Flat Rocks frequently stopped by to help. Nagar was in her End Days. It was a miracle that she lasted as long as she did, no doubt because of Zura and Saba's ministrations.

It was also the creation of the new Flat Rocks that revitalized her. They were creating the kind of bode that she had long dreamt of where people worked together to build a safe living place. She was surprised how the Agreements not only brought less fear but also increased the laughter and lightness of their lives. It was surely something to keep always, and she longed to stay a part of it.

Nagar was now barely conscious. Saba and Zura sat watching over her. Esri was nearby working on some new scraping tools. Saba said, "I'm so relieved that the Violent Ones are going far away. I want them to be gone soon, and we can feel peace again and not have to worry about fighting them or having them take any of us as slaves."

Zura said, "Yes, it's good for us, but I worry they may find other Ash Rain survivors and make them slaves."

Nagar heard them talking and tried to push herself up, gasping, "We . . . must . . . stop them."

Saba said, "Mother, lie down. It's good they are leaving us. They are few now. Flat Rocks can keep growing peacefully."

"Get . . . Esri."

"She's right here."

"Bring . . . her . . . close."

"Saba said, "Hurry, Esri. Come here. It's important."

Zura spoke to her friend. "You're right, Nagar. It is dangerous if the Violent Ones leave and become a big, powerful bode. We tried, but they did not want to change their ways and join us. What do we do?"

Esri came and sat by Nagar. Nagar spoke to Zura and Esri, "Divide . . . them." Nagar clutched Esri's arm, "You cannot . . . let . . . Ulun . . . leave. He will . . . keep . . . spreading . . . his evil."

"How can we do this?" asked Esri.

THE PARTING

CHILDREN'S SERVICES

The end-of-term papers and projects were piling up for Esri. If only she could survive until the Christmas holiday break. Navigating life in Flat Rocks while trying to carry on like a normal high school student during her awake hours was increasingly stressful. And, after the flint-cutting incident with Troy, Esri's reputation was anything but normal.

She faced increased scrutiny and notoriety from both teachers and students. It felt like her dad and teachers analyzed every small sign from her to see if it was a signal that she was screwing up again. She tried to stay on top of her school work, but she had trouble focusing and her grades were slipping. Many students either gave her a wide berth or wanted to high-five her for "kicking ass." Esri didn't know how to handle either reaction.

And, further complicating her life was the move to the one-bedroom apartment with her dad and Jilly.

The day Esri's alarm interrupted Nagar's End Days and her plea to stop the Violent Ones, Esri could barely pay attention in her classes. She tried keeping an attentive expression on her face even as she was thinking of Nagar. Esri's mind was awhirl. She had to talk to Clea and Thomas before tonight. Though it would surely would get her into a pile of trouble, she skipped her last class.

"Esri, we didn't expect to see you so early. What's going on?" asked Clea.

"Many things. I left school early. No, don't say it," Esri held up her hand. "I know, I shouldn't have, but I have to talk to you. Nagar is dying. I worry what will happen. Even as she got weaker, everyone still listened to her and respected her. I'll miss her terribly, and her death will leave a big hole at Flat Rocks. She was asking for me, just as I woke up I know she'll want me to do something about the Violent Ones, but how can I?"

Clea said, "It's not up to you alone."

"Of course, yes, Zura is there. She's my rock," said Esri.

"And, Tars and Saba and Barsa and Kai and Nat and Grilu," Clea ticked them off. "And many others. They trust you and believe in living by the Agreements."

Thomas said, "Clea and I have talked and thought a lot about what might have occurred with the Flat Rocks people the first time, without your Mending. I believe what happened is that the Violent Ones stayed together as a tribe and became one of the core groups of homo sapiens that left Africa after the Toba volcano eruption bottleneck. And, in time, they went on to populate the rest of the world."

"But not everyone is like Ulun today. There are lots of good, kind people in our world," said Esri.

"As there are good, kind people with Ulun. Look at Geslo," said Thomas.

Clea said, "But by keeping Ulun's bode together, it allowed for the perpetuation of cultures of violence and greed to the point where we now throw up our hands and say, we've always had war, always had warrior cultures. It's just the way it is and, anyway, even if you want peace, you have to 'fight fire with fire.'" She sighed.

"At the moment in time of your Flat Rocks people, the numbers are clearly on the side of those who believe violence is wrong," said Thomas.

"And your Mending is about seizing this moment," said Clea.

Esri took this in. "And dividing the Violent Ones." She sat quietly for a minute, then nodded. "Why not? It won't be easy, but why not?"

■ ■ ■

Esri worried that when she got home there would be a message on the phone for her Dad to call the principal about her skipping her last class. No messages were waiting, someone might call later, or, fingers-crossed, maybe she wouldn't face any repercussions.

Talking with Clea and Thomas was reassuring and bolstered Esri's resolve to do everything in her power to carry out Nagar's final words to divide the Violent Ones. Clea and Thomas were right. The numbers were on the side of those who wanted to live peacefully. She just had to rally their support.

After supper, Esri and Jilly sat at the kitchen table. Esri did homework, Jilly drew pictures of fairies with her smelly markers, and Joe sprawled on the couch in the living room reading a book. He was insistent that they all have some quiet time every day after supper dishes were done. Esri was still on edge worrying about a call from school about cutting her last class.

There was a knock on the door.

"You expecting someone?" asked Joe.

"No, Luca's at work this evening. I doubt it's Ada. I'll see who it is."

Esri looked through the peephole. There was a woman dressed like she worked in an office and a police officer. It was Officer Calvino. Esri groaned.

"What's the matter?" asked Joe.

"It's a police officer and a woman in a sort of business suit."

"Well, let them in. You didn't do anything did you?"

Surely, they wouldn't come just because she skipped her last class. "Ah, not really," she said and she opened the door.

The woman spoke, "Good evening, Esri, is it? I'm Sue Bradley from Children's Services, and you know Officer Calvino. Is your father at home? We'd like to speak with him and you and your sister."

"Why?" said Esri. "What's up?"

Joe came to the door. "It's okay, Es." He turned to the two at the door. "Please, come in." Everyone moved into the living room area. "Have a seat. Esri, grab a couple of the kitchen chairs. Is there a problem?"

Sue Bradley said, "Thank you. We will sit for a minute. We'd like to talk with you and ask you and the girls a few questions. I understand Esri's already met Officer Calvino." They sat on the chairs Esri brought.

Jilly stopped colouring, saw the grim expressions on everyone's faces and went to her Dad and Esri. The three of them sat on the couch, Jilly in the middle. "Why is everyone so sad? Did someone die?"

Joe smiled at her and hugged her. "No honey. It's okay. They just want to talk to us. Don't worry." But he was worried, very worried.

"Joe. Is it all right to call you Joe? You can call me Sue. We received a report from someone who had some concerns about your parenting."

Esri burst out, "What did you hear? Someone is telling lies about my Dad!"

Sue said, "We had a call. We follow-up when we get a call from the community."

Joe tried to sound calm. "Esri, it's fine. Go ahead, Sue."

Sue started by questioning them all together about their daily lives, who fixed meals, what they ate, who looked after Jilly when Joe wasn't around, their morning routine, Joe's work, how the girls were doing in school. Joe encouraged the girls to answer the questions, filling in if he felt more details were needed. He tried to appear normal, but both Esri and Jilly could tell he was anxious, saw his jaw muscles tensing.

"Joe, do you mind if I take a quick look around?"

"Sure, help yourself, anything you want. It's just a one-bedroom. We're trying to save some money for the next little while. This is temporary. The girls have the bedroom and I sleep on the couch."

Sue Bradley walked into the kitchen, opened a few cupboards and the refrigerator, and went down the hallway to the bathroom Joe and Esri looked at each other. Jilly piped up, "Good thing you made us clean our room, Daddy."

When Sue came back she said to Jilly, "Do you want to show me your room, Jilly?"

Jilly clung to Joe. He squeezed her knee, "It's okay, honey. You go on and talk to Sue. Why don't you show her your princess castle and some of the sparkly fabric Farhana gives you. I'll bet Sue'd like to see some of costumes you're so good at making."

"Okay. You and Esri will stay here?"

"We won't move."

After Sue and Jilly left, Officer Calvino asked Esri how things were going for her.

"I'm doing okay. You know we did the mediation and now I've done some training that Mr. Romero organized, so maybe I can help with other mediations. There's been no more trouble with Brad or Troy or their friends. I'm staying focused on my schoolwork."

"And no more carrying arrowheads?" Officer Calvino smiled at Esri.

"No ma'am."

"She's been really good, officer. She's a super kid," said Joe.

"And you Joe, you've had some financial setbacks? Must be tough raising two girls on your own?"

Joe spoke carefully about their financial situation and his plans for finding another part-time job. He knew he was appearing nervous, but there was nothing he could do about it.

Jilly and Sue came back. Jilly said, "The lady thinks I could be a fairy godmother when I grow-up!" Sue winked at Joe and Esri.

Joe said, "I'm sorry, I should have offered before. Can I get you two something to drink?"

Sue said, "No, no, I think we're done. Don't you officer?" Officer Calvino nodded. "We'll get going. Thank you for your time."

"But, what happens next?" Joe asked.

"I'll be in touch soon. I assume it's best to phone in the evenings?"

"So, we'll never know who filed a complaint and what they said?" challenged Esri.

Joe put his arm on Esri, "Es, it's okay."

After they left, Joe sat with his head in his hands.

Esri walked to the door. "I'm going to talk to them and tell them about Randi. I bet it was her."

"Esri, no," said Joe, but she was already gone.

When Esri stepped into the hall, she could hear Sue Bradley and Officer Calvino talking by the elevator around the corner from their apartment. She quietly closed the apartment door and moved silently toward the elevators but remained hidden. She heard Officer Calvino say, "Well, what do you think, Sue?"

"There's nothing wrong going on there. The little girl, Jilly, told me when I was talking to her alone that her dad had been seeing a pretty woman, but she was mean to Esri so he stopped seeing the woman. The woman's name is Randi, and that's who made the complaint."

"Ah. I figured it must be something like that. Yeah, there was no reconciling what the complainant described with what we saw and heard in there."

"It's always interesting watching families interacting with each other. It's clear those girls are fond of their dad, and Esri is super conscientious about looking after her little sister. I was expecting Esri to be different after the school incident you described. You know, full of attitude or something."

"She's an interesting kid. You should see those boys she stood up to at school and then convinced them to chill out and go through mediation. That takes character. So, next steps here, Sue?"

"There is no previous record with this family. I'll talk to my supervisor. I believe it was a false complaint. I don't think there's anything here."

The elevator doors dinged open. Esri returned to her apartment. Jilly was curled up next to her Dad. Joe was leaning his head on the back of the couch, eyes closed. One hand stroked Jilly's head and the other wiped away tears from his eyes. Esri had only ever seen her dad cry once, the night her Mom died. "Dad," she said and ran over to him. "It'll be okay."

FIRST PARTING

Esri leaned over Nagar, "How do we divide the Violent Ones?"

"You must . . . or it is . . . over. Riga . . . can . . . help." And Nagar fell back and never again opened her eyes or said another word. Her breathing became increasingly laboured. The three women stayed near her. Saba rested Nagar's head on her lap, and Esri and Zura held Nagar's hands.

Gradually, all of Flat Rocks gathered around Nagar, paying their respects. Some only knew her as an ailing, sometimes crotchety, old woman, but all of them understood that it was Nagar and Zura who were behind the Agreements that made them feel safe and more hopeful than they ever thought possible.

Nagar stopped breathing.

Zura said, "Look, the Evening Star is up. It's come for Nagar."

Saba and Esri prepared Nagar's body, and she was buried near Dara's grave. Though the bode had long known that Nagar's death was imminent, it cut them deeply and stirred up painful memories of others who had died.

Esri and Zura wanted nothing more than to spend days mourning Nagar, and Dagan, but the urgency of Nagar's last words plagued them.

Zura said, "At first, I was glad to hear that the Violent Ones are leaving. But Nagar is right about Ulun and the Violent Ones. If they all go, they will find others to make into slaves and kill those who fight them.

And once their bode grows large and strong, they will come back to Flat Rocks and harm us. It may not happen quickly, but it will happen."

Esri said, "Nagar said 'divide them.' I've been thinking about that and thinking that without Ulun, the other Violent Ones could be like Geslo. Riga says Hanu is good to her. I wonder how Hanu might be if he was not around Ulun?"

Zura was thoughtful. "We've talked in the last days about starting another bode. New babies are coming. The children are growing. Before long we'll be too many here. A good place for the new bode would be in the direction of the Rising Sun."

"And some would go with Ulun's group?"

"Divide Ulun's group. Convince some to stay at Flat Rocks and some to go to the new bode."

Esri mused, "Ah, yes, if Ulun knows many are leaving, he may see it as an opportunity to take over Flat Rocks. Geslo says that what Ulun covets most is Flat Rocks, but he knows we are too many. Geslo thinks that even if Ulun goes toward the Rising Sun, he still wants to come back and take over Flat Rocks someday. If Ulun knows there will be a Parting soon, maybe we can convince him and the rest of his bode to join Flat Rocks."

Zura said, "We need to make sure that it's a good division for the Parting between those staying and those going so that the Agreements remain strong in both. And then, work at dividing the Violent Ones between Flat Rocks and the new bode. The two bodes must be far apart . . ." Zura's eyes filled with tears, "It could mean that you and I will have to separate."

"I know" Esri said.

They continued the conversation with the Elders Council. Initially, many wanted to let the Violent Ones leave, but they could also see the problems that could cause later on.

Zura asked, "How do we get the Violent Ones to agree to pledge to the Agreements, join Flat Rocks, and then divide them at the Parting?"

Barsa said, "It's all about Ulun. He tells them what to do. How do we get him to agree? He wants to keep all the power."

Piram said, "He'll agree if he feels he is getting more power."

Saba said, "We can't give him more power."

"I said if he feels he's getting more power."

Esri looked at Piram and nodded. "Maybe Geslo could help us understand Ulun and how we could talk to him."

Tars said, "Can we trust, Geslo?"

"Since the Healing Talk, Kai and I have spent more time with Geslo. I believe he would do anything to show others that he is a good person for Flat Rocks."

The conversation expanded to include everyone at Flat Rocks. People were in agreement that it was time to start a new bode, but most were reluctant to leave Flat Rocks. This changed when Esri announced she would be going with the Parting to find a new place for a bode. People who had never imagined leaving the safety and abundance of Flat Rocks began to view the Parting as a more compelling opportunity.

Approaching the Violent Ones again to join Flat Rocks was another matter. Most wanted nothing to do with the Violent Ones and thought, anyway, it wouldn't work. Geslo's Healing Talk had helped people become more comfortable with him, even some who were captives of the Violent Ones were starting to interact with him. But Geslo came to Flat Rocks of his own will and begged to be allowed to live with them and had done nothing wrong since.

Nat said, "Ulun will never be like Geslo. Ulun will never pledge to the Agreements. But I have thought about it and I understand. It's better if he doesn't go away and we know where he is and what he's doing."

Esri took Kai aside. "Let's talk to Geslo about Ulun. Maybe he can help us. And bring Piram too."

"Piram? You don't like Piram."

"Since Dagan was killed, I've tried to think differently about Piram. He still says things I don't like, but he hasn't bothered Wilki and he has a better understanding of people like Ulun than many of us."

Kai said, "Piram grew up in a bode similar to the Violent Ones. He never talked about it very much. When I was little I didn't like that he was mean at times, but he did teach me a lot about hunting."

Piram was surprised when Esri asked him to come with her. The three took Geslo for a walk. They went to Dagan's grave by the golden rock and the four unlikely collaborators came up with a plan.

Geslo said, "Ulun must be made to believe that he will gain something for himself. He thinks of himself as a great warrior. He kept talking about Dagan, how he had never seen anyone hold off so many for so long and so calmly. You know he comes here to Dagan's golden rock and sees how the buffalo carving grows as many honour Dagan. I think Ulun is starting to feel his age and would like to know that he'd be so honoured when he dies."

Esri said, "If we promise to bury him well, will he pledge to the Agreements?"

Geslo laughed, "I doubt it will be that easy, but maybe if he thinks that somehow, in time, he can get control of Flat Rocks, he might agree. Though he and the others talk about walking to the Land of the Rising Sun, I think Ulun would rather not try to start a new bode someplace far away. "

Esri said, "So, if he felt he'd have a good burial and a place on the Elders Council?"

"That might be enough for him to pledge to the Agreements, but he'll never agree to a Healing Talk."

Esri queried further, "What about others around Ulun? Would any of them join us to start a new bode and pledge to the Agreements? Would they do a Healing Talk?"

"I think there are others who would leave Ulun if they could. The Agreements are good. If Ulun had no power over them, I think others would pledge the Agreements. It will be hard for them to do a Healing Talk, but maybe some could in time."

Kai said, "You did it."

"I didn't want to. You remember at first in the Healing Talk? I didn't want to talk about the bad things I had done. I was ashamed. I wanted people only to know the new Geslo. But I was lonely. No one at Flat Rocks wanted anything to do with me. People don't forget when you hurt them or those they care about or hear you've done bad things. You can't change what happened in the past. The Healing Talk helped me understand what I could do to make things better for those I hurt. Ulun and some of the others don't think there is anything wrong with hurting people."

Piram said, "It will make a difference who talks to Ulun and how."

Kai said, "It needs to be someone who is like Dagan. Maybe Tars or Barsa."

Piram said, "And no women. Ulun does not listen to women."

Geslo said, "And I shouldn't go. I'm sure Ulun wants nothing to do with me. You're right, Piram. Ulun is not good to women. He does listen sometimes to his mate, Carthan. Esri is good with our way of speaking. She could go and . . ."

". . .talk to the women," said Esri.

"Yes, exactly. Try to speak with Carthan."

Kai said, "Do you think Ulun can be convinced to join Flat Rocks? And if he does, it will be hard for you, Geslo."

"I understand why it's important to try to control Ulun and to know what he's doing, but I worry how he might change Flat Rocks. We have to be careful. As for me, if Ulun comes to Flat Rocks, I'll go with the Parting. Or if he goes with the Parting, I'll stay here," said Geslo.

Esri said, "Before going to the Violent Ones' bode, maybe Dagan can help us. If Ulun sometimes visits Dagan's golden rock, some from Flat Rocks could wait nearby for Ulun to come and speak with him there first."

Piram nodded at Esri and to her surprise said, "Yes, Ulun may speak and listen better with fewer people around and in the shadow of Dagan's golden rock. We can watch for Ulun and make a group to meet him that is only a little larger than his. It may be just him and Hanu or Otom. So only this many of us go." He held up 4 fingers.

Geslo agreed, "It would be good to speak about Dagan with Ulun. And before a large group goes to the Violent One's bode, Ulun should know that Flat Rocks is planning a Parting. It will start him thinking about how to use this."

Piram grinned. "We should make it seem like we weren't going to tell him about the Parting."

"I can do that. I'm good at saying too much," said Kai. They laughed.

The four returned to Flat Rocks, conferred with the Elders Council, and set plans in motion to engage with Ulun.

A small group kept a discrete vigil near Dagan's golden rock. In a few days, they saw two people cautiously approaching the rock. It was Ulun and Hanu. Tars, Piram, Barsa, and Kai crept away from the watching spot and circled around to appear as if they were coming from Flat Rocks. They moved casually toward Dagan's rock.

Kai dropped his spear and ran ahead to Ulun and Hanu. "We're not here to fight. We're here to honour Dagan. If you put aside your spears and flints, we'll put aside ours."

Ulun glared at Kai and looked behind Kai at Tars, Barsa, and Piram coming nearer. From Ulun's observations, he knew that Tars and Barsa were among those strongest against killing. Ulun didn't trust Piram, but knew he listened to Tars.

Hanu moved to leave. Ulun said, "We stay. Our ways are as honourable as yours." He turned and walked toward the golden rock, struck his spear in the ground after several steps, signaling Hanu to do likewise. Ulun sat down in the shadow of the rock.

Kai turned to Tars, Barsa, and Piram and nodded. The four sat a short distance from Ulun and Hanu. Initially, the six men were quiet. Then the Flat Rocks men sang and chanted songs of Dagan's bravery and prowess as a hunter. While they sang and chanted, Kai stood and worked on carving the buffalo.

Ulun and Hanu didn't stay long after the singing ended but long enough for Kai to have a few words with Hanu, asking after Riga, and letting slip about Flat Rocks planning for a Parting to happen soon.

Ulun was subdued. As Barsa spoke again of the Agreements. Ulun looked coldly at him and motioned to Hanu that they should leave.

STRAINED MEETING

Several days after encountering Ulun and Hanu at Dagan's golden rock, Flat Rocks organized a group to visit the Violent One's bode, large enough to comfortably outnumber the Violent Ones but not overwhelming numbers. Esri and Saba were the only women who went. Saba would speak with Riga, and Esri would try to talk with Ulun's mate, Carthan.

The Flat Rocks group made no effort to hide themselves and timed their walk to arrive mid-morning at the bode.

Esri and Saba grasped each other's hands as they neared the place where they last saw Dagan's body. Esri leaned toward Saba, "Let's not look. We'll stay back, see where the women go, and sit near them."

Ulun and the other men from the Violent Ones' bode sat in an arc in front of the largest cave, their spears within reach. The men from Flat Rocks sat opposite, with Tars and Barsa in the middle. Esri noticed Ulun tracking her movements. She said to Saba, "Ulun is watching me. It's better if you try to speak with Carthan and I'll go to Riga." Saba nodded.

The four women remaining in the Violent Ones' bode sat off to one side of the men. Esri and Saba joined the women who, though not welcoming, didn't motion for Esri and Saba to go away. The women sat mutely, faces turned toward Ulun.

Barsa and Tars did most of the talking, explaining that the people of Flat Rocks sought to heal the past and live peacefully from now on. They repeated much of what was said before to the Violent Ones about the way of living at Flat Rocks, how it was in many ways better than before the Ash Rain. And, as other times, Ulun stared at them uninterested.

Barsa shifted the conversation to talk about issues that appealed more directly to Ulun. The plan was to tell stories about how people were venerated and remembered for brave deeds. Use this as an enticement for Ulun to live by the Agreements and earn similar honours. Barsa was delegated to take on this delicate task. He started talking about Dagan and hardly began when Ulun held up his hand, cut off Barsa, and pointed at Tars. "You, we'll talk alone. Inside." He motioned to the large cave behind him.

No one moved for a moment. Tars stood and briefly turned to Barsa, who spoke quietly. "It was to be expected that Ulun would demand control, even when out-numbered. Geslo is right. We must be careful. But if Ulun is finally choosing to speak, we should listen." Tars nodded and followed Ulun into the cave. It was risky but unlikely that Ulun would try to harm Tars with so many from Flat Rocks at the bode.

At first no one outside the cave spoke. Gradually people shifted into small groups. The men stayed separated in their bodes. Esri began speaking with Riga, and Saba sat near Carthan, waiting for some acknowledgment from Ulun's mate.

Riga said, "Why did Saba not come sit by me?"

Esri said, "She wanted me to tell you about Nagar and her End Days. It's still hard for Saba to speak about Nagar."

"Nagar is gone?" Riga gasped, tears forming.

"She talked about you, right at the end."

"She did?"

"She wanted you to come back to Flat Rocks - with Hanu."

"Nagar was like a mother to me." Riga paused. "But what about you, Esri. Do you want me to come back to Flat Rocks?"

"It's hard with everything that's happened, but I've seen with Geslo how he lives by the Agreements. We are starting to trust that his violent ways are done, and that the days ahead can be good with him." Esri laid her hand on Riga's arm. "I know you're good, Riga. You took Wilki-Dumu from Ulun and handed him to me when it was dangerous to do so. I don't know Hanu. He has to decide how he wants to be."

"What happened with Geslo?"

"It was hard for him at first and for those he hurt in the past. It still is, but every day is better, especially since the Healing Talk." Esri explained the Healing Talk to Riga.

Before she finished, Ulun and Tars came out of the cave, and Tars motioned that they should go.

It was mid-afternoon. The Flat Rocks group walked until nearly dark before setting up a sleeping place. Tars looked grim when he left the Violent Ones' cave and didn't speak until they were seated around the fire that night.

"Soon Ulun and his bode will move near Flat Rocks, and we'll talk further about how they will live with us," said Tars.

Nat said, "And the Agreements? They're going to be at Flat Rocks and not pledge to the Agreements?"

Kai said, "We can't have that."

Tars continued. "I agree. Ulun is not saying he will pledge to the Agreements and it troubles me, but something has changed for him. We should allow him to be near us, at least for a while, and watch him closely."

Piram smirked, "You don't understand the ways of someone like Ulun. He will do more to change Flat Rocks than Flat Rocks can change him."

Esri said, "From speaking with Riga, I believe there are some in Ulun's bode who would pledge to the Agreements and go through a Healing Talk. I wonder if Ulun knows this."

Kai said, "But would they do a Healing Talk if Ulun is near? It was different for Geslo."

Barsa said, "It will bring troubles to have Ulun near, but it makes it possible to divide them with the Parting. Nagar was right. We can only end Ulun's ways if he loses power over others. But I don't understand why he has chosen to come close. He can try to influence us, but he knows we are so many more."

"They're hungry," Saba said.

"They didn't seem hungry to me," said Piram.

"True, but they offered us no food. That was strange. Ulun likes to show how they are great hunters," said Tars.

Kai laughed, "And they didn't look fat!"

Barsa said, "Let's let Saba speak. What did you hear?"

"First I sat near Carthan and the old slave woman. When Tars went into the cave, Carthan moved away from me and the slave woman began speaking. At first, I thought it was strange what she was saying, but slowly I understood that she wanted to ask me about a big white cat."

Esri said, "Grilu's cat!"

"Yes, Grilu's cat. She knew the cat helped you and Wiki get away. She also said that the white cat was stopping their hunters from killing any large animals. Their bode is hungry and she thinks Ulun is afraid of the cat."

Tars stared into the fire. "That explains it."

GOING AND STAYING

Within days, the Violent Ones moved to a place near Flat Rocks. Life be-came more difficult at the bode. Ulun and his group moved freely about. Those at Flat Rocks who had been captives of Ulun were terrified. Many were angry at the Elders Council for bringing the Violent Ones near Flat Rocks, and outraged when Ulun was allowed on the Council. Ulun kept making excuses why he and others from his bode could not pledge to the Agreements.

Geslo set up a sleeping spot a short distance from Flat Rocks to avoid contact with Ulun. More people started to spend time with Geslo because they too wanted to avoid Ulun. A few times, Hanu and Riga came to see Geslo when not many others were around. And Riga started reconnecting with her former Flat Rock friends.

It turned out that the older woman slave who spoke to Saba about the big cat was the creator of the fine bead bracelets and belts that the Violent Ones traded. The old woman soon attracted many at Flat Rocks to watch her work, and while she spoke little, she patiently showed how she formed the beads and strung them together. Many of the children eagerly scanned places in the river to find her the shells she needed. Now they no longer had to worry about being captured and enslaved by the Violent Ones.

With the addition of Ulun and his group, the plans for the Parting gained urgency. The guideposts and markers in the Thinking Circle indicated that the next Traveler, Fighting Cat, would soon arrive in the pre-dawn sky, providing an auspicious time for the Parting to happen.

Zura and Esri spent their days and nights speaking to everyone, planning and speculating about the division of Flat Rocks – who would be in the Parting and who would stay. A good division was needed to ensure the continuation of living by the Agreements and ending the ways of the Violent Ones, both at Flat Rocks and the new bode.

Zura and Esri made a place near the Thinking Circle with two piles of rocks to represent those staying in Flat Rocks and those leaving with the Parting. They wanted to make sure there were enough strong people in both groups.

Zura said, "Fighting Cat is coming in the morning. We'll have the final bodefire tonight. Is everyone ready for the Parting?"

"Yes, almost. I still don't know about Riga and Hanu," Esri said. "I think they want to join the Parting, especially Riga because Saba is going. I can't tell with Hanu. When I talk to them about the Parting, Riga talks about going and he says nothing. If he didn't want to go, he would say something. He is normally not one to stay quiet."

"If Hanu is going, he does not want Ulun to know. We need to find a way to help him leave in the morning."

"How are we going to do that?" asked Esri.

"Leave that to me. Come, let's look at our rocks again and who is going and who will stay."

"Oh, Zura, I'm frightened. I don't know what I'll do without you. I would be dead if it weren't for you, and we would all be dead without you and Nagar. You two made the Agreements that have made Flat Rocks a good place to live after the Ash Rain. You see what others don't. Who will have your dreams and visions in our new bode?"

"You will find all that and more in yourself and the others going with you, Esri."

They stood by the pile representing those remaining at Flat Rocks. "Here we have Tars and Piram. I think often how much we owe to Tars for not harming us when he first found you and me and Dagar. He's a good man. I'm glad he's staying. And Piram," she chuckled. "He's still Piram in the way he talks, but not his actions. You've seen, haven't you? Piram has found a mate among the people we've brought to Flat Rocks. She's a good hunter too. She sees his strengths but doesn't put up with his gruffness."

Zura continued, "Grayla and Jolam, Sela, Muni, and the two children we saved will also stay. Sela feels better knowing exactly where Ulun is and watching what he is doing."

Esri said, "She follows you everywhere, like I did when I was her age."

"She told me you gave her your Huti stone, Esri. Sela will be a great Skywatcher and healer one day. And Wilki and Wilki-Dumu are staying."

"I'm surprised that Wilki is staying at Flat Rocks after what happened to her at Ulun's bode. Maybe it's like with Sela, Wilki wants to know where he is."

Zura said, "Wilki told me she's done with long walks, at least until Wilki-Dumu's naming. After the Parting happens, she told me she'll insist that Ulun pledge the Agreements and make a Healing Talk. He won't, but she and others will keep pushing. He remains blind to the influence that she and others who he hurt have at Flat Rocks."

"What will happen with Ulun?"

"Ulun does not understand how his power becomes smaller every day he stays at Flat Rocks. Those he used to control are starting to turn to others who are not like him. He thinks that after the Parting, with fewer people at the bode, he will become powerful again."

"If Hanu and Riga join The Parting, that won't happen."

"Which is why it's so important that they leave with you."

"Let's look at the other pile. Those who are joining me on the Parting. I'll tell you again what each one said to me." Esri picked up the rocks one by one.

"Geslo said, 'I can't stay at Flat Rocks with Ulun. Being around him makes me feel such shame. People will always remember that I came from the Violent Ones, but maybe they'll think less about it in a bode far away from Ulun. I hope that when I'm an old man, they will remember other things about me.'

"Kai: 'Esri, I would miss you too much if I didn't come with you and make you laugh and sing. And, yes, you've seen it. Geslo is like me. I'm happy to be with him. Some may never forgive him, but he's a good man. We'll be good together.'

"Nat: 'Esri, if you go, I go.'

"Barsa: 'I'm getting old but to be on a journey to find the Ancients' Land of the Rising Sun makes me feel like a young man again. And I want to stay with Nat. What a gift from the fates to have been with Zura again and be a part of what she and Nagar started at Flat Rocks, bringing us through the terrible times of the Ash Rain and making us stronger and better. The Agreements will always stay with me.'

"Grilu: 'I know Sela and Muni and most of the other children are staying but I want to stay with you. When you came to Flat Rocks, your singing started to make people smile again. I want to keep singing with you and, anyway, if I go, my cat will come too and protect us.'

"Saba: 'Flat Rocks has always been my home and Dagan's golden rock is not far away. But those who are still alive and dearest to me are going in the Parting and I want to be with them. And I can help with the new babies when they start coming. You need to know that the first baby may be mine. I'm with child. It may slow us a little but it will also give us hope.'"

Esri took a deep breath, "And then, if Riga and Hanu come . . . I never liked Hanu. At the tradings, he would want to show how strong he was and talk all the time. But now, around Geslo's sleeping spot, when he and Riga come, and it's just a few of us, I've seen someone a little different. I'm thinking he might want to be that different person if he's not around Ulun. That's what I want to talk to him and Riga about tonight - even if it takes until Fighting Cat appears."

IN THE RAVINE

In the last few weeks, Esri's Toronto awake times had been consumed with thinking about what was happening at Flat Rocks, where life was increasingly intense. Growing the bode had gone reasonably well for a long time, but trying to blend in Ulun and his group was a struggle and threatened to destroy their peaceful community. Esri worried that all the months of her Mending might end up unraveling.

Everything was building toward tonight, her last night at Flat Rocks and then the Parting in the morning. Because it was Saturday, she would be able to sleep late tomorrow - hopefully until after the Parting happened. Esri needed time alone with Clea and Thomas this afternoon, and made arrangements with Ada to pick up Jilly and look after her until Joe got home from work.

"Hey, Ada, thanks for doing this," Esri said when Ada arrived at Clea's.

"But I want to stay here!" said Jilly.

"I need some quiet time with Clea and Thomas. We're talking about some complicated stuff. Trust me, you'd be totally bored," said Esri.

"Oh, okay. Ada is nicer than you anyway" Jilly took Ada's hand, "Bye, Clea, bye Thomas, bye Willa, bye boring Esri."

After they left Clea said, "Did anything further happen with Children's Services? How is your Dad doing?"

"The CS worker called and stopped by a week ago and said she'd make no further visits. She talked to my Dad alone, and he seemed way less tense after she left. I hate to think what Randi might have said about him. Are Disruptors even human?"

"Good question," said Clea. "I'm not sure. When my Mending was done, I looked for my Disruptors and couldn't find them or anyone who knew them or remembered them. It was as though they never existed, or had moved onto someplace else."

"Or went fallow until the next Mending," said Thomas. "But that won't happen yet with Randi or the Tall Man. Your Mending is not over."

"But it could be after tonight," said Esri. "It's the last bodefire and then The Parting in the morning."

"And how are your Flat Rocks people?" asked Clea.

"Everyone is pretty anxious. Ulun and many, though not all, of those around him are not nice. They keep putting off pledging to live by the Agreements. Many people at Flat Rocks are angry with those of us on the Elders Council who were pushing to bring him and his group into the bode. But I also think there're too many of us now at Flat Rocks. It was better when we were smaller."

Clea said, "And the Parting will fix that. How are you feeling about being able to divide Ulun's group?"

"I'm worried. I do think that Riga and Hanu want to go, but Ulun will freak out for sure. Zura told me not to worry. She said she'll take care of Ulun and others in his group and I should concentrate on ensuring that Riga and Hanu are ready to go tomorrow morning."

Thomas grinned, "I wonder what she has up her sleeve?"

Esri laughed. "Except she doesn't have any sleeves."

Clea said, "It's quite a dramatic Parting. Many of the old ties that predate the Ash Rain are breaking apart: Kai, Riga, and Grilu are parting from Tars and Piram; Barsa and Nat parting from Wilxi, Grayla and Jolam; and you from Zura. It's a good division of the bode, and it hinged on you and Zura splitting up."

"I haven't even allowed myself to think about leaving Zura. She's been my anchor throughout everything. But then, if this is the end of my Mending, won't it also be the end of my Flat Rocks dreams?" asked Esri.

"Yes, all the signs point to this being the culmination of your Mending. But still, we never know with Mendings," said Clea.

Thomas said, "Esri, I believe that your Parting group will walk a long distance to form a new bode. And a few generations later they will be that first group of homo sapiens to leave Africa and through the millennia populate most of the planet. The Flat Rocks bode will then spread out across other parts of Africa."

Esri asked, "And without the Mending, the Violent Ones kept on with their ways and they were the ones to leave Africa?"

"Perhaps, or more likely both the Violent Ones and Flat Rocks bodes spread out, forming different cultures around the world and throughout Africa. If the Violent Ones grew and spread, so too did their aggression and brutality that we see in our world today," said Thomas.

"As important as weakening the influence of Violent Ones, your Mending is also about strengthening the peaceful, sharing ways of Flat Rocks," said Clea.

"I've thought about that a lot, the Agreements, and how the Toba volcano eruption, though it was really bad, gave people the chance for a fresh start. It's kind of a miracle that Zura and Nagar were among the survivors and that they found each other," said Esri.

Clea said, "I agree. They shared a vision, but you and many others at Flat Rocks made it a reality."

"And do you think I'll stop dreaming about Flat Rocks after the Mending?" asked Esri. "I want to. I want my life to get back to normal, though I'm not sure what that is anymore. At the same time, the people at Flat Rocks are a part of me now. I'll miss them and I want to know what happens to them."

Clea nodded, "It's quite possible that you'll stop dreaming after tonight, unless the Parting doesn't happen or something extraordinary occurs. I know how hard it is to leave behind the people of your Mending. But you'll always remember them." She patted Esri's arm. "You've done well, Esri."

Thomas said, "Yes, my dear. I wish this old body could be of greater use to you."

"You've both done tons. I would've made a mess of the whole thing without you. But, one thing, explain to me again. What happens to history if the Mending works?"

Clea said, "The changes start from our time now. It doesn't affect who has lived and died in the past. That would be too disruptive. People's attitudes start to change. It's like an awakening. People begin questioning their behaviour and gradually shift their actions."

"Wow, I hope I get to see that!"

"You will. It will seem at first like nothing is happening, but then small signs will start showing up and you will begin to see lots changing all around you."

"But then things stopped changing with your Mending?"

"Yes, sadly, so much seemed to be shifting for the better for a while, but then the Disruptors started gaining traction again. Let's hope we can push them away more permanently this time."

"I'll do everything I can. Thank you both. I think I'm ready," said Esri. "I better get going. I told Dad I was going to hit the indoor track at the rec centre before I come home. He'll worry if it gets too late."

"What are you doing tonight? Will you be with some of your friends? You shouldn't stay out late," said Clea.

"No, no, don't worry. I kind of blew everyone off. My plan is to go running, get pooped out, go home, eat a light supper, read in bed, and then off to Flat Rocks. And since tomorrow is Sunday I can sleep in if a lot is happening at the bode."

"That sounds like a good plan. Thomas and I will be here. I wish I could go to Flat Rocks with you, but I know you'll be fine. And you'll have lots to tell us tomorrow, I'm sure."

Esri ran for a long time, keeping a steady cadence, pushing herself to do one more lap and one more lap and yet one more. As she ran, Esri thought about the people at Flat Rocks, recounting each of their stories to herself from when she first met them. She saved thinking about Zura until her final laps. Esri slowed her pace and began remembering how her dreams started by finding Zura in the chilly pre-dawn sitting in the Thinking Circle of their old bode, waiting for Angry Snake Traveler to appear.

With the lengthening days of mid-February, it meant that there was still a little daylight left when Esri walked out of the rec centre - maybe just enough light to enjoy a detour through the ravine on her way home. The setting sun reflecting off of the snowy landscape created an alluring lavender passageway. Enough walkers, snow-shoers, and cross-country skiers had passed through the ravine that the pathway appeared reasonably passable.

By the time Esri got to the halfway point on the trail, it was nearly dark. She was lost in her thoughts and misjudged how quickly the night set in down in the ravine and how much longer it took to negotiate the wintry path. But it didn't make sense to turn back. There were no lights in the ravine. Esri was anxious to get home. Seconds after she grasped her situation, the dead mouse smell hit her. It came from ahead of her on the trail. She'd have to turn back and go out the way she came in. Her Dad would be starting to worry.

Esri turned around and picked up her pace, hoping she wouldn't slip. The smell was getting stronger. The Disruptor must be close. Clea said the Disruptors would not hurt Esri, but she was scared to run into one in the dark ravine. Esri scurried back in the direction she came from, rounded a couple of turns in the trail, and thought she was in the clear when she tripped and fell down. She was covered in muddy snow but otherwise unhurt. As she sprang to her feet, another wave of dead mouse smell hit her, but this time it came from the opposite direction, the way she was now running. There must be two Disruptors. They were squeezing in from both sides. This could not be good.

"She's here. I see her. Hurry up!" It was Randi. Esri could barely see Randi ahead in the growing darkness but knew her voice well.

"Grab her," came a gruff male voice from the other direction, farther away. Esri couldn't see the man. It was likely the Tall Man she first saw in the donut shop, or maybe it was Jerome's promoter guy. Either way, she wasn't going to wait to find out. Esri dropped her gym bag and plunged into the woods next to the trail.

326 R. J. MOERSHEL

If only she knew where Clea's house was. Esri launched ahead in what she thought might be the general direction of Clea's backyard. It meant first crossing Taylor Creek which was only partially frozen but fortunately shallow at that point. Esri slipped and scrambled across the creek, several times breaking through to the icy water. In her panic, she hardly noticed the wet or cold or mud. She had to get away from them.

The thickly wooded ravine was covered in several inches of crusty, slippery snow. In the dark, the leafless trees and bushes created a prickly, tangled mass on the steep slope. Esri crawled up on her hands and knees, clawing at the snowy, frozen ground to prevent herself from sliding back. She looked down. She hadn't made it far. They had flashlights and were right below her. They'd find her for sure. And they did.

"Stop, Esri," it was the man. "You know you have no chance of getting away from us. It's over." She was lit up in their flashlight beams and they were starting up the side of the ravine. The horrible, horrible dead mouse smell was overpowering. Though she knew it was futile, there was no way Esri was giving up. Maybe by some miracle she could make it to Clea's. She pushed on. The Disruptors' flashlights kept focused on her. They weren't losing sight of her. They were coming nearer. Almost on her. She gagged at their smell.

A large hand grasped her ankle, "Gotcha. What a stupid girl. It will be a pleasure to get rid of you."

Then, yowling, screeching noises came from many directions. Many smallish, clawing creatures leapt onto Randi and the man. They screamed and dropped their flashlights. Esri could hear them flailing around and what sounded like the loudest cat fight ever. Faintly she heard, "Esri, Esri, come in the direction of my voice." It was Clea.

Esri continued scrambling up the side of the ravine. The noises of the cat fight continued below. She could see the Disruptors' flashlights lying on the ground, and hear their screaming and shouting as they fought off the army of creatures attacking them.

Clea kept repeating, "Esri, Esri." Gradually Clea's voice got louder.

"I'm here, Clea. I'm coming to you," said Esri when she finally made it to the top of the ravine. A short distance away she could see a lantern swinging and soon found Clea.

"Oh my dear, Esri. They tried to hurt you, didn't they? I'm so sorry. I thought you were safe. I was wrong. From the beginning, your Mending was different. If something had happened to you, I never would have forgiven myself."

"Clea, it, it was Randi and the Tall Man. He grabbed me, I think they were going to kill me," Esri quivered.

"You should be safe inside. Thomas and I have not been bothered by Disruptors. It must mean that the protections are working. I can only hope . . ." They made their way through the dark garden toward the back kitchen door.

"Something protected me in the ravine. It was like a herd of cats or raccoons or something attacked the Disruptors. That's how I got away."

Clea grinned, "Ah yes, she is quite resourceful." They stepped into the kitchen. "Goodness, look at you! Here, let's get you cleaned up." There was a scratching at the back door.

"Willa wants in," Esri opened the door for the cat. "She's kind of messed up too." Esri turned to Clea. "My Welcome Disruptor?"

"Well, she is very fond of you. Esri, you must spend the night here. Otherwise, you'll be in peril and your Mending may not finish."

"But, I have to let my Dad know. I'm sure he's already worried about where I am. And, Clea, if the Disruptors were going to harm me, what if they try to harm my Dad and Jilly?" Esri sobbed.

Clea looked worried, "I'll go to your Dad and Jilly and bring them here. I'll tell them you're sick. No matter what, you must dream tonight."

"But the Disruptors? Won't they hurt you?"

"I'll go with her," Thomas shuffled into the room, leaning on his cane.

Esri looked at the elder Clea and ancient Thomas. "This is crazy."

"I stopped a Disruptor not all that long ago. I'm sure I can do it again," said Thomas.

"When?" asked Esri.

"In the big library," said Thomas.

"That was you?" exclaimed Clea. "You never told me. I always wondered why we got away so easily. What did you do?"

"I tripped him with this," Thomas laughed and waved his cane. "He was furious but he thought I was just some doddery old man. My dreams had only just started again so he didn't realize who I was. Anyway, no one notices an old man with a cane."

"But the Disruptors will notice you now, won't they?" asked Esri.

"And they will under estimate me again," said Thomas. "Clea and I still have a few tricks up our sleeve. And, unlike Zura, we do have sleeves."

Clea said, "We'll go right away. The Disruptors are probably still getting themselves sorted out after the animal attack. We'll be back before you know it. In the meantime, get yourself cleaned off and ready for bed. I'll put a nightgown out. You can sleep in the little room off of the kitchen. As soon as you hear us return, lie down, and pretend you're sound asleep. That will help convince your Dad to stay. Don't worry. I'll figure out a way to keep him and Jilly here for the night."

Clea and Thomas left. Esri cleaned up and put on one of Clea's old, flannel nightgowns. She got into bed, tried to stay awake until she heard them return, but immediately fell sound asleep.

LITTLE THRUSH BIRDS

At the last bodefire before The Parting, Esri wanted to spend the night singing songs, listening to stories, and sit next to Zura for hours so she would always remember what that felt like. As people started drifting off to their sleeping spots, Esri sought out Riga and Hanu and spoke with them until late in the night. Though she felt they wanted to join The Parting, they still had not committed. She hoped it was to prevent Ulun from knowing their plans, yet she couldn't be certain.

Esri slept a few hours, and Zura woke her in time to see the first stars of Fighting Cat on the horizon before Sun-Man appeared. Esri thought about the morning long ago when she and Zura and Dagan started the long walk from their old bode and all that had happened to them since then. It was unbearable to think that she might never see Zura again. If The Parting group walked to the Ancients' Land of the Rising Sun, that would take them far, far away - too far to ever return to Flat Rocks.

Zura urged the Parting group not to linger. Ulun, Carthan, Otom, and a few others from their bode were still sleeping and everyone moved quietly to avoid waking them. Riga and Hanu went to stand with the Parting group.

Barsa said to Riga and Hanu, "We'll start. The rest of you come soon. We have far to walk today." He embraced Zura.

Zura said, "The Travelers were good to bring us together again." Barsa, Riga, and Hanu began to walk.

Esri looked at Zura, "How is it that Ulun and the others are still asleep?"

Zura smiled, "Sometimes the fates need a little help. Go now, song-bird. I have given Grilu a Sun-Man Stick to keep for your walk and you have the Sky Bones, yes? Don't look back. Think about where you're going, not what you're leaving behind. You and Grilu must make a song of your journey and now that the little thrush birds have returned, they will carry it back to me. Whenever I hear them, I'll know that everything is well with you."

And the rest of The Parting group left. Esri and Grilu brought up the rear. They held hands and began to sing. Zura watched them go. Even after she could neither see nor hear them, she kept standing and looking.

Sela gently pulled Zura's arm, "Come, we can't see them anymore. It will make you sad to keep watching."

"Wait."

Far off, bounding out of the underbrush following after the Parting group, they saw a large, white cat.

"Look, Zura! Grilu's cat!" said Sela.

"She'll keep them safe and prevent Ulun or any of the other Violent Ones from trying to follow them. Come, Sela, now we can go. Ulun and the others from his bode will sleep for a few more hours, but we'll have much to do when they wake up."

THE MENDING

Clea and Thomas moved as hastily as they could manage to Esri's apartment. Thomas said, "I know I'm slowing you down, Clea, but I can't let you go by yourself. It's too dangerous. At least with two of us we can create more diversion if we need to. Besides, there's nothing I enjoy more than disrupting a Disruptor," he chortled.

When they got to Esri's apartment, Joe opened the door. "Clea, Thomas! Come in, what brings you here? Esri's not home, but I'm expecting her any minute."

"I know. She's at my house. She was walking home and started feeling dizzy and nauseous, so she stopped by and I had her lie down. I said I'd come get you," said Clea.

"What? What's wrong with her? She seemed fine when she left."

"I do think she'll be fine, Joe. I don't want you to worry. I think it's one of those stomach flu bugs. Sometimes they come on fast. I'm guessing she'll be through the worst of it in several hours, but instead of moving her, it would be good if you and Jilly came over. You can even spend the night. It's no trouble on my part. I've got plenty of room."

"Ok, yes, of course we'll come. But I don't want to impose on you, Clea. Maybe Esri will feel well enough to come home soon. Hey Jills," he turned around. "We're going to Clea's for a little while. Esri stopped there because she got sick on the way home." He turned to Clea. "We need to get you a phone. I'm sorry you two had to walk over here."

Thomas said, "Ah, Joe, we should get going. I'm sure Esri's fine, but we should get back. I didn't want Clea to go out on her own."

They rode down on the elevator. Clea and Thomas worried what they might find when they got to the lobby. There was no dead mouse smell by Esri's apartment. Maybe the Disruptors were still regrouping after the incident in the ravine. The lobby was empty but the smell of the Disruptors was overpowering. Thomas leaned close to Clea and muttered, "They're inside someplace, maybe in the stairwell or the other elevator."

Clea said, "Joe, look, you and Jilly should hurry on ahead. I'm worried about Esri. Thomas and I are slow. We'll be along shortly."

"Sure, c'mon, Jills. I'll carry you and we'll go fast." Joe thought it odd that Clea and Thomas had left Esri alone if she was so sick, but didn't say anything. He was anxious to get to her.

Joe picked up Jilly and ran ahead to Clea's. Thomas opened the lobby door and pushed Clea outside, "You go on too. Esri needs you. I'll take care of things here. Joe and Jilly will be safe in a few minutes. I can delay them for that long."

"But, Thomas."

"You must not challenge me. This is why I came back to be with you. It couldn't please me more to do my part. Don't deny this to me." He closed the door. Clea stood outside and watched as Thomas rapidly pushed his cane through the front door handles, stood with his back against the doors, and his arms looped around either end of the cane. Randi and the Tall Man emerged from the stairwell.

Clea heard them yelling, "Get him away from the door", "We don't have time.", "Pull him off the door!" Randi worked at pulling Thomas's arms from around the ends of the cane. The Tall Man began punching Thomas, landing many blows to his head.

Clea stood outside the door and cried, "No, Thomas, no." Yelling as loud as she could manage, "Help him, someone, help him! Call the police." She knew Thomas would hang on with every last molecule of strength left in him.

Thomas's head lolled down and the Disruptors unwound Thomas's arms from around his cane. Soon they would be through the door. But Thomas had succeeded in stalling the Disruptors a vital few minutes. Joe and Jilly should be safe or would be soon. Clea did not move and kept yelling.

"Clea! What's the matter?" She turned. It was Luka.

"Thomas needs help."

Thomas lay by the front door. The Disruptors were gone. Luka called an ambulance and the police. They arrived in minutes. Thomas was unconscious and not moving. The ambulance crew carefully transferred Thomas to a stretcher and sped off to the hospital. Clea described the assailants to the police. She was doubtful the Disruptors would ever be found, and they never were.

While Clea and Luka were talking to the police, Luka contacted Ada. He asked her to go to Clea's and let Joe know what had happened, and that Clea would be much later but to please wait for her even if Esri was feeling better. Clea was relieved when Ada returned and confirmed that she spoke with Joe and that both Jilly and Esri were asleep. Joe would sleep on the couch, and Clea should wake him when she got home.

Clea tried to present a reasonable story to the police about what happened but it was difficult to concoct something that made sense of why Thomas's cane was threaded through the front door handles. She bought time by appearing flustered and confused and the police agreed to talk to her further tomorrow. Plus she was anxious to get to the hospital. Luka came with her. Once they got there, they were told that Thomas was stable for now. There was little they could do but watch the beeping monitors connected to Thomas's motionless body.

It was well past midnight by the time Clea arrived back at her house. Joe was stretched out on the couch and sat up when Clea came in. They talked for a long time, and he finally convinced her to lie down for a while. They would go back to the hospital in the morning and let Esri and Jilly sleep through the night.

Esri woke in the bed in the small room off of Clea's kitchen, with Willa nestled in the covers beside her. Clea sat on a chair next to the bed, "You slept a long time. That's good."

"Wow, I really conked out. I fell asleep before you got back. Clea, is everyone all right? Dad and Jilly, are they here?" Esri sat up.

"Yes, yes, they're here. Your Dad and Jilly spent the night. They're still sleeping. We stayed up late. I wanted to speak to you first. I hope that's all right."

"Yes, as long as they're safe. Did anything happen with the Disruptors?"

"First, tell me about your dream. What happened with the Parting?"

"It worked. I think it worked, Clea! The Parting happened. Riga and Hanu came with us. I talked with them a lot until late in the night." She grinned. "Zura gave Ulun and his group something to make them sleep. We were able to leave without waking them."

"And you don't think Ulun or Otom or someone will go after Hanu as soon as they wake up?"

"They'll be scared off," said Esri. "At the end of the dream, I was walking with Grilu and we were holding hands and singing. We were sad and a little scared. Zura told us not to look back until we were well away. Finally, I did turn around, and far behind us we saw his cat - Grilu's big white cat with the crossed-eyes. And it felt like everything would be all right."

Clea sighed deeply and looked down at her hands circling the mug of tea on her lap.

Esri said, "What's wrong? It's good what happened, don't you think?"

"Yes, I believe it is good. It's very good. Your Mending will start a new ripple of how humans behave, and before long we should start seeing the effect. As Thomas said, 'it will bring a peace tsunami.'"

"Why are you crying?"

"I didn't want to tell you right away. But I have to, you'll know soon enough. It's Thomas. Thomas saved us last night, but . . .' she couldn't continue.

"What?"

"Thomas is in the hospital. He's not conscious and they don't know if he'll pull through."

"Oh my god, Clea, no!"

She told Esri what happened.

"Oh Clea. That's terrible."

"Thomas is very old and frail. But he still has the heart of a hero. But I don't know if that will be enough this time."

Tears ran down Esri's face. "Clea, I'm so sorry. He's your Guide and your good friend. And he's been my Guide and friend too."

"Yes. He is all of those things and so much more. I'm sad and heart-broken. But Thomas told me frequently that he was ready to go. I know he may not survive this but, Esri, I do know how good he felt about being able to do this one last great thing for you and me, and most importantly, for the Mending."

PEACE TSUNAMI - EIGHT YEARS LATER

"Honey, I'm home!" Esri called inside Clea's front door.

"Oh, Esri!" Clea's beaming face appeared in her kitchen doorway and she made her way down the hall. "My dear girl, how wonderful to see you." The two women hugged long and hard.

"I've missed you, Clea."

"And I've missed you." Clea pulled back a little and stroked Esri's cheek. "I shouldn't call you a girl anymore. You're such a beautiful young woman. You're so good about writing this old lady, but it's not the same as seeing you in person."

"I know. Same for me." Esri smiled at Clea. "You look great, Clea."

"I'm doing well. A little slower, but enjoying watching the changes, aren't you? We have so much to talk about. I was thinking that we should go right away, and then come back here for tea and muffins after. Will you have time for that?"

"I do have some time. I promised Dad I'd be home for supper, and my flight doesn't leave until ten tonight."

"Good, I'm glad we'll have time to talk. How long will it take you to get to your excavation?"

"A few days. It's in a pretty remote place. I'm told it will take planes, boats, cars, and feet to get there. I'm meeting up with someone else from the team tomorrow morning in Munich, and we'll make our way there together. He's been at the site before so knows the way."

"And when will you come back?"

"I don't know, Clea. I know it's farfetched, but I want to look for Dagan's golden rock. It's the one landmark from Flat Rocks that I think I could have a chance of finding. My big plan is to make myself indispensable on the site and find a way to stay in the area for a while."

"I'm so thrilled for you. But manage those expectations. That all happened such a long time ago." Clea handed Esri a pair of garden shears that were sitting on a small table. "I thought we could cut some iris to take with us." She reached for a worn, wooden cane leaning in the corner. "And I'll bring this to make sure I don't topple over."

After a half hour ride in a taxi, Esri and Clea stepped out and made their way along the winding paths. Esri held the iris bouquet and gave Clea her other arm for support.

"Do you get here often?" Esri asked Clea.

"A few times a year. Jilly takes me. And the last little while I've come with your dad and Pauline. I'm enjoying getting to know her better. You didn't write much about that. Was it a surprise for you when she and your dad got together?"

Esri laughed, "Well, Luka and I were kind of thrown at first. We were like, huh? What? But now I think it's great. My Dad, he's so happy and relaxed. And you know, Jilly always liked Pauline. She's good for Jills. And now Luka and I are brother and sister. It's pretty funny. But it's nice, really nice I think, for everybody."

"I agree. They're good together. It adds to all the nice things I'm seeing and hearing about these days, though I'm sure your Dad and Pauline would have happened without the Mending."

"Do you really think the Mending is working, Clea? It felt like nothing was happening at all for a long time, but now it's like there's something in the air, a turning in how people approach things - less anger, more compassion, and sometimes from the least likely places. I started noticing changes and thought it was because I was looking so hard for some signs of the Mending. But it's pretty big. I don't think it's a fluke."

"No, it's not a fluke."

"Do you think it will be enough?"

Clea was silent. Her cane kept tapping on the path.

Esri paused their steps. "Clea?"

"I want it to be enough. It must be."

The last stage of their walk took them down a steep incline to a small open area in the wooded, hilly graveyard. The two women stopped in front of a tan marker among the several dozen headstones in the hidden glen.

Esri knelt and placed the iris on the grave. Her fingers traced the carved outline of a cape buffalo etched in the tombstone. She whispered. "Your peace tsunami, Thomas, I think it's coming."

ACKNOWLEDGEMENTS

When I began *The Mender* I had no idea what an engaging and fulfilling journey it would be. I started writing in library branches in my neighborhood with frequent trips to the downtown Reference Library. With no distractions, no nagging house chores calling out, the library setting proved ideal for writing – so ideal that I decided to visit and write in all 100 Toronto library branches. I finished the epilogue in what was then the newest branch at the Scarborough Civic Centre.

Writing *The Mender* provided an excuse to spend umpteen hours noodling into all sorts of odd-ball research trying to imagine life at Flat Rocks. What we know about homo sapiens, circa 75,000 BCE, is that people knew how to control fire and make tools with stone. They were physically just like us only lacking our technology. And we can reasonably assume that there were individuals within groups or clans who would have been highly intelligent, curious, and natural leaders.

To imagine the social, cultural, and spiritual life at Flat Rocks, I took great liberties with paleoanthropological findings as jumping off points. The oldest evidence of Thinking Circles and Tally Sticks is much more recent than Flat Rocks. But who knows, some day we may find indications of sophisticated cultures dating back farther than what we have found to date. We are discovering more every day.

The Mender also gave me a reason to engage with many interesting people about a load of topics, and prattle on to many more about cave-people, ancient cultures, volcano eruptions, population bottlenecks, hunter-gatherers, star-gazing circles, tally sticks, and human nature.

The writing and research was a solo journey but contemplating and revising the draft involved a Flat Rocks sized bode.

Thank you --

To Paul Thompson for a beautiful cover. I'm still amazed how brilliantly you rendered it from my vague description. It exceeds what I imagined.

To my lovely, wonderful readers: Michele Arnold, Allyson Bomber, Kay Bomber, Julie Goldstein, Paul Mero, Sharon Oosthoek, Phyllis Robinson, Sha Shifford, Marilyn Tate, Roseann Tos, Lynn Tullis, Wendy Wright. I am so fortunate and grateful for your candor and encouragement. Many others helped me along the way simply by caring enough to ask: what's happening with your book? Any writer should be so lucky to have such a dedicated group of friends and supporters.

To editors Judith Diehl and Marnie Woodrow, your excellent and detailed advice was invaluable.

To the many who generously gave their time and expertise on topics such as prehistoric childbirth, wheelchair life, Bangladesh names, teen life, children's aid, restorative justice, star-gazing, construction work, talon-pierced eyes, and a whole lot in between: Justin Conley, Sam Coulavin, Matthew Fox, Xavier Fox, Anil Kanji, Farhana Khan, George Kostic, Emma Lewzey, Eden Gladstone Martin, Margaret Anne McHugh, Cole Mero, Noah Mero, Fran Odette, Ingrid Randoja, Jonathan Rudin, Dusha Sritharan, Adam Tate-Howarth, Dylan Tate-Howarth, Cheryl Wagner.

To my sister Marianne Moershel, for that early morning out on the lawn chairs by Lake Ontario trying to understanding what it must have felt like for Clea seeing Angry Snake again after the Always Cloud came.

To my partner, Larry Gordon, and our daughter, Ellie Gordon-Moershel, for their unflagging encouragement, reading many versions of Esri's story and accompanying me on numerous peculiar field trips. Without you, I never would have started nor finished *The Mender*.

ABOUT THE AUTHOR

The Mender is R. J. Moershel's first novel. She was inspired by the many dedicated Menders she has worked with during her 30+ years at various non-profit organizations. Now retired, she wrote *The Mender* during visits to all 100 branches of the Toronto Public Library System.

R. J. Moershel was born and raised in Homestead, Iowa (population 148). After sampling life in a number of North American and European cities, she settled in Toronto where she resides happily with her partner, Larry, and enjoys the frequent company of their daughter, Ellie.

www.ingramcontent.com/pod-product-compliance
Lightning Source LLC
Chambersburg PA
CBHW060354260626
47160CB00006B/2307